Wish for a Sinner

by

Lynn Shurr

The Sinners Series, Book 2

Wish for a Sinner

Cover Art by *Diana Carlile*

The Wild Rose Press, Inc.
PO Box 708
Adams Basin, NY 14410-0708
Visit us at www.thewildrosepress.com

Publishing History
First Champagne Rose Edition, 2014
Print ISBN 978-1-62830-340-7
Digital ISBN 978-1-62830-341-4

The Sinners Series, Book 2
Published in the United States of America

"Concerning my list—"

She cut him off in a voice turned frosty. "In last week's tabloids, number forty-seven among your list ladies, who wished to remain anonymous—I can't imagine why—said you were a real stud muffin and lived up to your reputation. You also believe in wining and dining and took some time for foreplay."

"You shouldn't believe the tabloids."

"Which part—the wine or the foreplay?"

"Uh, no. I hate the term stud muffin. I'm nobody's muffin. I prefer just being called a stud."

She had to laugh. "Don't you ever give up, Joe Dean Billodeaux?"

"*Mais*, *cher*, no. Dat's why I gonna win anoder Super Bowl, me."

"Oh, the cute Cajun routine. Number twenty-two reported the week before last that she found it adorable." There, that should show she knew all his tricks and deflate his enormous ego. She heard the sound of turning pages. He was reading during their conversation? Then, the sound of paper tearing.

"That was Tami Blair, flight attendant, three stars. I won't be calling her anymore. Look, I'd like to see you again. I'd like to do something for your patients. Sincerely. Why don't you come over to my place? We'll talk."

"I don't think so, Joe. I have no interest in being number fifty-five or whatever."

"Number seventy, but you're not on my list. You aren't just a number. I could come over to your place—to talk. Where do you live?"

Praise for Lynn Shurr

"Shurr is a wonderful storyteller."

~The Romance Studio

~*~

"Wish for a Sinner is a fun romance that takes place in both New Orleans and Cajun Country, providing readers with quick witty dialogue and a sexy story."

~Chere Coen, Louisiana Book News

~*~

"Very easy reads, well written, combined with conflict, believable plots and secondary characters that make the story come alive."

~Jane Lange, Romance, Reads & Reviews

Dedication

For my daughter, Caroline,
inspiration for Stevie Dowd and a darn good writer, too;
and for Kris Harding, contest judge,
who wanted to read beyond the third chapter.

Chapter One

His mama always said, "If you have ice cream for breakfast, chocolate cake for lunch, and a big ole sack of candy for dinner, y'all will soon be craving the good green beans your pawpaw grew just for you."

Joe Dean Billodeaux, star quarterback of the New Orleans Sinners, ruffled the pages of his little black book. The football season ended a month ago, and he had done as promised. Beginning with A, he contacted each and every female who had written a name and number in his book during his six months of celibacy.

When he thought back on it, that vow to remain celibate for the entire season seemed hasty, but he did have to admit St. Jude delivered. Connor Riley, his favorite receiver, had recovered from a broken neck and played again, almost as good as raising the dead…or at least a dead career. Keeping his own mind off women had increased his concentration on the game, and the results had been spectacular.

Joe Dean paused in flipping the pages to admire his Super Bowl ring, heavy gold, a circle of diamonds and a black enameled S with a sinuous row of small rubies running down the center, red and black, the Sinners' colors. S was for Super Bowl. S was for Sinners. S was for stud. Women loved to try on his ring.

By doing two, sometimes three a day, he had reached number sixty-nine on his list, and he was only up to the E's. A few had cancelled on him. One was now engaged, another pregnant, and a third giggled so much he quickly figured out she was underage. He had drawn thick, dark lines through their names. Joe Dean Billodeaux did have his standards—only he had broken one tonight.

His nooner had gone well. Carly Eglund, a pert blonde secretary, asked her boss for a long lunch hour. They enjoyed a light repast on Joe's terrace overlooking the Mississippi from his top floor condo, then passed a pleasurable time together. It was understood he would not be getting back to any of the women any time soon. He gave Carly two stars in his book, an average rating.

He had gone out of order a few times. At the end of the B's, he decided impulsively to call the three names at the end of the book, Zelinsky, Yablonsky, and Xavier. Zelinsky and Yablonsky were good time girls, but Latasha Xavier turned out to be a hot UNO senior with many talents. He put four stars by her name. Still, the very first one and the very last had left him feeling like someone put pins in his Halloween candy.

He'd been true to his word by letting Margaret Stutes, a publicist for the Sinners, be the first woman he bedded directly after the Super Bowl. That was taking one for the team in the name of friendship. When Connor Riley's fiancée, Stevie Dowd, asked him to put Margaret at the top of his list in order to get herself a job as an official Sinners photographer, he agreed reluctantly. Having Stevie nearby helped Connor overcome the spates of temper that nearly cost him his career as a wide receiver when not even the neck injury had kept him out of the game. He had done his best to help his friends.

Well, to be honest, that night was not Joe's most stellar. He had put away two bottles of victory champagne and was starting on a third when Margaret dragged him from the locker room and hailed a cab to take them back to her hotel. He sort of remembered polishing off that third bottle on the trip to her room with the help of a doorman who was holding him up. Margaret tipped the fellow with a bill large enough to gain his help in getting Joe to the bed and partially undressed. After that, the evening was pretty much a blank.

He recalled waking in the early morning hours to Margaret's nasal voice complaining that Joe Dean Billodeaux was just a flash in the pan, and she would let everyone know unless she got a re-do. Her thin-to-the-point-of-bony body with its small, flat breasts and freckled skin, her purple-red hair, her overbite and her whining had necessitated a quick trip into the bathroom.

Afterward, he was able to carry on and defend his reputation. Talk about playing hurt. As he picked up his rhythm over Margaret, his brains seemed to slosh against the top of his skull. Keeping his eyes closed mitigated some of the piercing pain he felt when he opened them. In this situation, stamina and training paid off. Margaret, shrieking and clawing, was finally satiated. On the way back to his own room to pack and meet the team for a return to New Orleans, Joe Dean pulled out his black book, found Margaret's name in the S's, and crossed it out as he had once before, this time so hard the page ripped.

That was one bad experience and tonight brought another. Nicole Everard, a lady lawyer as he found out when he called her office number, remembered putting her name in his book one evening when she'd been having drinks with a few of her friends. She wondered when he was going to get around to her. Tonight after work would be fine. Her office sat only a short way from his condo.

Nicole required no drink, no food, nor any foreplay. Telling Joe Dean, wearing nothing but his boxers, to relax against the pillows, she undressed for him at the foot of the bed. Watching her strip down from her navy blue lawyer's suit to nothing but a garter belt and black stockings easily aroused him. Nicole, long and lean and lightly muscled, looked like a woman who worked out regularly. Though small-breasted, what she had was firm and up-tilted, always a feature he admired. Her skin was lightly tanned and her teeth perfect.

When she let down her long, brunette hair from its twist, never taking her dark, intent eyes off of his body, Joe gave a growl of appreciation. She started out on top, but after a small tussle for domination, she submitted to the bottom position. They were both satisfied at the end. Nicole rose from the covers.

Usually, Joe left the bed first. Normally, he headed for the shower and gave the woman a chance to relax, dress, or join him in the water, whatever they wanted. Nicole pulled a perfumed, lace-edged handkerchief from the pocket of her suit, dabbed at her thighs, and proceeded to dress rapidly after checking the slim gold watch she'd left on the night table.

"Must run, Joe. Harry always works late at the firm, and I told him I was going home to spend some time with the kids. I'll have to give my nanny a bonus to keep her mouth shut."

"Harry? Kids?" he'd asked blankly.

"My husband and the two boys. I've crossed one more thing off my life list, thanks to you," she said while shrugging into her blue jacket.

"Life list?" He was clueless again.

"Yes, sex with a major athlete. Done. But, there's still skydiving, a trip to Nepal to seek my spirituality, and sex with a famous musician, among other things. If musicians are as easy as you, that last one should be no trouble at all. Thanks a million, Joe."

She went out the door before he could shuck off his condom. He liked to send his women off with a kiss and a smile and no hard feelings. He never knowingly slept with married women, virgins, the under aged or the girlfriends of his teammates. He did not coerce or play rough unless his partner started it. This was supposed to be fun and games for both of them, but tonight he felt used. If he associated Margaret with the taste of regurgitated champagne, then Nicole left behind the lingering flavor of sour grapes.

No wonder Joe Dean Billodeaux had an appetite for someone fresh and wholesome. He thumbed through his book again. Where, where, St. Jude, where? A business card tucked into the binding fluttered to the floor. It read, *Nellwyn Abbott, Volunteer, Louisiana Wish Kidz.* The card listed three telephone numbers—office, home, and cell. This woman wanted to be contacted.

Joe recalled her now, a small sylph of a woman with large, dark eyes and a pixie haircut. She was the Wish Lady chaperoning the desperately ill children who wanted to meet their football heroes, a request granted by the Wish Kidz Foundation. Mistaking her for another groupie, he had hit on her in front of a room full of sick kids, their families, three friends, and Margaret Stutes in one of life's most embarrassing moments. Nell looked not much older than the children she accompanied, but the authority in her voice when she put him in his place let him know she was a woman grown.

Covering his humiliation by giving her his autograph, and then unable to resist teasing her, his phone number encircled by a devil's tail heart, he moved on to spend a few hours with little Patrick, a childhood leukemia victim. He left the kid with one of his jerseys, an autographed football, and a promise he would win the Super Bowl for him. Joe Dean Billodeaux always kept his word. For the first time since the big game, Joe wondered how Patrick was doing. The Wish Lady would know.

Let's see, home or cell phone on a Friday night? If she was out on a date, the cell phone was a bad choice. She worked with sick kids and should have an answering machine. Call the home number, then. Joe punched out the digits that would connect him to Nellwyn Abbott.

Chapter Two

Nell, wrapped in a flowered cotton afghan, lay on her sofa and watched for the hundredth time her favorite comfort film, Disney's *Beauty and the Beast*. The main characters danced in the ballroom, light and colors flashing by. She closed her eyes and imagined twirling with them. Her telephone rang, destroying the magical moment. Putting the old VCR tape on pause, she picked up the phone and made a wish that this would not be more bad news.

"Hey, Nell," a deep, masculine voice said.

"Hello?" she answered not having the vaguest idea who it was.

"This is Joe."

"Joe?"

She sorted through all of the Joes she knew—first, her supervisor at the hospital, but for a man, he had a rather high voice, very unlike this one. Joe, the maintenance worker at her apartment complex, spoke with a heavy foreign accent, and besides, his name wasn't really Joe, but a substitute for something unpronounceable by Americans. Joe, the pharmaceutical salesman, or representative as he liked to be known, would have identified himself formally with his full name immediately before asking for an appointment or a date, if he was contemplating cheating on his wife again. None of them fit the warm, deep

7

voice on the phone.

"Joe Dean Billodeaux, quarterback for the Sinners." He sounded a little peeved at having to identify himself. That was just too bad.

"Oh, yes, Mr. Billodeaux."

"Joe," he said again.

"Joe. Do you need my help with something?" Nell could have kicked herself. She was so used to offering help any time, day or night. A guy like this would positively take her offer the wrong way. She absolutely did not need football players to mess up her life again.

"Um, yes. I was sitting here alone wondering…"

Nell had absolutely no time for this stuff. "Look, Joe, this is a bad time for me."

"Oh, you have somebody with you?"

"No, I attended a funeral this afternoon. I'm feeling a little low and am not in the mood, okay?"

"Okay. I was wondering about Patrick, the little kid at the Super Bowl. How's he doing? With my bonus I bought a small ranch out by Chapelle. It's not cleaned up yet, but I plan to keep some horses. Maybe you could bring him and his family out to ride sometime this summer." He got this out in a burst as if he figured she was about to hang up.

"I'm so sorry, Joe. I misunderstood."

Still, she had to be cautious. As a quarterback, he was probably much, much brighter than people gave him credit for—dumb jock being the designation that usually came to mind because of his off-field antics. However, when watching games with her dad, she knew Billodeaux could switch plays just like that, and the other team hardly knew what hit them.

Her voice grew very soft. "Joe, I attended Patrick's

funeral today."

"I should have called sooner." Real regret tinged his voice.

"Wouldn't have made any difference. He was too ill to do much but sit in his chair and watch life go by. He wore your jersey every day. They put it in his coffin along with the football. You made that little boy very happy."

"How's the black kid doing? The one the Rev met with."

"Passed away about a week after the Bowl. Rev Bullock came to his funeral."

"Yeah, the Rev should have been a Saint," Joe Dean said, referring to the Sinners great cornerback and would-be preacher. "I really did mean it about kids coming to the ranch. I'll stand by that. When Joe Dean Billodeaux makes a vow, he keeps it."

"That's great. Let me know when you are ready for guests. I'll pass the word along to the Wish Kidz Association and some of my patients."

How nice of him to offer and to call on a Friday night when he probably had better things or sexier women to do. Maybe the guy wasn't as bad as the tabloids claimed. Nell relaxed her guard.

"You're a doctor? The Rev is marrying a doctor next week," he said in that rich, seductive voice.

"Yes, I know. I met her at the funeral. She's a lovely person, inside and out. They invited me to the wedding, me and, I guess, a few hundred other people."

"Great. I'll have someone I know to dance with if you come."

"Aren't you in the wedding party? Won't most of the team and their families be there?" Nell shook her head against the phone. He was moving in for a pass. She saw through that play.

"Well, Doc, I meant I won't be taking a date. The seventeen-year-old I'm escorting is off-limits, and most of the other women are likely to be relatives of the Rev's or belong to other players."

"First of all, I am not a doctor. I'm a child psychologist at Ochsner. I deal with patients who have life-threatening illnesses, and their families. Secondly, I am not fair game because no one on your list is attending." Always best to be clear and direct with persistent people. She put the about-ready-to-hang-up tone in her voice.

"Concerning my list—"

She cut him off in a voice turned frosty. "In last week's tabloids, number forty-seven among your list ladies, who wished to remain anonymous—I can't imagine why—said you were a real stud muffin and lived up to your reputation. You also believe in wining and dining and took some time for foreplay."

"You shouldn't believe the tabloids."

"Which part—the wine or the foreplay?"

"Uh, no. I hate the term stud muffin. I'm nobody's muffin. I prefer just being called a stud."

She had to laugh. "Don't you ever give up, Joe Dean Billodeaux?"

"*Mais, cher*, no. Dat's why I gonna win anoder Super Bowl, me."

"Oh, the cute Cajun routine. Number twenty-two reported the week before last that she found it adorable." There, that should show she knew all his tricks and deflate his enormous ego. She heard the sound of turning pages. He was reading during their conversation? Then, the sound of paper tearing.

"That was Tami Blair, flight attendant, three stars. I won't be calling her anymore. Look, I'd like to see you again. I'd like to do something for your patients. Sincerely. Why don't you come over to my place? We'll talk."

"I don't think so, Joe. I have no interest in being number fifty-five or whatever."

"Number seventy, but you're not on my list. You aren't just a number. I could come over to your place—to talk. Where do you live?"

Nell took a look at herself in the mirror by her front door. She wore her tattered Tinker Bell nightshirt, the one she'd gotten at Disney World when she was a Louisiana Wish Kid a dozen years ago. Tink was fading away. Chocolate ice cream stains dribbled down one side of the garment. The armpits had holes. The thing was practically a rag, yet she held on to it, wore it each time one of the children died. It reminded her that some survived.

"I live in Metairie, but you can't come over. I'm not dressed."

"You don't have to get dressed for me, sugar."

She could imagine his sexy leer having experienced it at the Super Bowl meeting. Nell shook her head. The mirror reflected the light from the tiny diamond earrings she had forgotten to take off. They were the only things sparkling in her apartment tonight. Her dad had given them to her when she went into remission. Enough nonsense from this over-sexed jerk.

"I'll see you at the wedding, Joe." She disconnected.

Joe Dean Billodeaux stretched out his six-foot-

Lynn Shurr

three frame on the leather sofa long enough to accommodate his entire length with a few feet to spare. He tried to recall the last time a woman had hung up on him. The answer was never.

He still had plenty of time to call number seventy if he wanted, but his desire just wasn't there. That was the trouble when you craved something healthy and all you were surrounded by was bags and bags of candy and one or two sour grapes.

Chapter Three

The sun shone down on the nuptial day of Revelation Jeremiah Bullock and Dr. Arminta Green. The fuchsia and purple flowers of the mountainous azalea bushes surrounding the red brick AME church in Chapelle, Louisiana, opened under its rays in glorious profusion. The crowd of guests overflowed from the sanctuary on to the lawn and pooled into a another burst of color—people of all shades of brown, tan and white dressed in their Sunday best clothes of red, gold, bright blue or green. Nell Abbott stood among them, sweating in the afternoon heat of a late March afternoon, but enjoying the scene.

Speakers placed outside the church allowed those who could not be seated to follow the service intoned in Reverend Bentley Bullock's stentorian voice. When the organ blasted out the recessional, the visitors lining the sidewalk armed themselves with handfuls of rice from a five-pound sack someone had remembered to tote along. Too short to see over the crowd, Nell wiggled her way to a space by the church steps. She threw her rice as the couple exited after a long photo session inside the sanctuary. The grains came down like hail, and the Rev and his bride ran for the limousine waiting at the curb.

One joker threw an entire box of Minute Rice, which the Rev caught and tossed back to a teammate.

Ten dollars exchanged hands. Nell overheard the Sinners' Coach Buck say, "Told you he'd catch it. The man has great hands," as he pocketed his bet.

Two little girls dressed in bright pink trotted behind the bride holding up the long train of her gown. When they flipped it up and down to clear the rice, the expanse of seed pearl and crystal embroidered cloth threw off a burst of sparkles nearly as bright as the bride's diamond choker. The rice jumped around like popcorn. Giggling and still flapping, the train-bearers were drawn into the limo as Arminta—often called Mintay and now Mrs. Revelation Jeremiah Bullock—gathered up the cloth. The sisters of the church, talking among themselves nearby, claimed they had never seen such finery outside of Mardi Gras. Why that train had dragged halfway down the aisle of the AME sanctuary. Nell believed them.

The hail of rice ending, the attendants emerged from the wide, red-painted doors. Connor Riley, wide receiver for the Sinners, escorted the bride's matron of honor, her sister, Edwina, according to the program. As they came down the steps, someone dumped a handful of rice into Connor's long, blond hair. He shook his mane and sent rice flying. His sports photographer fiancée, Stevie Dowd, was the culprit. She laughed at him now and stretched her long legs after spending an hour crammed into a seat at the back of the church. Nell stood among all these celebrities she'd seen in the tabloids and marveled at their size and physical beauty.

The attendants continued to pour out of the church, eight couples in all, the last, a pairing of Joe Dean Billodeaux with one of the Rev's cousins. All the Bullocks were on the large side, Nell observed. The young woman probably tipped the scales at one-hundred eighty and unfortunately chose to wear the bright pink gown rather than the royal purple dresses like four of the other bridesmaids.

Joe caught sight of Nell and paused. "Hey, Nell. This is Larisha. Doesn't she have a great smile? And you should hear her laugh. You could shill for a comedian, sugar." He squeezed the delighted girl's pudgy arm and coaxed out that laugh.

"I can see you are an experienced groomsman," Nell said. He had most likely experienced a number of bridesmaids, too. She had to remember under that nice guy routine lurked a hardened womanizer.

"I was in all four of my sisters' weddings. Got to go, but you save me a dance, *cher*."

Ducking a handful of rice throw by Stevie Dowd, he escorted Larisha toward the line of white limos stretching down the street. His eyes scanned the crowd again before taking his seat, but she felt safely obscured by the Rev's stout family members. Once the wedding party reached the Mardi Gras ballroom—the only place in the small town big enough to hold several hundred guests—she would find a nice, dark corner table, have a little food and drink, then be on her way home.

****

Nell thought the decorators had done a wonderful job of turning the somewhat shabby hall into a wedding wonderland with bolts and bolts of white tulle, tiny white twinkle lights, and banks of potted azaleas matching the colors of the bridesmaids' dresses. The band and bar were in full swing by the time the last limo pulled up. Guests who had decided against standing out in the afternoon sun to hear the service had

15

claimed the best tables.

Some newcomers oohed and aahed over the six-tiered wedding cake and a groom's cake shaped like LSU's Tiger stadium where the Rev had gotten his start toward pro ball. Others fanned out looking for seats. Nell was one of these. Dressed in spring green, she floated like a leaf looking for a place to light. She didn't know a soul in the crowd and regretted having come to the celebration even though the security guards at the door assured her the bride had placed her name on the guest list. Well, she could always wish Mintay and the Rev the best of lives together and head for home as soon as possible. Why had she been tempted to come?

"Over here, Wish Lady!" A long, slim arm waved her to a chair currently being occupied by a camera bag at one of the reserved tables up by the seating for the bridal party. Stevie Dowd called to her. Tall enough in four-inch silver heels to be seen over the mob, Stevie beckoned. "I have a seat for you."

Nell squeezed her way between the guests and arrived by Stevie's side. "Mintay asked me to save a place for you and be on the lookout. I remember you from the photo shoot before the Super Bowl. Sorry I don't recall your real name, but you are responsible for one of the priceless moments in my photographic career—a fantastic shot of Joe Dean Billodeaux being turned down by a woman."

"I'm Nellwyn Abbott and you are Stevie Dowd, famous sports photographer. Sorry, lots of my patients, especially the teenagers, are addicted to *People* and some of the tabloids. They keep me informed," Nell admitted. "One of them had the cover with you and Connor Riley kissing after the Super Bowl hung up in her room."

"Would that be Cassie, one of the Wish Kidz we met? The picture was taken by an old friend of mine who likes to exploit me for profit. How is she doing?" Stevie asked.

"Great, thank heaven. I think she'll make it."

"And the boys?"

"Didn't. You have to concentrate on the ones who do, Stevie."

"I understand. Anyhow, I'm likely to be neglected by Connor most of the afternoon while the wedding photographer pushes the bridal party around. I brought my camera to pass the time and maybe get a few candids. We can hang out together, okay?" Stevie slouched down in her elegant silk pantsuit of pearl gray and played with a series of silver and gold chains around her throat.

"No fabulous engagement ring from Connor Riley yet? I need to collect some gossip for sassy Cassie while I'm here. Maybe that's why I came," Nell questioned herself.

Stevie pulled on one of her chains and fished a large ring from her cleavage, which began at the first of the rhinestone buttons of her top. "Connor's Super Bowl ring. It's all I wanted."

"So you are like, going steady forever?" Nell asked doing a good imitation of Cassie.

"Exactly. I thought you came to be with Joe Dean, not to admire my ring. Oops. I can tell by your expression the bride neglected to mention how she thought a kiddie shrink would be perfect for Joe who is a tad immature. I was supposed to make sure the two of you connected. Sorry."

"A tad? Make that a ton. I have no intention of being his number seventy, thanks anyway." Nell started to rise from her specially held seat.

"I believe the man is up to seventy-five now. Really, Joe needs to grow up when it comes to women," Stevie agreed.

The eyes of both women turned to where the quarterback had his arm around the waist of his plump bridesmaid. Several relatives took pictures with the disposable cameras left in baskets on the tables.

Joe Dean saw them watching. He sent Nell a special smile from across the room. The force of it made her blink. His beautiful dark eyes glinted. His black hair shone with blue highlights. All six-foot three inches of quarterback focused on her...ordinary Nell Abbott. With her mind glazing over, she sat down again. Stevie waved a hand before her eyes.

"I'm breaking the spell," she claimed. "Do not sleep with this man unless he marries you."

"That's how you handled Connor?" Nell asked.

"Uh, no. With us, it was sort of sex, proposal, sex, breakup, sex, engagement. Connor says we were meant to be together. After all we've been through, I believe him. Let's get something to eat."

Beyond the chilled shrimp and salad choices, servers carved rare roast beef and southern hams. The melon baskets were many and each was attended by a ring of mammoth strawberries dressed in black and white chocolate tuxedos. Evidently, the Rev's kin preferred their food plain but plentiful. Stevie and Nell filled their plates and returned to their prime seats.

Toasts were made. The champagne flowed, along with a vast variety of beers, colas: regular, diet and un-, and any easily mixed drink. Thus loosened up, the wedding party began to dance. Joe Dean danced with his bridesmaid, then Mintay's married sister, then all of the other bridesmaids. Connor followed suit. With the obligations finished, both men felt free to gravitate toward the table where Stevie and Nell sat chatting with three pair of the Rev's aunts and uncles.

Moses Bullock kept the champagne glasses filled even though his wife, Ethaline, announced she was a teetotaler and did not approve. Nell had reached her two glass limit an hour ago and took only tiny sips from the ever full third flute. As a small person, she did not hold her liquor well and had learned in college even three drinks pushed the limit for her. As it was, she felt a giddy thrill when Joe Dean came up behind her and put his large hands over her eyes.

"Guess who?"

"I have no idea. Ahh, maybe Connor Riley. I hear he has great hands."

"Well, I have a great arm. It's Joe."

"Joe, who?" she answered sending Stevie, way past her third glass, into a fit of giggles at this lame repartee.

Giving up on cute, Joe pulled Nell's chair back. "Let's dance, Wish Lady."

He took her with him all too easily into the space in front of the band and snuggled her up against his chest. Glad she had worn her highest heels, she took two steps back and tilted her head upward to see his face.

"Just one dance. I really must leave soon. It's nearly three hour's drive back to Metairie, and if Uncle Moses fills my glass again, I might not be fit to do it. I wasn't planning on spending money on a motel."

"There are no motels in Chapelle anyhow. You'd

have to drive to Lafayette, and that wouldn't be a good idea in your crazy, drunken condition." Evidently, Joe Dean recognized a convenient excuse when he heard one. "I'm a native here. You can stay with my family. They got an extra room. It's right next to mine," he added and felt her startle in his arms, a dead giveaway that he had some effect on her.

"I wouldn't want to impose."

"No, no. They like company. My mama has been after me to bring a nice young lady home for years. I'm staying over to check out the ranch I bought. See about getting a few horses. You could help me pick out gentle ones for the children."

He gave her a Gotcha' Wish Lady grin and drew Nellwyn close against his chest again, her head resting on his heart. She felt herself go warm and soft and boneless like her friend's orange tabby cat who loved to sit in her lap and purr. No purring! She had to keep up the conversation.

"I don't know anything about horses. I can't ride."

"Even better. If you can handle the animal, it must be safe for kids."

"We'll see how late the reception goes."

By the time Mintay and the Rev piled into their limousine and headed for a charter flight to their "undisclosed honeymoon destination" as the papers would say, Nell felt, not drunk, but woozy and very tired.

"Go ahead and stay at Joe's place," Stevie urged. "His mama will protect you, guaranteed, as Joe would say."

"Guar-an-teed," Joe repeated with a sparkling grin promising just the opposite. "My Porsche is right out back. We can collect your car tomorrow."

Nellwyn Abbott soon found herself bumping along the substandard back roads of Chapelle, Louisiana in a red sports car that did not handle potholes very well. With relief, she saw they were slowing down before a modern ranch-style home sitting on a large lot carved from the cane fields on either side. The security light was on and the front door open.

Joe Dean hollered as they entered the house, "Mama, guess who I brought home!"

Chapter Four

Hospitality at the Billodeaux home turned out to be spontaneous and friendly. In short order, Mrs. Billodeaux provided Nell with a bedroom not next to Joe's, an oversized t-shirt to sleep in, which did belong to Joe, and a fresh toothbrush. As Nell moved from the bedroom to the bathroom in the hallway, she heard his mama making a late phone call starting with, "Allie, you won't guess. Joe brought home a girl, a nice one." No way was she leaving her locked room again until morning.

When the Sunday light spread across the white eyelet comforter, Nell roused herself from a fairly decent sleep and did what she had been urged to do last evening, rummage through two identical chests of drawers for casual clothing to put on. The Billodeaux girls—who had once shared this room with its matching twin beds, dressers, and night tables, and souvenir cluttered bulletin boards—were a heftier breed than Nell. The smallest pair of jeans required a tightly cinched belt to stay up and had to be rolled into substantial cuffs at the bottom. She tied a large chambray shirt faded to a pale blue-white at her waist and pushed its cuffs up to her elbows. Bare-footed, Nell padded down the hall following the scents of breakfast in the making.

Forking bacon from a cast iron pan, Mrs.

Billodeaux turned to her husband who was deep into reading the Sunday sports section. "Ain't she darlin', Frank? *Tres petite.* No?"

"Cute as newborn calf, Nadine," her husband answered. "Coffee, *cher?*" He held up a pot sitting at his right elbow.

"Please." Nell took a seat at a round oak table lit by a wagon wheel chandelier. She took a sip. "Maybe with a little milk and sugar."

"Frank likes it strong enough to stand the spoon," Nadine Billodeaux testified while getting a carton of milk from the refrigerator and pushing a sugar bowl Nell's way. She poured a bowl of beaten eggs into the bacon grease and buttered some freshly popped toast as the eggs bubbled up.

"Could I help with breakfast?" Nell offered.

"Manners, too, Frank," Nadine remarked. "No, *cher*, I got it under control. I used to cook for seven. Now it's just me and Frank except for hired help during the cane harvest. Of course, my grandkids stay over sometimes, but all they ever want is Pop Tarts and Fruit Loops." Holding up a saucepan, she offered, "Grits?"

"Just a little bit," Nell replied, watching Mrs. Billodeaux piling on the scrambled eggs and adding toast and bacon strips to her plate.

She served her husband twice the portion, then shouted down the hall, "Joe Dean, eggs are gettin' cold."

Wearing nothing but striped pajama bottoms that sagged low across his pelvic bones, Joe wandered into the kitchen.

"Go back and put you on some clothes before you sit at my table, boy. Wear something decent. We can still get to eleven o'clock Mass," his mama ordered.

Nell bit into a piece of bacon. Saliva flooded her mouth as a heavy-eyed Joe ran a hand through his thick, tousled hair, scratched his heavily muscled chest and turned, giving her a fine view of his slim rear end as he returned to his room. She did not eat bacon very often.

"Spoiled by his sisters, but not by me. Cat'lic, dear?" Mrs. Billodeaux inquired.

"Me? No, Episcopalian." Nell blotted her lips on a handy paper napkin.

"Almost Cat'lic." She gave a "can't have everything" shrug. "All's I want for my Joe is a nice girl to settle down wit'. I don't approve of what I read at the grocery store, no. We didn't allow none of that when he was living at home, did we, Frank?"

"Nope." Frank poured more coffee and hid behind the comics.

"We scrimped to send him to parochial school. He says he would have been noticed sooner by the scouts if we let him go to public school, but those nuns did teach that boy morals. He's got 'em somewheres. I keep saying there is more to life than sex and football, Joe."

"Aw, Ma. Nell doesn't need to hear all this." Joe, now decently attired in a plain white shirt unbuttoned at the neck and clean, new jeans, but still barefooted, slid into a chair at the table and began digging into the farmer's breakfast sitting at his place. His mama set mugs of orange juice, milk, and coffee down in front of him.

"And you wonder why I never bring anyone home," he groused.

"The kind who would put their name on a list for sex I don't need to know. Milk or juice, little darlin',"

Nadine said to Nell.

"Just coffee is fine, thanks." Nell ducked her head to stay out of the crossfire. She could see where Joe got his strong features and thick, dark hair, though his mother's was shot through with silver. In build, he more resembled the long-limbed Frank who knew when to stay out of matters. Frank offered her the comics and went on reading the front section of the paper.

"Nell is nice. She's a child psychologist who works with sick kids. And she doesn't want to have sex with me," Joe answered petulantly.

"Good girl. You save yourself for the weddin' night," Mrs. Billodeaux said with approval.

Nell felt herself turning red and practiced the Frank technique of pretending to read the comics. Joe dropped his fork and leaned her way during its retrieval. "But it's just a matter of time for us," he whispered. More loudly, he asked, "Ready to go over to the ranch, Nell? A guy is bringing by some horses for me to look at in about an hour."

"Oh, yes! I'm ready." Nell took her plate to the sink. She had devoured the bacon, most of the eggs, some of the grits and one piece of toast, more breakfast than she ate in a week of breakfasts.

"What about Mass?" Nadine Billodeaux asked.

"No Mass, Ma. I have to take care of business, then get Nell back to her poor, sick kids in New Orleans. Let's find some boots, Nell." He rose from the table and motioned toward a side door. It opened onto a mudroom with a row of dirty boots shoved under an old bench.

"Try these." He tossed her the smallest pair. They were red and pointy-toed with a rearing stallion embossed on both sides. "I think they belong to one of my nieces."

Joe pulled on his own no-nonsense cowboy footwear of scarred brown leather. He took down a stained Stetson from a wall peg, looked over the selection, and chose a pink cowgirl hat for Nell. "Probably belongs to the same niece, no taste, that girl."

"I'm supposed to wear this stuff?"

"Smallest we have. Make do." Joe led the way out of the mud room to the double carport where a new Silverado and a nice, clean white Honda sedan sat side by side.

"I got my parents those with part of my bonus. They won't let me buy them a new house, but I'm building one for myself on the ranch. You hear what went on in there? And Mama wonders why I don't come home more often. I'd stay with one of my sisters, but they're just the same. Joe, when are you gonna settle down? Joe, when are you gonna marry?"

He held the door to his Porsche open for Nell, then got in and backed his car down the gravel drive between two young live oaks about the same age as the house and just starting to spread their limbs.

"They're concerned about your lifestyle. You know you could get something much worse than a football injury."

Joe glanced over at Nell as they bucketed along the road. "I take precautions. The Sinners have me in for checkups all the time, if that's what's holding you back."

"Nothing is holding me back. I have no desire to sign your book," Nell said.

"Don't want you to."

The Porsche hit a pothole throwing its passengers against their shoulder belts. "Damn, I'll need another alignment. I need to get a truck for when I'm home."

They drove for a mile or so between endless rows tufted with low clumps of winter-planted sugarcane.

"My daddy farms this acreage with his two brothers. Three Brothers Plantation they call it. The ranch is right down here. Used to belong to my Uncle Hal. He kept a dairy herd, but the dairy industry in Louisiana isn't what it used to be." He gave a sharp laugh. "I sound just like Uncle Hal. Anyhow, he wanted to retire to a place on Toledo Bend Reservoir, so when I came into money, I bought him out. Better than having family land go for a sub-division. Their son, my cousin Bijou, is taking care of the ranch for me. He's still living in the old family place."

Joe gestured toward a white frame house set up on stacks of old brick. Its gingerbread trimmed porch and the moon window on the second floor said latter nineteenth century to Nell. An added-on bathroom with a butterfly screen jutted out of one side of the building. The place needed paint, but sweet olives framed the walkway and large camellia bushes still bearing a few pink blooms dotted the yard giving it a less neglected look.

"Looks like Aunt Flo's daffodils came up without her help. She'll be upset with Bijou for parking his truck in her patch of yellow iris. Bijou, he isn't as ornamental." Joe gave the man lounging on the porch a brief wave.

His cousin sported a greasy mullet of black curls and a small pot belly. Looking like Joe Dean gone to seed, the unshaven Bijou had on a dingy sleeveless

27

undershirt and worn jeans. He saluted them with a cold, sweating beer and a flash from his large pinkie ring as they passed on to dirt side road and under the rusting wrought iron arc that read Lorena Ranch.

"Lorena was my great-grandmother. Looks like Bijou isn't going to Mass either," Joe explained as they bumped along the farm road sadly in want of grading. He pulled over into a grove of granddaddy live oaks, all stretching their long, low arms to the brown bayou flowing by slowly at the bottom of a gentle decline of the land.

Parking in the shade, Joe got out and patted one of the oaks. "Best climbing trees ever and over there is a good barn with a sound tin roof. I can keep half a dozen horses, maybe some Charolais cattle just because they're pretty. I'm setting my house in this grove. Used to be a place here before the Civil War. The family claims the Yankees burned it down when they brought the gunboats up the river. Later, they rebuilt out near the road." He tested a stout oak limb by chinning up on it.

"Look at this. I could hang a swing here for my kids or a tire to pass a football through."

Nell was touched. "Planning on a big family?"

"Am I Cajun? Some day. Plenty of time for that. In the meantime, maybe your patients would like to visit here," Joe said, backing away from the idea of his own kids.

"I'm sure they would love it." Nell put her foot into the crotch of the tree and pulled herself up on to the second branch where she settled into a patch of resurrection ferns.

She pushed aside a curtain of dangling Spanish

moss and gloated, "Look at me. I'm taller than Joe Dean Billodeaux."

He took her by the waist and bumped her down to the lower branch, pulling himself to a seat beside her. "Not. You know what I thought when I saw you yesterday wearing that green dress with the raggedy hem? You look just like Tinker Bell—you know, in *Peter Pan*."

"It was a handkerchief hem, and Tinker Bell was a blonde."

"Yeah, I go for blondes. I never could figure out what Peter Pan saw in Wendy when Tink was so built."

"Maybe he had problems with interspecies marriages or any marriage at all."

"I can understand that, but what about interspecies fooling around?"

He was coming in for the kiss when an SUV pulling a horse trailer sounded its horn. Joe jumped down to saunter over to the trailer. Her heart thumping wildly, Nell stayed put.

The burly driver wearing boots, jeans, and a red western shirt pumped Joe Dean's hand and said, "Earl Goody here. We spoke on the phone. It's great to meet an athlete like you."

Then, he thumped down the tailgate of the trailer to make a ramp and carefully backed out an enormous sorrel horse whose copper coat gleamed even in the shade of the oaks. Its mane was trimmed in what looked to Nell like a long row of bangs and his tail was squared off.

"This here is Three B's Lazy Boy. Did some racing in his early years up at Evangeline Downs. Good record, don't let the name fool you. He's eighteen hands and look at the rump on him. Smart, too, retrained for cutting, but the owner was thinking of putting him out to stud when you called. He'll pay for himself in fees."

All the while, Earl Goody walked and turned the horse, showing him off from all angles. "Flashy, too, if you do any parade riding, four white socks and a blaze. Could let his mane and tail grow out."

Nell came up behind Joe but kept her distance from the gigantic hooves. Joe curled up the horse's lips and checked the big yellow teeth for wear. He felt up and down the legs, lifted the hooves, nodded, and asked Earl Goody what else he had. Tossing the halter rope to Joe, Mr. Goody backed out another horse.

"Nice little Arabian mare, used to be my daughter's ride until she up and married and moved away. Got papers if you want to breed her, but she's a good, gentle riding horse, not quite fifteen hands."

Earl Goody did the walking and turning routine again. Joe repeated the teeth, leg, and hoof check and led the mare over to Nell. "What do you think?"

Nell patted the coat dappled faintly like the shade under the oaks. The horse, its long white forelock and mane fluttering in the breeze, turned a mellow dark eye on her. Nell stepped back. Joe opened her hand and gave her a sugar cube filched from his mama's bowl.

"Hold it out flat on your palm."

The mare lipped up the sugar with her soft pink nose rubbing against Nell's hand. The animal crunched the cube and nosed for more.

"Her name is Fatima, but if she doesn't get some exercise and lay off the sugar cubes, we might have to rename her Fatty," Mr. Goody joked.

"She's like a fairy tale horse, Joe, with that white name and dainty feet."

"Hooves, sugar. Want to ride?"

"I brought their tack. Take 'em for a spin," Earl offered.

Nell stood way back while the men saddled the mounts. Joe tossed Nell onto Fatima and vaulted himself on to the tall Lazy Boy. With the reins knotted over the horn, Nell sat there terrified.

"I don't know what to do here!"

"They're western trained, sugar. Lean left for left, right for right, back for whoa, and give her a good kick to get her started."

He turned his animal and walked him out along a faint path running along the bayou. Fatima came along without urging, her nose stuck almost in the stallion's tail. They ambled along until they reached a meadow with space to turn. Lazy Boy turned on a dime. Fatima settled in to graze.

"Give her a nudge, Nell," Joe Dean shouted.

Nell flailed her booted heels. Fatty kept eating. She flapped the reins. Nothing. "Joe, don't leave me! It's like she doesn't even know I'm here."

"Well, pull her head up."

Nell jerked the reins up. Fatty continued to strain for the spring grass. Finally, Joe circled, took the reins and got the mare's attention. They headed back to the grove where Mr. Goody waited and hoped for a fat check from a rich quarterback, but the sales debate continued.

"Not a proven stud, then."

"No, but he got what it takes," said Earl pointing to the part needed which had decided to come out and take a leak. Embarrassed, Nell turned her head. "What do you say, little lady?"

"Ah, I can see he and Joe are two of a kind. Fatima is beautiful, but she should watch her weight."

"See, your girlfriend likes 'em."

"Sold, but I'd like to get a sperm count on the big guy before we finalize."

"Done."

The rich man wrote a big check.

****

Sneaking back into the Billodeaux home while his parents were at Mass, Nell changed back into her wedding clothes and folded his sister's jeans and shirt neatly on the bed she had made that morning. She could hear Joe Dean jiggling his keys and thrumming his fingers against the doorframe.

"In a hurry, Joe?" she asked as she opened the door.

"My parents will be home from Mass soon, and we don't have time for any foolin' around. Let's get out of here."

"I wasn't planning on doing any fooling around."

Joe glanced into the tidied bedroom. "You could keep the shirt if you want. It was mine before my sisters stole it. Wouldn't fit me now anyhow, and you looked so sweet in it."

"I can't take clothing from your parents' house. Besides, just because I'm little doesn't mean I'm sweet. I can be a fighter when I have to be."

"Whatever you say, sugar." He prodded her toward the carport and his escape route. They made it as far as the mudroom door when a car turned into the drive crunching gravel beneath the tires. Joe all but carried her to the Porsche, got the sports car in gear, and backed up before his mama could block him in.

"Don't you want to stay for Sunday dinner, Joe? I got a pork roast and cornbread dressing in the oven," Mrs. Billodeaux called after them. "Your sisters might come over."

"Nell has to get back. Gotta hurry."

They were slamming down the hardtop before Nell could shout her thanks for the hospitality. Oh well, she could send a bread-and-butter note later.

At Joe's rate of speed, they got back to the Mardi Gras ballroom in minutes. Evidently, the Chapelle police slept late on Sundays. Nell's reliable Toyota sat a little distance from the dumpsters out back, which now overflowed with black trash bags. A few busy yellow jackets crawled over the rims of soft drink cans and beer bottles. The lot was dotted with cars belonging to those who had overindulged or found someone interesting to escort home.

"It was kind of rude running out on your mother like that, Joe." Nell rolled down the window of the Toyota to let out the March warmth.

"That was a trap for sure. I guarantee you don't want to be interrogated by my sisters."

"But you looked so adorable sticking your little, curly head into their prom pictures. They still have your photos up on the bulletin boards in their room after all these years. Besides, your mother said they spoiled you."

"Ma never packs anything away. You were staying in Allie and Eenie's room."

"Eenie?"

"Yeah, my sisters, Alise, Darlene, Lizette, and

Isabelle—or Allie, Eenie, Lizzie and Izzy among the family." Joe leaned against the side of her car.

"Gee, I wonder what they would call me."

"Tinker Bell, Tink for short."

Nell turned pink. "As it so happens, someone else calls me that."

"A guy?" Joe inquired with a shrug, indicating he had no trouble with a little competition.

"My dad. If you will remove your carcass from my ride, I need to get going."

"I'll follow you just to make sure you get back to Metairie safely."

"No need. I drive these roads all the time."

"As a gentleman, I have to see you to your door. Mama taught me that."

Nell gave up. Maybe she could lose him on the Atchafalaya Causeway or in Baton Rouge when the traffic got heavy.

****

Three hours later, Joe parked beside her in the apartment complex lot. No matter how slow she had gone, he stayed behind her. Now, he followed her up the stairs to her second-story home. She turned her key in the lock but did not open the door.

"Joe, this was fun, the reception, meeting your parents, the horses and all. Thanks." She turned his way.

He caged her with his arms against the door. Nell squirmed trying to reach the doorknob. He lowered his head to her level. His lips, firm and warm, touched hers and stayed there. He prodded gently with his tongue. When she opened her mouth to protest, he was in. Joe raised her by the waist to a more comfortable height and sandwiched Nell against the door. He was as ready as the stud he had purchased this morning. Her hand found the knob and they tumbled into the apartment. She fell free.

"Out, out, out!" Nell pushed against his chest to no avail.

Joe looked around her place. Nice, warm, cozy, small. On the balcony sat an aluminum table and chairs pressed with a rose pattern to look like wrought iron. The window boxes hanging on the railing burst full of freshly planted purple petunias, golden marigolds, and trailing ivy. An overstuffed floral sofa with a matching chair dominated the living room. Her refrigerator blossomed with magnets holding up pictures of her patients.

Finally deciding to take notice of her pushing efforts, Joe looked down and asked, "What would it take to get you to let me stay the afternoon?"

"A health certificate!"

"I doubt if I can get one on a Sunday, Nell."

"So, go call number seventy-five."

"Seventy-six, actually." He shrugged as if to say Joe Dean Billodeaux did not have to force himself on anyone and she was a lot of work. An eloquent shrugger that Joe Dean.

"If you insist. So long for now."

Nell locked the door behind him.

Chapter Five

He should have known number seventy-six was a ringer by her name alone, Fanny Goodenwilling. Who named their girls Fanny anymore? But then, New Orleans bulged full of women with stage names like the famous Blaze Starr.

Joe cranked the weight machine up another notch trying to work out his annoyance in the Sinners' training facility. The place stood fairly empty with most of the team indulging in their off-season pleasures: golf, deep-sea fishing, whatever—as he had been indulging in his, women—and having a good time, too.

When little Nell Abbott had pushed him out her door he had called the next person on his list, Fanny. The headlines in the tabloids last week read *Call Girl Says, "I did Joe Dean for free."*

No wonder she knew her way around a man's body and had given the best swirly in town. Today, he crossed through her name and all five stars following it. The woman had sent him a thank-you note, pink and perfumed, saying her business was up by fifty percent because so many wanted to be where the Sinners' quarterback had been.

He guessed that was a compliment, but somehow, it disgusted him.

On silent athletic-shod feet, Coach Marty Buck came behind him and positioned himself, arms folded, by the side of the Nautilus. Great, on top of everything, he was going to get a lecture. Might as well be done with it. Joe sat up, wiped the sweat from his hands and face and prepared to have his ears chewed.

"Son," Coach Buck began, "you've got a problem with women. It's just not healthy, what you're doing. If you catch something serious, you know the suits will find a way to cancel your contract. Probably, they'd use that clause about pursuing dangerous off-season activities. Could cost you millions…and your career, too."

"I'm careful, Coach. Besides, I don't hear any complaints from the general manager or the publicity people. They told me women are buying up season tickets, supposedly for their husbands."

"Don't let it go to your head. This isn't being careful." Coach Buck unrolled the tabloid he had tucked under his arm and bared the damning headline. "Boy, if I had a son instead of the three daughters by two wives, I'd be telling him the same thing. Why don't you go have another talk with Dr. Funk? He got your pal, Connor, straightened out."

Joe Dean gritted his teeth. The last time he had been dragged into the team psychiatrist's office, the doctor had theorized that Joe overcompensated with women because he felt insecure in his role of quarterback and team leader. That was one Super Bowl and six fuckin' months of celibacy ago. Besides, he felt he and Stevie Dowd had helped Connor with his head problems, not any shrink.

He had nothing to prove or to say to Dr. Mind Fuck, as Joe liked to call him, but all he said to Coach was, "I don't have a sexual addiction. I'm making up for six months without sex is all. When the season starts, I plan to cut way back on dates, but that celibacy thing, it's just too hard. I've been thinking about getting a health certificate though."

"Good idea, son. You might think about settling down to maybe one or two girlfriends after you get it." Coach Buck ran his hand over his silver bristle cut in a gesture that said the uncomfortable issues that went along with running a football team most people would not believe.

"Look, Coach, when I settle down, that's it for good. Billodeauxs marry forever. I figure forty is a good age for a man to find a wife and start a family. In the meantime, I don't want to worry about child support for illegitimate children or messy divorces. I just want to have a good time between now and training camp. Unless of course, you'd like to introduce me to those daughters of yours. Who knows…"

Coach Buck took a step back. "Oldest one is married. The other two live with their mother in Florida and are way too young for you—not that I wouldn't like to have you in the family. Take care, son."

Marty Buck retreated, shaking his head all the way to his office. Joe Dean laughed all the way to the showers, but he did schedule that health test.

****

Joe's cell phone vibrated in his pocket as he stepped out into a pleasant April day where the humidity sat at probably no more than eighty-five percent, great for New Orleans.

"Hey, Joe Dean Billodeaux at your service," he answered.

"Hey, your fine self," the Rev's deep voice came

back. "Where you at?"

"In the city. So you and Mintay are back from the undisclosed destination."

"Yeah, a day or so ago. She didn't want to be away from her patients too long, but I tell you, we had paradise on earth there for a while. I booked this private island off of Cozumel. No one there but a few Mexican families and their kids to tend the place. We could have walked around naked all day."

"Did you?"

"Naw, but we did hit the beach a few times at night. You want to meet me at the Versailles course for some golf and maybe have us a cookout tonight, do up some ribs? Between the sex and the fresh fish and fruit, I must be down ten pounds."

"Sounds good. Give me a few hours to get there. Book a tee time around two."

****

The day ahead looked so good Joe gave no thought to calling number eighty-one. Instead, he swung the red Porsche out of the parking lot, picked up his titanium clubs at the condo, and headed for Morgan City on the new highway.

In Hahnville noted for its great high school football teams, he pulled up at a Burger King, got two Whoppers with cheese, a large serving of fries and a jumbo drink. Why not help the local economy? The off-season had arrived, and he resolved to enjoy every minute of it.

At the gated community near Chapelle where the Rev and his bride had set up housekeeping, the guard waved him in with barely a glance at his identification. Revelation Bullock waited at the pseudo-French villa serving as the clubhouse. They decided to walk the course since Joe wanted to burn off his cheeseburgers, and the Rev figured he should pay in advance for his planned dinner by using up some calories.

It occurred to Joe Dean as they followed the little white balls from hole to hole, that he was somewhat tired of the company of women. With Connor all tied up planning a wedding with Stevie and the Rev on his honeymoon, he'd missed uncritical male camaraderie.

"That's the place I bought for me and Mintay." The Rev gestured to a huge brick home with an impressive terrace overlooking the fairway. "You should have seen the look on the neighbors' faces when the black folk moved in, but I have to say everyone has been nice and polite, bringing over cookies, inviting us to barbecues. My relatives, though, are already complaining about being scrutinized when they visit. Auntie Ethaline got mistaken for one of the cleaning ladies. Now she says I've gotten uppity."

"I recall Aunt Ethaline from the wedding—the only one not having a good time."

"That would be her. She sat with Uncles Moses, Stevie and the Wish Lady. So how did that go?"

"What go?"

"You and the Wish Lady. Mintay kept bringing that up on the honeymoon when her thoughts should have been purely on me, brother."

"We danced. She stayed the night at my folks' place. We did some riding."

"Car, bike, horse or sexual?"

"Horse. She was afraid to kick her mount too hard. Man, I loved watching her flail around, those little breasts bouncing." Joe Dean smiled at the memory.

"And no foolin' around at your mama's neither, I'll bet."

"Are you kidding? Mama put Nell in the front bedroom right across from hers where there's this big, squeaky board in the hallway. I found that out when I was a kid. I had to go out the window or forget sneaking out altogether."

"So no bing-bang with the Wish Lady after Mintay went to all that trouble to get her to the wedding and had Stevie sit her right up front like bait for suckers like you."

"You're the one who got married, not me. Besides, I called her before the wedding. That's why little Nell came—to see me again. Mintay's plans had nothing to do with it."

"Yeah, right. Mintay won't be happy until all my friends are married. She thinks you need a woman with character, not round heels."

"Women just don't understand. Men don't need character to have a good time."

"Sad, but true."

"Besides, I'm thinking she might be a virgin. That would explain the reluctance."

"That would be one explanation, yes."

"She asked for a health certificate. Can you believe it?"

"Yes, I can."

"I might just get one and shove it in her face. I'm thinking she needs patience, reassurance, and a gentle hand."

"That's you, Joe Dean, the soul of patience."

"Are you laughing at me?"

"I am. Mintay said you would never get over a

woman who didn't fall at your feet."

"That settles it. I'm calling number eighty-one as soon as I get back to the city."

****

Joe did not make his call that evening. Instead, he lingered on the Rev's terrace and sucked down ribs cooked in an oil drum smoker with a small chimney sticking out the side—a family heirloom, the Rev said. Mintay after a hard day at the clinic only had to toss a salad and sip a glass of red wine. The Rev took care of everything else.

"You spoil me, honey bear." Mintay sighed so full from dinner she could burst. She stretched out, her feet up on a lounger, another glass of wine in her hand.

"That's why I was put on God's green earth, sweet thang," answered the Rev, tossing a foil-wrapped baked potato from hand to hand. "Anyone want another spud?"

He lobbed it at Joe Dean who snatched the potato before it could tip over his beer.

"I been thinking, Joe. You, me, and Connor should rent that honeymoon island and give the whole team a long weekend vacation as a sort of thanks for a great season. It would be good for morale. What say?"

"I'd say don't spill beer on me when I have a long drive back to New Orleans and the smokeys are likely to be out." Joe Dean leaned back and watched the purple martins scooping up a crop of mosquitoes in the dusk. "But sure, count me in on the island. Any women to be had there?"

"None that I noticed. The guys could bring their girlfriends."

"Or their wives and families," Mintay added. "I'll

bet Nellwyn Abbott would love to lie around in the sun for a few days. Her job is very stressful."

"Yeah. Stress and Nell sort of go together. Let's do it."

Chapter Six

"Hey, it's Joe."

"Yes, I recognized your voice." Nell Abbott rolled her eyes. Now what did he want?

"That's progress. My ma said you sent her a real nice card and note. She's impressed with you."

"Just common courtesy for letting me stay over at her house."

"Yeah, that's what Mama said. Most of the women I date don't have common courtesy. She said that, too."

Nell refrained from commenting on his taste in women. "It was nothing."

"So, the reason I called is a few of us have rented an island down near Cozumel for a week around the first of May. We have a plane chartered to fly the team and anyone they want to bring out of New Orleans. You interested in some vacation?"

Nell closed her eyes for a minute and envisioned palm trees, beaches, surf and a couple of dozen hunky men to gaze at, then came to her senses. "Wish I could, but I'm scheduled to work that weekend. We have a couple of recent liver transplants that are touch and go. I really can't leave them on such short notice."

"Kids have bad livers?" He sounded as if she were making up excuses.

"Yes, from heredity diseases, congenital birth defects, sometimes from a previous severe illness. Not from drinking, Joe."

"I guess I knew that. It's a no then?"

"Sorry. Really. Sounded great. Have a good time."

"Yeah, I will. Good-bye, Nell."

****

Joe wished he hadn't been using a cell phone so he could have slammed down the receiver. Two weeks he'd spent setting this up. Then, he delayed calling Nell for a few days while debating endlessly with himself if she was worth the trouble. Well, she would be sorry. He decided to call numbers eighty-one through eighty-six and invite them all along. Let the Wish Lady read that in the tabloids.

Stretched out on his leather sofa, Joe finished setting up Shelley Havers, Dawn Henderson, Lori Holmes, Jenny Hu, Selena Jaspers and Tabitha Johnson for the trip. This effort had taken most of his day and brought him up to number ninety-two on his list, but the effort would be well worth it.

A few of the women had other plans that could not be broken, like being their sister's bridesmaid. Some said they needed to check with their bosses. Tabitha Johnson was the first to call back after offering her manager at McDonald's the creative excuse she had to attend her great-granny's one-hundredth birthday in North Carolina. She made the cut. One called back and cancelled because she was having a herpes outbreak, but now the list was complete.

Herpes. Joe shivered. Close call. He checked for any other messages that might have come in while he was assembling the week's entertainment. A voice mail from Dr. Phillips' nurse asked him to come in for his health test results. He had plenty of time to do that tomorrow before he packed and headed for the island.

****

Doc Phillips kept Joe Dean waiting for half an hour during which passage of time, he wondered why the doctor had asked him to come in rather than give the results over the phone. That uncomfortable thought made his palms sweat. Finally, the nurse showed the Sinner' quarterback to a chair in the doctor's office and closed the door behind her.

Phillips, his white lab coat open to display a Daffy Duck necktie worn with a pink shirt, came in shortly. He shook Joe's clammy palm and smiled. Glancing down through his bifocals, Dr. Phillips began. "On the questionnaire, you say you've had intercourse with eighty women in the last three months. What are you thinking, young man?"

"I'm careful." Joe Dean studied his fingertips. Were his nails looking a little blue?

"You know what's out there: AIDS, herpes, gonorrhea, not to mention a recent outbreak here in the city of that all time favorite, syphilis, a drug-resistant variety." The doctor paused to let that sink in while little beads of sweat formed near Joe's hairline. "I can only say you are one lucky devil because your blood test came out clean…along with the rest of the examination. I have a copy for you right here." When Joe reached out a hand to take the report, Doc Phillips snatched it away.

"Have you been with anyone else since the exam was done?"

"I've had other things to do." Joe felt almost shamefaced about not keeping up his with his womanizing.

"Good, because this paper is valid only until the next time you have intercourse. Remember the adage—you are having sex with everyone your partner has had sex with before you."

"And I'm taking advice from a man wearing a Daffy Duck tie."

"My daughter gave me this tie. I treasure it, and all the other children I deal with seem to love it. That's another thing. Ever think about your offspring? Some of these diseases can do major damage to an unborn fetus: stillbirth, blindness, retardation and so on."

Joe felt queasy now. The nuns at the Chapelle parochial school had not been this specific. Their basic theme was God would strike you down if you had sex out of wedlock, no details given. Of course, he knew the doc told the truth, but he just didn't want to think about blind, retarded babies. He put out a hand for his report.

Doc Phillips leaned back in his chair. "You know, I follow football. I have season tickets to the Sinners games. Your performance this past season blew me away. I could see you growing as a quarterback every week until you were showing some real team leadership. I think it's time you grew up in your relationships with women. Remember, this certificate is good only until the next time you have sex." He offered the paper held out between two fingers.

"Thanks for the good news, Doc." Joe folded the certificate over until it fit in the rear pocket of his jeans and left the office shaking his head. He paused just outside the door and leaned against the wall for a minute. Jesus, blind babies. Doctors, they sure knew how to ruin a vacation.

Dr. Phillips made a call on his office phone. "Marty, this is Phil. I appreciate those season tickets. I think I did as good a job on Joe Dean Billodeaux as I did on my own son when he left for college. No, don't thank me. I was very happy to do it."

Ah, so that was the strategy. If a shrink didn't work, Coach would try a real doctor. Joe Dean shook his head. He was on to them. But still, blind babies.

Chapter Seven

Here he sat on an island with six women, not all pretty but certainly willing, and Joe Dean Billodeaux possessed no desire to have sex with any of them. Still, the girls seemed to be having a good time. He'd taken all six snorkeling and played some touch tag under water. He enjoyed watching the gorgeous and well-endowed Dawn Henderson and Shelley Havers play beach volleyball. The men teamed up against the women simply for the view. Who wanted to look across the net at some big-bellied lineman?

Little Jenny Hu, a free-lance massage therapist, walked on his back and it felt great. She was off practicing her trade with a few of the other team members. Now and then, Joe heard her high voice ask, "You like?" from one of the nearby cottages.

Selena and Tabitha, both black women in their early twenties, had nothing else in common. Selena worked as a personal trainer and had the muscles to prove it. She possessed a deadly volleyball serve. Tabitha, her head covered in short orange dreadlocks that made her look like a demented, black Raggedy Ann, had a great sense of comic timing. She did her standup routine about working at Mickey D's one night after the pig roast. The guys loved it.

Blue sky above, frothy surf at his feet, a breeze rustling through the palm fronds, what more could a man want? Taking in the rays, Joe Dean sank deep into his beach chair. The icy sweat off the glass holding a cool, minty mojito trickled down his arm, and all he could think of was children who had to undergo liver transplants.

Through the lenses of his mirrored sunglasses, he watched Lori Holmes frolic in the surf and wished she hadn't confessed she'd saved every penny of her manicurist's salary and tips to pay for a boob job. He thought she should have had her nose done first. Not every man's eyes went straight to the chest. Himself, he liked large, dark eyes.

He was getting to know these six women too well. They were no longer names and phone numbers and easy lays. He'd already promised Tabitha Johnson he would speak to the management of some of the clubs he frequented about getting her a gig, no strings attached. Her look of relief when she realized she didn't have to sleep with Joe Dean Billodeaux to further her career stung a little. Hell, he might as well give Lori the money for her nose, too, and expect nothing in return.

A shadow fell across his mid-section as a tall, thin woman settled into the next beach chair. A nasal voice greeted, "Hiya, lover boy."

He'd stayed in one place too long, and Margaret Stutes had sacked him. She'd come along as the guest of the second-string lineman who seemed to believe publicity rather than talent, hard work and just plain luck would move him up to starter. So far, Joe Dean had managed to avoid her advances. He dug his feet into the sand and got ready to stand up and say he was going to seek some shade.

"Don't move on my account, Joey. I'm just visiting

for a minute."

No one called him Joey. Ever. Joe gritted his teeth and managed a weak smile. "You're lookin' good, Margaret."

He did not lie. A light tan covered her freckled skin. Her breasts looked bigger in that under-wired, padded bikini top, but Joe had enough experience with bras to know sometimes the package held very little inside. She'd put on a few pounds. Her pelvic bones no longer jutted out sharply enough to impale a man. The henna rinse had grown out and been replaced by blonde streaks over dark brown. Still, Margaret did not tempt him.

"What's the matter, Joey? Run out of energy? You bring six women along and aren't doing any of them, not even the one with the big knockers and bleached blonde hair. I thought she was just your type. Here, rub some lotion on my back." Margaret tossed him a tube from her straw beach bag.

"I have plenty of energy. I'm half way through my list and wanted to take a break—Maggie."

Somewhere in his dimly recalled one-night stand with Margaret, he seemed to remember she hated to be called Maggie. Joe squeezed gobs of white cream out of the tube and slathered it between her sharp shoulder blades. Her back remained as bony as ever. Maybe she would stick to the chair and he could make his getaway. He tossed the tube back into her bag and stood up.

"I need to cool off." Joe headed for the surf where Dawn Henderson bobbed with the young wide receiver, Jared Forte.

"I don't think we'll ever get back together, Joey, but you just remember, I was the first on the list to screw Joe Dean Billodeaux," Margaret called after him, not bothering to lower her voice.

In a rush, he dived head first into a small wave and lost his sunglasses to the sea.

****

Back at the airport, four of his six ladies stayed to line up and say thanks. Dawn Henderson left on the arm of Jared Forte as soon as the plane touched down. Shelley Havers, the prettiest of the bunch, had hooked up with a halfback on the island and stayed behind with him for another week.

Jenny Hu stood on her tiptoes and kissed Joe's cheek. "*Merci beaucoup*, Joe. I got lots of new clients."

Selena Jaspers bopped his arm. "One or two of the men are going to recommend me to their wives. Seems they don't trust male trainers."

Lori Holmes held the check for her nose job to her immense chest and cried. Tabitha Johnson pulled Joe's head down to her level and gave him a huge smacker right on the lips. Her orange dreadlocks tickled his nose.

"You're a great guy. Be sure to come opening night, you hear?"

Joe waved good-bye and went to retrieve his car. He wondered if Nell was working this coming weekend. He had some show and tell he wanted to do at her place and he was not going to wait much longer. She owed him for a wasted week at the beach.

Chapter Eight

The hospital confirmed Nell was not on duty. Her car sat in the complex lot not far from the staircase leading to her apartment. Joe Dean parked his sleek Porsche next to her dumpy Toyota and bounded up the stairs. He figured he would take her to lunch first. Then, they could go back to his place or hers, whatever she wanted. He banged on the door.

"I know you're in there, Nellwyn Abbott. I got something to show you. Don't bother gettin' dressed if you're naked, sugar. Just open the door."

The door opened. A frowning middle-aged man asked, "You're here to see my daughter?"

"Ah, yes. Just jokin' around with her. Would you tell her Joe is here, sir?" Joe rocked back on heels and put his hands behind his back.

Staying in the doorway, Nell's father turned and shouted, "Tink, a young man named Joe is here to see you. Should I let him in or throw him down the stairs?" Mr. Abbott gave Joe a large, toothy grin.

"Throw him down the stairs, Daddy," Nell answered from her bedroom.

Nell's dad was tall and on the heavy side, but no way did he have the muscle to throw Joe Dean Billodeaux down the stairs. Could he? In a scuffle, either one might get hurt.

"Don't worry. She always says that. We've been

doing this routine since she brought her first beau home when she was sixteen. Come on in. Sit down. The women are using the powder room. It could be a while." Mr. Abbott led the way to the floral sofa.

Nell stuck her head into the living room. "Only this time I meant it. Not a good time, Joe. I'm going shopping with my mom and sister." She ducked back into the bedroom.

A petite older woman with a head of soft gray curls and dark eyes set in a net of fine wrinkles came from the back of the apartment to act as hostess. "Could I get you something to drink, Joe? I could make coffee for all of us."

She smoothed her mauve blouse tucked neatly into slim gray slacks, then toyed with the gray freshwater pearls around her neck. "I'm Nell's mother, Ann. You've met my husband, Gary."

Joe stood up and offered his hand. "Joe Dean Billodeaux. I'm enchanted to meet you, ma'am. I can see where Nell gets her looks."

"My, you're a big one." Mrs. Abbott stared up at Joe and appeared worried.

"Everyone, sit down," Gary Abbott prompted. "Billodeaux? You look familiar."

"A Cajun name, I believe. Do you come from a large family, Joe?" Mrs. Abbott asked making polite conversation.

"Four sisters and me if you consider that a large family." Joe refrained from telling her Billodeaux meant "love letter" in slightly corrupted French as he did most women. A good opener in a bar might not go over so well with a mother.

"Why, yes, I would consider five children a lot. I

guess you are Catholic."

"Raised that way, yes."

"Billodeaux," repeated Nell's father. "Got it! Don't you play for the Sinners?"

"Yes, sir. Quarterback."

"Joe Dean Billodeaux sitting right here in my little girl's apartment, what do you know! Aren't you the one who recently got back from spending a week on a desert island with six women?"

"You can't believe those tabloids, sir. We were at a nice resort with lots of other men and women around playing volleyball, swimming, and such. I invited Nell, but she was too busy at the hospital."

"She works too hard. I worry about her. Of course, beach swimming has its dangers, too. Undertows, jellyfish, shark attacks," Mrs. Abbott fretted.

Another woman entered the room. A larger version of Nell with long, dark hair worn lose, she shot him a very cold smile. "Always worrying about little Nell, Mom is. Emily Abbott, Nell's sister. Yes, the one who saved her life in the flesh."

Joe jumped up again. He felt as if his mama was pulling his good manners strings over and over. He pressed her hand. "Charmed, sugar."

Mama would not have approved of that greeting or the warm eye contact. It came to him so naturally.

Emily's well-plucked eyebrows went up. "Nell gets him, and I'm stuck with Todd Washburn. Life is so unfair."

"Todd is a very nice young man, Emily. He earns a good living as a computer programmer. He's not very flashy, of course, but completely reliable. You play football, Joe? That's a rather dangerous sport, isn't it?"

Obviously, Mrs. Abbott considered Joe to be flashy.

"Jeez, Mom. The Sinners won the Super Bowl this year. His picture was everywhere." Emily Abbott slammed herself into Nell's overstuffed chair and slung her jean-clad legs over one of the arms. She presented Joe with a nice profile of her breasts in a tight red tank top. This earned a frown of disapproval from her mother.

"It can be dangerous, yes. Good training and good luck help, but careers can be short, yes." Joe eyed the hallway. Where was Nell? This was worse than being home with his ma.

"Do you like baseball, Joe? I think a Braves game is coming on. I guess you know Garrett lives in Shreveport. Married a girl from up there. We have a great little grandson we don't get to see as much as we'd like. I miss watching the games with my son. Why don't you grab a beer, and we could check out how the Braves are shaping up while the women go over to the Galleria." In a loud aside, Mr. Abbott whispered, "I really don't want to go sit around in the mall. Bet you don't either."

"No, sir. A baseball game would be great."

At last, Nell appeared wearing low-slung jeans and a small pink top exposing an inch or two of belly that Joe Dean zeroed right in on. She tugged at her top, but it wouldn't go any lower.

"I'm sure Joe can't stay, Dad. He probably has to go train or catch the next plane for the desert island or something. He should have called first."

"I should have called, but I had something I wanted to show Nell."

"What?" asked her sister, showing intense interest.

Joe stood and took a well-folded paper from his hip pocket. He offered it to Nell. She looked it over carefully.

"This is dated more than a week ago. Let's see, was that five or six women with you on the island? You know your vacation activities make this invalid."

"We went swimming. We played volleyball. We didn't do anything else. Hell, Dawn went home with Jared Forte. What kind of proof do you need, Nell?" He knew his exasperation showed.

"I believe you, Joe. Want to date me?" Emily offered.

"You are lovely, sugar, but Nell and me are working something out here."

"No, we aren't. Let's go, Mom. At the rate we're moving, the stores will be closed."

"Are you coming, Gary?" Mrs. Abbott asked.

"No, Joe and I are going to watch a game. We'll be here when you get back." Mr. Abbott fondled the remote control.

As Nell led the way to the door, Joe said, "What do you think of a bucket of fried chicken to go with that beer, Gary? I'm paying."

"Too much cholesterol, dear," Mrs. Abbott shouted back.

"How about buffalo wings, Joe?"

Joe liked Gary Abbott. Nell's daddy worked as the head manager for the Wal-Mart over in Covington. He'd had his own appliance store at one time.

"If you can't beat 'em, join 'em, I say. A lot of people put Wal-Mart down, but their foundation was a big help with medical bills when Nell got sick. Sure we hire more part-timers than full-timers, but my health plan took care of most of my girl's expenses. The corporate jet took her up to that famous charity hospital for children, you know."

"I didn't know she was sick." Joe put down the bones of the chicken wing he had been sucking.

"Now I'm in trouble. She hates when her mother or I bring that up, but she beat childhood leukemia. She's a survivor. Been in remission for ten years now and helps those who are fighting the same battle. I'm so proud of her I could bust, but I wouldn't relive those years for anything. It's hard on the whole family. Her mother still gets upset over every bruise or head cold Nell comes down with. No wonder Tink decided to live over on this side of the lake."

"No wonder," Joe echoed. "I'm done. You finish up the rest of these wings, Gary." He suddenly wanted to leave, but the game was only in the seventh inning and he had made it so clear he'd wait for Nell.

The women returned in the bottom of the eighth, announced by their chatter and the rustle of shopping bags coming up the stairs. The apartment filled with their noise and their purses and their tissue-wrapped bundles.

Holding up a Victoria's Secret bag, Emily stood in front of the TV and flourished its contents. She dangled a short nightie, deep burgundy red and satiny, by its spaghetti straps and hooked the matching bikini pants over a finger.

"We got this for Nell, Joe. You know how she's always wearing that ratty old nightshirt she got at Disney World. It's time she threw that out. What do you think?"

"Well, it's not see-through." Joe gave his honest

opinion.

"This is Nell we bought it for. Want to see mine?" Emily rooted something sheer and lipstick red from her sack.

"Emily. Enough," her mother prompted.

Gary Abbott waved his hand. "Get away from the screen. I want to see the replay on that move from third base. Sit down and have a chicken wing."

Nell grabbed the bag, gathered up a few others, and retreated to her room. "Want to go to Middendorf's for dinner, Tink?" her father called after her. "You're invited, Joe. This will be my treat since you paid for the wings."

"No, I can't stay after all. Let me tell Nell I'm going." Joe pushed out of the sofa's deep cushions and went to tap on her bedroom door. "Nell, look, I don't want to bother you so I'm going."

The door wrenched open. "Get in here." She pointed to a spot at the foot of her bed. Joe went to stand on a throw rug patterned with sunflowers. He took the chance to look around, as this would probably be the only time he'd see the place. She had painted the room a deep yellow and covered the moldings in forest green. The sunflowers on the spread matched the rug under his feet. Old bottles of violet, deep green and amber glass sat on the windowsill and dresser.

"Nice room," he complimented blandly.

"What did my father tell you?" She was for sure angry.

"You call me and show up at my door. Now you're not going to bother me. What did Dad say?"

Joe felt his temper rising, too. He found his health report in his shirt pocket and waved it at her. "You made me get this. You don't believe I haven't been with other women since, but you're the one who's sick."

"Was sick, Joe. Was. Ten years in remission."

"You should have told me up front."

"Sure, the first thing I tell my dates is that I'm a cancer survivor. It makes lovely dinner conversation. I describe my chemo treatments during the appetizer, my baldness during the main course, and the bone marrow transplant with dessert. Or, maybe I don't say a word because this has happened to me before. Are you one of those people who think they can catch cancer? Is the great big football player afraid of sick people?" she shouted.

Nell got in his face, or more accurately, went for his throat.

"I know you can't catch cancer from another person. I know that. It's just I don't feel easy around sick people, is all. My family is real healthy. I mean we were together a whole day, and you never mentioned your disease."

"I am not sick! Get out, just get out."

Joe tripped over the throw rug in his haste to leave, caught himself on the dresser, and set the antique bottles clinking. He went straight for the front door, past the appalled faces of Nell's family.

"Nice meeting y'all," he managed to get out before Nell came roaring after him and slammed the door in his face. He bolted down the steps, hopped into the Porsche and roared away.

****

Nell's dad came up behind her and put his arms around his little girl. "Aw, I'm so sorry, Tink. I blew it for you, didn't I?"

"Doesn't matter, Dad. Joe is only a big, dumb jock." She buried her face in his chest. "We weren't even dating, and if we had, it would never have worked out anyhow. I know it's normal for people to shy away from disease. Some animals drive the sick from the herd. It's a survival mechanism that keeps disease from spreading. I know that. I've studied it. I can't get used to it."

"That's because people are not just animals."

"Some are."

"Poor Tink." Gary Abbot patted her back.

"Yeah, it's always poor Tink," added Emily.

"For shame, Em," said their mother.

****

Joe Dean tore across the causeway in his red Porsche aiming for Connor Riley's place on the other side of Lake Ponchartrain. Eula Mae, Riley's housekeeper, buzzed him into the gated estate on the shore.

"You stayin' for dinner, Mr. Joe," she asked, "because I can set another place before I leave for my Sunday off."

Joe paused in taking the shortcut through the kitchen to the deck where Connor and Stevie were sunning. "What's cookin', Miss Essie?"

Eula Mae's mother listed the menu. "Chicken fricasee, rice and gravy, green beans with bacon, salad, hot bread, and strawberry shortcake for dessert. That suit you?"

"Sure does. Set another place, Eula Mae." He moved out to the deck where Connor and Stevie lounged away the hot May day.

"Hey, bro. Aren't you afraid of burning that lily white skin?" he called to Connor.

"Too late, I think." Connor regarded his broad fair shoulders capped with the red of sunburn. He pulled a t-shirt over his head. "What brings you across the lake?"

"Women problems."

Stevie Dowd raised her sunglasses to get a better look at Joe, then framed his face with her fingers as if snapping a picture. "Stop the presses! New headline! *Joe Dean Billodeaux Admits to Having Problems with Women*!"

"Very funny, Stevie. I need to talk to Connor about the Wish Lady."

"Oh, the Wish Lady. Do you want me to leave?"

"No, stick around. Maybe a woman would know how to handle this."

"A novel idea. Should we call our old friend, Jackie Haile, and get a lesbian viewpoint, too?"

"I don't think so. That only worked when I thought you might be a lesbian."

"Spare me from another of your plots, Joe."

"Okay. Well, here's the problem. Nell and me, we spent a nice time together after the Rev's wedding. But, she put me off saying she wanted me to get a health check because of my list, you see."

"I see," said Connor nodding his head gravely.

"I did what she asked and I'm clean. I go over to her place to show her the proof and maybe make some progress, you know. Her whole frickin' family is there except her brother. Anyhow, I watch the ball game with her dad."

"How did the Braves do? We were out sailing."

"Wiped 'em, eight to two. So, we're eating chicken

wings, and her dad says about how Nell is a cancer survivor, how brave she is and all."

"Joe, would you stop pacing and sit down. I'm going to injure my neck again watching you."

Joe flopped on to another lounge, put his feet up and leaned his head back against his folded arms. "It sort of threw me hearing that. I needed to think about it. Then, Nell comes home. Her sister is showing me nighties and sort of coming on to me. I decided maybe I had better to leave. I go to say bye to Nell and she tears me to shreds over the cancer thing when I never said a word about it."

"What do you think the problem was?"

"Oh, she told me. Men leave her when they find out about the cancer thing."

"Were you leaving her?"

"We aren't a couple. We spent one day together and didn't even hit the sheets. How can I be leaving her?"

Connor nodded. "Are you going to see her again?"

"I don't know. Sick people make me nervous. Of course, she's not sick. She made that clear enough."

"If it's a problem for you, it would be best to let her alone."

"She's different, interesting, but what if her cancer comes back?"

"Did it ever occur to you that she is different because of what she has been through?" Stevie chipped in. "Joe, your life and your women have been too easy."

"Maybe so, but it sure has been fun."

Stevie sighed. "We invited her to our reception. That's in two weeks. Why don't you think things through for a while and see how you feel then."

At the mention of their wedding, Stevie looked into Connor's eyes and squeezed his hand. "In sickness and in health is the way it goes, Joe."

"Sounds good and easy when you say it. Let me wash up for dinner. I think I still have chicken wing sauce under my nails." Joe sprang up.

"Who invited you for dinner?" questioned Stevie as she ran her fingers through Connor's long, blond hair all the way down to the scars it covered on his neck. She gave him a small kiss.

"Eula Mae. Okay, huh?" Joe hung his head like a little boy who had forgotten his manners.

"Maybe a child psychologist is exactly what you need, Joe. Mintay thinks so, too."

"I thought you and Mintay liked me."

"We do. But this is an exact quote from Mrs. Revelation Bullock, a. k. a. Dr. Arminta Green, 'That boy can lead my man down some wrong alleys and I'm having none of it. The sooner Joe Dean says 'I do' to someone nice and steady, the better I'll feel'."

"Does that go for you, too?"

"You bet."

"Nice impersonation of Dr. Mind Fuck, by the way, Connor."

"I thought so. Go wash up for dinner, bro."

His problem solved, Joe Dean trotted off to the kitchen.

Chapter Nine

Nellwyn Abbott wondered for the second time why she was attending the reception of people she knew only vaguely. Stevie Dowd had tossed out the invitation very casually at the Rev's reception and gone on to grouse about having her wedding turned into a media event by the Sinners' publicity department. Stevie intended to have a small, private non-traditional service for the family at Connor's lakeside home, but with four hundred people invited to reception, one more would make no difference. Still, Stevie remembered to follow up with the engraved announcement, the address copied off of one of Nell's business cards.

Afraid her green dress would make her too easy to spot, she'd worn the only other party gown she owned, a summery nearly sheer white number with a print of tiny blue flowers that swished around her hips. Beneath it, she had on her best lace cami and matching accessories. A necklace of enameled forget-me-nots purchased at the NOMA gift shop after a Faberge' exhibit encircled her neck. White sandals with sensible heels carried her into the fray. If she hoped to remain unnoticed by staying low, it hadn't worked. She stood out like Persephone, the goddess of spring, doing her time in Hades among all the sophisticates who had worn black to a wedding.

Her teen patients would relish an eyewitness

description of the event, that was for sure, but she could not quite keep her mind on the details while being intent on avoiding Joe Dean. Surely, that would be easy in this mob filling the Fairmont ballrooms. Then, why did she sense him immediately when he entered the room—as if he were sending out pheromones to every woman in attendance? He wore a white dinner jacket and aped James Bond in an imitation that sent his audience of three busty blondes into gales of giggles.

Nell slipped behind a group of Sinners linemen and felt much safer. Truthfully, all that testosterone in the air was making her a little horny, but no, she would not succumb to a football player. Instead, she would run swiftly under their cover to the next exit and be out in the lobby reclaiming her car from valet parking in minutes. The big men in their custom-made suits shifted. She found herself caught in a pocket moving her toward Joe. Nell stepped back, assuming the group would go around but instead, trod on the feet of the Sinners' nose guard, Calvin Armitage.

"Oh, I'm so sorry," she apologized.

"No problem, little lady. I get stepped on worse at every practice. Here, let me take you where this crowd won't trample you." He held out his arm. What could she do but accept his offer? Calvin drew Nell to a table near the dance floor only yards away from where Joe Dean entertained his current harem.

"Meet my little woman, Precious. That's Sharlette Dobbs across the table from you. They'll take good care of you, honey." Calvin moved off purposefully for the hors d'oeuvres table.

Precious Armitage, who had a sort of Queen Latifah grandeur but could be called a "little woman" only by someone as large as Calvin Armitage, turned her large, purple-draped bosom toward Nell. "So this tiny thang is the Wish Lady we been hearing about."

"Looks like," purred the sexy Sharlette Dobbs, clad in a leopard print and lots of bling.

"I don't plan on staying very long. If I'm taking someone else's seat, I'll move along." Nell got up to leave. She'd lost sight of Joe Dean, and that made her nervous.

"Sit, baby. Stevie asked us to look out for you. She even gave us a picture." Precious dug into a beaded bag that seemed to be a replica of an eggplant and drew out a slightly bent print of Nell's first meeting with Joe Dean. Stevie had captured the look of amazed embarrassment on his face as Nell handed him her Wish Lady volunteer card. The infamous little black book lay open on the table before him, the pen he had offered her still clutched in his hand.

Sharlette Dobbs moved over to take a look. "Why, I don't think I've ever seen Joe Dean's jaw drop like that unless he was being hit in the stomach by a tackle. You must deliver quite a wallop for your size. You're no bigger than—"

"My name is Nellwyn Abbott. Please call me Nell." There, she had headed off any comparisons to fairies, Tinker Bell or gnats.

"One of my breasts," Precious Armitage finished Sharlette's sentence.

Both women roared with laughter. Nell joined in as a white-jacketed waiter moved toward their table with a tray of filled champagne glasses.

"Drink up, ladies." Joe Dean set his prop on the center of the table. "I had to fight a server for this. I want to get Tink out on the dance floor."

"Tinker Bell—that's the name I was looking for." Sharlette Dobbs raised a glass and clinked it against one held up by Precious Armitage.

Nell looked back at the women as Joe whisked her to the dance floor. No help came from their direction. She would have to resist him all by her lonesome self.

"Not afraid of catching cancer today, Joe?" she attacked.

"You know, for a psychologist you sure don't give a person much time to adjust to a new situation. As it happens, I adjust pretty quickly. That's a good trait in a quarterback. I think I can deal with your *past* illness if you give me a chance. In fact, I think you and Connor Riley must be the bravest people I know."

"Connor, maybe. Coming back from an accident like that, playing again, that's hard to do. He almost didn't make it as I recall. As for me, I wasn't brave. I cried, I whined and made life even harder for my family. At least, some good came out of it. I know how my patients feel. I don't expect them to be brave and nice all the time. I can point to myself and tell them they can beat disease and have a life."

She looked up at him earnestly and he leaned over and gave her a kiss on the forehead. Nell shied back. As commandingly as he had handled the balky mare on his ranch, he drew her up against him and tucked her under his chin. He hummed along rather tunelessly to *When I Fall in Love* and returned Nell to her table at the end of the song.

"Sugar, this soiree will be wrapping up around five because the Rileys are leaving for the honeymoon about then. I'll check back with you, see if you need a ride home again."

"Forget about me. I'll be fine."

"Sure you will." Joe moved off grinning.

About that time, Calvin Armitage returned from the shrimp bowl with an overflowing plate to share with the table.

"Cal, the buffet line is open. We don't need all this shrimp," his wife told him.

"I'll dance it off. Come on Wish Lady. It's a fast one. You'll have a better chance of not getting crushed."

Nell gyrated around the huge nose tackle like one of the lesser moons of Jupiter circling the largest planet in the solar system. She repeated her introduction, "Please call me Nell. I only get to play Wish Lady a few times a year, but working with Louisiana Wish Kidz is very rewarding."

"You could grant Joe Dean his wish tonight and make our Cajun boy very happy. We like our quarterback to be happy," Calvin suggested.

Nell was certain her blush could be seen from his wife's seat at the table.

"Calvin Armitage! What are you telling that child?" Precious called out.

"Just the truth, Precious."

"She don't need to hear it, Cal. You come back and eat this shrimp before it spoils."

Nell danced with other team members, the handsome groom himself and the groom's brother, a man just a little too touchy-feely for her taste. An Italian named Marcello, who obviously adored women, seemed to be trying to recruit models and show off pictures of his baby daughter, Gabriella Stefania, simultaneously.

"So very gamine. You are like the young Audrey Hepburn, but short, too short. Would you like to see a *fotografia* of my child? *Bella*, no?"

Nell admired his photos, but was relieved when Asa Dobbs, prodded by his wife Sharlette, came to her rescue. She danced with no one twice, not even Joe Dean.

She took advantage of the fine buffet with its chilled rock lobster tails, hand-carved roast beef and crepes made to order with a choice of fillings from savory to sweet. Over the course of the next four hours, Nell limited her drinks to three. She laughed along with everyone else when Joe snatched Stevie's garter in mid-air and declared he would not marry until he turned forty. The quarterback, completely soused, staggered back into the crowd immediately after claiming this prize. Good, he would not even remember she'd come to the reception.

Sharlette and Precious urged her to participate in the bouquet toss, but Nell held her ground at the table. Some poor, desperate woman in a baggy animal-print dress ripped the daisy clutch from the air and called pathetically for Joe Dean to come bestow the ritual kiss. She'd fought like a linebacker for the privilege and probably would have crushed Nell underfoot without a thought. How pathetic to be so enthralled by the man.

Nell felt fine enough to drive home when the newlyweds left in a sendoff filled with confetti and streamers released from small poppers shaped like champagne bottles. She would not be trapped by another false offer of assistance. She gathered up her purse and the silver box of chocolates embossed with the Sinners' red devil insignia. Precious Armitage tucked a daisy centerpiece under her arm like a football and said good-bye to Nell. Sharlette Dobbs gathered up extra boxes of chocolates for her daughters.

Suddenly, as if it were midnight on New Year's Eve instead of five on a hot June day, Joe Dean appeared at Nell's side, scooped her up and gave her a big, sloppy, celebratory kiss. Recovering her feet, Nell told him sternly, "I don't need a ride home."

"No, but I sure do." He gave her a silly grin and wobbled into Precious Armitage's breasts. "Whoa, big and purple. How's my Precious?" He reached out a hand to touch. Calvin intercepted the fingers before arrival.

"Do us all a good deed, Nell, and drive this boy home. He'll kill himself in that Porsche, and there go our chances for another Super Bowl. Besides, if he stays much longer, I might have to break his wrist myself."

"Go on, girl. He can't do much damage the shape he's in," Sharlette Dobbs said, having reclaimed her tight end husband from the bar where he was watching a ball game.

"Go on, girl," Joe mimicked. "I'll follow you anywhere."

He did—through the thinning crowd of guests, down the long, magnificent vaulted corridor to the entrance where the doorman summoned her car from whatever distant lot they had found to park the vehicles of four hundred guests. Joe said farewell lavishly to all he encountered and informed them he was "going home with the Wish Lady." Cameras whirred around them, but Nell moved fast disassociating herself from Joe.

Coach Buck waited nearby for his Mercedes sedan. She hid behind him.

"Going home with the Wish Lady, Marty. She's a nice girl, a good girl, Coach," Joe told him. "She works with dyin' children."

"I can see she's not your regular type." Coach Buck turned around to look at Nell. "You take good care of him, you hear, young lady. He's like a son to me."

"I'll see he gets home safely. That's all I can guarantee."

Her Toyota barreled to the curb stopping inches from the bumper of Coach Buck's Mercedes. The extra help hired for the event, a ponytailed college student, got out, handed Nell her keys and left his palm open. Nell dug into her small purse for a couple of ones, but Joe slapped a twenty into the hand and made it go away. He melted himself into the front passenger seat and fumbled to adjust it for more leg room. Then, he reached over and squeezed Nell's knee as she slid behind the steering wheel.

"Seat belt," Nell prompted. "I don't drive in New Orleans unless everyone is strapped in." She leaned, pushing his hands away, and stretched the belt across his wide chest and latched it. That should keep him in place while she drove. "Where's your place, Joe?"

"I'm not sayin'."

"Don't be ridiculous. "Where do you live? We're holding up traffic."

"Let's go to your place."

"I'm sure your place is much nicer and has a big, strapping concierge to help get you to your door. Give me directions."

"Go up Canal and get on the interstate."

"Joe, I know you live in the city."

"We're going to Nell's place. I want to see your sunflowers—and your bottles again."

Horns blared at the Toyota that failed to move from the curb and make way for incoming cars. Nell pulled out and, giving up, headed for Metairie. Joe closed his eyes and slumped further in his seat, his knees jammed up against the dashboard. He stayed mercifully quiet for the trip.

Nell arrived at her assigned parking space. Joe, suddenly alert, sat up as the engine stopped. He bounded out of the car before she came around to get him.

"I can make it up the stairs with a little help," he assured her.

Leaning heavily on Nell as if she were a crutch under his arm, they made it to the landing. Joe slouched against the doorframe while Nell opened her locks. They stumbled inside. Joe flung himself on the floral couch, sinking deep into the cushions. He splayed his legs over one of the arms, loosened the formal bow tie and unbuttoned his white jacket. Shucking the silly blue garter off his arm, he spun it around his finger a few times, then tossed it away. All comfy now, Joe put his hands behind his head and closed his eyes.

Nell hurried to her tiny kitchen. "That's right. You nap for a while. I'll make coffee. We'll have you out of here and home before dark good as new."

Joe smiled and hummed his off key-version of *When I Fall in Love* as she poured water into the coffeemaker. The smell of ground coffee filled the room as she spooned it into the paper filter. With a click, she turned the machine on. The brew began to bubble.

"How old are you, Nell?" he asked.

"Twenty-five. Why?"

"I'm twenty-six."

"Good for you, Joe." She got mugs from a cupboard. The cups clattered together.

"You know, I don't do virgins. Too many complications and probably not much fun. But in your case, it's just not right—you going to waste and all because of the cancer thing. I think I should help you out."

"What!" The bustle in the kitchen ceased.

"We can take it real slow, get you prepared and all."

Something brushed against Joe's legs. He opened his eyes and there Tink stood between them, her hands on her hips.

"What makes you think I'm a virgin, Joe?"

"Well, the cancer thing and men avoiding you and all."

"There is something you might not know about this teenage cancer victim. I had my bone marrow transplant when I was fifteen. It took me nearly a year to recover and get back to a normal life. All that time, I told myself if I ever got the chance, I wouldn't die a virgin."

She made her point by prodding him in the starched shirt with a finger. "But when I got back to class, a sixteen-year-old in the tenth grade because of all the schooling I missed, no one talked to me or sat with me in the cafeteria. I certainly did not get invited to any parties. I was the cancer kid. Hell, the cheerleaders had bake sales to help my family with medical expenses. Everyone knew."

"I begged and pleaded with my father to move to another school district so I could have a social life. Can you believe he did that for me? My parents took a loss on their house and I got to be popular in a way as a sixteen-year-old sophomore. How dumb was she? Fresh meat for the senior boys."

"Aw, Nell, you don't have to tell me this."

"Listen up, Joe." Her finger poked at him again. "A football player snapped me right up. He must have felt pretty macho when he got lucky on the first date. We went together his entire senior year. I went to the prom, but no after-the-dance parties for Nell. We went to a motel and did it all night long—because Joe, I liked sex and did it really well. This was living. Brady dumped me because I had to take summer courses to catch up with my class and didn't have enough time to do what he wanted. Didn't matter. He'd done a lot of locker room bragging before he went off to football camp at the University of Mississippi. I had a new boyfriend before he tore his first ligament."

Nell worked off one of her sandals with the toes of her other foot, then kicked off the shoe. She hitched up her diaphanous skirt, hooked her fingers in her white lace panties and lowered them. She gave him a quick glimpse of the dark curls between her legs and her bikini wax before the dress floated down, hiding the view. Nell held the panties in front of his face making him inhale the scent of perfumed powder and sexual desire. She tossed the scrap of lace over his shoulder.

"I was well on my way to being team slut, as my sister Emily would say, when one of the nicer guys came to pick me up and actually walked to the door instead of honking his horn. My dad told him the whole cancer story while he waited. You know, Joe, I find athletes aren't afraid of injury. But disease, it just turns them off. After that, I had plenty of time to study and catch up. I graduated top of my class and went off to college."

Nell grasped the collar of his formal shirt and tore it open. Studs went flying into the TV screen and skittered across her glass-topped coffee table. She ripped off the cumberbund, commenting, "Velcro, how convenient," and opened the front of his pants.

"I had a couple of boyfriends in college. One cried off because of the cancer thing, as you would say. The other stuck around for the sex. We didn't have much else in common. I went to graduate school and got engaged to another psychology major I met there, but Drake wanted to go on for a psychiatry degree and a lucrative practice. I wanted to help sick children sooner rather than later. We parted ways. I haven't had sex for more than a year, Joe, and as I said, I like it."

"I know how that is," Joe answered, dumbfounded. "Honest. I did the celibacy thing for six months last year. It was hard."

"So are you." She lifted his erection free of the zipper and eased the dress slacks down enough to give him moving room. Then, she raised her skirt again and prepared to settle on his shaft. "I'm tough, Joe, small but mighty."

"Condoms, left rear pocket," he prompted. "I told you I was careful."

Nell felt around for the little pockets of protection while Joe enjoyed the search. She came up with a packet, ripped it open with her teeth and smoothed it over his penis while he throbbed beneath her hands. She pushed his knees together, knelt on his hard-muscled thighs and lowered herself.

He let her do the work as she moved against him with her eyes closed. He removed her hands when she clawed at his chest, scratching at the dark hair between his nipples, and slid the top of her dress and the camisole down over her shoulders in order to cover her small breasts with his hands. He rubbed his callused fingertips over them in a circular motion. Nell moved faster determined to show him what she could do.

Joe leaned back, supporting her with his grasp, closed his eyes and let it happen. Nell kept moving even after he spent himself—until the fuse she'd lit sent up the fireworks inside. She gasped and moaned and finished. Her head sank to his chest and she rested over the wild beating of his heart.

"Yeah, small but mighty." Joe stroked her back.

They dozed together just like that, her legs dangling over the side of his, and his hand cupping the short, silky hair of her head.

****

Someone knocked. The doorbell rang. A pleasant voice sang out, "Nell, it's your mother. I saw your car outside. Are you in the shower?"

Mrs. Abbott raised the flower pots on either side of the door and clunked them back into place. She peeled up the doormat and let it spring back against the concrete landing. "Where is the spare key?" Ann Abbott said aloud.

"My mom! My God!" Nell vaulted over the sofa back, scooped up the red cummerbund, the blue garter and the white lace panties, and raced for the bathroom. A second later, water roared in the shower.

Joe Dean, always calm in a tight situation, righted himself, tucked in and zipped. Good thing he'd only faked being drunk to get into Nell's apartment because now he had to think fast. Not much he could do about the gaping, studless formal shirt. He sauntered toward the kitchen and called out to Mrs. Abbott, "Just a minute. Nell has herself locked in here like a fortress. Let me find the deadbolt key."

"Who is that?" Nell's mom queried from the other side of the door.

"Joe. We met the other Saturday, Mrs. Abbott." He took a large red barbecue apron from a bentwood coat rack. The illustration on the front showed two happy crawfish stirring up a big pot of gumbo. Why the crawfish should be happy when they were listed among the ingredients that followed, Joe had no idea. Obviously, the apron, still stiff and creased from the gift box, had never been worn. He put it on and tucked his shirttails in beneath its covering.

Joe picked up the full coffeepot and sauntered to the door. Nell's deadbolt key sat in the lock. He opened the door for Mrs. Abbott. "Hi, there. I was just making us some coffee."

He lowered his voice. "Nell overindulged a little at the wedding reception, but I got her home safely. Good, you brought food. Now I won't have to cook after all." He gestured to his apron before taking two large Styrofoam boxes from Ann Abbott's hands.

"Gary and I had dinner downtown at Ralph and Kacoo's. He shouldn't have all that fried food and couldn't finish the seafood platter anyway. I brought my leftover shrimp fettuccini, too. Nell rarely cooks when she gets home from work. I thought she might appreciate the leftovers."

Ann followed Joe behind the sofa and across to the kitchen. The heel of her pump crunched down on foil. Joe reached for the floor, scooped up the condom wrapper and balled it in his fist before Mrs. Abbott could remove it from her shoe.

"Not much of a housekeeper, is she, our Nell?"

"Well…" Mrs. Abbott looked around the apartment. "The place has always looked tidy to me. If she's not feeling well, perhaps I should check on her." She hurried to the bathroom door and shouted over the torrent of the shower. "Nell, it's your mother, baby, can I do anything for you?"

"Just sit down, Mom. I'll be out in a minute."

For a second there, Joe had a vision Nell naked, frantically washing off the scent of sex under a stream of warm water, maybe rubbing a bar of scented soap between her legs. If they had been alone, he'd have joined her by now. Good thing a stiff apron could cover a stiffie, now likely to melt like ice on a barbecue grill with her mom in the house.

Nell appeared with her short dark hair slicked back, her small but perfect body swathed in only a large terry bathrobe. She smelled of flowers, those kind that looked like little bells, ah—lily of the valley. His erection didn't go away.

Ann Abbott sat perched on the edge of the sofa. She picked a small object off the floor. "Did you lose an earring, dear?"

"That would be mine, ma'am. It's a stud. From my tuxedo shirt. I don't wear earrings, not that I have anything against men who do. I was in the wedding and wanted to get comfortable afterwards so I took the studs out. Coffee?" Joe held up the pot again.

Ann put her hand down on the sofa and stooped to pluck another stud from the floor. "They are all over the place, and the upholstery has a damp spot."

"That would be mine, too. I mean I knocked the studs onto the rug while I was trying to get Nell to take a little water. Then, I spilled the water trying to pick up the studs. I can be clumsy."

"I see," said Mrs. Abbott as if she really did. "Actually, Gary said you had fine feet in reference to your football playing, I believe. Which reminds me, Gary is waiting in the car. I told him I was going to drop off the food, not visit. He thinks I visit too much."

She stood and walked toward the door. "I'm glad you and Nell made up. She can be overly sensitive about her—past. You will take good care of her, won't you, Joe? Make sure she eats some of that food."

"I will, Mrs. Abbott. Don't you worry." He closed the door behind Nell's mother and relocked the deadbolt. "Coffee," he offered the pot in Nell's direction, "or should I make a fresh pot?"

Nell sank into her overstuffed chair, tucked her legs beneath her, and checked her robe to make sure it closed over all parts of her body. "Give my parents a chance to get out of the lot and then you can go."

"I think we should have coffee." Joe filled the two mugs that had been sitting on the counter for a couple of hours. "Sugar?"

"Don't call me that," Nell snapped.

"For your coffee. I'm afraid to ask if you want milk."

"Sorry. Black is fine. Assign me a number. What would I be? Ninety-one or two? Then, go. Your irresistibility is affirmed."

He handed her a mug and, avoiding the damp spot on the sofa, sat on the arm nearest her chair. She took a sip and winced at the bitterness of the dark roast made too strong when she thought she had a drunken man to get sober.

"The number would be in the nineties if I had done those girls on the island. I sort of got hung up in the early eighties, but I can't give you a number."

"How about stars? How many stars did I get?"

"You know about the stars?"

"Doesn't every man who has a little black book give stars? So how many?"

"I can't rate you."

"Why not?"

"Because that was, well, not a pity fuck, more like an anger fuck if there is such a thing. I never had one of those before—not that it wasn't great."

"Joe, Joe, Joe. I had it all together before you came into my life. Now, I'm a mess again." She placed the coffee mug on the table and used her hands to cover her face.

"You're not like the other women. Don't say so."

She tried to straighten him out. "You know, all those other women, whether bored with their everyday sex life or out for a thrill or just plain curious, have life stories, dreams, careers, hopes of marrying and having families."

"But you had—"

"Cancer. It's a disease, not an excuse, though heaven knows I used it that way for a while."

"When I took those girls on vacation, I got to know them a little since we weren't doing anything else. One was funny. One was sad. She hated how she looked. Two were proud of how well they did their jobs. It's a new way of thinking about women for me. I know I been spoiled by fame and my sisters. I was the big football stud in high school and college like that Brady dude. Say, are we talking about Brady Grant who played for Ole Miss? We beat the hell out of him when I played for LSU. He never made it to the pros. Weak knees."

"That would be Brady. I am so ashamed I told you that stuff."

Joe lifted her, settled into the chair and placed her on his lap. "Sugar, if we are talking about shame, you got nothing on me. Coach says I should try to settle down with one or two women. I think I'd like to give that a try. Are you willing?"

"Depends."

"On what?"

"Who the other woman is."

"Lord help me. This one is funny, too. We need to go back to the bedroom and give this another try before I bust up laughing."

Chapter Ten

The fresh tabloids came out early in the week. Joe usually ignored them as he walked past the newsstand on his way to get hot beignets for breakfast, but this morning his name fairly jumped off the page. *"Billodeaux Drunk at Best Friend's Wedding. Takes Home Teenage Girl for Sex."*

The picture of Stevie and Connor exiting their limousine at the Fairmont looked pretty nice. Unfortunately, the paparazzo had gotten a good single shot of Nell in her floaty dress and little white sandals. She did look very young and childlike. Taken at an angle with his bow tie askew and dinner jacket flapping open as he pursued Nell, Joe appeared very drunk. That did not bother him. He had been photographed carousing when he served as reserve quarterback for the Sinners, but he had watched the booze very carefully since he became the starter, the Super Bowl winning starter. He seized a copy and paid the blind paper seller.

Joe's anger rose as he stood reading in a long take-out line extended by a busload of elderly, sightseeing women dropped off at the Café du Monde for breakfast. Once he had grabbed his greasy bag of donuts and large go-cup of café au lait, Joe charged back to his condo. Tourists gave way before him as if he were a tanker cutting through Mississippi waters. He had his game face on and could not to be bothered. Those who recognized Joe Dean Billodeaux snapped pictures they would later narrate by saying, "I was almost run down by the Sinners' quarterback right there in the French Quarter. You can see the statue of Andy Jackson just behind him."

He used up half an hour getting through to a tabloid editor with enough clout to authorize a retraction. Joe finished his coffee and wiped the powdered sugar from his fingers as he made his demands.

"Look, I don't care what you say about me, but you leave Nell alone. She's no teenager. I don't do teenagers. She's twenty-five and has a responsible job at Ochsner's Hospital."

"How do you spell her last name?" the editor asked.

Joe hung up. He should have known better than to mess with the press himself. He'd call the Sinners' PR department. They knew how to put out fires by stomping on the fuel. Who would be mean enough to do the best job? Margaret Stutes of course.

Joe found his black book. The cover had gathered a thin layer of dust over the last few weeks, but no matter, he knew Margaret had signed listing both her office and cell numbers so she could be reached day or night.

Where would Margaret be at nine on a sweltering June morning? Probably in her air-conditioned office where she thought up good ways to keep the Sinners in the news during the off-season—nice things like having players visit the Boys and Girls Club or hold day long football camps for little kids. As the phone rang, Joe thought he might suggest that he go visit sick children at Ochsner. He should learn to be more comfortable in that sort of situation like the Rev was.

A young man answered the phone. Had he called her cell by mistake and gotten the second-string lineman Margaret cultivated? What the hell. "Is Margaret around? Tell her Joe Dean is calling."

"Margaret? Oh, Ms. Stutes. No, she is no longer with the Sinners organization. This is Shawn Kyle. They gave me her office," the voice reported with glee. "I would be more than happy to help you with anything, Mr. Billodeaux."

"What happened to Margaret?"

"Ms. Stutes said she was taking a long vacation, then starting her own agency in the fall. She expected to come into some money. I would love to help you, Joe Dean."

Shawn seemed a little too eager and a mite limp in the wrists even over the phone to do what Joe wanted done. "Ah, Shawn, could you get together a sack of those little foam footballs, some of the stuffed red devils and a few teddy bears for me to take over to the hospital? I'll be by to pick them up."

"I'll have them ready for you, Joe. Should I arrange for a photographer? I'm much better at this job than Margaret, you know."

"I'm sure you are, Shawn, but let's skip the photographer. Thanks for the information." Joe hung up and considered the situation. He might have to do the stomping himself.

****

Nell showed some annoyance when paged about a guest who wanted to visit her patients. Do-gooders were always dropping in wanting instant access to the children. She took her time and finished an exit interview with Cassie. The teenager was being released—one of their success stories.

She had asked Mrs. Thomas to wait in the hall at the very end of the conversation in order to have a few private words with the girl. They had been over how others might react when she returned to school in the fall. Nell suggested Cassie find a few summer activities and make some friends, perhaps join a youth group at church, and ease back into a normal teenage social life. Keep in touch with friends she had made in the hospital by all means, but find new ones who would stand by her when classes started.

With Mrs. Thomas safely out of earshot, Nell discussed sexuality. Cassie looked thirteen, but her age and hormones were fifteen. Nell had the personal knowledge to counsel her well. Interview ended, she walked Cassie and her mother to the lobby where she sighted Joe Dean, sprawled in one of the plastic chairs, passing the time by taking little foam footballs from a plastic sack and autographing them with a black marker.

"Hey, Nell. Hey, Sassy," he greeted them.

"Mr. Joe, you remembered me!" Cassie beamed, the freckles across her nose almost glowing.

"How could I forget you, sugar? The one woman in the world who thinks Connor Riley is sexier than me."

"Not sexier, more romantic. He didn't wait for me. I saw his wedding picture in the papers today. I hope Stevie is good enough for him."

"And then some. Besides, he'll be a crippled old has-been by the time you grow up. Me, now, I'll be young and still playing at forty. Maybe you should reconsider who your favorite player is."

"But I saw you and Miss Nell are—"

Nell could have sworn the child was about to make an obscene gesture with her hands, but Cassie's mother gave her a look and the gesture changed to two intertwined fingers. "You know, together," Cassie concluded.

"Sad but true. You might pin your hopes on Jared Forte. He hasn't settled down yet."

"Like you have. Well Cassie, call me any time if you need to talk. You have my card." Nell hugged the girl.

"Bless you, Miss Abbott, for being there for us," Mrs. Thomas said while grasping Nell's hand. Her face with its watery blue eyes, faded red hair and freckles, was taut with sincerity. "Come along, Cassie. Your brothers and sisters are waiting to throw you a party."

"Little kids." Cassie rolled her eyes. "Got to love them. Bye, Mr. Joe. Bye, Miss Nell." Mother and daughter walked out into the world.

"So, you are the visitor who wants to see my patients." Nell eyed the sack of toys. "I hope all of those are new and clean because we can't risk infection with any of the children. You'll have to scrub up like a surgeon and wear a face mask. Keep the visits brief. We'll see how you do." Nell led the way to the elevators.

She remembered seeing Joe over a year ago trailing the Rev and Connor Riley as they visited less critical children. Joe had looked as if he were afraid of catching celiac disease or cerebral palsy, but he'd put his time to good use hitting on the more attractive nurses. Nell had prepared herself to waylay the players before they got to her kids, but the big men turned and got on the elevator before they reached her sector. Joe's eyes had passed right over her. He'd not made a good first impression. Their meeting at the Super Bowl went even worse, thanks to his cheesy come-on.

Scrubbed and gowned in paper, Joe pulled up his face mask and left the restroom. He caught a glimpse of himself in a window as they passed along a quiet corridor. "Calling Dr. Billodeaux, calling Dr. Billodeaux. Bring that heart you have for transplant to the operating room," he whispered.

"Stop clowning. Don't tell anyone to get well soon. These kids aren't that stupid. They know the odds," Nell snapped.

"Yes, Miss Nell. Whatever you say, Miss Nell."

All in all, Joe did fairly well. He asked names and personalized the footballs for little boys with their arms stuck full of needles. He autographed the plastic red devils on their butts and made a few of the kids laugh. Where allowed, he gave out furry teddy bears and signed their ribbons with his name underscored by a tail that ended in a heart.

"Well, that was…" he began.

"Depressing." Nell filled in his sentence.

"I was going to say uplifting. Okay, it was sad."

"You did fine, Joe. Thanks for coming. I appreciate you didn't bring a photographer."

"Speaking of which—do you have time for lunch?"

"If we don't go out, I can spare a half hour. How about the cafeteria?"

"Great. Hospital food, my favorite."

"I recommend the chicken wrap. Stay away from the special and the grill."

In the end, Nell had the wrap and unsweetened iced tea. Joe had the jumbo cheeseburger and fries, good and greasy from the grill.

"Hey, it's the off-season. I get to have some fun."

"This past weekend was no fun?"

"About that." Joe took a bite of cheeseburger big enough to bring on a Heimlich maneuver. Nell braced herself for first aid on either Joe or her heart.

"Have you seen the tabloids this morning?"

"No, I've been here since seven."

"Good. Well, you might prepare yourself." He took one last item from the deflated plastic sack and spread the tabloid out on their table.

"Oh, no! They mistook me for a teenager!"

"If that's all that bothers you, you'll be fine, sugar. Just don't talk to the press if they track you down. Okay?"

"For my good or yours, Joe?"

"Both. It will blow over."

"If you say so."

****

When Nell Abbott completed her shift and emerged from the hospital, she discovered she *had* been tracked down.

"Hey, Miss Abbott, are you Joe Dean's latest?" one reporter called out to her.

She made the mistake of turning toward him and heard the camera whir. Head down, Nell kept moving for the parking garage.

A pushier version of the first reporter, this one a woman, shouted, "What number are you? My paper will pay good money for an interview."

Nell took a firmer grip on the files she carried and

walked so fast her lab coat flew open in the breeze she created. She approached her car, sure her followers were going to jot down the license number of her rather ordinary Toyota, when Joe's Porsche roared up the ramp. He popped the door and she jumped in. They peeled out, leaving the entourage groping for their cell phones.

"That was awful."

"You get used to it. Spend the night at my place. The concierge will keep them out. Better yet, if you can get some time off, we can hide out in Chapelle where I'm just one of the good ole boys. Since Uncle Lester warned the scum of the press off our land with a shotgun, no one bothers me there. We can visit Mintay and the Rev. They're living in a high class gated community now."

"I can see why. I can't leave my kids though, and I work this weekend. Just take me to your place for a few hours. We can sneak back and get my car after dark. I'll treat for Chinese take-out, and then we can…"

"Yes, we certainly can. It will be my pleasure. I'll pay for the take-out, too."

****

As it turned out, Nell did not have to work the following weekend. Her decision was made for her. Joe Brunner, her supervisor, called her into his office late on Friday. "Nell," he began, feeling his way. "You are great at your job and your personal life is none of our business so long as it doesn't affect your performance. But, the reporters hanging around the front doors are causing a disturbance and a few of the mothers, just one or two, have called to say they don't think you are morally fit to guide their children."

Nell gasped. "Am I going to lose my job?"

"We've had many more calls in your favor. Cassie Thomas' mother was particularly supportive. We have no intention of firing you, but the administration has suggested we put you on a leave of absence—a paid leave of absence—until this quiets down. That might take a while." Brunner unfolded a fresh tabloid out just in time to catch the eyes of the weekend supermarket shoppers. He shoved it across the desk.

"*Joe Dean's New Girl is Nurse Nelly,*" she read in the banner. They hadn't run the picture of her fleeing in her lab coat. No, they used her high school yearbook photo. She realized she had changed very little: same short pixie haircut, same big eyes and minimal makeup. Nell wished she had taken Emily's advice and let her hair grow out now that she had hair. She should have gone for a makeup makeover at Dillard's, too, when her mother offered to pay for the deal. She wondered which friend or acquaintance had sold her out.

Except for her job title, the article was fairly accurate. The reporter portrayed her as a "valiant cancer survivor." Ha! They had tracked down Brady Grant who sold real estate in Mobile. He called her his "wild child", but made sure everyone knew they hadn't seen each other in years because he was a respectable businessman with a wife and small son. All things considered, Brady could have been much more explicit.

The writer cited her work with sick children. The last paragraph speculated, "Has Joe Dean reached the end of his list?" and reviewed his sexual excesses, noting his longest affair had been with a model named Amber who lasted three months as Joe Dean's woman.

Brunner began talking again. "We think six weeks

would do the trick. Football training camp starts the beginning of August. The Sinners will be out of town. The scandal should blow over by then. What do you say, Nell? Myself, I'd love to have six weeks of paid vacation." He gave her a friendly smile.

"Some of my children might come up for transplants during that time. I have a couple in recovery right now. I can't leave."

"Well, uh, we have a graduate student who was looking for an internship this fall. She's willing to start early. I'll work with her directly. That should cover things."

"I guess I have no choice."

"Nell, don't make things any harder than they need be. This is no more time than we'd give you for surgery or maternity leave."

"Yeah. Right. Maternity leave."

****

Joe waited in a borrowed car by the cafeteria exit exactly as promised. All week long, he had been devising ways of avoiding reporters. Nell never left by the front door. He drove a different vehicle each time, some rented, some loaned from friends, all low key transportation. She could hardly deny she was having an affair with Joe Dean Billodeaux. They stayed at his place and to stay with Joe was to have sex with Joe. Where had all her resistance gone?

Nell slid in next to him and immediately turned her head toward the window and pretended to scan for paparazzi. She blinked her eyes rapidly and made a quick swipe of the hand across her cheeks to get rid of the two escaping tears.

"You're crying. What happened?"

"I was laid off, given a leave of absence for six weeks."

"That's not fair." Joe turned off the engine. "Let me talk to your boss."

"Let it go, Joe. There have been complaints about the uproar, complaints from a few parents about my morals. All true." Nell slumped against the armrest and kept her face toward the glass.

"It's my morals, not yours. What—a couple of guys in high school, two in college, one in grad school, none for over a year. You're practically reformed. Me, I was up to number eighty-two, not counting all the ones that came before the list."

"Could we leave before someone sees us?"

"Sure thing, sugar." He took care to pull out and drive as normally as possible to keep people from noticing them. "Looks like our trip to Chapelle is on."

Chapter Eleven

Nothing had changed since her last visit to Chapelle. Joe said it never did.

Joe's mama greeted her with a big hug and a "*Mais, cher*, it's good to see you again. You stay in Allie and Eenie's room like las' time across from me and Frank."

She gave her son a meaningful look and relegated him back to his childhood quarters filled with dusty trophies and faded ribbons for high school athletic achievements at the end of the hallway. He stepped on the squeaky board on his way to toss his shaving kit and an overnight bag on his old single bed and winced.

Nell settled herself in the front bedroom. She found a few dresser drawers not stuffed with winter clothes packed in plastic and put away her underwear, hung up two modest dresses Joe told her to bring in case, as he said, they were forced to go to Mass. This trip, she placed athletic shoes, sandals and a few pair of low-heeled practical work pumps in the bottom of the closet. Maybe, she should have invested in cowgirl boots.

She took another look at Allie's old bulletin board on the wall across from the bed. There was no doubt about its ownership. The teenage Allie had written her name in glitter glue across the top of the cork board. Twelve years older than her baby brother, Allie had pictures of herself holding baby Joe Dean and later of her brother, a curly-haired six-year-old squeezing in between her and her prom date. The curls had been subdued by brushes and a short styling, hair spray and gel, but Nell already knew if he missed a haircut, one or two of those curls would spring to life and end up on his forehead. With one hand on the wheel of the Porsche and the other pushing back those curls every now and then, Joe had driven them to Chapelle.

Nell emerged from her room to find a lunch spread on the kitchen table and Nadine and Joe waiting for her behind a stack of cayenne-spiced pimento-cheese and egg salad sandwiches on white bread, a glass dish of hot-sweet homemade pickles and a red bowl of potato salad.

"Lemonade, milk or tea, *cher*?" Joe's mama asked.

"Beer," Joe answered.

"Milk for you. What you want, baby?" Nadine asked again.

"Lemonade would be fine, thank you, Mrs. Billodeaux."

"You call me Nadine. Help yourself to sandwiches. I get your lemonade."

Nell selected half a pimento-cheese, a few pickles and a dab of potato salad. She finished her meal and watched Joe Dean wolf down sandwiches with his milk.

"Mr. Frank isn't coming?" she asked as the pile of sandwiches lowered.

"No, honey, he's workin' Wylie's back acres today and took his lunch wit' him. We'll see Frank tonight."

"Want to walk off the lunch, Tink? The ranch is about a mile down the road. I want to show you the progress we're making," Joe offered.

"Tink?" his mama questioned.

"Short for Tinker Bell, Mama."

"Ain't that sweet. You don't eat no more than a fairy either. That's why you're so small, I guess." Shaking her head, Mrs. Billodeaux cleared the table. "Go on. I don't need no help."

The cane along the road now grew well above Nell's head, but not over Joe Dean's tall frame. He held her hand as they walked. She felt like breaking the contact, still riled over her forced exile. Now and then, a pickup truck passed with a honk and a wave. Joe waved back.

The old homestead had been repainted a brilliant white trimmed with dark green. Wicker chairs in the same color as the trim sat in place of cousin Bijou's plastic seats. The camellias, dropping a few yellow leaves on the newly mowed lawn, were long past their bloom. The spring flowers had vanished, replaced by a blaze of yellow daylilies along the walkway. The rusting Lorena Ranch sign was gone, replaced by a new arch of wrought iron spanning the dirt road.

"The old place looks nice," Nell commented. "Especially without Bijou on the porch."

"Yeah, my mama took it in hand. I have to admit Bijou did not get the Billodeaux looks. He can be a hard worker, though, when he wants to be. He did a good job overseeing the renovations on the barn."

They approached the grove of live oaks. The frame of a huge house raised up right in the middle of the trees. Dust coated the small, shiny leaves and darkened the Spanish moss from a silvery gray to a light brown. A few workmen were on the job even though it was Saturday. This was what money could buy: six bedrooms with their own baths, a home gym, a game room, a four car garage, formal dining, an immense living area, a kitchen big enough for a whole family to eat in, galleries on top and bottom, front and back, and enough white pillars to satisfy Scarlet O'Hara.

"Nice, huh?" Joe Dean asked as he pored over the plans laid out across a pair of sawhorses.

"Big. Trying to restore the Billodeaux name to its former glory?"

"The Billodeauxs have no former glory. As far as we can tell from the old foundations, a four-room cottage probably stood here. Maybe they had a *garconniere* in the attic for the boys of the family. No, the Billodeauxs are known for their good looks and their outstanding fertility is all." Joe waited for a smart remark, but Nell said nothing.

She wandered off toward the barn, its old gray boards now painted a deep red and its peaked metal roof as bright in the summer sunshine as if it had been scrubbed with Brill-O pads. The broad doors on both ends were open and a slight warm breeze moved between them. Nell stepped into the shade and sniffed the aroma of horses, manure and straw. Joe came up behind her.

"I thought about having it air-conditioned, but that just spoils your stock, I think."

Cousin Bijou backed out of a stall with a barrow full of muck. "Yeah, but it wouldn't spoil me any," he complained, closing the door behind him. Fatima stuck out her finely-formed gray head and nickered. Lazy Boy stirred in his big box across the way.

"So, did L.B.'s fertility check out?" Nell asked.

"L.B.? Oh, yeah, Lazy Boy. You bet. He's fit to be a Billodeaux earning his keep as a stud. We'll have some living, breathing results next spring."

"Not Fatima!" Nell looked at the small mare with pity. "He's so big."

"Not Fatty. Some racing mares up by Opelousas. Here you go," Joe fished out a sugar cube from his shirt pocket. Fatima accepted it with pink-lipped delicacy. Lazy Boy snorted and hung his head over the ledge. "You, too. Got to keep your energy up. Want to ride, Nell?"

"Not again."

Joe ignored her. "Bijou, saddle up the horses while Nell and I take a walk around."

"We added on a tack room, and there's a nice overhang where you can groom and wash the horses." He led her back toward the house but closer to the bayou. "My barbecue pavilion is going up right there."

He pointed to another slab sitting among some small pecan trees. "We'll have a built-in pit and a side-well with piped in propane. You can sit your crawfish boiler right down in there, fry turkeys, whatever, and won't have to worry about little kids getting in the flames or knocking over the pot. The floor is big enough for dancing, and we'll have screens to keep the mosquitoes down and ceiling fans to stir the air. Great view of the bayou, too."

Joe stood in the middle of the slab and spread his arms. "Boathouse and dock will go there." He pointed in the direction of the water.

Bijou came over leading the horses. Joe tossed Nell up into the saddle despite her protests, but did take the time to position her hands on the reins and run through the instructions again. "Just follow me and L.B. I like that...L.B."

Once again, Fatima followed the stallion without any encouragement from Nell. They came to the meadow where they had turned around the last time. Half of it was now fenced off. A white bull, curly-haired and pink-eyed, watched them, his blocky body half in, half out of a new open-sided shelter that gave a little shade. Beyond the bull, six cream-colored cows, some with calves nearly their own size, grazed in their own field that stretched away to the tree-line along the road.

"Who is that fellow?" Nell asked as she bounced along.

"I call him Snowballs. He has some fancy French name, *Neige de-* something on his registration papers. Pure-bred Charolais, the prettiest cattle you'll ever see."

"Looks like he has been busy."

"Those calves aren't his. Some of the ladies came with company, but he'll get his chance soon. We'll keep a few steers for table beef and all the heifers for breeding. I figure on giving some of the calves to 4-H kids to raise."

"Table beef?" Nell echoed. "Those pretty animals?"

"I know you grew up in the suburbs, but you do know where hamburger comes from, I guess. I don't need but one bull and all a steer does is eat. That was your country livin' lesson for today. How about some riding instructions?"

"I'm fine. No need."

"Really?" Joe put his heels to L.B. and picked up the pace to a trot that mowed down the waist-high meadow weeds and orange and yellow cone flowers around the perimeter of the field. He glanced back at

Nell clutching the saddle horn as Fatima kicked up her heels and followed. He eased into a slow canter and heard Nell gasp. When Joe pulled up, Fatima went flying by to one side and continued around the meadow.

"That's it, Nell! Take her around a few times and get the hang of it."

He watched Nell saw back on the reins. Fatima slowed to a trot, then stopped altogether. "Good, good. Now bring her head up and start out with a walk. Put her through her paces."

"Easy for you to say, Joe Dean Billodeaux," Nell shouted, but she did manage to get Fatty moving again and ventured into a trot before stopping once more. Nell slid down the horse's side and led the mare to where Joe Dean stood to do his coaching in the center of the field.

"Fun, huh?"

"Sort of. I guess I do need lessons."

Joe threw the reins over the heads of both horses and let them graze in the dry grass for anything they might find tasty. He pulled Nell farther into the tall weeds. "Here's something else us country boys like to do." He lifted her off her feet and fell back into a patch of yellow daisies making sure Nell landed on top of him. "We call it a roll in the hay."

"Out here—with cows watching? What if someone comes along the path or up the bayou?" Her words came out a little muffled because he was already pulling her red cotton top over her head. Joe unhooked her bra with one hand while working on her jeans snap with the other.

"I thought you were a wild child."

"*Was*. Years ago. And another thing. How come

I'm always on top? It seems to me I'm doing all the work."

"Didn't want to crush you, sugar, but if you insist." Joe was busy shucking off his own clothes, but he stopped to lay her clothes across the flattened grass where he had fallen. He added his shirt and jeans to the pile. "There you go. No blackberry brambles in your ass."

He shoved her from a huddled kneeling position to flat on her back. "You look like one of those Greek goddesses, all white—but rosy here and here—dark hair, here and there." He knelt between her legs and ran his hands over her torso. "What was her name— Pandora?"

"Pandora opened the box of troubles, Joe. Get your classics straight."

"Well now, that might be the case. I should stick to what I know: Disney films, Tink."

"You called me that in front your mother."

"She thought it was cute. Let's forget about nicknames because I am so ready for this, and we aren't likely to get any tonight at Mama's house." Joe sank into that hot, snug but yielding place only a woman could provide. He withdrew again and rummaged under Nell's hips for his jeans.

"You get no points for staying power, Joe."

"I need a condom. Just give me a minute."

"You don't need to…"

"I do. I told you I'm always careful. There, on in a jiffy. No more interruptions."

Snowballs put his head over the fence and bellowed. All the cows turned to stare in their direction.

"Ignore him. He's envious."

Nell closed her eyes to the hot sun overhead and gave herself over to the sensations of Joe massaging her breasts, kissing her lips and meandering down her neck. He raised her heels to his shoulders and kept his weight off of her that way. The new angle made her push against him and claw his hips with her nails. Her legs slid down and she sat almost upright on his thighs, her legs wrapped around his waist. Joe held her against him as he finished with a series of quick, powerful thrusts that brought her along, too. They fell back into the pile of clothes.

Joe rested his whole weight on the lower half of Nell's body, his head on her stomach. She toyed with the two dark curls on his forehead. "First class roll in the hay, I'd say."

"Me, too," he managed to get out. They rested for a while, getting a tan in places usually left covered. The sound of horses tearing at the grass, the cicadas singing in the trees, and their heavy breathing were the only noises in the meadow until a boat with a small engine putt-putted up the bayou.

Joe rolled over and snatched his jeans out from under Nell when it sounded as if the boat might be coming to shore. He stood in a hurry, ostentatiously zipping himself.

"Ah, dere you are Joe. I t'ink your horses might of got loose. Was going to bring dem back to the barn for you. What are you doing dere?" questioned a man about Joe's daddy's age and build, but thinner and grayer. Nell hunched behind Joe's legs and peeped out through a tiny gap in the weeds.

"Just taking a leak, Uncle Wylie. I thought you and Dad were working today." Joe motioned to Nell to stay quiet as she rustled the grass trying to get her clothes on.

"Don't ya know we got indoor plumbin' now, Joe? Dat new house of yours gonna have six bat'rooms?" Uncle Wyle put his engine into idle and sat back to chat.

"Like you never took a leak over the side of that boat. Actually, seven baths, one downstairs, too. And a shower for the horses in the barn."

"Gaw! You ridin' bot' dem horses, Joe?" Uncle Wylie chortled and spit some tobacco into the water.

"Nope. Nell must have had something bad to eat. She's off in the bushes. Don't embarrass her now."

"*Mais jamais!* Poor *bete.*"

"Catchin' anything?"

"Few catfish. It's too damn hot to plow and too damn hot to fish. We broke off early. Your daddy's probably home by now havin' a cold beer and watching a ball game. Dat's where I'm headed." Uncle Wyle used a paddle to push off from the bank where the little aluminum boat had drifted. He cranked up his engine again and crept out of sight around a bend in the river.

"That's it. Take your time, Joe. Just let me lay here covered with insects," Nell whispered from her nest in the grass.

"You look sweet as a fawn curled up down there. Besides, those are just sweat flies, not red ants. Up you go." He helped her dress, did a booty check for grass stains, and plucked weed fragments from her hair. "Mama will be on the lookout for signs," Joe told her. "But you're okay."

They mounted up, and the horses ambled back to the barn where Joe tossed the reins to Bijou and ordered a good rubdown for both animals. He and Nell strolled back to his parent's house. They were hand-in-hand again, no tension between them.

****

Nadine Billodeaux saw them coming up the drive from her kitchen window. "Ain't that sweet, Frank?"

Glued to the small television, Nadine used to watch her soap operas while she cooked or sewed, Frank took another handful of pork rinds from the bag on the table and washed the snacks down with beer. "What?"

"Look, quick, quick. They holdin' hands."

Frank tore his eyes from the screen and took a brief glance. "So, Nadine. Don't get all excited. Joe Dean got women in hand all da time."

"He never brings 'em home, no. This one is special."

Frank shrugged at his wife's comment.

The young couple came into the kitchen. Joe sniffed. "Smells good. What's for dinner?"

"I got a pot roast in the crock pot for after four o'clock Mass." Nadine crinkled her nose. "I smell— horse. Get you a shower before we go. You'll go wit' us, *cher*?"

Nell, who had been holding her breath about what Mrs. Billodeaux might be smelling, nodded and hurried through the kitchen, calling out, "Dibs on the shower, Joe."

Joe started after her, but was waylaid by a mixing spoon across the stomach.

"You ain't going in the shower wit' her, no, so just sit down and watch the game wit' your daddy."

His father passed the pork rinds and opened another beer.

"No more snacking and get that beer off your breath before Mass, you hear?" Nadine snatched up the cellophane bag, folded it over and closed it with a chip clip. She stowed the pork rind bag on top of the refrigerator. "I'm going to get dressed. Mind, you hear?"

****

Nell made it through the Mass in Chapelle's historic church fairly well. The service was not all that different from the Episcopal version except for the extra "and ever" in the Lord's Prayer. When the congregation rose to file up for communion wafers, Nadine Billodeaux leaned across her husband and whispered. "You just sit, Nell."

Also in a stage whisper, Mrs. Billodeaux called across to Joe on the far side of Nell. "Joe Dean, when you las' been to confession?"

"Aw, Ma!" He refused to look at his mother.

"Joe Dean, you answer me," she said a little louder.

"For Christ's sake, last September, I guess."

Two elderly women, eighty-five if a day and sitting in the pew directly in front of Joe, turned and raised their eyebrows. "For shame!" the one with the shoe-shine black hair said. "The language!" her redheaded companion chided.

"Miss Lolly, Miss Maxine, sorry," Joe Dean said.

"You stay on your knees and pray till we get back, son. Next week, you do your confession, you hear," Nadine Billodeaux ordered as the usher came to help Miss Lolly and Miss Maxine down the aisle. Her husband in tow, she followed the old women to the front of the church.

As soon as his mama got in line, Joe Dean slipped

off his knees and seated himself next to Nell again. "It was worth coming to see you down on your knees, Joe," she mocked him.

"You've seen me on my knees plenty, just not in church." He preened when she blushed and checked behind to make sure that pew was empty, too. The service ended with the recessional and blessing shortly after Nadine and Frank returned to their seats.

"Now we got pot roast waitin' and a nice quiet evening ahead. Tomorrow, we all going crabbing at the Point early, so get your sleep," Nadine informed the couple in the back seat of her Honda sedan as Frank drove sedately down the back roads to their home. Nell ended her first day in the warm clutches of the Billodeaux family the same way, sedately.

Chapter Twelve

Nell enjoyed crabbing at the Point despite the fact that the tip of her nose turned red and was sure to peel. About half the participants came home with a sunburn making them look as red as the catch boiling in a pot. The baseball cap Nell borrowed from Joe hadn't done much good in keeping the sun off her nose, but his old blue shirt, rolled up at the sleeves and tied at the waist protected her back and shoulders very well. Frank, of the perpetual farmer's tan, and Nadine, who had the sense to wear a large straw hat and long sleeves even in the heat, went unscathed.

By the time crabs filled three coolers, the children had lost interest and were chasing each other in a game of tag involving hitting their target with the bedraggled turkey necks tied to string for bait. Frank called an end to the catching phase and a beginning to the eating phase. He stopped at a roadside gas and grocery and picked up an extra bushel of crabs to make sure no one would go hungry.

Now, the men stood around under the carport at Allie's house dumping ice-stunned crabs into the boiling water and sipping beer. The women spread the Sunday papers over two long, redwood picnic tables under the oaks and had cold drinks and conversation. Allie bragged on her oldest boy who was starting at the university at Lafayette in the fall and would major in petroleum engineering. That same eighteen-year-old son, mingling with the men, had a beer can covered with an insulated purple and gold LSU holder in his hand—as if his mother would be fooled.

Allie's sixteen-year-old daughter leaned against her mama's chair and boasted during a lull in the conversation, "Uncle Joe says he'll put me through veterinary school at LSU if I keep my grades up."

"Better do something about those math grades, then, honey, and don't go telling your daddy Joe is going to foot your bills. He makes good money in the oil patch. We don't need the help," Allie said. Her daughter went off to sulk with Eenie's three girls who sat under the oak trees passing around teen magazines.

"That one girl is more trouble than all three of her brothers. Boys, you can put them outside and they find something to do. Girls, they're on your feet and in your face all day. I tell you Nell, don't have girls," Allie recommended.

"Oh, girls aren't so bad," said Eenie who had only daughters. "But Darryl worries about who'll take over Three Brothers when the old men are gone and he needs some help." Nell had swiftly been informed that Eenie's husband, Darryl, was the only one of the sons-in-law who continued to farm sugarcane.

"Your girls are only starting their teens, Eenie, so you just don't know. Darryl can always sell out to one of the big corporations or the development people, then we can all split the pot." Allie resembled her mother in all ways and dominated her younger siblings. It didn't take a psychologist to figure that out, Nell thought.

"Sell the Billodeaux land!" Eenie looked horrified.

"Maybe Joe will buy him out, too, like he did

Uncle Hal," suggested Lizzie who worked hard as a LPN and had four kids to put through college.

Her oldest girl wanted to be a real nurse, she told Nell. The two boys said they were going to play football like Uncle Joe, but at ages ten and eight, what did they know? Six-year-old Lisa wanted to be a mommy. What did she know either? Liz confessed she had not married well, but she stuck it out for the kids. Charlie over in the carport was getting a buzz on already and she'd be driving him home again.

Izzy, who had gone to college and taught the third grade for several years before marrying a high school history teacher, pulled her toddler's hand away from the bright red hot sauce bottle on the table and gave him a ring of keys to play with. The child bounced against her full belly.

"This one was an accident," she confided in Nell. "Looks like I'll be sitting out the first few weeks of school if she doesn't get here soon."

"Don't say my number thirteen grandchild was an accident." Nadine patted Izzy's stomach. "You come out when you ready, *cher* heart."

"How many children do you want, Nell?" Izzy asked.

Nell spilled a dribble of Diet Coke down the front of Joe's blue shirt. Her head buzzed with the Billodeaux family dynamics and confidences thrown at her in such a short time.

"I don't think about it." She looked over at the driveway to where Joe and Allie's oldest organized a basketball game around a rusty hoop and tattered basket. Joe held up Lizzie's eight-year-old so the boy could dunk the ball. "In my situation, you take one day at a time."

"That's right. You work with all those sick kids, don't you?" said Eenie. "It must be hard."

"Sometimes. What I do helps."

"Of course it does."

The group edged away from the topic and went on with their husbands' strengths and failings until the men approached the table with trays of steaming crabs. The aroma of the boiling spices rose off the pile and permeated the taste of the red potatoes and corn mixed with the seafood. Soon, cracking and crying began as smaller children begged for help getting at the meat and the adults compared the best techniques for opening crabs.

When the shells piled high, the men rolled up the newspapers and put the waste into the covered trash barrel. The women went inside to bring out the desserts: a plate of watermelon slices, a yellow sheet cake with a brown sugar and pecan topping and homemade vanilla ice cream melting in the heat. After the children, who had spent more time pinching each other with crab claws than eating, filled up with goodies and grew drowsy, the party broke up. The old folks stayed until the mosquitoes got bad at dusk, then headed home with Nell and Joe again riding in the backseat.

"I'm turning in early," Frank announced as they pulled into the drive.

"Me, too," Nadine said.

"Nell, what say we take the Porsche out for a spin? The night is young, and the moon is coming up full," Joe suggested.

His mother frowned. "You be careful. Don't go too fast, Joe Dean."

"Who, me?" He laughed and extracted Nell from his mother's car and placed her into his own.

They drove only a few miles before Joe turned the Porsche on to a tractor path between two fields of cane. They bumped along, the deep ruts hard on the undercarriage of his low-slung vehicle. As soon as Joe came to a crossing, he turned the bend, parked and turned off the lights. The tall stalks formed a wall between them and the world. He leaned over and put Nell's seat back as far as it would go and paused for a kiss on the way.

The kiss went on and on with tongue and teeth coming into play. Joe's hand slid under the knot in her shirt and rubbed her stomach before continuing upward to unhook her front-snap bra. He rubbed one of her nipples between his fingertips and the other pebbled up in envy. He slipped a hand into her jeans and stroked lightly with one finger until he caught an elbow on the gearshift.

Getting out of the car, Joe circled around to her side, paused for a minute with his backside pressed against her window as he struggled with a condom, then folded himself on to the floor between Nell's legs. His position was so incredibly awkward, Nell laughed.

"What's the matter—remind you of your high school days?" Joe said.

"Oh, no! My high school years were about anger and proving something. This is about fun."

"It's about more than fun, I think."

Nell continued to laugh. He slid her farther up the seat, took off her jeans with one pull and dove in head first between her legs. As soon as his tongue touched her most sensitive spot, the laughter stopped. She sighed and moaned as he loved her in and out. When she writhed and her back arched upward, he rose over her and entered. He sustained her orgasm as long as he could before giving up and letting go.

When he collapsed over her, his head close to her ear, he whispered, "Who's laughing now?" but the trouble he had getting up and out of the car set her off again.

"Damn, tomorrow I'm getting a truck with an extended cab and a long bed. I need one for the ranch anyhow."

****

Next day, they did drive to Lafayette to shop for a truck. The dealer had nothing in stock meeting Joe's specifications, but said he could check around on the computer and maybe have something by the end of the week if Joe wasn't particular about color.

"I don't care if it's purple so long as it's roomy," Joe Dean grumped because they had nothing he could drive off the lot that afternoon when he offered a cash deal.

On the return trip, Joe pulled up before the church on the square and went in to do his confession because he had promised his mama. "You can wait here. I won't be long," he assured Nell.

"Really?"

"Look, I'll pick a number, say one-hundred-one acts of fornication, and throw in the sin of pride. It keeps things simple and gives me a little credit for the next few weeks."

Joe did return in a fairly short time. "Told you so."

"And what was the penance?"

"A large check for the church restoration fund and

one-hundred-one Our Fathers on my knees. I'll put the check in the mail, but I got to save the knees for football. God will understand."

"I'm sure."

They picked up hot loaves of French bread from Pommier's Bakery across the street from the church and a bottle of wine, some sharp cheese and red grapes from the Winn-Dixie on their way to the building site. Joe and Nell picnicked on the slab laid for the pavilion and went riding afterward.

When an afternoon shower blew up out of the west, Joe gave Bijou the rest of the day off and they holed up in the barn. On the picnic blanket spread over the straw, they made love as the water drummed on the metal roof and curious barn cats, eyes glowing in the twilight of the storm, watched from safe corners.

"Better than the beach, don't you think, Nell?" Joe asked her as she curled on his chest and he warded off the cats closing in now that the action had stopped.

"Don't know. We'll have to try the beach."

They set off to Grand Isle in the morning and returned in time to pick up his new truck on Friday. Joe took communion on Sunday because, he said, he thought his confession was good for a few more weeks.

The pattern continued for the next five weeks: family gatherings on the weekends, church on Saturday or Sunday and sex on the sly which made it all the more delectable. Nadine soon caught on and suggested Joe's daddy could use some help on the farm because he wasn't getting any younger. She rousted Joe out at dawn before the heat of the day got too bad. He came home covered with sweat and grit, the edge taken off his boundless energy.

"Hard exercise," Nadine confided to Nell, "is what boys need to keep themselves in control. That's what sports are for. That's why Joe got so good at football."

Nell helped around the house when Joe was gone, offered to cook occasionally and usually ended up taking lessons on how to make Joe's favorite foods. At one point, Nadine, while supervising her roux-making, actually said, "Lovin' don't last, good cookin' do," a favorite saying from her grandfather. All of this did not stop the lovemaking, even if it meant climbing out of windows at night and taking off with a blanket from the bed for the cane fields. Afterward, Nell stayed awake wondering why she could not get enough of Joe Dean Billodeaux.

An old-fashioned Fourth of July celebration came and went with ancient veterans marching down Main Street, a concert given in the square by the community band and sky rockets over the bayou. Lizzie's husband, Charlie, bought a fortune in fireworks and the family went to their house to set them off. The shabbiness of the place didn't show up too badly at night. Lizzie told Nell she waited for the day when her sons could paint and do a good job of mowing the lawn, but tonight—tonight was fine.

The other men made Joe and Charlie sit on the sidelines and watch because, they said, Joe couldn't risk his fingers and Charlie's breath might set off an explosion. Charlie, too drunk to care, slung an arm around Joe's shoulder and cheered at the brilliant lights like a child. His famous brother-in-law, seated, kept the tippler out of harm's way. A caring family taking action without spoiling the fun or embarrassing Lizzie, Nell analyzed before she could stop herself.

All the children but the babies were allowed to have sparklers, and they played writing their names in streaks of golden sparks or green smoke. The teens shot off bottle rockets until some of the boys started aiming them at each other and Nadine ended that. Finally, Allie's husband, who had already lost a finger out on the rigs so it wouldn't make any difference if he lost another, set off the grand finale of Patriotic Salutes, Angry Alligators, Swimming Fish, and One Bad Mothers that popped and sizzled over the cane fields. When the concussion ended, the tree frogs took a full five minutes before they felt they could resume peeping.

On the way home, Joe executed a successful escape from the family down a side road and made love to Nell in his old double sleeping bag rolled out over padding in the long bed of his new silver truck. Afterward, he and Nell watched for shooting stars, made their wishes and kept them secret from each other.

Tired of being separated for most of the days, Joe woke Nell at dawn one morning, packed a double lunch and took her out to the plantation for a ride in the high glass cab of the cane tractor. They rolled along the rows on man-high tires in air-conditioned comfort, the cane swishing under their seats.

"My daddy, Uncle Wylie, and Uncle Ross went deep into debt for this farm equipment. With Wylie's diabetes and Ross having high blood pressure, they thought the time had come to add comfort, and maybe some years to their lives. I paid off the balance owed last year and they forced me into taking shares in the plantation. When the old men pass on, I plan to give my shares to Eenie's husband because I sure as hell do not want to farm cane."

"You are a better man than you let people know, Joe."

He shrugged. "They're family."

Nell caught on to driving the tractor easily. Compared to riding a horse, this was no problem at all. One afternoon, having left Frank under the single, wide oak in the center of a field to take a break, Joe and Nell rolled off in the massive machine and were gone more than an hour. Joe's daddy, still sipping hot coffee from the cup of his thermos when they returned, gave them such a look Nell felt compelled to check her buttons, and Joe glanced down at his fly to make sure he was zipped.

The next day, Frank suggested Nell stay at the house and help out Mama who wanted to jar some okra. Allie came over to help because Eenie was working part-time at the Wal-Mart now that her girls were old enough to stay alone. She and Darryl needed the second income. Izzy sat at the kitchen table with her swollen ankles propped up on a chair and helped Nell cut the fuzzy green pods into seedy circles. The last of the home-grown tomatoes dipped in hot water also fell to Nell to peel and dice. They'd do some of the okra with tomatoes the way Frank and Joe liked, then pickle the rest whole, Nadine decided.

The second batch of steaming jars was coming out of the hot water bath when Nell's cell phone rang from the bedroom. Washing okra slime and tomato seeds from her hands with a quick spurt of the kitchen faucet, Nell dashed to catch the call but arrived in time only to receive a voice mail message. Joe Brunner informed her that one of her patients had died. The funeral was tomorrow at eleven in New Orleans, at Bultman's, if she could make it. When Nell failed to return to her chopping duties, Izzy heaved herself up and went to find her crying on the bed. One by one, the women came from the kitchen and clustered around Nell, patting and consoling. Joe found all of them in Allie's old bedroom when he came in from the fields.

"Let me take care of her," he told his mama and sisters. Reluctantly, they went back to the neglected canning. Nell made his sweat-damp shirt wetter when he took her on to his lap.

"You expected this to happen if the transplant didn't come through in time." Joe kissed the top of her head.

"I know, but I wasn't there for the child or his family."

"We'll drive into the city for the funeral. Then, I was thinking we could pick up Cassie and some of her brothers and sisters and bring them to see the ranch. Bijou says the ponies arrived late yesterday. We haven't been out to see them. We could cook up some hot dogs and hamburgers, easy stuff. We can't do anything for the other little guy, but Cassie might like some company."

"That would be good." Nell kept her face pressed against his chest. He eased back against the old maple headboard and stretched out his legs on the white eyelet spread. Letting Nell rest against him, Joe rubbed her back until she slept.

When his mama checked on them a few minutes later, she nodded and mouthed to her son, "Good boy, Joe."

****

Cerise and purple crepe myrtles brightened the Garden District and pink banana blossoms, glorying in the heat and humidity, topped the walls, but the air inside Bultman's Funeral Home stayed chilled and redolent with the fragrance of hothouse carnations and lilies. Christopher's family had money and prestige enough to guarantee many bouquets and a large attendance of mourners, but no amount of either had gotten their son the heart transplant he needed so urgently. Joe, shivering in the sudden cold, cringed at the thought. Money and fame couldn't make everything right in the world.

Nell apologized to the family for being away when the crisis had come. Christopher's blonde, stylish and totally devastated mother answered saying, "There was nothing you could have done, but thank you for coming."

Nell pressed one of her cards into the mother's hand. "Call my cell if you want to talk or if I can help in any way."

Christopher's father took the card from his wife's damp palm and put it in the pocket of his dark suit. He shook Joe's hand. "Joe Dean Billodeaux. I don't know how you knew about my son, but thank you for being here. We went to some of the games together when Chris was well enough, watched them on television when he wasn't. I bought two tickets for the opener in the Dome." The father turned his head away, fumbled with a handkerchief he tried to conceal, wiped his eyes and turned back to Joe. "Thanks for coming."

Joe and Nell took seats for the brief service about a short life. Most of the funerals he'd attended had been for relatives who died of the diseases of old age except for the teenage cousin killed in a car wreck. That last one that been awful. This, the funeral of a child, was worse. He wouldn't be here if not for Nell's sake.

He breathed easier when they went out in the heat again and headed for Cassie's home in a much less fashionable section of the city. Passing from the Garden District through areas devastated by Hurricane Katrina, he wondered if he had done enough to help. Sure, he'd donated money, even slung a hammer to put up a few houses when the Rev asked him to help, but he had so much and what did he do with it—build a mansion, buy cars and chase women. The drive made him almost as uncomfortable as the funeral.

Following telephone directions, they found the address posted on what looked like an old boarding house, big and square with no frills on the porch. A gray van that had lost most of the shine on its finish sat parked outside.

As soon as the Porsche pulled up, redheaded children began pushing out of the front door. Cassie stood out as tallest of the bunch. Short auburn curls covered her head in a style that seemed almost intentional. She'd been experimenting with blue eye shadow, mascara and goop to cover her freckles. Nell's patient had become lanky with a sudden growth spurt, and her breasts were an unlikely size in what Joe decided was a very padded bra.

"Miss Nell, Mr. Joe! These are my younger brothers and sisters." She pointed to each redhead. "Ben and Brian and Bridget and Nora and Kathy. Don't we look like the Weasleys?"

Joe drew a blank. He looked at Nell.

"From *Harry Potter*," she whispered.

"Sure do," Joe answered, still having not the slightest idea.

"Bonnie has a summer job, the oldest four are in the service trying to earn money for college and Dad had a chance at overtime, so it's just us who will be going."

Small hands left fingerprints on the gleaming red hood of the Porsche. Joe didn't say a word. Mrs. Thomas came from the house carrying a huge plastic jug of red punch and a large brown paper grocery bag.

"Snacks for the trip. Peanut butter sandwiches. It's such a long drive. I can follow you in the van. Get in, children! The house is such a mess, or I'd invite you in. Cassie gets the front seat. No complaining. You wouldn't be going if it weren't for her. Don't argue with your mother."

"Mom, I want to go in the sports car with Joe!"

"I'd be happy to ride with you, Mrs. Thomas. I can pour the juice as needed," Nell offered. Looking a little flummoxed, Joe agreed to a change of passengers.

He led the caravan the shortest way to Chapelle. They stopped once at a gas station when the twelve-year-old van overheated. The children lined up for the bathroom while Joe waited for the radiator to cool before adding water and antifreeze. Nell came to stand beside him while Mrs. Thomas supervised the bathroom brigade. They watched the steam rise from the engine.

"How are you doing with Cassie in the shotgun seat?"

"Fine, except for going deaf in my right ear from the chatter. She's put out that I didn't invite Connor, but hey, he and Stevie are still honeymooning. It's only a week or so before training camp. They need their time alone. At least, that's what Stevie told me the last time I barged in on them. The Rev is coming. I gave Bijou the keys to the truck so he could go on over to Versailles and pick up the big grill since mine isn't ready yet. I hope they let him in. How about you and the redheaded gang?"

"It's great to be around a family with so much energy, sort of like yours."

"You don't find my family—overwhelming?"

"Yes and no. They're good people, Joe."

"I think so. Funny, isn't it, how many kids Mrs. Thomas has and hers gets well. Christopher, he was an only child, right?"

"Yes, born with a severe congenital heart defect. They did what they could with surgery, but it wasn't enough. His mother was afraid to have more children. I can assure you, though, if it had been Cassie in that casket, the grief would have been just as severe."

"I know, but sometimes life isn't fair." Joe reached over, removed the loosened radiator cap with a rag, and fed fluids to the ailing van.

"There are no referees to call a foul and make things right, Joe. I figured that out a long time ago."

Joe hugged her to his side and leaned to place a kiss on her cheek.

"Hey, break it up! That's my counselor you're mauling." Cassie had returned. Red-haired Thomases surrounded the old van like a Celtic hoard ready to attack. They loaded up and moved out toward Chapelle.

****

The ponies, one fat and spotted, the other shaggy and palomino, won the hearts of the children merely by mooching sugar cubes from small, open hands. They answered, more or less, to the names Boo and Buttercup and wore spiffy tack in red and blue leather. For Shetlands, they were very good-natured. The younger Thomas children rode the animals into exhaustion, going round and round the dirt practice ring that had materialized from the scrub and rotting posts on the far side of the barn where an old Cajun racing track once stood.

Leaning against the new, white-painted rails, Joe told Nell, "In my grandfather's day, the men would come to bet cash on match races on the two-lane course and maybe fight cocks in the barn. Big tracks like Evangeline Downs and people disapprovin' of cock fighting put an end to all that at Lorena Ranch. They still raise game cocks all over the parish and supposedly ship elsewhere to fight."

"You'd never fight chickens, would you?"

"How stupid would I be to get caught doing something like that when I have almost everything I want in life?"

Nell started to ask what else he needed when Boo decided he'd enough and stopped dead, allowing Brian to slip over the pony's head and end up a heap in the dirt.

"Get up, get on and show him who's boss," Joe prompted the boy.

Brian dusted himself off and remounted determined not to lose his turn, no harm done at all. Cassie flew by on Fatima. One lesson with Joe behind her in the saddle and she rode like an Indian.

"How come you put me up alone on that huge animal and Cassie gets the babe in arms treatment?" Nell had to ask.

"Since you are always trying to impress on me how tough and fierce you are, maybe I didn't want to insult you by implying you might need help."

"I did."

"Still do."

Bijou, who had dressed up for company in a clean western shirt with a red rose embroidered on the pocket and pearl snaps down the front, took a place on the other side of Nell, removed his snuff can from a worn jeans pocket and filled his lip with smokeless tobacco. Five assorted rings sparkled on his blunt fingers.

"She's a natural, that Cassie. Look at her go. Probably, I could train her to be a barrel racer, win some prizes."

"She lives in the city, Bijou, and is supposed to start at a Catholic girls' school at the end of August. Her mother got her a scholarship. I don't think she'll be doing much barrel racing."

"Just sayin'. Girl has spirit." Bijou spat on the ground. Nell moved her feet.

Mrs. Thomas came around the barn and called out the food was ready. Her younger girls, who had finished riding, placed plastic knives and forks on red-checkered table cloths covering the plywood and sawhorses forming a long table. Green resin stack chairs surrounded the table. The Rev flipped over hamburgers and got ready to fork hotdogs on to a plate. He had declined a chance to ride by saying he didn't like the look in the eyes of the big red horse, and he couldn't afford no broken bones just before training camp.

Nadine arrived with a trunk full of potato chips plus enough crock pots full of baked beans to feed the

Confederate army. A long, green-striped watermelon floated in the ice and water of a large cooler along with bobbing cans of cold drinks. Dinner was served.

Nell, stuffing hot dogs into buns, felt herself falling in love with Joe Dean Billodeaux, his large and generous family and his enormous, warm-hearted friends. That simply could not happen. This was supposed to be fun, a summer romance. Nothing more could be allowed.

The Thomas family departed around eight with Cassie's mother turning down an offer to be followed by Joe. "I'm used to this cranky old van. We'll be fine." Nevertheless, Nell scribbled her cell phone number on a napkin and gave it to Mrs. Thomas.

Cassie had to be routed from the barn where she was saying good-bye to the horses. "Bijou says if I can come over more often, he'll show me how to barrel race once I get a better seat. He says I have the build for it."

"You call him Mr. Bijou, Cassie," her mother said. "We have no money for riding lessons."

"He won't charge. I can drive up here alone once I get my license."

"You told her to get involved in things, Nell. What does she choose? A driver's ed class, and she won't be sixteen until September." Mrs. Thomas rolled her eyes. "I didn't have the heart to turn her down."

"Can I drive on the way home? I wanted Joe to let me drive the Porsche, but he said I don't know standard. I could learn though. Bijou says I'm a quick learner."

"Mr. Joe, Mr. Bijou," her mother corrected again. "Thank them for the nice day."

"Already did. Nell, I passed my written exam last

week and already have my permit. I could come here to visit you as soon as I get my license in September."

"Cassie, I won't be here in September, but you can visit me in Metairie."

Joe stood behind Nell, his hand resting on her narrow shoulder. His fingers clenched for a moment. He removed his hand to wave to the red-haired Thomases as Cassie took the wheel and pointed the van down the lane after backing up in a large half-circle.

Nadine packed the dirty crock pots and half full bags of chips in the trunk of her car. The Rev and Bijou maneuvered the grill on to the bed of the Silverado. Nell went to fold the tablecloths and stack the resin chairs. Mrs. Thomas had made sure her children picked up the trash and bagged it in two black plastic trash bags before leaving. Joe drained the cooler and placed it on the back seat of his mother's Honda.

"Bijou, when you get back from taking the grill, you can park the truck up at the old place. Keep the keys. I need to report to camp next week and won't be needing it."

Bijou gave a happy nod and headed out to take the Rev and his grill home. Mrs. Billodeaux took a good look at her son.

"Nell tells me she'll be leaving in a couple of days, so why don't you two spend some time together alone this evening?" With that blessing, she went to take leftovers to her husband.

Joe circled Nell with his arms and drew her back against him. "That almost takes the fun out it."

"No, it won't. Let's try and see."

They retrieved the sleeping bag from the tack room where Joe had stowed it and carried the sack up the double-wide steps that would someday be an elegant staircase in the new house, but were now just rough boards with no railing. The roof was on and most of the insulation nail-gunned to the frame.

"Voilá." He unrolled the bag with a flourish. He held out his arms. "Would you look at the view from the master bedroom?" Gazing out a large gap in the walls, Joe put his arm around Nell and stood awhile appreciating the scene over the low tops of the live oaks toward the bayou, then up the opposite bank, across the field of cane to the hot red ball of the sun sinking behind the tall stalks.

"With the roof on, things should move fairly quickly now. We could be in this place for Christmas."

"We?" Nell questioned.

"Ah, you know. Just talkin'. I brought condoms." He held out three.

"I've been trying to tell you, Joe. We don't need them."

"Sure we do. I told you I want a family some day, a big family, just not today. You know us Billodeauxs, super fertile. No sense taking chances even if it is near that time of the month."

"Joe, sit down."

He lay on the sleeping bag and stretched out with his hands behind his head inviting her to pounce and prove how feisty she was. Instead, Nell sat beside him and bunched up her knees.

"You know about the cancer. You know I had chemotherapy and a bone marrow transplant from my sister. That's why I'm alive today. When you go through all that, Joe, they have to kill off all the bad cells in your body. Some of the good ones die, too. It's very unlikely I'll ever have children."

Nell watched him swallow hard. He continued to stare out at the setting sun, not saying a word for a moment. Joe cleared his throat. "But it's not impossible though."

"When I was trying to prove my womanhood, I wasn't very careful, tempting my fate, I guess. When I was engaged, we didn't use anything. Drake studied medicine. He knew. He said we could always adopt."

"Sure. Adoption." His voice still seemed hoarse as if something were stuck deep inside and cutting off his air.

"Oh, Joe, you aren't exactly the man I thought you were."

"What, not a sex maniac after all?" He rubbed his chest as if trying to lighten a pressure building there.

"You are that. I mean once a day, every day, and twice on Sundays if you can get away with it." She shook her head and tried to give him a little smile.

"Training and playing take the edge off. I'm not nearly so horny during the season. I wouldn't be cheating after away games." He still wasn't looking at her.

"I believe you, but Joe, I've seen you with your family. I know what family means to you. You deserve to have children of your own. Most women could give you that."

She brushed back the curls that fell near his now closed eyes. He was like a child who thought shutting his eyes made bad things go away. "And don't tell me I'm not like most women. I know that."

"Nell, you are all women to me."

"Let's just have fun tonight." She started to

unbutton his shirt. He stopped her by grabbing her wrists.

"Nell, you're doing it to me again, not giving me a chance to think. There are other ways people can have children."

"All of them expensive, messy and often unsuccessful. I did some work with infertile couples. I've seen men walk out after experiencing failure after failure and find another woman who could reproduce. Some women put so much effort into conceiving there is nothing else left for their marriages. You enjoy life so much. I couldn't do that to you."

"Hey, so let's enjoy life." Joe opened eyes that were dark and glittering. He crumpled the condoms he still had clutched in one hand and tossed them away. He made love to her with his hands, memorizing every inch of her body so tenderly she cried out long before he entered her. A night bird answered.

He moved over her slowly. In the darkness, his sweat dropped on her lips and tasted like salty tears. When the end came, the farewell went on and on. She almost wished he had been silly or rough. Afterward, they lay naked in each other's arms and watched again for shooting stars.

"There's one bright enough for two wishes." Joe pointed to a streak in the sky that seemed to burn out in the cane field. "You tell me yours, I'll tell you mine."

"Is that like playing doctor, show me yours, I'll show you mine?"

"We've seen each other's. No, this is much more serious."

"Joe, wishing won't make it so."

****

Joe and Nell stayed out all night. Mrs. Billodeaux said not a word when they straggled in at dawn. She offered them coffee. Frank came yawning to the table.

"Don't think running around all night is an excuse to get out of helping with the farm this morning," he said to Joe. "I'm counting on you."

"Sure, Dad. Let me get a shower and some coffee."

After the men left for the day, Nell asked Nadine to drive her back to Metairie.

"Has my son done wrong by you?" Joe's mother asked.

"No. He was the perfect gentleman."

Chapter Thirteen

Coach Marty Buck watched his team work. After a few more minutes, he signaled to Connor Riley to come off the field. "Billodeaux, practice handing off to Harvey."

Connor wiped his face and hands with a towel and gulped down half a bottle of water. He watched the Sinners' top draft pick, DeLong Harvey, take the ball from Joe and sprint down the field avoiding the defensive players trying to stop him. "You wanted to see me, Coach?"

"What do you think of Harvey?"

"The commentators won't be calling him De Long Shot Harvey anymore once they see him working with our offensive line."

"Takes some pressure off of you, too. Not that you and Joe Dean haven't been connecting."

"The more options we have, the more we'll win."

"My thought, too. Still, something is off with Billodeaux."

"He's been throwing well. Considering how he spent his spring, he came to camp in good condition. Farm work must agree with him." Connor finished the bottle and threw the container into a trash barrel.

"It's not his playing. It's his attitude that's bothering me. Where's the spark? Where's the We Can Win the Super Bowl spirit we saw last year. I was hoping he'd fire up the new recruits, but he's just out there doing his job. Where's the mouth?"

"Maybe he's figured out there's more to life than football."

"Wash your mouth out, boy! You're saying this is about sex, Joe Dean's only other interest. God, I hope it's not AIDS."

"Not that. He stayed with one woman all summer, the one who made him get a health certificate. They broke up just before camp started."

"Christ! You last year. Him this year. He helped you out of your slump. Can you return the favor?" Coach Buck raked his silver crew cut with splayed fingers.

"I'll do my best."

"That's what I'd expect. Get back out there." Coach waved Connor Riley toward the field.

****

Coach Marty Buck did what he could to restore Joe Dean Billodeaux's spirit. He played the eager, new would-be backup quarterbacks in most of the exhibition games using his star only if the Sinners looked like they were losing. Competition put the edge on most men, but Joe trotted out when called, did his job, and sat back down. The team seemed to be cool with this, but Coach Buck wanted to see some fire in the regular season. Gung ho attitude could turn a loss into a win and Joe wasn't providing it.

Connor called in the women for advice during a short break before regular season play began. Out on the deck of his lakeside home, the men poked and prodded the chicken halves on the grill waiting for the exact moment to add Connor's special barbecue sauce.

Their wives hauled the rest of the meal from the kitchen where Miss Essie, the cook, had left the sides wrapped in plastic and foil. Strategically placed bowls held the blue tablecloth in place when warm air came gusting off the lake.

"We never used tablecloths befo'. Did we, Connor?" The Rev stuck a long-tined fork deep into a chicken thigh and studied the color of the juice coming to the surface. "A mite longer, I think."

"That was before marriage, Rev. I'm surprised we don't have candles." Connor stood by with a basting brush and bowl of sauce in hand. "I need y'all's advice on something."

Stevie and Mintay looked up from arranging the table. "It's too windy for candles—unless we bring out some hurricane lamps later this evening," Stevie suggested.

"That would be lovely," Mintay agreed.

"No, no. This is about Joe Dean. He'll be here any minute. You know he and Nell broke up."

"A shame," said Mintay. "I thought we almost had him married off."

"A damn shame," Stevie added.

"I'd like to get them back together. You know, return the favor he did for Stevie and me."

"What broke them up?" Mintay asked.

"Other women, weird sexual practices?" Stevie suggested.

"Neither," Joe Dean Billodeaux said coming up behind the group. For a big man, he could walk very quietly when he desired. It wasn't his usual ebullient approach full of motions and greetings. This stillness was unusual, so not Joe Dean, the women looked at

132

each other.

"No other women. As for sex, you wouldn't believe what that little lady could do. Nell looks so tiny and fragile, but she was one of the best…"

"Don't want to hear it." Mintay covered her ears.

"It was about children, having children. She says she can't."

"Joe Dean Billodeaux, you dumped Nell because she can't have children? That is one of the cruelest things I've ever heard." Stevie clenched her hand around a steak knife and seemed ready to stab the quarterback, star or no star. "A woman who survived cancer deserves better than that. Better than you!"

"Oh no. Cancer." Mintay put her fingers to her lips. "I had no idea when I was pushing you two together. I suppose she had chemo or radiation therapy."

"Chemo and a bone marrow transplant. She says she's sterile. And Stevie, get this straight, she dumped *me*. Said I deserved to have children of my own, then ran away when I was out in the fields with my dad. Any beer in this cooler?" Joe went up to his elbow fishing for something besides Diet Coke and un-colas.

"There is adoption, in vitro fertilization and a few other alternatives," Mintay listed.

"I said as much. She claims things like this can tear people apart." Joe with a triumphant look hooked a bottle of Turbo Dog from the ice. "But I've handled it. Everything will be all right."

"Just how?" inquired Mintay.

"This I have to hear," said Stevie. "It's not like one of the crazy schemes you used to bring Connor and me together, I hope."

"One of them worked and you have yet to thank

me for it. But no—no schemes with Nell. Any of you Catholic, do time in parochial school?" Joe surveyed his group of friends.

"You know I'm African Methodist Episcopalian," the Rev answered.

Mintay raised her hand. "AME by marriage."

"Lutheran by birth. My father was Catholic but never bothered to take us to his church. Mom won by default," Connor said.

Stevie shrugged. "Whatever."

"Then, you don't know how this works. See, I just got back from Chapelle where I owed a big penance. I paid the cash, but I was sort of fudging on the one hundred Our Fathers on my knees." Joe rolled the cold beer bottle across his shin. "I'm still sore. I hope this doesn't mess up my game. Anyhow, after I finished humiliating myself before the Lord…"

"I think the word is humbling, humbling yourself before the Lord," the Rev corrected.

"No, it was humiliating. Two ladies from the perpetual prayer group were there the whole time, Miss Maxine and Miss Lolly. When the next team tagged in, they stood in the back of the church speculatin' on my sins. They got pretty close, right down to the details. Who would have thought those old biddies read the Bible *and* the tabloids? Anyhow, when I finished, I went over to the Mary Altar and lit enough candles to burn the place down. They don't have an altar for St. Jude, but the BVM will see he gets the message."

"The BVM?" asked Stevie.

"The Blessed Virgin Mary," Joe answered with a look that appeared to ask if she had ever been in a church.

"And what message was that, Joe?" Connor gave the Rev a worried look.

"I see God lookin' down..."

"You're seeing God?" the Rev interrupted, perhaps a trifle jealous.

"No, this is just how I imagine things go. God says, 'Joe Dean Billodeaux, I gave you a loving family, good looks, a great arm, and a chance with a wonderful woman. Why should I give you anything else?'"

"Good question," Stevie couldn't help but say.

"But then, the Holy Mother says, 'Dear Lord, he isn't asking this favor for himself, but for Nell. You remember Nell. You gave her a really hard childhood full of sickness, but she turned out so well and now she helps others who are sick.' Now, St. Jude gives her backup. 'Oh God, grant our Nell the blessing of being mother to the Joe Dean Billodeaux children. Joe Dean has made me a promise, and he always keeps his promises.'"

"Not another celibacy vow! How are you going to have children if you are celibate?" Connor asked. "Immaculate conception?"

"No, no. I don't want God to do that part for me. I vowed to be a faithful husband and a good father to all our children. But you, you shouldn't be laughing at my celibacy vow. Look at you, healthy and playing great ball, just what I asked of St. Jude. And unlike you, I stayed celibate for the whole damn season." Joe straddled the picnic bench, seized a whole dill pickle from the relish tray, and pointed it at Connor.

"It wasn't a vow for me," Connor objected.

"Enough! Break it up!" Mintay held up her hand. Right before their eyes, she went from being Mrs. Rev

135

Bullock to Dr. Arminta Green. "Joe, you shouldn't get your hopes up. Science may be able to do something for Nell over a long period of time, but even in vitro fertilization has only a twenty percent success rate. You hear about the wonderful results, never the failures."

"Mintay, don't go dissing the power of prayer. Miracles do happen." The Rev squeezed his wife's hand.

"That's okay. It's my faith that matters, not hers. Besides, Nell may be pregnant already. Our last night together we had unprotected sex—more than once."

"No details!" Stevie clamped her hand over Joe's mouth. He removed her fingers.

"What I mean is, it's been about a month now. She may not realize it yet. If she doesn't call me in two weeks, I'll hunt her down. No secret love child for me."

Joe unwrapped his long legs from the bench and sauntered toward the grill.

"Oh, and guys, I promised St. Jude if he made it twin boys, I'd give him all the credit for our next Super Bowl win which should be coming along in about five months."

He stuck his finger in the bowl of barbecue sauce and tasted. "Needs more cayenne pepper, Connor."

"Doesn't! Get your hand out of my sauce." Connor went to defend his concoction. Stevie tagged along to referee.

"Poor Joe. He is going to be so disappointed. I feel responsible for this mess, pushing them together the way I did," Mintay whispered to the Rev.

Her husband engulfed her in his arms. "Maybe, but Coach Buck will be one happy man. Looks like the old Joe Dean is back."

Chapter Fourteen

On a small private island near Cozumel, the same island that great big jerk, Joe Dean Billodeaux had rented as a playground for the team, Margaret Stutes basked in the sun. She appreciated the irony of her location. The guest cabins were clean, lovely and amazingly cheap. When she came here with the second-string lineman who would be her first client when she opened her own agency, Margaret took out a six-month lease on one of them. Her plans were going so well.

"Jorge!" she called out, knowing the little Mexican would be hanging around to answer her every beck and call. "Another pina colada."

"*Sí señora* Margarita." Jorge scuttled off with her empty glass and returned minutes later with a fresh drink.

Margaret sipped. As she suspected, the drink had been made with only fruit juice and ice. Still, the pineapple and coconut cream mixture was refreshing. Just to have a little fun, she reprimanded Jorge again, "It's *señorita*. Sorry if that upsets you."

"*Sí. Sí.*" Jorge backed away.

Margaret, unsure if he was agreeing to address her as *señorita* or assenting that he was upset, shrugged. It hardly mattered what Jorge thought. The beach, deserted now that American children were back in school and the families had stopped coming, belonged solely to her. Soon, she would have to dig her feet out of the sand and pee again. Maybe, she would go down into the water, closer than her cabin, and do it there.

Digging a little crater in the beach, she plugged her drink in the hole and then set the feet she could not see beneath her and heaved out of the beach chair using both of her hands. Margaret stretched her arms out. She had the best tan of her life and her boobs were bigger than they had ever been, but shit, she hated being so fat. Public relations people should be sleek and shark-like predators.

Oh well, she wouldn't be huge much longer now. On her last trip to the main land, her obstetrician had told her in no uncertain terms she had to come in for checkups once a week now that she was starting her last month of pregnancy. He wanted her in the city near a good hospital, no more flying back to New Orleans once a month. She should have stopped doing that weeks ago.

What did he know? Margaret felt great. Down here, she could gorge on fresh seafood and tropical fruit, all dirt cheap. She had been very careful back home in her first three months—no booze, no cigarettes, no caffeine. Here, as soon as she started to show obviously, Jorge had conspired with the bartender to weaken her drinks and started addressing her as *señora*.

Margaret trundled down to the water's edge finding the going at little easier when she was out of the softer sand. She ran her hands down her distended belly. The baby rolled and kicked again, a real athlete. He kept her up nights. She had hoped for a boy, the better to trap Joe Dean Billodeaux with, and her ultrasound confirmed the sex of the child. When the little devil kept her up, she passed the time calculating how much money she could get out of the quarterback for child support, and how long to suppress the story of his love child. She needed enough to set up her own business. She'd retained a sharp lawyer to handle Big Deal Joe Dean. The quarterback would never marry her, but with his son in her power, Joe would be part of her life forever.

When the scandal broke, the free publicity would make the name of Margaret Stutes famous long enough to give her business a free boost. Timing was everything. and so she'd had to be first on Joe Dean's list. She'd monitored her fertile periods for months and laughed out loud when she saw it would fall on Super Bowl week. Reluctant and drunk, Joe Dean had been such easy prey. She used his bruised ego to get him to screw her twice when she complained about his performance, both times without condoms. Who knew? Maybe that six-hour interval had made all the difference.

Margaret waded out only to the waist-deep water so the waves would not threaten to knock her over. Must be oh so careful with Joe Dean's child. Her bathing suit had a bikini bottom and a long flowing top covered in a wild tropical print that floated up around her. She splashed herself to cool her face. She emptied her bladder into the surf. Fish do it, why not Margaret Stutes? She stretched and started back to the beach.

Something bumped against the back of her legs, then slid along her thighs like sandpaper over a board. It knocked her belly down, her feet flailing, her arms out in front of her. Margaret went under, came up and spit the bitter sea water from her mouth. She struggled to move forward, but something held her back. The water around her took on a strange red tinge.

"Jorge!" she screamed.

She could see the little man she loved to order around. He always wore white cotton clothes and sandals like some Mexican stereotype but without the sombrero. The horror on his face clearly visible, Jorge grabbed a paddle from one of the kayaks the younger guests loved to take into the water. He splashed toward Margaret and began beating at the surf like a madman. Finally, he drove off the shark and towed her to the beach.

She spurted blood from a ghastly wound in her leg. He tied a towel tightly around her thigh and shouted for help. Javier, the bartender, came running. They carried Margaret to the little infirmary where semi-retired Dr. Lopez treated jellyfish stings and heat stroke in return for room and board.

The lady was going into shock, but she screamed very clearly, "Save my baby! Save my baby! I need this baby!"

Those were the last words the *Americana* uttered before losing consciousness. Jorge, Javier, and Dr. Lopez, all good Catholics, understood her meaning. In fact, they felt deeply touched that an unwed mother would care so much for the child who had caused her to hide her shame on the island for months.

While Dr. Lopez prepared for an emergency Caesarian section, the manager called Cozumel for a medivac. They requested a priest as well. Dr. Lopez, competent enough on a day-to-day basis, had not done surgery of this nature for many years.

Pleased when old skills came back to him, Dr. Lopez lifted the lady's bladder without nicking it and sliced into the uterus without touching the fetus. As soon as he removed the child, tied off its cord and dealt with the placenta, he put all of the senora's organs back in place and sewed her up with tight little stitches. Very good under the circumstances, he thought. Yes, perhaps, he should have attended to the monstrous wound first, but the woman had made her wishes very clear, "Save my baby!" His English was quite good enough to understand that.

He wrapped the baby, still un-cleaned, in a white towel and placed him in his mother's arms. Small, but not dangerously so, the infant boy breathed well. *Gracias a Dios.*

The priest, murmuring last rites accompanied by the thump of helicopter rotors, finished one sacrament and began another. "*Señora*, a name for your child?" he asked trying to rouse the mother.

Margaret's eyes opened but began to glaze. All her plans, all her schemes faded away into a realm where they did not matter. Or perhaps, it was the other way around. She was fading and going to another place while her wishes remained behind. She'd had Joe Dean Billodeaux's child, but she would never profit from it. She tried to tell the priest. She should confess her sins, or had they passed that part already? A name, the priest wanted a name, not her name. She wanted say Joe Dean but only the second word made it past her pale lips, "Dean." She attempted again, pushing the word out, "Joe."

"*Excelente.* Dean Joseph, I christen you in the name of the Father, the Son and the Holy Ghost. A

141

good saint's name for a fatherless child, Joseph. Rest, rest, your sins are forgiven, Margarita Stutes."

Padre Angelo closed her eyes. So sad. All he knew of this woman was her name and the fact she was unmarried, her baby illegitimate. Jorge had given him these few details as they raced for the medivac. An American woman, who in her pride, had boasted to her servant that the father was a rich athlete who would pay for his child.

Chapter Fifteen

The two weeks were up, and Joe had not heard from Nell. He debated an approach. He would break down and phone *her*. Should the call be casual and friendly? Like: did you see the season opener? Great game, right? They could talk about football for a while, a topic where he felt sure of himself. Then, he would ask Nell how she was doing, no, feeling. The more he thought about it, the more muddled he became. He needed to take action and work the rest of the play from there. Picking up the phone, he punched in her number, all the while holding the old business card she had given him like a lucky charm.

"Hello," a voice lower and huskier than Joe expected answered. Maybe she had been crying— crying over him—or an unexpected pregnancy.

"Nell? Are you all right? Please, please don't hang up."

"This is Emily. Who is calling, please?"

"Joe, not her boss. Joe Dean Billodeaux."

Nell's sister, Emily, covered the phone and shouted to her sister. "She can't come to the phone right now, Joe. Can I help you?" The voice went softer, sexier.

"Uh, no. I really need to talk to Nell. I'll hold."

"Joe, it's like this. She really doesn't want to talk to you, but if you're lonely, I'm available. We were going to a movie, but I can get out of it," Emily whispered.

"Ah, tell Nell it's urgent."

Again, the hand covered the phone and the voice shouted the message. "Exactly how urgent, Joe?" Emily relayed.

"Look, tell her I may have given her a social problem." The words just popped into his mind.

"Ooooh! Herpes, syphilis, AIDS?" Emily whispered again.

"No!"

"Vaginal warts, gonorrhea, chlamydia?"

"You sure know your social diseases, Emily. Get Nell to the phone, please."

This time Em did not bother to cover the receiver. "Nell, Joe says he might have given you a social disease." He could hear the patter of Nell's feet doing a quick step down the hall.

"Joe, how could you! Did you fake that health certificate?"

Nell was very unhappy with him, sure, but in a minute or two everything would be fine. "How are you feelin', Tink? I just wanted to check up on you."

"Up until a minute ago, I was fine. What's going on, Joe?"

"No nausea or vomiting, swollen breasts, missed periods?"

"Joe, I'm not pregnant, but thanks for being concerned. Is that the only reason you called?"

"Hell, no. Nell, you and me, we could work this out. I've got St. Jude, the BVM, and God working on it."

"I'm overwhelmed, truly. But, Joe, I've had my miracle. I survived cancer. Don't you think it's asking a lot to want more?"

His phone signaled an incoming call. Why now? Still, few people had his private number. He never gave it to the women he dated except for Nell. He needed to check this out because he didn't recognize the number. "Hold for just a second. I'll be right back. We aren't done talking."

"Joe, this is Nicole Everard, the attorney. We need to discuss a very important matter. You do remember me?" The voice came across as precise, chilly and no nonsense as he recalled—the sour grape lady.

"Yes, I remember you, Nicole." Great, one of the list ladies was going to cause trouble. Never screw with a lawyer. The possibilities ran through his mind: venereal disease, pregnancy, rape charges. Coach Buck had tried to warn him. Now, when he was getting his act together—this, whatever it was.

"I want to see you at my office tomorrow."

"I don't do office visits, Nicole."

She laughed in a way that made the hair stand up on his arms. "Oh, Joe, ever the big ego. No, this is a legal matter. Would ten o'clock tomorrow be good?"

"I have practice in the morning. I could make some time after lunch. Do I need to bring my own lawyer?"

"That's up to you, Joe, but I'd like to keep the initial contact friendly. Hear what I have to say first. This could be a very simple matter."

"Okay, fine. I think I have your office address in my book."

"Well, I wouldn't have given you the one for my home, now would I?" she said in a superior voice.

"Yeah, I guess not. When you cheat on your husband, that's a poor idea."

"That's right, Joe, make it harder on yourself. I'll see you at one. Don't be late." Nicole Everard disconnected.

Frantically, Joe switched back to Nell's line. She'd hung up. He called again. No one answered. The voice mail intervened. Presumably, Nell and Emily had gone to the movies. She'd left her cell phone behind. Maybe, he should let her be until after his appointment with Nicole Everard. Nell did not need to take on his problems, too.

Chapter Sixteen

Joe Dean would have been the first to admit he put in a lousy practice. Coach Buck did not let it pass. "You hung over, son?"

"No, sir. I have some things on my mind is all."

"Way you played Sunday, I thought your troubles were behind you. Great game. You had the boys all fired up, maybe more than necessary considering the opponent. Save some for later."

"I'll try. I might be late coming back this afternoon. I need to see a lawyer."

"Shit, boy, what you done now? You want to go to my office for a talk? You want a team representative to go with you?" Coach Buck shook his head like a bobble-head toy.

"Not yet. Let me see what she wants."

"Hell, I might have known it was woman trouble. Not one of your list ladies, I hope."

"Maybe. Don't know. I'm really sorry this time, Coach."

With his prize quarterback head down and shrinking before his eyes, what else could Marty Buck do but give him the old slap on the back. "Come see me when you return."

****

The sign on the narrow old building wedged between two banking behemoths on the edge of the financial district read *Hait, Everard & Everard, Attorneys at Law* in classic gold lettering. Joe Dean walked up worn marble steps to the red door and entered.

No one attended the mahogany reception desk. Maroon leather chairs and up-to-date, glossy magazines awaited to help clients pass the time. Joe declined to sit and twiddle his thumbs. He wanted this over and done. He looked down a hall to where a middle-aged woman in a smart gray suit made coffee in a fancy stainless steel machine.

Next to her, a young woman with short blonde hair and a shapely bottom cooed over some employee's baby wiggling in a car seat. Maybe the kid was hers, or maybe Nicole's. Joe counted backwards. No, too soon to be his by the attorney. Maybe she'd been pregnant during their encounter, but Nicole Everard did not seem the type to bring a baby to work. He remembered her kids had a nanny. He cleared his throat and the two women looked up from kid and coffee.

"Joe Dean Billodeaux. I have an appointment with Mrs. Everard at one."

"Of course, Mr. Billodeaux. Please have a seat. Can I offer you coffee, tea, water?" the older woman responded.

"No, thanks. Just tell her I'm here." Joe remained standing while the receptionist opened one of the four hall doors and murmured the announcement.

"Ms. Everard is taking a call right now. She will be with you in a few minutes."

The witch was probably checking her makeup and putting him in his place at the same time. He would give Nicole two minutes, then he would charge into her sanctum.

The blonde abandoned the baby for a moment and slid toward Joe Dean. "I'm Stacey Smits, the paralegal." In a low voice, she added with a furtive glance toward Iris, "I signed your book, but I guess you never got to the S's."

"No, I only got to one S. Sorry. You sure are pretty, but I'm in sort of a serious relationship now. My loss, sugar." He gave her a smile to remember. Even the older woman widened her eyes. The intercom on the desk buzzed.

"Ms. Everard will see you now, Mr. Billodeaux. Third door on the left. Good luck," the receptionist said with feeling.

Would he need luck? Joe passed two offices bearing the names Jeremy Hait and Harry Everard before coming to Nicole's lair. He noticed Harry's door stood slightly ajar. With his back to Joe, this man really was talking on the phone. The overhead light reflected off the bald spot in his gray hair. The attorney tapped a manicured but pudgy hand on his polished ebony desk. He shot up his cuff and checked the time on a massive gold Rolex watch. So this was Nicole's husband. Joe stopped and stared into the room.

On a shelf holding weighty law books perfectly matched in size, two framed family pictures stood, one of two grown young women and another of Everard, Nicole, and two boys about six and eight—first family, second family and trophy wife, Joe figured. Sensing Joe lurking in the hall, Harry Everard spun in an office chair resembling a throne on wheels and asked, "Are you lost?"

"I have an appointment with Nicole."

"Next door." Harry's tone implied Joe could not read. "Would you mind shutting my door?" He turned his back once more.

Tired of lawyer games, Joe let Harry Everard's door remain open and walked into Nicole's presence without knocking. He didn't do doorman for her either. Joe played football. He understood intimidation and mind games. Attorneys had nothing compared to men who possessed nicknames like "The Refrigerator." Joe took a seat without its being offered.

"Nice to see you again, Joe." Nicole arched her finely penciled eyebrows as if she did not mean the greeting.

"Same here," Joe answered, making sure she knew the scorn was mutual.

"Fabulous game on Sunday. Harry and I were given tickets in a luxury box by Councilman Derise. He had intended to go with his son, Christopher."

"But the boy died. I know. I went to the funeral."

"So I heard—with little Nurse Nell. The councilman was very touched. Isn't it funny how a couple with only one beloved child loses their boy while other people carelessly bring children into the world without a thought of the consequences?"

"Look, I need to get back. Could we cut to the chase?" he said, remembering their brief encounter.

"Ah, yes, the chase. Do you recall a woman named Margaret Stutes?"

"Sure. She used to do PR for the Sinners. I ran into her several times."

"Oh, I think you did more than run into her, Joe. Margaret, it seems, gave birth to your baby two weeks ago."

He did not flinch. This was the old paternity suit scheme, then, and not for the first time. The blood tests never panned out because, as Joe had told Coach Buck, he was always careful. The kid probably belonged to the reserve lineman Margaret diddled along the way. That poor guy was in for a shock. Joe confessed, "I had sex with Margaret right after the Super Bowl. It's too soon for the baby to be mine."

"Then you admit to intercourse with my client."

"Sure—with you, too, if you want."

"You see, Margaret met with an unfortunate accident near Cozumel while she awaited the birth. The child came early. Poor, dear Margaret died shortly thereafter. I was named the child's guardian in a legal agreement we signed in June. Margaret was an only child. Her mother died of cancer three years ago. Her father walked out when she was two, whereabouts unknown. No contact with his family. Only two aunts in their sixties on the mother's side. The pitiful orphaned child has no one but me to defend him."

"So you were already figuring out your cut back in April when we got together, Nicole?"

"Oh, it will be considerably higher now. Margaret wanted a very good life for her child, and you can afford it. Before, this was only a routine paternity suit with my fee based on a percentage of how much we could squeeze out of you. Now as legal guardian, I can exact reasonable fees until the child reaches twenty-one. Sad, isn't it, that Margaret had to list her attorney as the person to contact in an emergency."

"Very sad it was you. I'll have my attorney get in touch to arrange the usual blood test." He kept his game face on, not letting his shock show, not blubbering about always being careful. He remembered so little about his night with Margaret. Joe rose to depart.

"Don't you want to see the boy, Joe? Margaret named him Dean Joseph with her dying breath. I was able to supply the Mexican authorities with the name of the father for the birth certificate." She slid a document across the slick surface of her desk.

Joe was no linguist, but he could read his own name filled in over the word *Padre*. He frowned, then blanked his features. "I'll be happy to see the child if he turns out to be mine." He turned toward the door.

"Iris, bring in the baby, please," Nicole ordered over her intercom.

Joe nearly collided with the receptionist who must have been waiting in the hall. She thrust the baby carrier at him like a woman who had once been a forward on a girl's basketball team.

"He's a little angel, Mr. Billodeaux, so good, so small. Just look at all that dark hair, would you?" Despite her eagerness to hand over the child, Iris paused to touch its soft, red cheek. The infant turned its head and made sucking motions with its tiny lips.

"Are you hungry, Deanie? Are you hungry, little lamb?" she said, dropping into baby talk.

"That will be enough, Iris. Leave the diaper bag, too."

Iris relinquished the denim bag with the yellow duckie on the side by placing in on Nicole's desk. She bowed out of the office and shut the door. Joe sank back into his chair, and then taking charge again, sat the baby seat on the oriental rug covering the hardwood floor. The child began to fret, but Joe stared straight at Nicole, refusing to break eye contact.

"Go ahead, Joe. Pick him up," she dared. "I see now he has your chin." Nicole checked her watch, a slim version of her husband's Rolex as if to say, "How time does fly."

Joe leaned over, unstrapped the child, and laid the baby on his knees. The lawyer's mouth opened, amazed no doubt, by his ease with children.

"Yeah, he has the chin. The hair, too." Joe ran a hand over the thick cap of curls. Felt like fine velvet. Beneath Joe's fingers, the pulse of the child throbbed under the soft spot in time with his heart. The baby blinked his eyes open for a moment. Their color was a blue so deep Joe knew it would turn to a dark brown within days. The same thing happened with all the Billodeaux infants. He offered his finger. Dean Joseph clutched it and tried to raise it to his mouth but failed.

"He's sort of small though."

"Weight at birth was five pounds, nine ounces. He's already up to six. Those Mexicans love their babies. They probably fed him every time he opened his mouth. If he's already spoiled, my nanny will be upset."

Clearly, Nicole enjoyed this moment. Who wouldn't when they were about to take a man for all he was worth?

"That won't be a problem. He's mine." Joe placed the baby in its seat, buckled the security straps, and raised the whole contraption by the handle. He sat his bundle of joy on Nicole's desk for a moment as he scooped up the birth certificate and placed it into the pocket of the diaper bag. He slung the bag over a broad shoulder, picked up the carrier and started for the door.

"Joe, you forget I'm his legal guardian," Nicole warned sharply. "Put the baby down."

"Seems to me his daddy has the stronger claim, Nicole."

"I'll have child welfare come pick him up. You aren't a fit parent—single, drinking, womanizing, always on the road." She listed the things she would bring up in a custody battle.

Standing in the doorway, Joe surveyed the plush office. "Nice place—a partnership in a law firm, a rich husband who lets you go your own way, two cute little boys." He nodded at a picture on her desk showing only her children framed in gold.

"I wonder what the partners, you know, Jeremy and Harry, would say about you being one of Joe Dean Billodeaux's list ladies. Everyone knows I got past the E's. Oh right, Harry is your husband, too. Think he'd be upset? Leave it alone, Nicole, and I'll pay your legal fees and any itemized expenses the boy and Margaret incurred. See she gets a nice burial if that hasn't been taken care of. Come on Dean, we're going home."

Joe passed a livid Harry Everard standing in the doorway to his office. "I can find my own way out, Harry. Thanks anyhow."

As he passed Iris, the receptionist bolted to his side. He took a firmer grip on Dean's carrier and prepared to block with his diaper bag arm. "Mr. Billodeaux, there are reporters outside," she whispered. "That bitch made me call them."

"Thanks, Iris. We'll be fine." He charged out the door and elbowed to the illegally parked Porsche. Getting the car seat settled was awkward even after he remembered to reverse its position. He did the best he could fastening the shoulder strap to hold it in place. All the while, cameras clicked and whirred and reporters shouted questions. Joe answered only one of them.

"Yes, this is my son, Dean Joseph Billodeaux." Then, he got in the Porsche and sped away. In his mirror, he saw Nicole standing in the doorway, her cold, calm face ruined by anger. Her husband stood behind listening to her words. Joe Dean could give a damn what she said. He had to report in to Coach Buck.

"I was supposed to be the one holding the baby. They were supposed to get a shot of Joe Dean Billodeaux walking out on his child, Harry!" Nicole Everard shrieked.

****

"Damn if he ain't cute," Coach Buck observed. "A lot of trouble in a small package."

Jared Forte, the youngest and least favored of the wide receivers, watched Joe lift his son's tiny buttocks off the training table's surface, swab his rear with baby wipes, and lower the infant on to a fresh newborn-size disposable diaper. "Nothing small about the 'nads on that kid. I think he has an erection already."

Joe pressed the diaper over the spouting penis. "Thanks for the heads up. My sisters' boys used to spray me all the time."

"That where you learned this stuff?" Forte asked, still in awe.

"Yep. Thirteen nieces and nephews as of last week. Dean will be the fourteenth grandchild for my parents." Joe shook out another diaper and fastened it in place with the tabs. The baby managed to get his thumb to his mouth and sucked vigorously. Not satisfied, the infant wailed.

"Here it comes. Here's your bottle." Joe took a

four-ounce container of formula from the duckie bag and reversed the nipple. Tucking Dean into the crook of his arm just like a football, he took a seat and let the baby nurse.

"Can I hold him when he finishes?" the Rev asked. "I want to get in some practice, you know, in case I can convince Mintay to start on a family."

"Take him now. Support the head. Keep that nipple filled. We don't want him sucking air."

"Sure is tiny though. I think my boys were twice his size, the girls, too. He won't make a lineman," Calvin Armitage predicted.

"But look at his legs." Joe measured the teeny thigh, no bigger than a chicken bone, between his thumb and forefinger. "Once they uncurl, he's gonna be tall like his daddy."

"So, who's the mommy?" Asa Dobbs asked.

"Nell is going to be his mama," Joe answered with certitude.

"Have you told her yet?" Connor Riley asked as he watched the intent infant, all closed-eyed and red-faced, pull at the nipple.

"I'll call her tonight. This is my miracle, Connor. I guess St. Jude wasn't interested in having the Super Bowl dedicated to him, but I might throw that in anyhow in appreciation for the quick work."

"Don't you think you should wait for the blood test, Joe?" Coach Buck cautioned. "The doc is on his way over to take samples."

"Doesn't matter. If he isn't mine, I'll adopt."

The wall the team made around the baby opened for the man with the black bag. Joe hardly felt the needle as the doctor took a blood sample from the crook of his arm, but he held on to Dean as the doctor pricked the tiny wrinkled foot of his son. The baby's toes splayed and his body stiffened with outrage as the doctor squeezed out a sample. The oversized men of the Sinners' team flinched when the baby began to howl.

Joe flipped the child to a shoulder covered with a training towel. "There, there, Deanie. We're gonna walk it off. Yes, we are."

He paced up and down gently thumping the infant's back. Dean Joseph belched, spewed up part of his lunch, then with a shudder, settled a cheek in the mess and closed his eyes. Gently, Joe lowered the child into the carrier and tucked soft flannel receiving blankets around the small body.

"Can I have the afternoon off, Coach?"

"Go. We aren't getting any work done with you and your boy around anyhow, but you make it up tomorrow."

"Sure thing, Coach."

Chapter Seventeen

Joe gave Deanie a change and a bottle at four and waited impatiently for Nell to get off work. Calling her there would be a big mistake, he sensed. He tried her cell at six, got no answer, and left a voice mail. "Nell, please come over. I have a surprise for you. It's Joe—not your boss or the maintenance man."

At seven, he offered the baby another bottle, but the infant fussed and took only two ounces. Around eight, Joe tried Nell again but used her land line at home. He spoke at the sound of the beep. "Please come over. We need to talk. I have something to show you. You know who this is."

Ten o'clock came and Deanie fretted. He'd suck, then spit out the nipple. His tiny bump of a nose filled with gunk and his dark hair stuck to his pink scalp with sweat. Joe put his lips to the little forehead the way he'd seen his mother and sisters do. Too warm.

He tried Nell's cell. She wasn't available at this time. Maybe, she had turned it off to go on a date. Maybe, she lay in bed with another man and they were both laughing at his increasingly frantic messages. Not Nell, not his Nell. He tried her apartment again and got the machine. What words would get her here?

At the sound of the beep, he blurted, "Nell, I think the baby is sick. Please, I need your help."

Before he could hang up, she answered, "What

baby?" into the receiver.

"Our baby," he said simply. "Come see."

****

The trip from Metairie to Joe's place should have taken twenty minutes depending on traffic. He swore his bell rang in less than ten minutes, sending Dean into frantic cries. The always well-tipped concierge had given him a heads up on Nell's arrival and he stood right next to the door waiting anxiously. She practically fell into his arms when he turned the knob.

"Thank God, you're here!" Joe handed her an enraged red bundle of baby, its face smeared with snot and its mouth open wide enough to see the uvula vibrating in the back of its throat.

"Joe, I really don't know much about babies. The children I deal with are older." She shoved Deanie back at Joe, but not quick enough to avoid a smear of baby saliva on her shirt. "I can call the pediatrician on duty at the hospital." She did.

Joe paced with his son while they waited for a return call. "Do-do, Deanie." He repeated the Cajun words that urged a child to sleep for all the good it did. The ten-minute interval seemed like forever. Over the screaming, Joe tried to tell her about Margaret and Nicole and the prayer to St. Jude, but it came out all garbled. Nell stared at him in astonishment. At least, it wasn't horror. She pounced on the ringing phone.

"How old?" she relayed to Joe.

"Two weeks."

"Weight?"

"About six pounds."

"Yes, yes, good. We're on our way." Nell looked around the condo. "Do you have a car seat?"

"Over there. The lady lawyer had everything ready. There's diapers and little shirts in the bag, two more bottles in the fridge."

Nell rooted in the bag and took out a wipe to clean the baby's face. They swaddled Joe's son and secured him in the seat. The child's feet, one with a tiny bandage, kicked out of the covers before they were out the door.

The concierge took it all in stride. Disregarding the screaming infant, he asked, "The Porsche, sir?" If he thought it no wonder that a baby had been left on Joe's doorstep after the daily and nightly parade of women making their way to the condo last spring, Gregory kept it to himself.

"My Toyota would make more sense. Is it handy, Gregory?"

"Just over there. I wasn't sure if you were staying the night, Miss Nellwyn." He handed her the keys taken from his vast pocket. Joe replaced the keys with a twenty and they hustled to Nell's car. Dean, as loud as a siren on an ambulance, rode in the back seat.

"Dr. Brown said it was probably just a cold, but an infant so young and small can dehydrate rapidly or go into pneumonia. It's safer to bring him in."

"Safer, sure." Joe drove like he was racing the Porsche instead of pushing the Toyota to go faster. At the hospital, he dropped Nell off with the baby. "I'll park and find you later."

Dr. Brown waited for them. "Good lungs," he joked. "No, really. From what I can hear, they sound clear. Whose baby is this, Nell?"

Joe tore into the examination room. Too impatient to wait for an elevator, he had run the stairs to the pediatrics floor and located his son by the sheer volume of his cries.

"Oh, I see," said Dr. Brown, recognizing a face as familiar in New Orleans as that of the Mayor.

"He was born in Mexico, premature. Maybe it's some foreign, baby-killing bug," Joe managed to get out. An instrument shoved into Deanie's ear beeped.

"Low grade fever, but no ear infection. Throat's a little red. I'd like to keep him a day or so since he was a preemie, get some fluids into him, keep an eye out for complications. I think this is simply a case of a very small baby coming into contact with too many people too soon. It's advisable to keep newborns at home for about six weeks. Keep that in mind."

"I let the guys hold him this afternoon. It's my fault."

"No, I think not. More likely he caught it on the plane if he was flown in from Mexico. No diarrhea, eh?"

"No, none," Joe said, taking every word seriously. "Just wet diapers."

"Wet diapers are good. Really. He's not too dehydrated then. He's going to be fine, Dad. Better sit down with Nell and finish filling in those admittance papers so we can get him settled. As it is, we did an end run around the front desk. End run, get it?"

"Yeah, like football. I appreciate it, Doc. If you're a Sinners' fan, call me if you ever want tickets. Here's my real number." Joe scribbled it on prescription pad along with his name underlined with the devil's tail because he was running on automatic.

Exit the doctor. Enter the nurse who tagged the baby with an identification bracelet and wrapped him up for transport to the nursery. "Finish your paperwork. I'll get him settled, and you can visit for a minute. Then, go home and get some rest. Come back in the morning."

Nell, filling in the information from Joe's insurance card, barely noticed the sudden silence in the room. When she looked up to ask his social security number, she saw the bereft look on his face. "Joe, your son will be fine."

"Our son. The one I prayed for. I just didn't expect him so soon. Marry me, Nell. Dean needs a mother."

"Joe, you can hire childcare. You don't need to marry it. What about his real mother? Run all that by me again."

"Dead. You remember Margaret Stutes?"

"Margaret, the big-toothed PR woman who took the Wish Kidz around at the Super Bowl? Oh, I'm so sorry. That was unkind."

"She was setting me up for a paternity suit. Something happened to her down in Mexico, an accident. I didn't get the details from Nicole. Anyhow, Dean came early and she died. Nicole said she was going to sue for custody. See why I need a wife quick?"

"Nicole? Were they a lesbian couple?"

"Hell, no. They were list ladies, both of them. Not like you. Nell, please."

"Joe, most women have nine months to get used to the idea of motherhood. As you can see, I wasn't a big help tonight. Maybe, I wasn't meant to be a mother, and that's why things are the way they are."

"Untrue. You didn't see Deanie at his best. When he looked up at me with those curly lashes and Billodeaux eyes, I knew he was mine, blood test or no blood test. He wasn't screaming then."

"Joe, you are a wonder." Nell shook her head. "And a natural father, I can tell, but me…"

"I'm rich and good lookin', too." He held his arms out to his sides as if letting her examine the merchandise.

"Both, to be sure." She laughed at him. "But, I don't think so."

Here they were in a small, sterile, brightly lit room. Both of them had baby snot and spit-up on their clothes. He should have proposed when they were making wishes on shooting stars, but no, he hadn't. Now, he desperately needed a mother for his child, the baby he'd prayed for, the baby he'd wanted for Nell.

"I promised God, St. Jude, and the Virgin Mary that I'd be a good father and a faithful husband if they gave us children."

"Bringing out the big guns now, Joe? The really hefty saints? What's Dean's middle name? I need it for the forms." She turned back to the counter to fill in the blank.

"Joseph. I'm sure his patron saint played a part in this, too."

"Certainly." Nell nodded without looking up.

Joe spun her chair around, dropped to his knees on the cold floor tiles and buried his face in her lap. He mumbled something into the denim fabric of her jeans. She raised his head with both hands. "What?"

"I love you, Nell."

"Was that so hard to say?"

Joe rolled the sentence around on his tongue, taste-testing each word. "No. It's just right. Perfect in fact. Try it for yourself, Nell."

She leaned over and kissed his lips. "I love you, Joe. You're right. Perfect."

He raised Nell and set her down on his lap before she realized what was happening he was that quick. "Great. We can fly out to Vegas tomorrow, be married, and back before Deanie gets out of the hospital and I have to leave for Dallas."

Chapter Eighteen

The wedding party arrived in Vegas on a chartered flight by early afternoon of the next day. If it had been up to Joe who shoved an expensive dark suit, white shirt, and silk tie into a garment bag and tossed his shaving kit, shoes and socks in the bottom, they would have been there by dawn, but Nell dug in her heels about asking her parents and sister to go along.

"Aren't you going to call and invite your family, Joe?"

"Hell, no. I'll have to listen to all that stuff about having a wedding in the church and how you should take instruction and why the rush. Then, I'll have to explain about Dean. After that, all my sisters would be on the phone, and we'd never get to Vegas. They'll be happy for us and thrilled about a new grandbaby after the fact. I'll set aside a whole day to listen to their lectures. So, no Billodeauxs at the wedding. I am definite about this."

Gary, stunned, and Emily, excited, phoned into work giving a family emergency as an excuse while Ann packed overnight bags and wrung her hands. They met Nell and Joe at the apartment where Nell still pondered what to wear while Joe tapped his fingers on the doorframe. Her mother held up the white dress with the cornflower print, the one Nell wore the first time she'd had sex with Joe.

Joe brightened. "I have some fond memories of that dress."

Nell shook her head. "No, too Monica Lewinsky," she said, leaving her mother to ponder the meaning.

"Buy a dress in Vegas, Nell. Let's move." Joe stood in the doorway jingling car keys.

"Did you leave numbers where the hospital could reach us?"

"Yes, both our cells."

Nell opened a drawer and plucked out the burgundy nightie from Victoria's Secret. She folded it and placed it in a small suitcase over a change of lacy underwear and next to her makeup bag.

Joe noted with pleasure the price tag still on the nightie. "Never wore this for anyone else, huh? That's all you need. We'll get whatever else in Vegas." Joe snapped the case shut and started out the door.

"Toothpaste. Did you pack toothpaste?"

"Nell, they have toothpaste in Nevada." He took her hand to move her on her way. It was shaking. He swept her up and held her close to his heart.

"Things will be fine, sugar, more than fine." Not wasting any more time, he carried his bride through the living room. "Gary, please bring her suitcase."

Emily objected. "Aren't you supposed to save that for the honeymoon?"

"You still coming, Em?" Joe said as he backed out the door and started down the steps with Nell held in an inescapable grasp.

He'd have to take them all in the Toyota or the group would never get to the airport. Joe deposited Nell in the front seat and started packing suitcases in the trunk as her family dribbled one by one down the stairs.

Laying his garment bag on top of the pile, he slammed the lid and opened both back doors of the car for his in-laws to be.

Emily pouted about having to sit in the middle until Nell screamed, "For crying out loud, I'll sit in the middle."

She unstrapped her seatbelt and slid into the back seat. That was the way the bride's family got on the road with the groom driving and his prospective sister-in-law gloating in the front seat. The more Joe got to know Emily, the more he disliked her. Nell gone bad, he thought.

At the airport, the Rev and Connor with an arm around Stevie waited. All three wore dark glasses and Braves ball caps, jeans and T-shirts. Stevie carried her camera bag and a small knapsack. The men stood with garment bags slung over their shoulders.

"Mintay couldn't get away from the clinic, but she sends her very best wishes," the Rev said squeezing Nell's hand.

"I wanted to get married in Reno, but Connor and the Sinners had to have a big party. I held out for the private wedding though," Stevie added.

"You've been to Las Vegas before, Stevie?" Nell asked in a small voice, taking in the sight of three gorgeous people who traveled light, and often.

"Yeah, when the golf tour went that way. Bright lights, good food, great entertainment. Very plush if you can afford it. He can, so don't hold back," Stevie advised with a nod at Joe who was unloading in-laws and baggage.

"Connor, some help here, man."

Connor draped his garment bag over the Rev's free

shoulder and went to assist by picking up two suitcases and shoving Nell's small bag under his arm. Herding Mr. And Mrs. Abbott before him, he headed for the steps of the chartered corporate jet.

"Watch your step, ma'am," he cautioned Nell's mother.

Hips swinging beneath a very short black skirt, Emily cut into the line and mounted the stairs, her butt practically in Connor's nose. "I don't think I like that one," Stevie muttered to the Rev and went to back up her husband.

Joe tugged Nell's hand because she seemed frozen to her spot and brought her along with the remaining luggage. The Rev tipped an airport employee to take care of the car and off they went for a wedding in Vegas.

****

Joe made the situation very clear to the management of the Bellagio as he gestured toward the group of women. "This is my bride and her maids. This is my platinum card. She can buy anything she wants. I'll need the closest thing you've got to a honeymoon suite and two more two bedrooms."

The staff happily honored his requests. Joe had been to Vegas often, usually with a well-endowed blonde or two on his arms. The manager eyed the rangy blonde, the short brunette in the tight skirt and the petite waif with the big eyes as if to say Mr. Billodeaux's tastes were expanding. Who did he think Mrs. Abbott was—their madam?

Regardless, "We are pleased to be of assistance," the manager said with an efficient nod of the head.

"Nell, you, Stevie, Em and Mom, get yourselves

dressed up. We meet back here at five and take cabs to the chapel. Rings, I'll take care of the rings. Let's go." Joe clapped his hands together and strode off leading the men.

"I'm surprised he didn't pat your behind and make you pump your fist in the air," Stevie drawled.

"Hey, he left his platinum card. I'm ready to shop." Emily rubbed her hands together.

"I'm not ready. Stevie, I'm not ready," Nell appealed to the tall blonde who looked so right when she stood next to Connor. She'd seem like a child standing beside Joe, all five foot-one, one-hundred and two pounds of her. What an absurd couple they would make.

"Been there myself." Stevie led her to a beautifully upholstered lobby chair away from Nell's anxious mother and mouthy sister. "Look, Joe can be childish and he is certainly spoiled and used to getting his own way. But I'll tell you, Nell, no one cares more for the people in his life or takes his vows more seriously. You will be fine."

"If you are finished with the pep talk, can we shop?" Emily complained.

****

Shop, they did. Nell dazed and seemingly without opinions allowed her attendants to drape her in white leaving one finely-boned shoulder bare and cinching in her waist with a gold belt. The hemline slanted to one side to show a glimpse of thigh.

Stevie and Emily found similar gowns in light blue and pale green that could be cinched in silver only after she and Em had a fight over a sexy red number that was totally inappropriate for a wedding. Well, maybe not in

Vegas.

Mrs. Abbott supported Stevie by saying, "I brought my pale pink silk-linen shantung suit that I wore for Easter services, Emily. We should all be in pastels, I think."

"Hell, buy the red dress and take it home with you. It's Joe's money. I vote for low heels. We might as well be comfortable," Stevie asserted.

"Fine for you, Miss Giant," Emily grumbled. "Nell will look like a child."

"Oh, no!" Nell gasped, the tabloid headlines that had surfaced after Stevie's reception coming into her mind.

"She's just jerking your chain because she wants stilettos. Would some nice bling-bling at the jeweler's shut you up?" Stevie towered over Emily.

"Oh, I can be bribed," Emily said.

"I brought my good pearls," Ann Abbott added. "I don't need a thing."

****

Stevie stood over the florist while he wove a crown of stephanotis with a wisp of tulle attached for the bridal veil. "I like real flowers. I wore a daisy crown for my wedding. Veils, trains and all that shit just get in the way, don't you think, Nell?"

"I guess."

"Stop guessing. If you want something else, say so."

"Really, it doesn't matter."

"Okay, then. Two more of these without the netting."

"We could have gotten tiaras at the jewelry store," Emily pointed out.

"The day you see me in a tiara, I'll be dead. Be satisfied you soaked Joe for a platinum necklace with an emerald drop."

"Well, you got one with a sapphire."

"I had to so we would match. A silver chain would have been fine with me."

"Girls, girls!" Mrs. Abbott interrupted. "Don't argue."

Nell smiled at her mother. "It's like old times, Mom."

"Who would have thought sickly Nell would marry before me? She gets a rich, hunky guy and a baby she doesn't even have to lug around for nine months. No stretch marks, no labor. Nell always comes out on top," Emily groused. The details of the marriage had come out on the plane ride and sister still showed her envy.

"Good for you, Nell. Joe is a great guy, and I'll bet that child of his is beautiful," Stevie countered.

"Well, Deanie was red in the face and full of snot the last time I saw him." Nell looked at herself in a mirror as the florist fitted the headpiece over her short, dark hair.

"Looks great." Stevie sniffed the flowers. "Make some of this stuff up as boutonnieres, four of them. And Mom here, will need a corsage. How about gardenias? We'll be back for the bouquets in an hour. Gotta make tracks, ladies. Hair and makeup next."

****

Joe arrived at the jewelry store with his groomsmen and almost father-in-law after they finished watching a baseball game on the tube up in Connor's suite. Baseball and a stiff vodka drink from the bar calmed him about the upcoming event.

"I need matching wedding rings and a diamond—a big one," Joe told the suited clerk who started to pull a velvet tray from the glass case. "And no crap, either."

The salesman shoved the tray back into place and selected another.

"I don't see the difference." Joe peered at the glittering stones.

"Cut, color and clarity," the Rev instructed.

Connor shrugged. "Stevie isn't much for jewelry. She says it gets in her way, and she doesn't like the idea of getting mugged in New Orleans or some foreign country for what she had around her throat."

"Also the number of carats," said the clerk. "These are top quality stones. Do you have any idea what cut the bride would prefer?"

"No idea. How about a really big solitaire? Can't go wrong there, huh?"

"Nell has such small hands. You don't want to overwhelm her," Gary Abbott cautioned.

"Oh, are you with the bridal party who came in here earlier? Two little brunettes, tall blonde, older woman? They selected a diamond choker for the bride—tiny girl, very nervous—and platinum necklaces with colored stones for the bridesmaids. I have matching bracelets if you are in need of gifts for the young women," the clerk hinted, obviously adding up the commission in his mind. He smoothed his nicely trimmed mustache. The gesture would have been his tell if he were playing poker.

"Do we need gifts for the bridesmaids?" Joe asked.

"Most definitely. I had to shell out for seven," the Rev answered.

"Yeah, I think so. The bride is supposed to do that,

but Nell was looking a little shaky. She might not remember," Connor added.

"Okay, then. Show me the bracelets, matching rings, and a really spectacular diamond that won't look too big on her hand. You guys need gifts? Want a Rolex?"

"Got a Rolex. How about diamond pinkie rings?" the Rev suggested.

"Pimps wear diamond pinkie rings." Connor elbowed his friend. They shoved at each other.

"If you break it, consider it sold," the clerk snapped. He presented the bracelets draped over a velvet cloth and suggested a ring set with a many-faceted stone so blue-white it could have put an iceberg to shame on a sunny day. Joe picked out a wide, plain gold band for himself and a slimmer one inlaid with channel cut diamonds for Nell.

"Think she'll like it?" he said, consulting Gary.

"She'll be overwhelmed. Our Nell, she hasn't asked for much since we moved the household for her. I think she still feels guilty about that."

"I know. Wrap all this stuff up. Guys, if you want something, you pick it out yourself. I am finished."

Connor and the Rev joked around about earrings and nose studs, then settled on Mont Blanc pens to commemorate the day Joe Dean Billodeaux promised to be faithful to one woman.

****

The women kept the up the traditions as best they could. Stevie sent Mrs. Abbott to meet the men in the lobby and insist they take a cab to the chapel since they were not to see the bride before the wedding. Ann softened those orders by observing how handsome they were in their suits and ties.

"Best lookin' groomsmen in the league," the Rev agreed.

Without any argument, the four men crushed themselves into a cab with Gary riding the hump between Connor and the Rev and left for the chapel.

Getting the women moving proved harder, Stevie found, but eventually, they crammed into a small powder room at the chapel where each made last minute adjustments to her clothes and makeup after the taxi ride.

"Are you sure I look all right? Not silly or childlike?" Nell fretted.

"You look lovely, dear," her mother assured, dabbing at her eyes with a tissue.

"Believe me, Joe will appreciate the nymph look. When this is over, you can go back to the room and play wine god pursuing dryad or maybe, Viking ravishing village maiden," Stevie encouraged. "Connor and I enjoy that last one."

"How about horny Cajun raping Evangeline?" Emily nudged her sister away from the mirror and added another layer of mascara to her eyelashes.

"He's so big and Nell is so small." Ann Abbott held her hands far apart, probably indicating the breadth of Joe's shoulders, or maybe not.

Stevie snickered. "Sorry. Mrs. Abbott, I think Nell and Joe have already established that they are compatible on the size issue. Stop worrying. There, that brought some color to the bride's cheeks. I hear the music cranking up. It must be our turn. Everyone out of here! Ann, you go in first and make sure the men are lined up. Send your husband out. I'll start down the aisle, then Emily, then Nell."

The effect was spoiled by Stevie glancing over her shoulder every few seconds to make sure the bride would make it to the altar. With Mr. Abbott holding his daughter's arm and looking very serious, Nell managed the short walk without fleeing or collapsing.

****

Joe, shifting on his feet, watched the woman he was about take as a wife walk slowly into his life forever. She looked pale and hesitant. Was marrying him so bad?

Joe glanced around the room. Sure, the entry to the chapel was surrounded by a pink neon heart, probably so drunks could find the door, but the place had plenty of artificial flowers and nice piped-in music.

Okay, you could call the place tacky compared to the mellow bricks and old stained glass of the church where the Rev had married Mintay.

The chapel didn't have the simple beauty of Connor's wedding by the lakeside either. Sorry, this was the best he could do right now. He'd make it up to Nell one of these days.

Nell's father stepped aside. Connor nudged Joe into position next to his bride. The preacher or facsimile thereof, guided the couple through a brief but traditional service read from a book that may or may not have been a Bible.

Nell's eyes widened at the opulence of her rings hanging loosely, a size too large, on her finger. Joe's ring, a perfect fit, slid on easily. "Are you sure, Joe?" Nell whispered as she put it on his finger.

"I, uh, just wanted to say I'll be a faithful husband like I promised and a good father, and someday, I'll

give you a better wedding than this. I love you, Nell."
Joe exhaled.

The presiding official, a stout man in a white suit
and black string tie, who, thank God, looked nothing
like Elvis, pronounced them man and wife in a slightly
offended tone. Nevertheless, he accepted the white
envelope stuffed with bills that the Rev handed him and
wished the couple a happy life together. He punched the
button for the recessional music and the group walked
out to make way for the next couple.

Mrs. Abbott helped herself to a handful of
complimentary rose petals from a china bowl by the
door. She scattered them over Joe and Nell as they
stepped out into the glare of a Nevada afternoon. "Rice
is for fertility. I wonder what rose petals mean."

"Rice attracts birds and all their mess. Rose petals
are biodegradable," Stevie told her.

"Stevie, dearest, always so romantic." Connor
hugged his pragmatic bride.

"The rose is the symbol for the Virgin Mary. She is
on our side," Joe said seriously.

"No foolin'?" That was the Rev talking.

"Throw the bouquet! Throw the bouquet," Emily
screeched.

Stevie could have snatched the bunch of miniature
white rose buds, stephanotis, and trailing ivy tied up
with gold ribbon from the air over Emily's head, but
she had her man and didn't need to start another fight
with Nell's obnoxious sister. "There's a nice garden
over here. Why don't I set up my gear and get a few
pictures?"

Stevie got her snaps and signaled to Connor to lug
her gear while she followed the bridal pair to the

waiting cab, Joe carrying Nell in his arms just because he wanted to. They waved to their guests from the cab window and took off letting the others find their own transportation back to the Bellagio.

The Rev helped Mrs. Abbott into another taxi. "Joe said I was to treat y'all to a nice dinner. The bride and groom are gettin' room service."

****

Joe insisted on carrying his bride past the Bellagio's dancing fountains and down the hall with its fabulous ceiling of glass flowers. With her head resting in the crook of his arm, Nell had a great view, but she began to feel seasick.

"Please, Joe, put me down. I'm getting a little nauseous."

Another paparazzo leapt into their path and snapped a picture. Joe kept right on walking with Nell in his arms. "It's faster and safer this way, I think."

Finally arriving at their suite, Nell saw Joe Dean had arranged for all of the woman pleasing amenities: lobster with plenty of melted butter to dribble down the chin and be licked off, white wine to get giddy drinking and a dessert having the sinful name of chocolate decadence. The maid had not forgotten to scatter red rose petals on the down-turned sheets of pristine white.

Nell retreated into the bathroom to change into her nightie.

"Sugar, you still in there?" Joe rapped on the bathroom door.

"There aren't any windows, Joe. Of course, I'm still in here."

"You plannin' to take a bath? I'll come in and scrub your back—and then your front."

177

"Have you called the hospital to check on the baby?"

"I called fifteen minutes ago. He's doing fine. We can bring him home before I leave for Dallas, they think."

"That's good news."

"Yes, it is. Tink, could we talk out here? The lobster is getting cold." He heard her sniffle and blow her nose. "Hell, I don't feel like eating either and cold lobster is just fine. Let's work up an appetite, what do you say? Come on out, sugar."

The bathroom door cracked open. Nell stepped out in her short, burgundy nightie. Two bows held it up on each shoulder. The satiny material came to a deep V between her breasts, then dropped down and ended just above panties consisting of no more than two satin swatches held on with more bows.

"Nice. I like the g-string you got there." He ran one hand over the swatch and untied a shoulder bow with the other. The nightie slithered down not quite exposing one breast. Joe Dean tugged it the rest of the way. Cupping, he said, "Half a handful, but perfect."

She usually countered with, "Well, you have enormous hands. If you don't like my breasts, don't mess with perfection." Then, she would jump him. He liked that, but she could not manage her usual repartee.

He took a hand and led her to the bed. He ran his fingers over the sheets. "Silk and rose petals." Joe picked up a petal and drew it down her cheek, down her neck and over the exposed breast. No response.

"Tink, darlin', please tell me what's wrong."

"I've never done this as a wife before and I feel awful." Her nose was pink on the tip. Her big, dark, worried eyes watered.

Joe Dean dropped his head into his hands. "Nell, *ma cherie*. We've done this on the sofa, in the Porsche, in the truck, both cab and box, in the straw, in an unfinished house, in broad daylight in an open field, and yes, even in a regular bed. I've never done it as a husband either, but I think it still works the same way, sugar. You just lean back and enjoy it."

He moved her to the center of the bed and lay down beside her. Starting slow, he kissed her forehead. His lips felt cool on her warm skin.

"Joe, I think I caught the baby's cold. And when we get back to New Orleans, he'll be sleeping in the next room. If we're loud, he'll wake up."

Joe flopped back on the pillows. "Nell, babies sleep pretty soundly. You could run the vacuum under my nephews' cribs and not wake them. Stop worrying. Enjoy." He leaned over and started to rub her stomach in small circles.

"I'm going to be sick!" Nell, one breast bobbing, made a run for the bathroom and kicked the door shut behind her.

He listened to her wretch, then got up and tapped on the door. "May I come in?"

"Uh-huh. I'm so sorry." She flushed before opening the door.

Joe wet a washcloth and sponged Nell's clammy face. He gave her a glass of cold water to wash out her mouth, retied her bow and carried her to the bed. "Just rest, then, Tink." He pulled the covers up to her chin.

While she slept, he ate his lobster, then hers, cracking the shells as quietly as possible. He was ravenous. Once he finished the meals and had two glasses of the wine by the window where he could watch Las Vegas glitter into evening, Joe called room service and had them retrieve the cart.

"Bring a box for the cake, would you? And a bowl of chicken soup with a pot of hot tea on the side right now. I'd appreciate that." He greased the palm of the server.

The knock on the door woke Nell, but Joe kept the waiter in the sitting room as he boxed the cake and accepted the tray with the soup and tea.

"Here, sugar, you try a little of this stuff. You'll feel better."

Nell sipped her soup and tea, then curled up on her side and breathing heavily through her mouth, went back to sleep. Joe lay down and slept with his bride, back to back.

****

In the morning, Joe forked scrambled eggs into Nell's mouth, tore off bits of dry toast, and insisted she eat them. She washed the food down with more tea and two decongestants. Nell looked so bedraggled he tried for some humor. "Say, Tink, do you think you might be pregnant?"

"No, I told you, no. You were so damned sure of your potency I actually bought a test two weeks ago. I'm not pregnant." Nell started to cry.

"It makes no never mind to me. Really, it doesn't matter, Nell. Let's get you dressed and to the airport."

The rest of the group waited for them. Joe knew they expected to see a radiant bride, the triumphant woman who had captured their elusive quarterback. Instead, they saw this sad creature with the dark circles under her eyes and a crumpled tissue hidden in one feverish fist.

"Hey, all is not lost!" Joe held up the cake box and unopened bottle of champagne. "We got goodies for the ride home."

Chapter Nineteen

"Hey, Ma," Joe said, pacing the living room. "Yeah, I know I don't call enough. You know how it is during the season. Look, Nell and me, we got something to tell you. No, she's not pregnant. We went to Vegas yesterday and got married. Sure, we can make it right with the church later. Want to talk to Nell?"

Curled in her warm, safe corner on the long leather couch, Nell adjusted the cotton comforter Joe had wrapped around her. She shook her head, but Joe tossed her the phone anyway.

"Hi, Mrs. Billodeaux. Okay, MawMaw Nadine. I'm so sorry you couldn't be at the wedding. Joe was in such a hurry and we had to get it done between games. Why? I think Joe should tell you. Thank you, thank you. I'm happy to be part of the family, too." She slapped the phone back into Joe's hand.

"So, Ma, what would you say about having fourteen grandchildren? No, I told you Nell isn't pregnant. I had a little surprise dropped in my lap a few days ago. Yeah, I guess there will be a paternity suit. I *was* careful. Right, not careful enough. The blood test hasn't come back yet, but you should see him, Mama, he has my chin and the Billodeaux eyes. Lots of dark hair, yes. He's a great little guy and he needed a mother, so Nell and I got hitched. Of course I love her. But, see, there's this lady lawyer wants to take Dean away from me. She says I'm not a fit father."

From her nook, Nell heard an outburst of French curse words.

"I agree with you, Ma. We'll be great parents. Sure, we'll bring the baby to see you as soon as we can. He's in the hospital right now, has a little bug, is all. Probably caught it coming up from Mexico. No, Mama, his mother wasn't Mexican. She was just living down there. She passed away when she had Dean. A woman who used to work in the Sinners' PR department. You never met her. Explain this all to Dad, will you? Guess it will be in the papers soon. Wanted you to be the first to know. Right, so long."

Joe scrubbed at his ear to take the ringing away. "Well, that's done and over with. She'll be fine once she sees him. Says I made a good choice with you. Look, your mom and Emily are coming back as soon as they drop off your dad. We're going to look for a crib and stuff for the baby. You feel up to coming along?"

Joe looked at his miserable bride sniffling on one end of his couch. "No, I guess not. Sugar, you rest this afternoon. I'll meet your kin in the lobby so you don't have to explain. I'll tell them you're contagious."

Nell looked up with woeful, watery eyes. "Don't. You'll panic my mom. Just say it's a really bad cold."

"Okay. Rest and think about where we should put the baby when we get him out of the hospital."

"Not in Joe Dean's Love Palace, that's for sure."

Nell had names for all the bedrooms in the condo. Joe's room, the Love Palace, was furnished with a round bed covered in black satin sheets and fake fur throws. It sat raised up on a platform two feet high putting it closer to the round mirror of equal size mounted on the ceiling. The walls papered with a red-flocked material set off the sleek, modern black lacquered furniture. An adjoining bath featured a round platform tub made of black marble and surrounded by black glass mirrors veined with gold. Even the commode and bidet Joe had installed especially for the women were a shining black. Nell refused to sleep in the Love Palace because so many others had slept there before.

They always used the Pompadour room. Nell said it looked like a place a French king would keep his mistress. The massive bedstead was ornate white and gold and the walls surrounding it papered with blue brocade also used for the bedspread and drapes. A large dresser, swooning couch by the window and several small, ornate tables continued the white, gold, and pale blue theme. A small crystal chandelier dangled from the center of the ceiling. The bath, also blue, possessed gold-washed fixtures.

The third bedroom had an oriental theme. Nell called it the Chinese Bordello Room. Here the black lacquered furnishings were intricately carved and stood out against the yellow silk walls. The bed, king-sized, sported an embroidered quilt on which green and gold dragons writhed. Over a bamboo-patterned headboard, a series of framed Japanese wood cuts depicted people in kimonos having sex in every way possible. Joe claimed the prints to be antique works of art and very valuable. Nell supposed so—for both their artistry and their suggestive content. She was quite sure Joe's designer had decorated the best whorehouses in New Orleans. Where in this decor would a person put a crib and a changing table?

"I guess you will have to sacrifice the Chinese Bordello Room. We might want to strip that fancy wall covering and paint the walls with something washable."

"And take the pictures down?"

"Most definitely."

The concierge rang to inform Mr. Billodeaux his mother and sister-in-law were in the lobby. Joe planted a kiss on Nell's feverish forehead and headed out to buy a layette.

Rest would have been nice, but the phone started ringing when Joe was barely out of the door. One by one, they called—Allie, Eenie, Izzy home on maternity leave, and Lizzie who had to keep it short because she was at work. Each welcomed her to the family. All offered used cribs and excess baby clothes. Since Izzy's second child was a girl she had scads of little boy duds to offer, but she wasn't allowed to drive yet so maybe Joe could come and get them when he had the time. Nell thanked them one and all.

She headed to the kitchen to warm a cup of broth in the microwave, but the telephone rang again. Gregory, the doorman, asked if Miss Stevie could come up for a visit.

"Sure, if she wants to take her chances with the plague I've got. Send her up."

Undaunted, Stevie stood at her door within minutes. She offered Nell a brown paper clasp envelope containing an elaborate gift certificate for baby pictures she had run up on Photo Shop as soon as she got home.

"I didn't know what you'd need, and people always want pictures of their kids, so there you go. Give me a call when Dean's snot clears up, okay?" She hesitated.

"Go on, whatever it is."

"Well, when we got back to the Bellagio, I saw a man arguing with a desk clerk in the lobby. From the back, he looked like my old partner and nemesis, Dexter Sykes. Dex has been doing a sideline of celebrity shots. He dogs me and Connor wherever we go. I'd punch him out, but Connor says the guy's old news. Anyhow, he might have followed us to Vegas and gotten word of the wedding. Don't be surprised if something shows up in the *Enquirer*."

"He wasn't the only one. Joe carried me across the lobby. He might as well have shouted to one and all that I was his new bride."

"That's Joe for you. Lots of enthusiasm. Look, the photos I took of the wedding are a gift from me and Connor. I think I should send official pictures to *People* and the *Star* and get that out of the way for you. I'll caption them with the names, date, place, but the reporters will want more. If they call, give them a telephone interview. You don't have to do any more. You look like hell. Get some rest."

Stevie, having kept a safe distance from Nell's contagion with her long reach, prepared to leave. "Oh, if you ever want anyone to strong arm Dexter Sykes for you, I'm your woman. He once sent nude pictures of me to the swimsuit issue and I still owe him one for that."

"I like you, Stevie. I really do."

Nell walked her to the door, then detoured to the kitchen after locking up. She put her mug of broth in the microwave and waited for the ding. The ring of the phone came first. Two delivery men had arrived in the lobby with a box for Mrs. Billodeaux. Should they be sent up?"

Giving up on both food and rest, Nell answered, "Why not?"

The thump of a heavy carton being set down in the hall announced their arrival at the door. Still in her robe and slippers, Nell let them in.

"Where youse want dis crib set up, lady?" the larger of the two men asked.

"Just a minute." She scuttled down the hall, climbed up on the bed in the Chinese Bordello room, took down the erotic pictures and stowed them in the back of the large closet.

"Okay, bring the crib in here. If we move this table and the floor cushions, we can put the crib along this wall."

"Lady, we get paid to deliver and set up. We ain't no furniture movers. It ain't in the contract."

Nell threw the large floor cushions on to the bed and removed objects from the top of a low lacquered table that looked as if it had been set for a tea ceremony. She tugged on the edge of the table hoping to slide it out of the way, but the squat legs remained firmly entrenched in the deep pile of the carpet.

"Give the lady a break, Bruno. You can see how sick and puny she is. It's like asking Tinker Bell to move the castle," the smaller man replied. He wore a wedding ring on his left hand. Bruno wore none.

"Tink would wave her magic wand and make da castle disappear," Bruno answered, gracefully flinging his big, hairy forearm in an arc.

Nell shoved harder. The table did not budge.

"You're my brother-in-law, Bruno. I won't tell the Teamsters on you."

"Christ, Murray, ya nag like my sister." Bruno

placed a hand on either side of the table, pressed it to his chest and set it aside.

"Thank you, really. I'll just get out of your way." Nell retreated to the kitchen while Murray got out his tools and Bruno went to get the changing table. He hauled it in on a dolly that left a trail of black marks across the rug.

Nell added crackers to her lunch and boiled water for a cup of tea. She'd just finished her lavish spread when she heard the men talking in the hall.

"Would ya look at dat, Murray, Joe Dean's bedroom. How many women ya think he screwed in dere? If I had a place like dis, women would be all over me."

"Bruno, you could get a woman if you took a bath more often."

"Why ya figure a guy like Joe Dean shacked up with a broad like dat one? She's all scrawny and sick. Joe is a legend. He coulda had any dame."

"We delivered a crib and a changing table. Marge always looks like the devil the first three months she's knocked up."

"Yeah, why ya got to knock my sister up so much?"

"If you're finished, you can go," Nell interrupted. She escorted them and the dolly heaped with crushed boxes out. As she closed the door, she heard one last remark from Bruno. "She's a snippy bitch, too."

Nell curled on the leather sofa, stretched the cotton comforter over her head and woke some time later to the sound of Joe's key in the lock.

"Sorry, didn't mean to wake you, sugar." Joe bumped the door open with two economy-sized bundles of newborn disposable diapers. Nell's mother, Emily and Gregory flooded in behind him riding a wave of bags and boxes.

"Look how adorable, Nell." Emily held up tiny jeans, a matching jacket and hat with a turned down brim she extracted from a bulging Baby Gap bag.

"They look big for a newborn, Em."

"The sales girl said to buy large because babies grow so fast." Emily dumped out what must have been the entire Gap inventory for six-month-olds on one end of the sofa.

"But in six months, it will be nearly summer here."

"Not to worry, dear. I got plenty of onesies with footsies and snap crotches for diaper changing." Ann Abbott held up a shopping bag from a large department store.

"I guess you can give these to the less fortunate or return them yourself," snapped Emily balling up the trendy baby clothes and shoving them back in the sack.

Gregory peered into the bag he carried. "I have a vaporizer, powder, baby shampoo and three containers of Boudreaux's Butt Paste in mine, Miss Nell."

"My sisters say Boudreaux's Butt Paste is the best for diaper rash. Looks like we're all set up to bring the baby home, Tink."

"Right. All set up."

Chapter Twenty

Dr. Brown saw no reason why Dean couldn't come home on Saturday morning. The baby was doing fine and since Nell's illness had probably been caught from him, the danger of re-infection remained low. The doctor prescribed the same pediatric cough syrup for both of them and added the usual caution about calling immediately if the infant seemed in any distress.

They peeled the baby from his paper gown, dressed him in a little footed suit patterned with tiny blue lambs and settled him on his back in the new crib with a whirligig mobile of plastic butterflies swooping overhead. Joe pecked Nell on the cheek, grabbed his overnight bag, and headed for Dallas to play the Cowboys. Here she was left alone with a three-week-old infant and the fear she couldn't handle him or her new husband.

Deanie slept most of the time and was not the best company when awake. Mostly, he sat in his infant seat and watched Nell when she crossed in front of him. He kicked, burped, and sometimes farted. He cried for his bottle every three or four hours round the clock. Nell moved into the Chinese Bordello Room to be sure she wouldn't miss a feeding. She kept him clean and dry and wondered what the hell was wrong with her.

She'd mourned for the children she would never have. She had considered adopting if she never married, maybe taking in an older special needs child someday. She thought she had lots of affection to offer. Where was the fount of motherliness she had expected to spring forth now? She'd been handed a baby, a perfectly good baby, a little crusty around the nostrils right now, but not one of those infants so colicky the women who bore them were driven into exhaustion. Where were her instincts? Where was her undying love?

On Sunday, Nell invited her parents over to watch Joe play football. Emily, still miffed over the Baby Gap wardrobe, said she had other plans. The elder Abbotts had no problems accepting Dean as their grandchild. They came in full grandparent mode with a washable terry cloth crib bear and a set of plastic keys Dean was too small to rattle but happy to suck. The baby spent most of the game in the crook of her father's arm having football explained to him.

"See Daddy had to throw that ball away because he was going to get sacked and all his receivers were covered." Deanie screwed up his face and gave a small yelp.

"Don't let it upset you, boy. Your daddy will get a long one out to Riley or Deets any time now."

"Oh, Gary, the child just has gas," her mother corrected. "Does Deanie want his belly rubbed?" She gained possession of the grandchild. Nell marveled at their ease with the baby and wondered if she would ever have their skill.

The Sinners took the game 17-14, too close for comfort. Gary Abbott got up to stretch and use the bathroom. Ann started toward the kitchen to check the refrigerator for dinner possibilities. Ignoring the baby seat on the floor, she sat Dean in Nell's lap as she passed.

As usual, the reporters interviewed Joe about the game. "Wasn't my best game, no. They nearly had us at the end. I'd like to thank the defense for holding the line and my great offense for being there when I needed them. I missed a few practices this week and had a lot on my mind, but I'll be making up for that against the Panthers next week."

"We hear congratulations are in order, Joe," Rita Fortunado horned in with her rich contralto voice. "Who is your lucky bride?"

Nell noticed how close Rita stood to Joe and wished the reporter would get her damned hand off his arm. They'd slept together, she simply knew it.

"Nell, her name's Nell. Hey, Nell. I'm sure she's watching." He sneezed and turned away from the camera to swipe his nose with the sleeve of his jersey. Rita's hand slipped away.

"Sorry," he apologized. Leaning closer to the lens, he smiled. Women watching wilted all over America, Nell was certain. "Hey, Deanie. Daddy's on his way home." He gave a little wave with his fingers.

"Deanie? Daddy?" Rita was right on top of things.

"Ah—no comment. Coach Buck wants to say a few words." Joe trotted off to the sanctuary of the locker room.

Deanie Billodeaux watched the flickers on the television screen, blinked his eyes, yawned, and snuggled into Nell's belly. She lifted him to a shoulder and rubbed his back the way Joe did. "What do you think, Deanie? Did Daddy sleep with that woman?"

****

On the trip back to New Orleans, Joe Dean paused in the aisle next to Calvin Armitage. "Nell and the baby are getting over a bug and truth to tell, I think I might be coming down with it, so no surprise receptions or anything, okay?"

"I'll stop the ladies. I think they were planning something. How's married life treatin' you?"

Joe leaned against the seat and considered. "Well, there's a lot less sex than I figured on."

In the space next to Calvin, Asa Dobbs cackled. "Oh, you married all right. Now you got to beg for it."

"Sharlette say you never get it on during the season 'cause both your heads is in the game." Calvin tweaked his buddy.

"Sharlette should keep her mouth shut."

"Really, Nell's been sick. We both been up with the baby, and I'm not feeling so well myself."

"That the way it go with kids. They catch some crud at school and bring it home." Calvin took out a handkerchief and blew his nose. "Wouldn't trade mine for another Super Bowl ring though."

"I would," Asa Dobbs claimed. "You want some more, come get my girls, Joe."

****

Joe got in late after Nell and Deanie had gone to bed. He took two aspirin and threw himself down on the round bed and cool satin sheets in the Love Palace without thinking there should have been a wife around somewhere. He pulled the fake fur throws over his feverish body and went to sleep. When Nell got up to give the baby a change and a bottle, she heard his phlegmy snores resounding off the red-flocked walls and let him rest.

In the morning, she plied him with orange juice and hot tea with lemon and suggested he call in sick just as she was going to do.

"Can't. I missed too much last week. Team meeting today." He took two decongestants and a hot shower, kissed Nell's head and said, "Bye-bye, Deanie."

Coach sent Joe to the doc. The doc sent him home an hour later. He put on his black satin robe, the one the chicks liked so much, propped his head up on two pillows at one end of the leather couch, and warded off the chills with the cotton comforter. He could review the game tape right here. Joe Dean fell asleep listening to Nell give an explanation to her boss.

"I know I took personal emergency time off last week, but I caught this virus, and I shouldn't be around the children until it's totally cleared up. Dr. Brown can vouch for me."

"That's not all you caught, Nell, now is it? According to this week's tabloids, you caught yourself a husband and spent last week in Vegas secluded in a honeymoon suite. I have the paper right in front of me." Joe Brunner rustled the paper near the receiver as if he could make Nell see it.

"We spent one night in Vegas. Since then, I've been home sick. Now Joe's come down with it."

"When did you have the time to give birth to Joe Dean's secret love child is what my enquiring mind wants to know."

"I didn't, but that's another thing. I'm going to have to ask for six weeks maternity leave. There's a baby, not mine, but I have to make some arrangements for childcare. Deanie isn't supposed to be around strangers for another three or four weeks. I really need your understanding on this. Yes, I know. This is only possible because the new intern is working out so well. Thank her for me." She hung up.

The doorbell chimed, waking both Joe and the baby. Nell raced for the crib. Whoever had arrived unannounced could wait. She returned with Deanie howling for a bottle. The doorbell sounded again and the phone rang. Bleary-eyed, Joe struggled off the couch, his black satin robe gaping open to show his most valuable assets.

Nell put the phone to the ear opposite the crying baby. "Miss Nell, I'm so sorry. She got by me. Just flashed her credentials and stormed over to the elevator. It's a child welfare lady. She'll be there any second," Gregory apologized.

"I appreciate the warning." The bell chimed again. She could do nothing but open it.

"Althea Alexander, child welfare case worker." The immense black woman, who made Precious Armitage seem small-boned, filled the doorway. Twice Gregory's weight and several inches taller, she could have taken the doorman down with ease.

"We've had a complaint filed by a Mrs. Nicole Everard, the child's legal guardian, against Joe Dean Billodeaux, the natural father. She claims he abducted the child and removed the infant to an unfit environment."

Nell clutched Deanie a little too hard, and he squalled in her ear. "As you can see, the child is fine, but you woke him. He does want his bottle." Official types, even four times bigger than her, did not frighten Nell. She could stare down a surgeon if one of her kids was involved.

"May I come in? I do need to check out these allegations."

Thinking cooperation would better serve their cause, Nell moved aside. From the corner of her eye, she saw Joe tightening his robe but looking shaky from the fever and chills. "Please sit down, Mrs. Alexander. I need to get Dean his breakfast."

Nell warmed a bottle in the microwave, tested the temperature of the formula on her wrist, and settled herself on the sofa. Terribly aware of the spot of baby drool on her pink t-shirt and her bare feet hanging out of cropped pants, Nell gave the social worker a plucky smile. Keeping Rita Fortunado in mind, she had put on a little makeup for her husband's return home and so wasn't a total slob. Deanie didn't care what she looked like. He latched on to the nipple. Nell took him to the rocking chair in a quiet corner of the room. Let Joe handle this mess, this cute little mess, he had created. Joe sat and covered his knees with the cotton comforter.

Mrs. Alexander selected one of the oversized matching leather chairs with arms substantial enough to give her a boost up and a seat large enough to accommodate her behind.

My, my, my, she thought, Joe Dean Billodeaux in the flesh, and what flesh. Those long, muscular legs showing a few cleat scars, that mat of dark hair covering his chest, the thick, ruffled hair, the sleepy eyes, they just made a woman want to run her hands under that black satin robe and touch the goodies.

Wait until she told the sisters at the Sunshine and Showers Social Club meeting about seeing the man in person. She couldn't discuss the case, but she sure could give a physical description. The man might be a womanizer, but she bet he had to beat them off with a broom. No wonder he kept a list. Althea patted her black wig into place over her short gray cornrows. She almost hated to bring up the allegations, but that was her job.

"Mr. Billodeaux, Mrs. Everard claims you ripped the baby from her arms and brought him to your apartment which is no better than a whorehouse full of easy women. She says you are a heavy drinker, a womanizer, and the nature of your career keeps you on the road half the year."

Althea Alexander looked around the condo. She had been in plenty of households where the evidence of heavy drinking was obvious, but no scattered liquor bottles littered the floor, no glass rings marred the coffee table, no signs of slovenly housekeeping stood out. Still, he did have the look of the hung-over—or maybe just the well hung. May the Lord forgive her for that thought.

"Ma'am, I don't drink all that much, even less during the season, though I have been known to party from time to time. For a year now, I haven't been doing the clubs very often because I made a vow to St. Jude. I made another vow recently to be a good father and a faithful husband…and I keep my promises. It's true I'm on the road a lot. I earn my living playing football and that's part of the life, but I've taken a wife. She'll be here for the baby. As for baby stealing, I told Mrs. Everard, as the child's father, I would be responsible." Joe sniffed to keep his nose from running.

Good answer, Althea judged. She turned to the wife, an almost child-like figure who held the baby in her lap as he nursed. "Mrs. Everard says yours is a marriage of convenience purely to put up a good front for Mr. Billodeaux."

"Then, she may not know I spent the summer with Joe's family. They are warm-hearted, wonderful people and have welcomed me to the family."

"Sure did. I knew Nell would make a good mother for the baby so I just moved my plans to get married up a little," Joe chipped in as cheerily as he could.

"Was Nell one of your—list ladies?"

"Hell, no. She wouldn't even sign my book. Nell works with dyin' kids over at Ochsner."

"You have a career then, Mrs. Billodeaux. Do you plan on staying home with the baby?"

"I've put in for six weeks maternity leave. Once that is up, I'd like to see about working part-time at least. As a survivor of childhood cancer, I have a special rapport with other victims and feel I should continue to help them. Joe, of course, has the means for the best of childcare, but he wanted to give Dean a family."

"What's the status of your health?"

"I've been in remission for ten years. There is no reason to believe I won't live to raise this child."

Althea Alexander nodded. "Could I see where the baby sleeps?"

"Of course." Nell pulled the baby bottle from Dean's lips with a little pop. He'd drained it and did not protest. She put him on her shoulder and led the way confidently to the Chinese Bordello Room passing the open door and rumpled covers of the Love Palace on the way. Mrs. Alexander took a quick peek in that direction. Her eyes widened when she noticed the mirror on the ceiling.

The erotic pictures had been replaced with nursery rhyme prints. Now, Humpty Dumpty sat on the wall, Jack jumped over the candlestick inches from an open flame, Jack and Jill started up the hill heading for a fall and baby rocked in the treetop—where once hung illustrations of cunnilingus, fellatio and a variety of sexual positions. The new pictures made fairy tales and nursery rhymes seem much more dangerous than sex, but Mrs. Alexander merely smiled at them.

She checked the crib and changing table and let her eyes roam around the room. "Very nice, but a little impractical for a child."

"I know. We plan to redecorate. Joe is building a house in the country, too. Dean will have a room there as well."

On the way back to the living room, Mrs. Alexander looked into the Pompadour Room. "Lovely, I wish I had a room like this in my house."

Joe stood in the kitchen swilling down what looked like a shot glass of red liquid. He held up the plastic cup. "Decongestant. Honest, I haven't been drinking. Just so you know, Nicole doesn't stay home with her kids either. She has a nanny. Look Mrs. Alexander, this is all an attempt to soak me for child support. I'm sorry Deanie's mother died, but you're welcome here anytime."

What gorgeous eyes he had, and those fine sculpted lips, how could they lie? Pull yourself together, Althea. Be objective. "One other matter, Mr. Billodeaux. Mrs. Everard says a blood test to prove the fatherhood of the child has not been completed yet. She is sure you are the daddy, but what if the tests show otherwise?"

Casually, Althea opened the refrigerator and inspected the contents: formula, orange juice, milk, fresh fruit, and no more than a reasonable amount of beer.

With no hesitation, Joe said, "My wife and I can't have children because of her cancer treatments. I'd like to adopt Deanie or be his foster father first if we can't do that right away. But, did you see the chin, his eyes?" Joe took the baby and held him out for Mrs. Alexander to inspect. "He's mine."

Althea took the child and sat down with him. She unsnapped the sleeper and patted Deanie's full, rounded belly. He burped. No signs of abuse, but it never hurt to check.

"Mr. and Mrs. Billodeaux, I see no reason to remove the child as this time, and I will say so in my report. However, if Mrs. Everard gets a court order, I can do nothing to stop her trying to get custody except give testimony of my findings."

She placed Dean in Nell's arms and picked up a briefcase-sized purse. "I wish you luck in keeping your son."

A shame the boy would be their only child, Althea thought on the way out the door. She smiled as she heard Joe say, "We passed, Nell."

"Yes, I think we did, all three of us."

Chapter Twenty-One

"I'm telling you, Hank, this sick roster explains it all. Would you look at the names we got here: Connor Riley, Rev Bullock, Curse 'em and Crush 'em Calvin Armitage, and last but not least, quarterback Joe Dean Billodeaux, down with something they're calling Deanie's flu. A few of the guys out there on the field are playing like they're about to be ill, too," the sports commentator covering the Sinners game raved.

"Al, the Panthers are eating the Sinners alive with a score of 47-7. The Sinners look like a college team trying to play the pros. Well, that's what most of them are, new draft picks with speed and talent but very little experience. And, you don't fill the gap made by 356-pound Calvin Armitage in your defensive line with some 269-pound reserve lineman. Derrick Foster gave it a good try, but he just doesn't take up enough space. The Panthers offense is running rings around him. That's the two minute warning, and all this agony will be over here in the Dome."

****

Joe Dean put his head in his hands. The new kid probably would have done a decent job with Deets and Forte still in the lineup, but he kept getting sacked. This was his fault, his and Deanie's. A little baby couldn't help what it caught, but he should have known better than to take the child to a practice. Himself, he should have stayed home at the first sign of illness. Next week, the Sinners flew off to play the Seahawks. He'd have to make it up to the team and to Nell, married almost two weeks and not bedded once.

Joe kicked the tabloid off the coffee table with his bare foot, but the headlines still blared, *"Joe Dean Marries Nurse Nell"* over the photo of him carrying Nell through the lobby of the Bellagio. That picture shared half the front cover space with another, of him striding out of Nicole's office with the baby carrier and duckie diaper bag over one shoulder. Nicole, framed nicely in the doorway, shouted at him. A teaser at the bottom read, *"Mother of Joe's Love Child?—Story Inside."*

A press release prepared by Nicole clarified the maternity of tiny Dean Joseph—a young career woman employed by the Sinners who had been seduced and impregnated by their star quarterback, another callous, thoughtless, overpaid athlete. Valiant Margaret Stutes had lost her life giving birth to Joe's son.

"I regard Mr. Billodeaux as an unfit parent, and I will press my right to be declared legal guardian of this poor child as his mother wanted," Everard swore. Of course, she had sent out the release and set Joe up for the photograph before he'd threatened to tell her husband about her one-night-stand as a list lady.

Nicole made good on her pledge to call Child Welfare, but he and Nell came through the interview with good grades. Still, this battle wasn't over. He knew that. The best news he'd all week came in the form of the blood test results. Deanie was his, not, as he had worried, Derrick Foster's child.

Nell returned from putting the baby down to sleep.

Over the worst of her flu, she had perked up considerably, and he was on the mend. Now, he needed something to take his mind off Nicole and the Sinners' dismal performance.

"Nell, do I feel hot to you?"

She leaned over and put her lips to his forehead. "No, why?"

"Because I am." Without warning, he pulled her on top of his prone body and ripped her baby spit stained T-shirt over her head. Beneath it, she wore a plain white cotton bra. No sense letting that homely thing obstruct the view. He tore it off in seconds.

She perched topless on his pelvis. His satin robe split open of its own accord as he grew big and hard beneath her.

"I thought you were too sick to play."

"I am. That's why you're on top. I can't get overheated."

Nell put both of her small hands around his penis and tugged. "Too late."

"Oh, Nurse Nell, I feel too weak to take off your jeans. Please, please do it for me." Joe flung a hand across his eyes and peeped out at her between the cracks in his fingers. Yes, he'd made her laugh, which explained why she was bouncing up and down on him, at least partially.

Nell stood up, bracing her legs on either side of the wide couch and slowly unzipped her jeans. She shimmed them down to reveal—full-sized white cotton panties. Joe grabbed an ankle and upended her. The jeans came off. He balled the panties in his fist and made a perfect basket into a nearby waste can full of used tissues.

Nell settled over him so lightly all of his awareness focused on how snug and steaming she felt to him. She began to move, drawing herself up high and coming down hard. He groaned and helped her move with his hands.

"Nurse Nell, I'm comin' home. Hold me tight."

"Not yet, you're not." She slowed down so she was barely moving.

"You just need to catch up and you can go home with me." He reached down with a wide thumb and stroked between her legs. When she arched and writhed, he humped his hips rapidly against her so they could both burst and meltdown together. Nell collapsed on to his chest and lay there panting.

Joe Dean put his arms behind his head. "I'm glad that's out of the way."

"Out of the way! That's how you feel!"

"No, sugar, you misunderstand. Our marriage has been consummated—finally."

"Joe, we consummated dozens of time before we were married."

"Didn't count. Now it's official."

Chapter Twenty-Two

On the road, the Sinners took the Seahawks 24-17 and went on to flatten the Falcons 35-10 as the team regained its strength. Joe gloated when the Panthers dropped a game because their ranks were thinned by Deanie's Flu. Football was a contact sport and evidently the Sinners had shared some germs with their rivals. Yes, the Sinners were on the way to the Super Bowl.

Joe called home. He asked Nell to put the receiver up to the baby's ear. "Daddy's coming home, Deanie. Then you, me, and Mommy are going to go to the country for a few days. But yes, we are. You be a good boy, Deanie."

Nell swore the child kicked and wiggled twice as much when he heard Joe's voice on the phone. She couldn't help but smile. So she wasn't blessed with the hormone rush birth mothers got gratis. Her feelings for the infant grew steadily. She tickled his chin with her finger. Deanie gave her a crooked grin. Startled, she laughed and the baby stretched his mouth even wider.

Fumbling the receiver, Nell shouted into the phone, "Deanie just smiled at me. Billodeaux eyes, my ass. He has your wicked grin. I guess it could just be gas—or hot air. No, he did it again!"

"Damn, I missed Deanie's first smile."

Passing behind the new father, Jared Forte mocked,

"Ooooh, Daddy Joe missed baby's first smile."

Joe shot his left elbow back and caught Forte in the ribs about where the wide receiver had taken a hard hit early in the game and fumbled the ball. "When Daddy Joe throws you a good pass, you try to hang on to it next time, boy."

Connor Riley had repeated his performance of the previous year against the Falcons and run in an amazing string of touchdowns that accounted for all but one score of the game. Forte went away sulking.

"Trouble?" Nell asked.

"No way. We have a bye week coming up, then a home game. What say we spend a few days in Chapelle, check out how the house is coming, exercise those lazy horses, and see if Bijou is putting down enough straw in the stalls while my mama spoils the baby."

Check out the straw, indeed. "We'll be ready to go, Daddy Joe."

****

The small family headed for a weekend in the country without bothering to call ahead. In Nadine Billodeaux's life there was no such thing as not having a room ready or being without food in the house for guests. "You just add more rice to the pot, *cher*," she told Nell. As for her grandchildren, she always had the time.

MawMaw Nadine came to the door with Izzy's new baby girl in her arms. "Come see whose visitin', Randi."

The child had been christened Miranda Marie, but the Cajun law of nicknames had come into force already. The chubby, bald little girl wearing a pink stretchy headband to designate her sex would be Randi to her dying day.

"Oh look, see. It's Uncle Joe and Auntie Nell and Cousin Deanie. Come to MawMaw, *cher bebe*." Nadine handed Randi to Joe and scooped Dean from his carrier. That left Nell holding the diaper bag, but she did not mind in the least. She'd had no outings in four weeks.

"So is Izzy around?"

"No, *cher*, she's gettin' her figure back, only it didn't go back to the same place. Never does." Nadine looked down sadly at her own robust body. "She went to the mall with Eenie to get some clothes. Me, I'd rather stay home and give some sugar to my grandkids." Nadine laid a smacking kiss on Deanie's forehead and the baby smiled.

"Ah, son, he got your smile. Jus' like the one your daddy gave to me first time we went out, only he had teeth. And here we are, five kids and fourteen grandchildren later."

"If you don't mind watching Deanie, we thought we'd go over to the ranch, see how the house is coming, do some riding." Joe lifted Randi high in the air. She opened her mouth wide with joy and let loose a string of dribble that landed on his shirt.

"Unless having both of them will be too much for you," Nell added quickly.

Nadine wagged a finger at her. "*Cher*, there's only the two, and they don't even walk yet. Wait till you have four under the age of six, then you see some trouble. The house is comin' along real well. It's been hot, hot with no rain. Makes for an easy harvest, but we could use some cold to bring the sugar up. Anyhow, the house might be ready for Thanksgiving. Go take a look."

Nadine turned toward the kitchen counter. "Take this leftover gumbo to Bijou, would you? He drinks more than he eats. How Hal and Flo got one like that, I don't know. The rest turned out okay, but Bijou, poo-yie!"

Joe took the Tupperware container of gumbo from his mother and pecked her on the cheek. "Thanks for watching Deanie, Mama."

Nell relinquished the diaper bag, and they went off to deliver the food and check out the depth of the straw in the barn. They caught Bijou, leaning up against the extended cab truck Joe had left behind, watching a horse and rider in the ring. He smirked at Nell's Toyota.

"Comin' down in the world, Cousin Joe? You trade in that Porsche for a mom mobile?"

"You know it's Nell's car, Bijou. We couldn't get the baby seat in the sports car."

Bijou chuckled. "Yeah, I heard you got caught in more ways than one."

The sound of hooves tearing around the exercise ring drowned out the conversation as the horse moved closer at a gallop. The rider pulled up sharply and lost a pink cowgirl hat to the maneuver. Dust obscured the scene, then the happy face of the rider emerged from the cloud. Trails of sweat rolled down like tears through the dirt on Cassie's face. "Surprise!" she hollered.

Cassie dismounted and led the heaving horse to a gate and over to Joe and Nell. "Isn't he beautiful? Bijou said you wanted to get more horses, and he picked this one out for me. His name is Copperhead."

The animal looked at Nell with a wild, blue eye. His head certainly was a copper color. It arched over a compact white body splotched with black and brown. A tail with all three colors switched nervously.

"Yeah, I did want more horses, but Bijou should have checked with me first. He's not too much horse for you, Cassie?"

"No, sir. We get along fine, don't we, Copper?" Cassie stroked her mount's nose and the horse calmed.

"But, what are you doing here, Cassie?" Nell asked the obvious question.

"Riding. Bijou is teaching me barrel racing and pole-bending. I was always the sickly one, but now I fly like the wind." Cassie threw out her arms and Copperhead spooked a little. Immediately, she patted his neck.

"She showed up here in early September wanting to ride. Just got her driver's license and managed to get that old van all the way up here alone." Bijou grinned as if pleased by Cassie's connivance.

"I paid for my own gas with babysitting money, but Mom wouldn't let me do it again." Cassie stuck out her lip. "She said I deceived her by coming all the way to Chapelle when there were closer places to ride if I had the money. Those places won't let me ride like I want to, and they cost more than I can make with after school jobs."

"So I said I'd come down and get her in the truck Friday night, and she could stay over all weekend at the house. Figured it would be all right with you, Joe. You brought girls to the homestead a time or two, didn't you?" Bijou poked Joe in the ribs.

Before Joe could answer, Nell cut in. "I think if Cassie stays the weekend, it would be better to let her sleep at Nadine's or with one of Joe's sisters."

"Fine by me." Bijou presented her with an oily

smile. The sun glinted off his bad front tooth newly capped with gold. "Hear that, Cassie?"

"I bring my own sleeping bag and help clean up the house and muck out the stalls, Nell. I'm not a burden. I feel so good and strong for the first time in years. You must understand."

Nell did, only too well. "Stay with Nadine from now on."

"I guess." Cassie looked down and rubbed a boot toe in the dirt.

"She's a natural, Joe. Look at her. No more fat on her than on a greyhound. She clings to a horse like hungry tick. Won't be long before she can compete." Bijou gave his professional opinion.

"I don't know, Joe. She should get her parent's permission. Is pole-bending dangerous?"

"Tight turns and fast speeds, so it can be if the rider falls off. It's not as dangerous as bronco or bull riding. Girls don't compete in those," Bijou said.

"Bijou should know. He did the rodeo circuit for a while when he was younger," Joe told Nell.

"While you were playing it safe on the high school football field, Cousin, I was making my way to the top. I tell you, it's just not right what you get paid compared to a bull rider. Sure, you get roughed up once in a while, but you got those big linemen protecting your precious ass. All I had was a couple of rodeo clowns protecting me. All I got was a bunch of broken bones that ended my career."

"I could end up the same way, Bijou."

"Yeah, after you bank millions. Didn't you buy my daddy's place with your last bonus?"

"I did it to keep the land in the family. You can

always quit if you don't like what I pay you."

"Let's see you ride, Cassie," Nell said to break things up between the men.

Cassie mounted and wove Copperhead around some barrels at a slow canter on the course Bijou had laid out for her.

Nell applauded. "That's great, Cassie. Joe, if that's all there is to it, I don't think it would be a problem if she competed."

"If that's how she rides in competition, she won't win, Nell."

"That wouldn't matter. I think it's the riding she enjoys."

"Okay, then. Clear it with her folks though. It might be a good idea to have them sign a waiver in case she gets hurt."

"If she got hurt, I'd expect to pay the medical bills. You know the Thomases don't have much money with all those children to raise."

"Whatever you say, Tink."

Bijou mumbled something in an undertone. Joe heard the word "pussy-whipped", but he let it pass for the sake of Nell and Cassie.

Joe and Bijou saddled L.B. and Fatima. Cassie on Copperhead followed them out to the hay meadow now deep in goldenrod, wild aster, and black-eyed Susans. With their company in tow, they rode farther along the bayou, then returned following the tractor path beside the recently harvested cane fields. They would not be testing the depth of the straw in the barn or having nookie in the meadow today. When they returned, Nell made sure Cassie collected her things from the old homestead and came back with them to Nadine's home.

****

Frank turned over two briskets—soaked with liquid smoke, rubbed with garlic salt and tightly wrapped in foil—on the grill. Allie brought coleslaw studded with tiny pink shrimp, and Eenie the mandatory potato salad. Lizzie promised to pick up hot French bread from Pommier's Bakery on her way home from work. Izzy put together a Watergate salad more like a dessert with its lime Jell-O and marshmallows because it was the only green stuff most of the kids would eat.

Cassie, easy to pick out by her bright red hair among the dark Billodeaux girls, held baby Randi. Joe stood near the grill, a cold beer in one hand, and Deanie, legs gripped under his daddy's arm, small head palmed like a football, in the other. The baby gazed at his father and tried out his new smile every time he was addressed.

"Deanie, see PawPaw cooking. Is Deanie hungry?"

Sitting in the late afternoon shade, Nell marveled at Joe's ease with the child. "I'm still afraid I'll drop him," she confessed to her mother-in-law.

"Comes wit' practice. Joe babysat for Allie's kids. First time, he comes to me hollering to help change a diaper, I said, 'Who's the one gets paid for this?' He caught on real fast. Always knew he would be a good daddy once he settled down."

Frank peeled back the foil and basted the briskets with barbecue sauce. "Be ready quick. Lizzie here wit' da French bread for sandwiches yet?"

"Not yet," Nadine called back. "Tomorrow, we go to Mass, then after, to the Pepper Festival in St. Martinville. You been?"

"No. I've been to the Strawberry, Rice, Frog, and

Jazz festivals plus a few others, but never one for peppers."

"I'll keep the baby for you," Allie offered. "Mine are getting so big."

Nell looked around the crowd on the lawn. "Bijou doesn't come over for the cookouts?"

"No, he's more likely to be at a roadhouse drinking on Saturday nights," Eenie said. "Here comes Lizzie, alone. I'll bet Charlie's out with Bijou. They went to high school together. Of course, Bijou never finished. Got a GED and a criminal record instead."

"Bijou's been in jail?"

"Minor things. Drunk driving, receiver of stolen goods. He couldn't pass up one of those fancy rings he likes to own. The first time he hocked it, he got picked up, but they couldn't pin the robbery on him. Said he got it off some black dude. As if," Eenie said with disgust.

"Joe is too kind-hearted letting him stay in the house and look after the ranch. Bijou is just plain trash," Allie asserted.

"He's your cousin, Allie. For shame," Nadine corrected. "The rest of Flo and Hal's children turned out fine."

"Bad apple in the bunch," Allie insisted.

Lizzie, still in her LPN clothes and white, thick-soled shoes, dumped six long loaves of French bread in white paper wrappers on the picnic table. She lifted the tea towels keeping the dust and flies off the food and gave an evaluation. "Yum, any night I don't have to cook is a good night."

Lizzie took a seat on the bench. "Did my kids get here?"

"Sure, Darryl picked them up."

Lizzie frowned. "Charlie was supposed to drop them on his way to pick up Bijou. He said they had to see a man about a horse."

"Probably going to the off-track betting parlor is my guess," Allie whispered to Nell.

"PawPaw, is that brisket done? We all starvin' here," Nadine shouted to Frank, turning the conversation in a different direction.

****

Lulled by the sound of the engine and worn out by well-meaning relatives, Deanie slept in his car seat as the Toyota passed through the smoke of cane fields being burnt after the harvest and down the long causeways over the marsh leading back to New Orleans. Cassie had fallen asleep, too, still wearing the garish necklace of bright red ceramic Tabasco peppers Joe had bought for her at one of the crafts booths. She slumped against the window behind the driver's seat, her head bobbing each time the car hit a pothole.

Nell watched a big, bloody harvest moon rise through the haze as she rested her head on Joe's shoulder. "Joe, do you think Bijou is a danger to Cassie?"

"You been talking to Allie, right? She has a low opinion of everyone. She's the one who told Mama you and I were probably sneaking out and doing it in the cane fields."

"And she would have been right."

Joe's smile glittered in the beam of light from an on-coming car. "Bijou is thirty-three or thirty-four, Lizzie's age. He had his brushes with the law when he was younger, but nothing for years now. He can be *canaille,* sly, you know. Like I bet I paid for that gold tooth somehow. Probably told the dentist it was part of his dental plan as my employee. But, he would never hurt a child."

"If you say so," Nell conceded. "If you're sure."

Nell sat up and turned her head from side to side stretching her neck and making her silver hot pepper earrings dance. "It was a nice day, a good day. Who would have thought watching grown men and women eat hot peppers off paper plates until the sweat ran down their faces would be so diverting?"

"Diverting from what?"

"Things we have to discuss."

"What things?" A note of instant caution entered Joe's voice.

"My leave will be up the first week in November. I want to go back to work at least part-time."

"You want to hire a nanny like Nicole Everard does?" Even in the dark, she could tell he frowned.

"No. Just find a good nursery to use for half a day."

"You know we haven't heard the last from Nicole even with the blood test being conclusive. If you don't stay home with the baby, she'll use that against us. The house will be finished around Thanksgiving. Would you think about moving to Chapelle and working in Lafayette? There are four or five hospitals up there. Heck, maybe Mintay could use your services at the clinic. Then, my mother or maybe Allie could take care of Deanie. You don't need the money anymore."

"It's not the money. I feel I have something special to offer sick children that will go to waste if I'm a stay-at-home mom."

"There's nothing wrong with staying at home with

215

our kids."

"I'm not pregnant, Joe."

"I know. I'm getting off to a slow start, kind of like this football season, but give me time. Just let the magic work, Tink, because we're going all the way, you, me, and the team."

Chapter Twenty-Three

Bruised and tired after another two-week road trip, the Sinners trudged through the airport. Having won both games, they were still the heroes, but they'd paid a price for the victories. Tampa Bay gave them no trouble, but the Philadelphia Eagles took a chunk out of the team despite their one point loss. Jared Forte with a broken leg might be able to play again if the Sinners reached the playoffs, but their new golden boy running back had pulled a hamstring on top of that. Joe was down two receivers and Connor limped with a slight sprain. At least the Rev, sound as ever, still forced fumbles and interceptions on the other team.

Even though the hour was late, a small group of autograph seekers crowded around the team as they exited the security area. A fresh-faced college boy thrust an envelope Joe's way.

He started to sign on the back when the kid said, "You've just been served, sir. Warrant to appear in family court. Tough game yesterday. Glad you won. Oh, and good luck in court. Hope they let you keep the baby." He dashed back into the stream of people moving toward the parking garage.

****

"Nell, could you ask for a few more weeks off until we get this hearing out of the way?" He didn't want to beg, but he would if necessary for Deanie's sake. Joe

217

could tell his wife was getting restless cooped up in the condo with a small baby and him on the road so much. Why, she'd even stripped the wallpaper in both the Chinese Bordello and the Love Palace Rooms while he'd been gone. The walls in Deanie's room glowed with a pale yellow paint job. A frieze of Disney characters paraded around the borders.

At this moment, he had no intention of asking where the Chinese furniture had gone. He only knew it had been replaced with a dresser and large toy chest matching the crib. A teddy bear about as big as the Rev sat in one corner. A large open area for playing had been created where the bed once stood.

As for the Love Palace, well, Gregory thanked Joe for the mirror on his way up to the condo. Nell had paint and fabric swatches spread out on the coffee table awaiting his input. Man, he'd loved that red-flocked wallpaper. Evidently, the fake animal fur throws were keeping the homeless warm down at the shelter. She'd left the round bed but exchanged black sheets for hunter green. He wasn't going to say a word about it if she'd only agree to stay home with Deanie a little longer.

Nell sighed. Joe hadn't made any remarks about her efforts to rehabilitate the apartment. He didn't want to talk about the game. All he desired was a few more weeks of her time. Not as gorgeous as most of his former lovers and probably not as exciting, she could grant the one favor no one else could do for Joe Dean. She raised the phone and called her boss.

"I'd like to claim another six weeks of family leave. Without pay, of course. I understand, but legally you have to grant it to me. Yes, I know how well the new intern is working out. I appreciate it. Thanks again." Nell disconnected and looked at her husband. "Done."

****

By her size and color, the judge could have been Althea Alexander's cousin, but she proved much less susceptible to Joe Dean's charms. Even though he gave her his best smile, Judge Andrews barely glanced his way.

"We've accommodated your schedule Mr. Billodeaux, so let's get started. It has been proven by means of a blood test that Mr. Billodeaux is the natural father of the child. The mother, Margaret Stutes, is deceased. Why, Ms. Everard, are you disputing the father's parental rights when he has shown he is willing to take responsibility for his son and has the means to do so?"

Nicole Everard sat alone at her table. She rose, looking as trim, professional, and deadly as always, and kept her eyes on the judge and away from the cluster at the other table made up of two attorneys, Joe and Nell.

"Your honor, as you can see, the mother of Dean Joseph Billodeaux stipulated that I was to act as the baby's legal guardian should anything happen."

The judge perused a document in front of her. "This is a contract, Ms. Everard, not a last will and testament. It appears you were to act as Miss Stutes' attorney in filing a paternity suit against Mr. Billodeaux asking for a substantial amount of child support and a settlement for the mother. You were to receive a percentage of that settlement if successful. Was it your suggestion you be made legal guardian?"

"Of course. The best interests of the child should be pursued despite the deceased status of his mother."

"But, she didn't name you guardian on her death bed before witnesses or in a will?"

"No. But, the child still needs my protection. I have also appended several articles from various newspapers and magazines that will give you a good idea of what sort of life Mr. Billodeaux leads. Partying, brawls and his infamous list of hundreds of women, all of whom he intended to have sexual relations with."

"Not the most reliable of publications, Ms. Everard. What do you have to say for yourself, Mr. Billodeaux?"

Used to defending sports figures on every type of unseemly behavior from rape charges to drug arrests, his attorneys sprang to life. "Our client had just completed a six month period of celibacy and sobriety and was merely letting off some steam at the end of the football season. Most of the incidents cited occurred more than a year ago and reflect a period of immaturity passed through by many young men. He has since married and been a model husband and father."

"I asked Mr. Billodeaux."

"Yes, ma'am, some of those things are true about me, but having this child has turned my life around. Ask Nell. Ask my wife."

"Mrs. Billodeaux? You married your husband quite suddenly and your marriage has been of less than three month's duration. How is it working out for you?"

"Joe has been a devoted father and a good husband, your honor."

"Their marriage is a sham brought into existence to wrest legal rights to the child without paying a dime to Miss Stutes' estate."

"Which you represent."

"Yes."

"Is your marriage a sham, Mrs. Billodeaux?"

"Joe and I were seeing each other prior to learning of Deanie's existence. We parted for a short time because I felt he should consider other women who could give him a family. Because of cancer treatments, I am unable to have children."

"Our marriage is not a sham. We've consummated it more than once, dozens of times..." Joe Dean's lawyers pushed him back into his seat as the judge wagged a finger at him.

"Your potency is not in question, Mr. Billodeaux. Sit down. Are you willing to give up your career as a child psychologist in order to be a mother to an infant conceived out of wedlock by your husband, Mrs. Billodeaux?"

"I have agreed to stay home while Deanie is small, but do wish to resume my career at some time. As a survivor of childhood cancer, I can provide support to my patients that others cannot."

"Well said. Mrs. Alexander, could we have your report on the conditions in the Billodeaux home?"

Althea Alexander moved from the back of the courtroom to center stage. "Your honor, when I first entered the Billodeaux home, I did notice the father seemed under the weather, you might say. I have since been provided with a doctor's statement that he suffered from a form of flu. I might have picked it up myself because I was down for a week following my visit. Anyhow, they have provided a clean, even luxurious, place for the child and the baby is well cared for."

"You saw no signs of the debauchery alleged by Ms. Everard?"

"Well, your honor, I did see one room that seemed to be a sort of bachelor pad, but on a return visit, I noticed this room had undergone a renovation and the baby's room had been made even more child friendly and inviting. They did keep that lovely place with the blue brocade on the walls for a guest room, though."

"In your opinion, does the Billodeaux marriage seem stable and likely to last?"

"I noticed Mrs. Billodeaux seemed more at ease in the role of mother and wife since my previous visit. I believe if Mr. Billodeaux can keep it zipped, they have a good chance. Sorry, I meant if he remains faithful."

"Given his history of past sexual excesses, there is little chance of that, your honor," Nicole Everard interjected.

"Ms. Everard, what I need to hear from you is what kind of life you would provide for this child. Are you planning on giving up your career in law? Is your husband willing to be a father to this baby?"

"I have two young sons of my own who are cared for by an excellent licensed nanny. My husband is unwilling to assume financial responsibility for Dean Joseph, which is why I will seek a judgment providing child support."

"In other words, you will continue to practice law and your husband does not want to be a father to the child."

"Your honor, I would like to present some information that became available only yesterday." The leaner and hungrier of Joe Dean's attorneys stalked over to the judge and handed her a sheaf of copies.

"As you can see, Mr. Harry Everard has filed papers for legal separation from his wife, Nicole. Cause given is adultery naming both Joe Dean Billodeaux and his law partner, Jeremy Hait as parties with whom his wife has had sexual relationships. Also," Leon Wiley continued, "I have here the famous list referred to in some the news articles. You can see Mrs. Everard's name on the marked page."

Nell flinched. Joe took her hand and squeezed. He spoke to her in an undertone. "I told them not to use that unless they had to. Sorry. She was one of my list ladies."

Nicole Everard charged forward and snatched the book. "This isn't my signature. Compare it to the one on the contract."

"We have a witness, a Mrs. Iris McNab, who will testify that at an after-hours event, Mrs. Everard ordered her paralegal, Stacey Smits, to sign Mr. Billodeaux's black book in her stead. The second marker shows the signature of paralegal, and they are the same."

"I notice Ms. Everard's name is crossed out."

"Yes, Mr. Billodeaux said he had no desire to sleep with Mrs. Everard again."

The courtroom crowd snickered. The judge rapped the gavel.

Nicole swore under her breath and seared Joe with an evil glare. Head down, staring at his hand clasped with Nell's, he tried to remain oblivious to her anger.

"The concierge at Mr. Billodeaux's condo, Gregory Barker, will swear Mrs. Everard did keep her appointment for a sexual tryst."

"As riveting and smutty as this is, Mr. Wiley, this is not divorce court, and I am not Dr. Phil or even Judge Judy. Put the book away and take these papers with you. What is your current marital status, Ms. Everard?"

"Separated as of yesterday. But, I still have possession of a lovely house and a very good nanny who would see the baby got the finest of care."

"I am unimpressed with you, Ms. Everard, *and* with Mr. Billodeaux as potential parents for this child. However, the stepmother seems to be the steadiest of the three of you."

Leon Wiley waved more papers at the judge. "Your honor, if custody is decided in the Billodeauxs' favor, they intend to sign adoption papers immediately which would make Nellwyn Billodeaux the legal mother of the child."

The judge nodded to show she would take this into consideration. "Ms. Everard, you had a legal contract with the birth mother. Her death ends that connection and as she made no other provisions for the child, I award custody of Dean Joseph to the natural father. Mrs. Alexander, your department will continue to monitor the situation in the home. Mr. Billodeaux, grow up. Adjourned." With a swish of voluminous robes, Judge Andrews left the chambers.

Joe gave Nell a hug that lifted her off her feet. He shook the hands of his lawyers and intercepted Althea Alexander on her way out of the room. "Thank you, thank you for the good report."

"It was an honest one, but mind what I said, you naughty boy." Althea gave a significant look at Joe's crotch. "I'll be watching."

"And I'll be watching, too, Joe," Nicole snarled as she passed. She stopped and continued her harangue to Joe's turned back. "You think you can ruin my career and my marriage and get away with it!"

"I didn't tell Harry." Joe kept his eyes on Nell.

"No, you dumb coonass, you left both office doors open, and he heard every word. You bray like a jackass."

"The guys tell me they can hear me call the plays over the roar of the crowd, that's the truth." Joe took both of Nell's hands, possibly to keep from striking out.

"After that he had me followed to find out if I was still seeing you and discovered my fling with Jeremy instead. The partnership is broken. We're all going our separate ways."

"Not my fault, Nicole." Joe kept himself turned away from her though every word felt like a sharp stab in the back.

"It's all your fault. Margaret went on and on about you. How great you were in bed and how hopelessly gullible. I came to your condo out of curiosity. You weren't that great in the sack, Joe."

"Well, they say curiosity killed the cat, Nicole. Let's go, Tink. We have a son to pick up at Granny's house."

"Don't expect to live happily ever after because I will see you won't. Do you hear me, Joe Dean Billodeaux?" The wicked witch, formerly of Hait, Everard & Everard, shrieked at them.

Joe Dean said a few words under his breath and crossed himself.

Chapter Twenty-Four

Nell finished painting the Love Palace a deep hunter green and put up a wallpaper border of burgundy, green and gold paisley. She couldn't do much about the dark, gold-veined mirror tiles or the black fixtures in the bath short of tearing them out and starting from scratch. She settled on hanging golden towels on the rack and putting a planter with sprawling vines in the bidet. The small high windows over the round tub should provide enough light for greenery and the pot would certainly be easy to water.

Joe had given her another project. "Since you think your taste is better than mine."

"It is."

"Why don't you go over to Chapelle and meet with Miss Ashleigh about decorating the ranch house. She did the mansion for that billionaire so she should be good enough for us. I like to spend my money in Chapelle when I can."

"If you call a place with six bedrooms and baths and all those pillars a ranch house, you do need my help."

"What I said." With that settled, Joe went on the road again.

****

Nell called Cassie to see if the girl wanted to ride with her to the ranch and found she had gone already, having been picked up right after school by Bijou. By the time Nell arrived at Nadine's, Cassie's overnight bag sat on one of the beds in the room formerly belonging to Lizzie and Izzy and very nearly identical down to the spreads as the bedroom Nell generally used. Naturally, Joe had pushed the twin beds together in the room they shared. Cassie, herself, was over at the training ring weaving a cloverleaf pattern around the barrels in the last light of the autumn day.

"That girl is here every, every weekend. Horse crazy, she is, like Lizzie once upon a time until she discovered boys," Nadine told Nell.

"There are worse things than being horse crazy, then." Nell shared a laugh with her mother-in-law.

Saturday, Cassie passed on going with Nell to Miss Ashleigh's Studio of Interior Design to consider paint chips and carpet samples in favor of more practice on Copperhead who stayed lean and fast. Meanwhile, Fatima and the ponies grew chubby and L.B. enjoyed life as a stud.

"That child," claimed Nadine, "she never eats, just rides, rides, rides. Packs herself a peanut butter and banana sandwich and a pop, and she's gone all day wit' Bijou. Says my food is too spicy for her. Still, she ain't no trouble. Cassie makes her bed and remembers to take those boots off before she comes in the house."

Fortunately, Nell and Ashleigh, who wasn't much older than her, hit it off. Yes, one bedroom could be done with a sunflower motif, and the Chinese furniture in storage could be put to use in a guest room with walls the color of old ivory netsuke and the French doors shaded with oriental screens. Ashleigh even knew a dealer who would consider a trade of the erotic pictures for some nice traditional floral brush paintings.

Because construction projects never go off without a hitch, the flooring was not installed in time for Thanksgiving, and the family gathered instead at the outdoor pavilion on a mild November afternoon. The Abbotts had been invited and insisted on bringing the pies, pumpkin, of course, and pecan plus a Mississippi mud concoction and a cherry cheesecake in a graham cracker crust. These offerings joined a fudge cake and a mound of iced brownies made by Eenie's daughters.

While hot dishes simmered on one side of the vast grill, the men gathered around the built-in crawfish boiler and debated whether the peanut oil had gotten hot enough for the whole fresh turkey to be lowered and fried. Gary Abbott seemed fascinated with the concept of frying a whole turkey. Nell's mother sat contentedly with the women and talked recipes and children.

There being no eligible men to flirt with except the eighteen-year-old college student who kept calling her ma'am, Emily soon grew bored. The college kid was no Jared Forte whom she'd hooked up with at one of the Sinners' parties. She could have helped Nell who flitted back and forth from the house carrying autumn floral arrangements to sit on the lemon-colored linens her sister was determined to use indoors or out. Em wandered off toward the barn where she could get away from the hoard of screaming children and her sister's sudden and stifling domesticity.

Joe noticed her exit. He stepped back from the group of men and told his father-in-law he wanted to check on the horses since Bijou had gone up to Toledo Bend to be with his parents. He found Emily stroking L.B.'s long blazed nose and murmuring, "So you're the big stud, you pretty boy."

"Figured that out by yourself, Em?" Joe asked her.

"Well, that one is a mare, the blue-eyed horse has his balls cut off, and it certainly wasn't either of those ponies. I know a stud when I see one."

She looked Joe up and down. A year ago, Emily would have had him reaching for his black book or saying the hell with it and doing a quickie before the party. Now, this woman simply made him uncomfortable. He had come out here to talk to her in private and that he would do.

"Em, you know there's a good chance Nell won't be able to have kids."

"I knew that long before you did." She continued to stroke L.B.'s nose. The horse blew his warm breath into her hair and she laughed.

"We haven't been using any birth control since we got married and nothing's happened yet." Joe leaned against the stall.

"What's the matter? Afraid it's your fault, big boy?" Emily insinuated.

"Seeing as how Deanie is sitting in his granny's lap right now, no. But, I'd like to have more children, children with Nell. I've been reading."

"Oh, do you read?"

"Yeah, I been to college." He gave his standard answer to the dumb jock inference.

"What did you major in?"

"Kinesiology. You know—physical movement."

"I'll just bet you did."

"I wasn't interested in academics. All I ever wanted to do was play football, and that's what I'm doing. Em, could we cut the crap? I want to ask if when we're ready for another child, you'd be an egg donor for Nell. You look a lot alike, and I know you donated your marrow for her transplant. Could you help your sister again?"

"Who's asking, you or her?"

"Me. Nell doesn't know about this. I'd like to tell her at Christmas you'll do this for us one day. I can't think of a better gift for the woman I love."

Emily snorted much like L.B. "What was I going to say when the doctors told my parents I was the best bone marrow match in the family, only one fucking antigen off? No, let my miserable little sister die. So, I save her life and what does she do—makes us move because, boohoo—she can't make friends at her school since they all know about her disease."

Joe shrugged. "Moving isn't that big a deal."

"Think not? I was a senior in high school. My boyfriend, too lazy to drive to another town to see me, dumped me. I don't go to the prom, but little Nell goes because she's putting out for Brady, another dumb jock. I don't get to go to LSU because my brother is halfway through up there, and we're still paying Nell's medical bills. I have to commute to Southeastern and live at home. I don't think I owe Nell any more favors. Go harvest your eggs somewhere else."

Emily dropped her hand from L.B.'s nose and started to stroke Joe's arm. "Unless you want to consider getting another child the way you got Dean." She cocked her head provocatively and waited for his answer.

"That would be breaking my vows. I don't do that."

Emily kept her hand on his arm and looked into his

eyes. "It's up to you."

Joe took a deep breath. "I'd be willing to pay you to donate those eggs, all the expenses of course, and a nice sum of money."

"How much."

"One million dollars."

Emily smiled. "Let me think about it. When are you free to discuss this some more?"

"We have a home game Sunday. Monday afternoon would be best."

"Great. Meet me in the restaurant of the Hilton at noon, lover boy. We'll see what we can work out."

"Joe, are you in here?" Nell called.

"We're here," Emily answered. She didn't drop her hand from Joe's sleeve until Nell came upon them. She gave Joe a conspiratorial smile and sauntered, hips swaying in tight jeans, back to the pavilion. No one could imply hanky-panky like Emily.

"What were you talking about, Joe?" Nell questioned, watching her sister go.

"Nothing. We talked about the horses." He felt like the old Joe Dean, the one always caught with a hand up a woman's skirt.

"Strange. Em has never been interested in horses before."

"Oh, she knows more than you would think. They get that turkey in the oil yet?"

"It's coming to a boil, your daddy said."

Joe stared at a clean stall deep with straw, but Nell tugged his arm. "We don't have time. Tonight after we've hauled out the garbage, I promise."

****

The Sinners won at home and Joe, feeling

231

confident, went to meet Emily on Monday. She sat alone lapping up a bottle of wine like a cat with a whole dairy at her disposal. Joe ordered the blackened redfish and helped himself to the beverage Emily had chosen. He was more of a beer man, but this wine had a dry, crisp taste with no harsh edge. He imagined the bottle would be expensive when the waiter presented the tab.

Emily told the waiter she would have the crab au gratin and a house salad, dressing on the side. Her first words to Joe were, "Two million." She took another sip of her costly wine.

"Two million to do something nice for your sister?" Joe shook his head with disgust. "I'd give any of my sisters a kidney for nothing."

"You aren't the one who has to have shots nearly every day for a month at some hospital. I could lose my job if I took that much leave."

"I'm considering the Mayo Clinic in Phoenix. They have a high success rate with in vitro fertilization. I'd pay for the process and your stay. With a million dollars you can quit your job and do whatever you want, go your own way."

"I intend to. Nicole, over here!" Emily smiled across the table at Joe. "My lawyer. Nell said she's a real barracuda. I thought, that's exactly who I need."

Nicole Everard slithered into the third seat at the table. Amazing her forked tongue didn't poke in and out testing the air for prey, he thought.

"Joe, so glad we could do business again. No, no food for me, only a glass of this lovely wine," she directed. "I am so sorry your stable, trustworthy wife isn't a complete woman. Giving birth to my own boys meant so much to me, my poor boys—victims of a nasty divorce."

"For this price, I can get a hundred donors, Nicole. I'm sure Nell has cousins I could contact."

"Just two young men on my dad's side. Mom was an only child. No, if you want the right genetics, there is only me, the sister whose mother stayed at a far away hospital while Nell got her chemotherapy. I got my first period while Mom sat with Nell. I stuffed my pants with toilet paper for three days because I was too embarrassed to tell my dad. My gym teacher found out after I soaked through my shorts. She cleaned me up and sent me home with a note. That's the kind of pain Nell has caused me," Emily claimed.

The waiter served Emily and sat Joe's redfish in front of him. Joe pushed it aside.

"When your attorneys got through red-lining my expenses on behalf of Margaret, I ended up with fifty percent of the total, Joe." Nicole rapped his hand with her sharp, manicured nails and left small marks in his skin.

"You had Margaret cremated in Mexico. You paid for an urn and a niche in the cemetery, not for the shipment of a body and a plot. Did you think they wouldn't check? I went out to see for myself in case Dean ever wants to visit. They allowed you a reasonable amount for your time. You got a fair deal, Nicole."

"I want a better deal. My fee to negotiate this contract will be five hundred thousand."

Joe stood to go. He was half way to the exit when Emily called him back. "Two million and I'll pay Nicole ten percent of that myself."

He returned to the table. "Five-hundred thousand

before the donation, the same after and another million if the procedure results in a live birth. You pay your own legal fees. Take it or leave it, Em."

Emily inhaled sharply. "Done."

"A toast, then." Nicole filled their glasses and stepped aside as Emily clinked hers against the one Joe held in his hand. A camera flashed and whirred. Joe looked up only to be caught by second blinding flash. The Hilton's security guards converged and escorted a paparazzo outside.

"What a shame," Nicole declared. "They let that riff-raff inside on such an important day in your life, Joe. I'll draw up the contract and get it to your attorneys. I still have their address."

Chapter Twenty-Five

Joe warned her there might be more trouble before he took off for an out of town game, but he declined to worry her with specifics. Nell made guesses: that Nicole had found new grounds to take the baby, that another paternity suit had been filed by an opportunistic list lady. Joe insisted he didn't want to ruin Christmas unless absolutely necessary.

"Believe in me," he said when he kissed her good-bye.

Because of the distance involved, Joe would be coming back Monday morning. That early December day dawned sunny and bright with the heat and humidity down to what in northern latitudes would constitute a lovely day in spring. Nell put Deanie in his stroller, tucked a light blue cotton blanket around his increasingly active little body and went out to enjoy the weather. She wheeled the baby along the River Walk through parks and plazas and around fountains, the great, gray Mississippi on one side, the sunken French Quarter on the other.

Taking her café au lait and beignets out of the crowded Café du Monde, Nell sat on the edge of a planter filled with the pansies and snapdragons that loved Louisiana's light frosts and winter sunshine. A humpbacked saxophone player wailed out a bluesy version of *Have Yourself a Merry Little Christmas* on one street corner and magazines held down with bricks fluttered in the off-river breeze at the newsstand on the other.

Nell decided to take the sidewalks home and enjoy the Christmas decorations, the blaring carols and window displays in some of the often strange and off-beat shops. Deanie's dark bright eyes winked closed while they sat in the sunshine. Perhaps, she could buy a few gifts before he woke hungry for a bottle. She guided the stroller to the crosswalk. The tabloid headlines at the newsstand pierced her to the heart before she got half way across the street.

"Joe Dean Trysts with Wife's Sister."

Paying for a copy, she pushed the stroller to a bench in Jackson Square even though a bum slept on the other end with a copy of the same tabloid spread across his face to keep out the light. In the front page picture, Emily smirked at the camera and held a wine glass high in a toast. Joe wore the same expression he usually had after being sacked by two three-hundred pound linemen.

The article said nothing and implied much. The couple had been seen wining and dining at the Hilton Hotel rather than at any of the famous French Quarter restaurants. The hotel management declined to confirm if they had spent the night. The occasion for the toast remained a mystery—but could Joe Dean be planning to divorce his wife of three months and wed her sister? An attorney, Nicole Everard, had been present at the festivities. Known to be one of Joe Dean's list ladies, could the lawyer be part of a bizarre ménage à trois?

"No, no, no," said Nell to the baby and herself so emphatically she woke the bum who demanded a dollar for having his nap ruined. She gave him the white paper bag containing a remaining beignet and he seemed happy with that. Nell moved out of the park and along the broken walkways propelling the stroller so fast Deanie's head wobbled. He was howling by the time she reached the condominium complex. She took a moment to pick him up and give comfort while Gregory brought the stroller to her door.

Inside, the phone rang. Nell hesitated to pick up. If the press called, she could take Stevie's advice and give them a terse statement that she was very happy with her marriage. The voice on the other end, however, spoke with Althea Alexander's mellow contralto.

"Mrs. Billodeaux, you need someone to listen this morning? Is there trouble in River City, honey?"

"Honestly, I don't know. Joe warned me a problem might be coming up, but I never expected my sister to be involved. She comes on to Joe all the time, but it's just her way of getting at me. Joe and I, we joke about it. I saw them at Thanksgiving in the barn."

"Doing what, dear?"

"Talking, but Emily had her hand on Joe's arm. She was rubbing it."

"Circumstantial evidence, I'd say."

"I need to go over to the training center and meet the bus from the airport. This can't wait."

"Want me to come over and watch the *bebe*? It's too fine a day to spend behind a mountain of paperwork. I can justify it as a home visit. After those headlines, no one will question me."

"I'd appreciate that. Truly, I would."

When she disconnected, Nell kept the phone in hand. She could make one call before she met her husband. "Hello, Emily. I need to know what's going on between you and Joe."

****

Thumping the folded tabloid against her leg, Nell sat near the entry to the training center. She stayed slightly apart from the other wives and they honored her isolation.

"You see this, Precious?" Sharlette Dobbs whispered. She surreptitiously showed her friend the front page of the tabloid held by her side. "That dawg did it with Nell's own sister and then celebrated in public."

Nell overheard but pretended not to notice. Jason Forte, newly out of his cast, spotted Nell as he came from the gym after working on his leg. He sat next to her and leaned over close to say, "Looks like Joe Dean has put his foot in some shit again, and this time the PR people will have trouble to putting a positive spin on the mess. Joe's fight to keep the baby and his marriage to a sweet, cancer-surviving wife has gotten all kinds of positive publicity. The fans ate it up. Hell, they hung banners over the railings in the Dome reading 'We're on your Side, Daddy Joe' or 'Win one for Nell and Dean.' Pretty sad he couldn't keep it in his pants, huh? Waiting to give hell to the old man?"

"Something like that," Nell said.

"You know, that's some sister you have there. Em and I got it on a few times after some of the Sinners' parties. Lazy though. After I broke the leg, I didn't see her again. She didn't want to do all the work. Joe says you're twice the woman she is even if you are smaller."

Nell stared at the door and willed Joe to arrive and make things better. Jared slid even closer and put one arm on the back of Nell's seat. "Ole Joe, he said I'd never get the chance to compare the two of you, but I don't know. I can't think of a better way to get even with a cheating hubby than to take a ride over to my place."

Nell stood up to move away without answering, but Forte seemed to take that as a yes. He put a steering hand on her elbow and a heavy arm around her shoulders and push-shoved them toward the exit to the parking lot. Nell dug in her heels, but on the slick surface they were crossing, it made no difference. Forte appeared to think of her resistance as part of the game. He swooped in to kiss the back of her neck and still nuzzled while Nell struggled to push him off with her elbows. The team bus pulled up with a screech of airbrakes.

Joe, shoving teammates aside, was the first off. He lunged straight for his wife and Jared Forte, separated them with one swipe of his arm and punched Forte in the jaw on the return. Forte slammed back into a concrete pylon and doubled over grasping his right arm.

"Goddamn, I think it's broken." Forte rocked back and forth cradling his receiving arm.

Coach Buck and Connor Riley got between the two men. The coach waved two trainers from the gathering crowd of Sinners, waiting wives and center staff. Riley held his friend back before Joe could make matters any worse.

"You trade that bastard, Coach! You trade him. It's him or me!" Joe shouted and jerked out of Connor's hold, but the Rev came up and grabbed the quarterback in a way that said he wasn't going anywhere.

"Get Forte in for X-rays," Coach Buck directed the

trainers. "Joe, you're out of line. Take your wife home. There will be disciplinary action for this whether you take us to the playoffs or not. No one tells me how to run my team."

Forte, grasping his arm and leaving behind a small puddle of puke, hustled off between the trainers. The Rev released his grip on Joe Dean. Joe shot forward to where Nell huddled in a small circle of team wives.

"How could you let that jerk touch you, Nell? How could you?" His arms flailed, but clearly he wasn't going to hit her.

"I thought I could shake him off, but he outweighs me by a hundred pounds," Nell answered biting off each word.

"Why didn't you yell? Why didn't you scream?" Joe shouted in her face.

Nell stood on her tiptoes and poked a finger into Joe's chest. "Because unlike you, I didn't want to make a scene." She punctuated each word with a jab.

"You tell him, sister," Sharlette Dobbs agreed.

"Stay out of this, Sharlette," Ace told his wife.

"Poke him again, honey, harder," Precious Armitage urged. "He done the dirty wit' yo' own flesh and blood."

"We going home, Precious. We all going home," Calvin Armitage ordered. "Go on, y'all get outta here." Calvin had a talent for moving folks. The crowd broke up. He steered his own wife across the street to where his van waited in the parking lot. His two youngest children had their wide-eyed heads sticking out the window.

Sharlette Dobbs left still fussing, "He cheated on her with her own kin. I'd kill you, Ace, if you done me that way."

"All your kin is ugly, baby. You the only pretty one." Ace kept her moving.

Finally, only Joe and Nell remained with Connor and the Rev standing by. "You can go, guys," Joe told them in a calmer voice. "I have some explaining to do."

"Yes, yes, you have, Joe Dean Billodeaux." Nell thwacked him with the tabloid.

Let him dare touch her or pull her up to his level and give her a kiss, and she'd sock him in the balls.

"I asked you to believe in me, Tink. That hurts. Truly." Joe rubbed his chest as if he had heartburn.

"You could have told me this involved Emily. The worst part was seeing you and my sister together celebrating with that bitch of a lawyer while I sat home with Deanie like the naïve little wife. I called Em for an explanation." Nell blinked her eyes rapidly to hold in the tears.

Joe rubbed his chest again. "What did she say?"

"She said you had lunch together and shared a bottle of wine. She said you didn't want to tell me anything until after Christmas, but I was in for a shock. Nicole Everard is handling all the details. Then, she hung up and wouldn't answer again."

"Let me thank Emily for making things so clear to you. Damn her! Who's watching Dean?" He looked around for someone holding the baby.

"Mrs. Alexander came over."

"That's just great. Mary, Jesus and Joseph, I could use some help here. Ride with me."

Joe led the way to his Porsche. Nell got in before he could open the door for her. He fought the traffic and made his way up shady Esplanade toward City Park.

Turning in at the pillars, he parked behind the art museum and beckoned Nell to come with him toward the lagoon as he searched for a quiet, romantic spot. This near the water, he figured could either dive right in and tell her, or drown himself if she rejected him.

He guided her to a bench by a broken oak hanging out over the water. Ducks roosting on the trunk started up a soft quacking full of hope for an offering of stale bread. He had nothing to give them rich as he was. He must explain somehow.

"Those mallards are like the Billodeaux men before they get married—always chasing any females who will have them. See the pair of swans swimming over there?"

Nell nodded. "Birds that big and beautiful are hard to miss. Everyone admires and loves them. No one notices that little night heron in the reeds, all small and brown."

"Well, night herons make a good gumbo so I wouldn't say they are overlooked by Cajuns, but let me make my point here. I was talking about swans. They mate for life, you know. That's how the Billodeaux men are *after* they marry. Faithful to their mates. Swans build a great big nest together and produce eggs and offspring."

"Joe, I may be small, but I am not a child. What are you trying to tell me?"

"Nell, I asked Emily to donate her eggs so we could try in vitro one day. I wanted you to be able to give birth to your own baby. We reached an agreement. That's what the so-called celebration was about."

"Oh, Joe, you didn't! Em donated bone marrow for me. I can't ask anything more of her. Mom was away from home taking care of me when she got her first period."

Joe held up a hand. "I know. Don't want to hear that story again."

"She didn't get to go to the prom or attend LSU because of me."

"Heard it all before."

"Isn't Dean enough for you?"

"I did it for you, Nell. You deserve to have your own baby."

"Dean is my baby now. Joe, if we ever consider in vitro, and it's far too early in our marriage for that, I'd rather we found some other donor."

"Too late. I signed the contract before I left this last time."

"Contract? You have a contract with Em?"

"That's where Nicole Everard comes in. Emily hired her to negotiate the price."

"You are paying my sister to do this?"

Joe shuffled his feet in the brown, fallen leaves of the oak and stared at the pool. "I think she'll be more pissed if we try to back out now. She wants the money so she can, this is a quote, 'shake the shit of Loo-siana off my shoes and never come back.' She has other stipulations, too. She wants the procedure done in the next six months because she isn't staying around here forever to serve us, and she'll do this only once. I said okay."

"Without asking me! Joe, human eggs don't freeze well. This will be a waste of your money and her time."

"I know. I've been reading up. See, you fertilize the eggs and implant or freeze the resulting embryos. It works best if the woman is young and the embryos are fresh."

"I know all that," Nell snapped. "Don't you think I did my own reading?"

"For all you've done for me and Deanie, I wanted to give you the best Christmas gift I could imagine, a child of your own, and a brother or sister for Dean— maybe more than one. Nell, you might think of yourself as small and ordinary, but you are the strongest and best woman I know. Hell, you've taken me on for life, and that's no easy task. I love you so much I'd give you the world if I could."

She hugged him around his slim middle and laid her head on his chest where she could hear his heart beat strong and steady. How could she deny him this?

"Okay. We'll give it a try in March when Deanie is a little older and the football season is over, but don't get your hopes up. The success rate is less than fifty percent. If this does work, I guess I won't be the first woman to have children a year apart in age."

Joe kissed her so hard Nell fell back on the bench. The startled ducks quacked as loudly as applause and took wing over the still water. Mrs. Alexander would be thrilled to know she did not have to report a failed marriage or find another home for Dean.

Chapter Twenty-Six

"If my man said he wanted to give me a baby for Christmas, I'd just have to kill him," Precious Armitage swore. "Don't think I couldn't do it either. Why I'd wait until he was nice and relaxed in bed, then I'd put my hands around that thick neck of his and smother him to death in my bosoms."

Precious demonstrated by pushing two huge brown fists against her enormous breasts covered in a holiday red sweater where Rudolph's red nose popped out on top of one nipple. Recent pictures of baby Dean went flying from her fingers. She picked them up one by one: bright-eyed Deanie clutching a handful of white beard as he sat on Santa's lap at the mall; Deanie on his belly among a mountain of gifts beneath the ten foot spruce his daddy special ordered from the Chapelle Optimists Club to decorate the new house; Deanie pushing up and giving a sloppy smile to the camera as drool pooled on a plush toy polar bear.

"Not that Joe Dean Billodeaux don't make a beautiful child, but this one is only four months old. You may not have given birth to the boy, Nell, but it ain't hardly time to have another when this one hasn't cut his teeth yet—or been potty-trained."

Word of Nell's extraordinary Christmas gift had gotten out, though none of the financial details such as the extraordinary price paid for the donor eggs were revealed. Joe Dean had taken care of that with a privacy clause binding Emily Abbott and her lawyer to silence. If they talked, they forfeited the second million regardless of the results of the procedure. Nell's jealous sister kept her pouty lips sealed shut and reaped praise from both families for her unselfish deed.

The team played on the road this weekend, so Nell took the opportunity to invite any wives not traveling to Utah to see the mansion built by the Sinners' quarterback and enjoy the game as a group. She tried hard to fit in with the other football player's wives, who for the most part were tall, blonde and beautiful which made her feel even shorter, darker, and below average in looks—but not in brains. She did have a master's degree in child psychology. Still, she thanked heaven people like Precious Armitage existed in this group.

The Sinners had their division sewed up tight but still had to meet the Salt Lake Saints in the last game of the year. The sports commentators always loved this match up if for no other reason than the numerous jokes they could make about the Saints playing the Sinners.

The women took over Joe's leathery den with its wall-filling hi-def television, easy to clean slate floors and close proximity to what Nell called the Sinners' bar and buffet. Not a single dainty sandwich graced the table. For starters, Nadine brought a two-gallon pot of turkey-sausage gumbo. Joe smoked and sliced two briskets before leaving the state. He would be surprised at how little of it was left when he returned. Bowls of chips and chili dip sat within easy reach. A bowl of creamy slaw served as the main side dish. Vegetable trays were available for any woman who couldn't get into the high-calorie spirit of the day. More than a few of the wives were mildly buzzed on iced beer and hot, spiced wine by the time they got to the Sinners' dessert table with its triple layer chocolate cake, sugary pecan pie and rich ice creams, neither fat free nor sugarless, with five possible toppings.

Nell sat cross-legged on one of the bright, washable throw rugs scattered around the room. She took a spoonful of chocolate cake capped with country vanilla ice cream, chocolate syrup, whipped topping, crushed pecans and a maraschino cherry, swallowed and gestured at the screen.

"I wish Stevie could be here." Connor Riley's wife was tall, blonde and gorgeous, too, but different since she was a sports photographer who could hold her own with the boys.

"Yeah, that girl can eat like a horse, then run it off doing her job, but she got this thang about being down there by the field when Connor plays. Thinks it helps him win. Look there, you can just see her ponytail bobbing behind the bench," said Precious Armitage stretched out in Joe's recliner.

With a bottle of beer in one hand and a plate of corn chips and chili dip at her fingertips, she did a fine job of filling Joe's space. "Aw, shit, Muhammad's done got the ball. Wake up, Calvin! Kick yo' boys' asses. They should have had him. Come on Rev, move that fine behind. We could use a turnover right now."

Mintay Bullock, light-skinned and usually serene, her medical beeper slung from a belt loop, took a sip of her ginger ale, then chastised Precious. "Don't be yelling at my man. He got that touchdown with his interception in the second quarter."

The Sinners hung on to a 17-10 lead into the fourth

quarter. While the commentators acknowledged the Saints were the weaker team, they threw out the possibility that intense rivalry might spur the underdogs to excel. Muhammad caught a second pass, sprinted across the goal line and did his little boogey dance for the roaring home crowd. The extra point was good. Tied game.

The wives, crammed on the sofa and sitting on the floor, groaned collectively. A few got up to use the powder room while Joe Dean and the offense trotted out on to the field and commercials filled the screen.

"What do you think, Al? Are we going into overtime, or will Joe Dean Billodeaux pull off a two minute blitz?" the commentator asked his companion in the booth.

"The blitz is Billodeaux's specialty, but he's down two receivers with Jared Forte back on the injured list and their first round draft pick running back proving to be mighty fragile and still out with hamstring problems. Fullerton's getting long in the tooth for this kind of play. Might be his last season with the Sinners. As for Riley and Deets, the Saints' defense will be covering them like blankets and hoping for an interception."

"I'll tell you, Al, Joe Dean hasn't been the fireball quarterback we saw last year. There have been rumors he might have been responsible for Forte's off-field broken arm. A hot temper can come back to haunt you."

"Judging by the big fine levied on Billodeaux that was no rumor. Let's see if being rash costs his team the game, Hank."

Nell cupped her hands around her mouth and shouted "Boooo!" at the sportscasters. The team wives took up the cry almost drowning out the next words.

"But Billodeaux has shown a steadiness we haven't seen in him before. Game after game, he pulls out those fourth quarter victories. Marriage and settling down must agree with him."

"Sorry about the boo, Al," Nell apologized to the screen.

Sharlette Dobbs sighed. "I wish Ace would break someone's arm for me, and say he doesn't care how much it cost him the way Joe Dean did."

"Don't wish. The fine was doubled after he said that. We have a child to put through college, you know," Nell chided.

"And another one soon to be on the way if you leave it up to Joe with all his candle-lighting nonsense," Mintay added.

"Fine could of been a lot worse, but half the team saw that dawg, Forte, mauling our girl here. Sure way to cause trouble on the team, going after another man's wife." Precious leaned forward to watch the action on the big screen.

"Here's the play. Two men on Riley, one on top of Deets. Fullerton's down, Billodeaux has no openings and decides to run it himself. He's down hard at the forty-five yard line. He could have fallen over and gained as much yardage. Second down."

"Booo!" Nell screamed again.

"Billodeaux is searching for a receiver and is sacked. Loss of two yards, third down and too far back for the field goal. Should punt, but no, Joe Dean is going for it again. Not a good decision on his part, Al. Deets and Riley shake free."

Sharlette Dobbs shot from her armchair as the camera homed in on Joe Dean dancing in the pocket, searching for a target.

"Ace is open, Joe! Throw to Ace!"

As if her shriek could be heard in Salt Lake, Joe glanced to his right and homed in on the dependable Asa Dobbs who had finished his blocking and punched through the opposing line to clear space. Joe lobbed a short pass into the tight end's hands. Ace, startled as if he had gotten the gift of a lifetime handed to him, took off, lumbering down the field toward the goal.

Connor Riley stopped searching the sky for the football, shoved one of his guards to the ground and went after the other. Deets threw his cover aside. The wide receivers opened a corridor for their slower teammate to charge through. Ace crossed the line and executed a ball spike, a short duck walk and three leaps in the air before being engulfed by the congratulations of most of the Sinner's offensive team.

"Excessive celebration? I think not, Al. Asa Dobbs scores his first touchdown for the Sinners."

"Al, baby, you don't know what celebration is. Just wait 'til Ace gets home." Sharlette swung Nell around in a wide circle while Ancient Andy Mortenson came on to the field and kicked the extra point as the buzzer sounded.

Some of the wives went in search of their children being entertained outside by Cassie and two of Joe Dean's older nieces. Nell offered sleeping space to anyone who felt they couldn't drive home but got no takers. Sharlette Dobbs remained glued to the screen for the post-game interviews.

Joe Dean, as usual, got the first word and gave it away. "I think the man you need to speak to is right over there." He pointed to the beaming Asa Dobbs.

"Deanie, tell Mommy that Daddy is on his way home." Joe gave a tiny wave to the camera.

"Awww," Precious Armitage said pushing out of her seat. "I guess I see why you couldn't turn that man down for wanting another baby, Nell."

"Hush, Precious." Sharlette Dobbs leaned forward to take in Ace's every word.

"I'd do it again if I got the chance, you know. Man needs to have a chance. I keep my mind on the game all season. That's how I am. And, uh—hi to my lovely lady, Sharlette."

Sharlette leaped into the air. "Did you hear? He said my name on the TV. Ace, honey, you in for the welcome of your life."

"Why don't I help clean up, Nell? Sharlette needs to get over her high before we hit the road with a van full of kids." Precious began collecting bottles and empty glasses.

"Unlike you, Precious Armitage, I have not been drinking. You know how many calories there is in a light beer?" Sharlette Dobbs ran her delicate mocha-colored hands down her slim hips.

"Know how much nourishment there is in lettuce, yo' scrawny thang?" Precious shot back. "Hoping Ace is gonna notice you during the season? You in for a disappointment, I declare."

"If he does notice, he'll love the view." Sharlette snatched up a stack of plates and sashayed for the kitchen, her slender rear swinging.

"Humpf. My Calvin likes a woman with a substantial behind. Told me so often. Childbearing hips, that's what I got. Had four babies practically fall out of me." Precious, carrying twice Sharlette's load, headed off to the dishwasher.

Nell eyed Mintay. They burst into laughter. Nell wiped her eyes on the edge of a napkin. Suddenly, she turned sober. "Mintay, do you think I'll have trouble with childbirth?"

"You are tiny, but it's what's inside that counts. Even though Joe is a big guy, the size of the mother often limits the size of the fetus. Once the child is born, their genetics kick in and the baby grows like wildfire. You know Joe is praying for twins? That's another issue altogether, but I'd say cross that bridge when and if you come to it." Mintay gave Nell a reassuring hug.

"Twins? He expects twins? Mintay, I think we'll be lucky to get even one child out of all this in vitro business."

"Oh, Joe didn't tell you he made a deal with St. Jude? He'll dedicate his next, and according to Joe, imminent, Super Bowl to him if you conceive twins. Can you believe it?"

Nell looked stunned. "I often feel like I'm in over my head with the Billodeaux family. What if I disappoint them?"

"Not your problem, honey. I say put your faith in modern medicine. The Rev would tell you not to discount prayer. Whatever will be, will be, and none of it is your fault. You understand me?"

"Thanks for the pep talk. I'm already edgy, and I haven't even taken the hormone shots yet."

"So, if you are going through with the I-V, I'd guess you aren't going back to work at Ochsner?"

"I called Joe Brunner before Christmas and told him I wouldn't be back. He has an eager intern waiting in the wings so it wasn't much of a problem for him. He said he saw it coming, to have a nice life. I think about all the seriously ill children I could help and feel guilty lying around in luxury." Nell gestured to the spacious den and game room.

"You know, Nell, the Chapelle Clinic doesn't have one psychologist that will work pro bono for us. I have sick people who have to go all the way to Lafayette to get help. Most won't do it because they have no transportation or think talking to someone won't do any good. If you want a job on your own terms, I can offer you one."

"I accept. Thanks, Mintay."

The gumbo pot crashed to the floor in the kitchen. "Sharlette, I said to move yo' skinny ass."

"Get your big butt out my way, Precious!"

"I think we had better go and referee before any arms get broken." Mintay led the way toward the gumbo calamity.

"Or asses kicked," Nell added.

****

Nell helped strap children into the Armitage van and waved the last of her guests down the lane, the noise of Precious and Sharlette still bickering ringing in her ears. Mintay left her with a hug and an open offer to listen whenever Nell wanted to talk. The party hostess walked over to the barn to pay off her babysitters.

Joe's nieces were grooming the two tired ponies who dozed under the curry combs like ladies getting a massage at a spa. Copperhead gleamed in his stall. Fatima, who had not been allowed out since Joe said she showed signs of coming into season, shifted restlessly around her box. L.B. had been put out to pasture for showing too much interest in the mare, but when he whinnied from his enclosure, Fatima encouraged him with an answer.

Nell stroked the mare's nose and gave her a sugar cube. "He's not your type, Fatty, too big and over-confident. Look at it this way, no weight gain, no labor pains, no problem."

She paid off the girls giving them forty dollars each, twice what they expected, and looked around for Cassie.

"She said she was tired and went back to MawMaw's house after she finished grooming Copperhead. We let the little kids time her when she did the barrel course. She's real good, but she wouldn't let anyone else ride Copperhead—just like he was hers and not Uncle Joe's horse. I could be that good, too, if I had a ten thousand dollar horse already trained," the younger niece tattled.

"Copperhead cost ten thousand dollars!"

The knowledgeable 4-Hers nodded. "Could have been more for a really great barrel horse, but I heard PawPaw tell Uncle Joe he should take it out of Cousin Bijou's salary for not getting permission to buy Copperhead in the first place."

Unwilling to encourage little pitchers with big ears, Nell shrugged it off. "I'm sure Joe and Bijou worked it out. I'll drive you home."

****

Returning from Eenie's farm, Nell passed her in-laws' house and was tempted to stop and reclaim Deanie, but his grandmother had been firm about her having a good time with her guests and getting a nice, long night's rest. They'd switch the baby for the gumbo pot tomorrow. Then, Nell would have to explain the dent in the cookware, the result of the Precious-Sharlette debacle. She put that off by driving directly back to Lorena Ranch where the house seemed too large and the bed too big whenever Joe was gone. Funny, everything appeared just the right size when her husband stayed home. He filled whole rooms with real friends and family, his imaginary children and dreams for the future.

Nell kept herself busy cleaning up the last of the party mess and even vacuuming up fallen needles from the Christmas tree close to midnight since she had no baby to wake in the house. Finally, she climbed into the king-sized bed that felt as cold as the silver moon hanging over the bayou and barren cane fields without Joe's heat next to her. Nell tossed half the night.

Still, she must have slept since the roar of a big engine and slamming truck doors woke her in the pre-dawn hours before the late winter sun crept over the horizon. Must be Bijou, she thought, coming back from a Sunday night binge. Or maybe, he was showing up early to do some assigned chore that had gone undone and had to be finished before Joe got home. The neigh of horses and the sound of hooves clattering on the trailer ramp confirmed the last guess. Nell pulled the covers up, put the pillow over her head and went back to sleep.

At half past ten in the morning, Nell finally crawled out of bed and dressed. She called Nadine in an attempt to reclaim her son, but Frank answered. Evidently, Deanie had been taken along to his MawMaw's Home Demonstration Club, a group degenerating over the years into a sewing and gossip get-together. Feeling the emptiness of the large house,

Nell put on a light jacket, went outside and wandered down the lane to see if the mail had come. She received a better package than the U. S. mail could have delivered: Joe turned the Porsche into their drive. Nell slid into the passenger seat and gave her husband a warm welcome home kiss.

"You're early!"

"What? Afraid I'll catch you messing around with Bijou? I left as soon as the team meeting ended. Didn't even go back to the condo. We get a few days off for the New Year with our families, then start training for the playoffs. But what have you done with my son, woman?"

"He's been kidnapped by your mother. I can't seem to get him back."

"Hmmmm. All alone and nothing to do."

Joe parked the Porsche in front of the mansion, threw his bag into the hall, and pressed his wife up against one of the substantial pillars of the verandah. Caught between hard surfaces, Nell pulled Joe's head back by the hair from its nuzzling place between her breasts.

"Bijou or your mom could drive up at any minute."

"Then, how about a walk in the woods?"

"We have a perfectly good bed upstairs. It felt so empty last night."

"Mine, too, but we can do it in bed anytime. Come on. Let's walk to the meadow."

"Least you forget, the meadow is now L.B.'s pasture where you exiled him before you left for Salt Lake. No more tall weeds, just a fine mixture of the best grasses for our stud."

"This Cajun boy knows lots of good places out that

way." He drew her around the side of the house toward the bayou path.

As they neared the meadow, they heard the scream of a horse, not a gentle whinny or a friendly neigh, but a scream. Joe dropped Nell's hand and took off at a speed she had no chance of matching. He stood at the fence cursing the act in progress when Nell caught up with him.

L.B. mounted a trembling Fatima. The pudgy little mare rolled her eyes and let out another scream of either pain or passion, difficult to tell which. The big red stallion held her neck with his teeth. His flanks heaved against her hindquarters and raised tail, both horses white-eyed and frothing.

"Joe, do something! He's going to kill her!"

"L.B. doesn't have killing on his mind, and Fatty isn't trying to kick him off. In the equine world, this is how it's done. I might kill Bijou though. How in hell did the mare get in here? Even if she got out of the stall, she's sure no jumper."

"I heard the truck before dawn. Maybe he was drinking and got confused."

"Confused, my ass. This was deliberate, and it's too late to do anything about it now. Looks like we're gonna have a little half-Arab foal come this time next year. Won't be the first one ever born, but I would rather have gone with insemination by some good Arab stud if we planned to breed Fatima. This is hard on the mare and sometimes both horses get marked up. Though by the look of him, L.B. isn't worried about a few scars on his beautiful hide right now."

They watched until the stallion disengaged from the mare, his impressive organ dangling close to the

257

ground until he gradually retracted it. Fatima eyed him and sidled away. After a few more nervous glances, the mare settled herself in the far corner of the pasture and began to graze on a lush clump of clover sprouting through the dull winter grasses.

"That's that, I guess. No post-coital cuddling in the horse world. Should we get Fatima out of there?" Nell asked, her eyes still wide from what she had witnessed, her pulse still pounding.

"No hurry now. In fact, I know a place just over in those woods under a big live oak where it's all mossy and easy on the knees. Want to try it their way?" Joe gave her a hungry grin.

"Joe, I'm not sure…"

He swept her up and trotted for the woods to the place where the moss grew in a thick cushion beneath the oak and a position on all fours was not uncomfortable. Joe had her jeans and panties down off her backside and his hands under her T-shirt before Nell could raise any more doubts. One of his large hands loosened her bra and fondled. The other ran a finger between her legs. She grew peaked and wet.

"Don't try to tell me you're not aroused, Tink."

"I am. I'm a little embarrassed about admitting it."

"No more talk, but you can scream if you want. It won't wake the baby."

He took her neck in his teeth and plunged into her. They heaved and panted together until she did scream, a sound that made L.B. and Fatima face the woods and Snowballs bellow as he guarded his harem of cows. Still only half unclothed, Joe and Nell relaxed against the cool moss. She ran her hand under his shirt, through the hair on his chest, then down to give a tender stroke to his flaccid penis. Joe cupped her backside and pulled her closer because people did enjoy a post-coital cuddle even if livestock did not. They stayed that way longer than they should have.

"Joe Dean, where you at, son? I got a baby here wants his daddy." Nadine's voice coming in their direction penetrated the woods.

Joe snapped Nell up and took care of his own problems, even kicking a few divots of moss back into place before leading his wife toward the pasture. They met up with his mama and a chortling Deanie who rode high on MawMaw's shoulders, his hands clamped in her thick salt-and-pepper hair, enjoying the bumpy ride along the bayou path.

"There's my boy. Come to Daddy." Joe held out his moss-stained hands.

"Don't you put those dirty hands on this nice clean baby. What on earth you been doing?" Nadine gave Nell the once over from the green on her hands and the knees of her jeans to the dead leaves in her hair. "Looks like something bit you on the neck. You got a big red mark."

Nell shrugged her neck down into the collar of her top and ran her fingers through her short hair. Forest debris floated to the ground. "Ah, looking for mushrooms?" she suggested.

"Only one big mushroom prob'ly came up in those woods. Aw, what's it matter. You married—but not in the church, of course. When you gonna take care of that, Joe?"

Joe ignored his mother and turned toward the pasture. He clucked to Fatima and held out a handful of clover. The mare came to the gate without a fuss, accepted the clover and allowed herself be led away by the halter as if she had lost all interest in the stallion who paced along the fence line snorting and whinnying suggestively. Nadine, nattering away at her son, braced Deanie with her hands and followed. Nell brought up the rear. She cast a sympathetic glance at L.B. who let loose with a deep-throated groan.

"You're not the only one who had their afternoon interrupted, so get over it," she suggested to the stallion.

While Joe put Fatima in her stall, Nell washed up in the family-sized kitchen with its warm cypress cabinets and matching trestle table possessing enough seats for a clan gathering. Nadine settled Deanie in his baby seat and tickled his belly. While the baby squirmed, she told him, "You gettin' too heavy for old MawMaw to carry so far, yes, you are."

Nell started placing yesterday's party leftovers on the table, half a bowl of slaw, the pitiful remains of the brisket, a quarter of chocolate cake. If she had a big appetite after their activities, she could imagine Joe being voracious by now.

"You want I should wake Cassie for lunch? Those teenagers sure can sleep when they got vacation and this one's always sleepy," Nadine claimed.

"Must be all that barrel racing. It's quite a workout. Cassie came over with you?"

"No, *cher,* she said she was stayin' here las' night. I figured that's why you went from the house to fool around 'cause she was still sleeping."

"Eenie's girls said she went to your place."

The same thought passed between the two women. Nadine voiced it. "That no good Bijou!"

Joe slammed into the kitchen. "Truck's gone,

trailer's gone. Copperhead and the two ponies are missing."

"Add Cassie to that list," Nell told him.

"This was nailed to Fatima's stall." Joe shoved a sheet of paper torn from a spiral notebook at Nell. In bold, black marker, it read: Get Fucked Joe Dean and Your Fancy Mare Too.

Nadine read over Nell's shoulder. "Such language!"

"God, what a mess." Joe picked up a phone. "Bijou isn't answering his cell."

"It's been at least six hours since I heard the truck, Joe. They could be in Texas. Isn't there some town across the state line that provides quickie marriages? But Cassie is only sixteen!"

"If anyone has the contacts to get her a fake ID, that would be Bijou. Hell, he got one for me when I was sixteen so I could bar-hop with him." Joe ran a hand through his hair.

"Joe Dean Billodeaux, you didn't!" Nadine said, outraged by the sins of the past.

"Too late now, Ma. Call Aunt Flo up at Toledo Bend and ask if she knows anything."

Nadine made the call. "Nuttin'. Says she's afraid Bijou got his self in trouble again. She don't want you to call the law on him."

"Ma, if it was only the horses and the truck, I wouldn't give a damn, but he's ruining a young girl's life here. We call the sheriff."

"Maybe they went to Cassie's family," Nell offered without a hope that it might be true.

"Call." Joe held out the phone.

"Mrs. Thomas? Put your mother on the line, please.

It's Nell. Has Cassie called you today? She hasn't come home, has she? I'm so sorry to tell you this, but it looks like your daughter ran away with Joe's cousin and a trailer load of horses."

Nell held the phone inches from her ear as the outrage broke loose. Then calmly, she said, "We're calling the sheriff now. Maybe he'll issue an Amber Alert. Please call around to Cassie's friends and see if they know anything. I'm so sorry. Yes, I know we're responsible." She disconnected, anguish apparent on her face.

A half hour later, the parish sheriff in person sat at the kitchen table with a glass of iced tea and a brisket sandwich in front of him. A deputy took notes describing the girl, her abductor and the stolen truck and horses.

"I'll try for a statewide Amber Alert, but the girl is sixteen and doesn't appear to have been coerced. Heck, they could be married by now and holed up in some no-tell motel in Texas. Great brisket, Joe Dean."

The sheriff wiped his chin to clear it of the slaw dressing seeping from the sandwich. "The child probably won't thank us when we do find them. Can't really hide horses and a big rig like that too well."

"Maybe they aren't eloping," Nell offered hopefully. "Cassie had some dreams about going on the rodeo circuit as a barrel racer. Would you like some cake and coffee?" Nell added, willing to butter up the lawman with any food available.

"Sure would. Well, there isn't much rodeo this time of year with the holidays and all. Even rodeo bums like to be home with their families. If they plan to do the circuit, we'll probably find them easy enough in a couple of months."

Sheriff LeDoux, son of the previous holder of that office, studied Cassie's parochial school picture. "That red hair and all those freckles should be easy to spot. The horse is distinctive, too." He studied the photograph of Cassie astride Copperhead and threw it on the table along side of Bijou's mug shot. "A ten-thousand dollar horse. Gaw, Joe Dean. You give that animal to a kid to ride?"

"Bijou found the horse for her. Said it was a young animal and well-trained, a bargain for the price."

"Well, Bijou does know his horses. I suppose he was right." Sheriff LeDoux blotted his mustache with a napkin and accepted a mug of coffee. He adjusted the brew's blackness with two heaping spoonfuls of sugar and a quarter cup of milk. "I just hope it is young love or a desire to rodeo, not white slavery. Bijou knows a lot of unsavory characters."

"Lord Jesus and Mary," Nadine gasped, crossing herself.

"Let's hope for the best," Nell said.

"Pray to God and hope," Nadine amended.

Chapter Twenty-Seven

January passed, though not in the way sports commentators and the tabloids figured. Cheap papers made the most of the latest scandal involving Joe Dean Billodeaux. *"Convict Cousin Abducts Teenage Girl from Billodeaux Ranch"* the banners shouted. The press chastised Joe Dean for allowing a child dying from cancer to be on his ranch alone with an ex-con who obviously had child molestation tendencies. The articles neglected to mention Bijou's offenses ran mostly to drunk driving and being caught with stolen goods, or that Cassie was in remission and had gone with the man willingly. Joe didn't care. He sent them the picture of Cassie aboard Copperhead and asked them to run it on the first page. Anything that would get Cassie back, he would do.

The sports commentators did not dwell on the sordid details. Instead, they predicted this newest upheaval in Billodeaux's life would affect his game adversely, and the Sinners would not make it past the first round of the playoffs. How wrong they were. Joe played with a steely determination. When the Sinners wiped out their first opponents, 34-10, Hank and Al admitted to being astounded. On-the-field reporters offered the quarterback hearty congratulations and asked what had driven him on to crush the other team.

"Every time we win big, I get air time with you

guys." Joe held up a picture of Cassie that was curled and limp with sweat. "I carried this with me all through the game. We need to find this young lady and bring her home. If anyone out there sees Cassie Thomas, call the Ste. Jeanne Parish sheriff's office with the information or contact the Sinners organization at this number immediately." Joe rattled off the phone number of the home office. In successive games, the number aired on the screen. The network said they would do it whether the Sinners won or not, but the Sinners did not lose.

The Sinners ruled all the way up to the Super Bowl. They restored the tradition of Super Bowl games being one-sided blowouts. Their defense held their rivals to one touchdown and a field goal. Riley carried for two scores, Deets for one and Ancient Andy couldn't seem to miss an extra point. Safely ahead, Joe tossed the ball to slow, but strong and reliable Asa Dobbs who took it home using the same play they'd worked against the Saints in the last game of the year. The Rev did his interception thing twice and ran one all the way for a sixty-two yard touchdown. The final score, 35-10.

With Nell tucked to his side and a beaming six-month old Deanie held in the crook of his very valuable arm, Joe Dean used most of his post-game MVP time to plead for the return of Cassie Thomas. At the last moment, he remembered.

"Oh, I want to give credit to Coach Buck and a great, great team. I also want to dedicate this win to St. Jude who sent me my wife, my son and hopefully, many children to come. Go Jude!" He raised his left arm and punched the air over Nell's head.

The bemused reporter responded as best he could. "That was the always interesting Joe Dean Billodeaux, this year's Super Bowl MVP. Let's see what Coach Marty Buck has to say about his team winning two consecutive Super Bowls out of three. Are the Sinners becoming a football dynasty?" He motioned for a cut to Coach Buck.

The Super Bowl public relations people considered all this emphasis on a missing girl a downer for the festivities, but Joe had steadfastly refused to participate in all the pre-game press conferences and publicity events unless he could have a few minutes for his cause. Since Billodeaux was what the crowds wanted, he got his time, even managing to put Cassie's parents on the air as well. Mrs. Thomas cried and begged Cassie to phone home. Her daughter did not call.

****

The first crumb on the trail leading to Cassie and Bijou came not from an informant, the private detective Joe Dean had hired, or the sheriff's department, but from Eenie's sharp-eyed girls. They claimed to have seen the ponies, Boo and Buttercup, at a street fair in Jeanerette.

"Save them from that cruel man," Eenie's daughters begged.

Joe called for a deputy, and they went racing in a squad car to check out the situation. At the carnival, Boo and Buttercup stood looking as tired and fly-specked as the rest of the rides. Boo, head down and eyes half closed and leaner than before, stood tethered to a rope ring. Buttercup trudged around the enclosure with a small, blonde child on her back. The little girl beat the sharp heels of her patent leather Mary Janes against the small mare's shaggy flanks. "Make him go faster!" she demanded of the carnie who held the lead rope.

"This hoss don't go no faster," the man told his customer. The ash from a cigarette held in one corner of his mouth dropped on the girl's frilly dress as he answered.

As the threesome turned a corner, the operator caught sight of Joe Dean and the deputy. Joe curled back Boo's lip and showed a tattoo to the officer.

"Oh shit, we got trouble." The carnie rubbed his bristled chin with a grubby hand. "Knew it was too fucking good to be true."

The mama, mortally offended by his language, huffed with enough force to move Buttercup's mane. As soon as they reached the opening in the ring, she snatched her little darling from the shabby saddle, set her down and hustled away.

The old man tied the pony and sank down on a bale of hay placed just out of Boo's reach. He sighed as if life was about to deal him another low blow and ground out his cigarette in the dirt. "What can I do you for, officer?"

"Mr. Billodeaux says these are his horses."

"That'd be right. Joel Beam Billodeaux. Says so on the papers I got back in my trailer. I checked his license before I give him the three hundred dollars. We traded his ponies for mine plus the money. Said he needed cash, that's why he was willing. These two are younger and in better shape than the ones I had."

"Bijou," said Joe. "Was he traveling with a young girl?"

"Had a wife, he said, but I don't figure they was

married. She had a big ole ring like a man would wear on her finger, but it weren't no wedding band."

"Thin, red-headed, freckles?"

"Brown hair, not all that thin, but not a fatty. Didn't notice no freckles. You know how women cover things up. Runaway?"

"Yes."

The carnie shrugged. "I ran away when I was fourteen. Look at me now. You gonna take my ponies?"

The deputy nodded. "Stolen from the real owner here."

"Can't earn a living without my ponies."

"Do you know where they might have gone?"

"No idea," the pony ride man said, looking away.

Joe Dean held out a check. He let the carnie study the amount before drawing it back. "That would get you some new horses. It's a reward for information."

"Those two traveled with the carnival for a month or so. We teamed up for the pony rides and split the take. Had another horse, real fine animal the girl exercised every morning. He was too jumpy to give rides. A paint with blue eyes. They kept him out of sight when we worked a fair. Stolen, too?"

Joe Dean nodded.

"Anyways, they had a fancy double cab truck where they slept. Two of 'em left when we got up around Many. I think Joel said they had family around there."

"Aunt Flo and Uncle Hal. I'll throw in another hundred if you load up these ponies and follow us back to my place by Chapelle."

The carnie nodded. "Got nothing left to lose."

****

The private detective questioned Joe Dean's aunt and uncle at their fishing camp on Toledo Bend. He drove up in a plain car and walked around the cabin a while before knocking. Lamott Sanders was polite and discreet. Joe Dean Billodeaux paid him well to go easy on the old couple, but he would get the truth from them. He gave them a card and asked if he could come in as if he were selling life insurance, not tracking a crook and a runaway. In fact, he had sold life insurance after getting out of the military, but much preferred his current job. He maintained his brush cut and the bearing of a retired sergeant.

The old lady made coffee. The old man showed Sanders his collection of antique fishing lures. When the chitchat concluded, Lamott said he noticed they kept horses.

"No, no horses," Uncle Hal said. "A horse can eat you out of house and home."

"Lots of old manure around considering." Lamott gave them a friendly smile. "Grass and brush is all chewed back, too. Looks like a big truck and trailer were parked out back. Left grooves in your yard."

"We had visitors. Some relations with a mobile home," Flo said.

"Well, you know a young girl went missing with your son. They stole a truck, some horses, a trailer. Joe Dean Billodeaux is one of the most reasonable men I've ever met. He could have sent the sheriff here to question you, but he's not interested in arresting anyone. He just wants the girl home with her family. You must have seen the Super Bowl and how her mama was crying."

Hal and Flo exchanged looks. "Yes, we saw the

Super Bowl. We're real proud of Joe Dean."

"If the girl is still alive, do you know where we could find her?"

"Of course, she's alive. Our son wouldn't hurt a hair on Cassie's head. They're in love and want to be together. They were going to Texas to get married. Cassie is going to be a famous barrel racer one of these days, and Bijou is going to be her agent. Joe Dean is rich. Like you said, he doesn't care about losing a truck and a horse."

"So they stayed here a while?"

"Left two weeks ago. For Texas. To get married," Flo emphasized. "As soon as possible."

Lamott Sanders swore he checked with every Justice of the Peace in the Great State. Not one recognized the pictures he showed. None of the names in their records indicted a Thomas-Billodeaux union. He tried Las Vegas and Reno and came up dry.

Chapter Twenty-Eight

February, the short month, progressed at a more rapid rate than usual, it seemed to Nell. Nadine and Ann squabbled over who would get to keep Deanie in March while she and Joe stayed in Phoenix for what Emily kept calling the Grand Insemination. Finally, the grandmothers compromised on two weeks each with Nadine taking the first shift since she wanted to be free to organize a novena the nine days before the embryos were implanted to ensure a healthy birth.

Father Ardoin was uncertain a novena should be used for that purpose. Nearly two centuries ago, God had provided a miracle child for the aging Madame LeBlanc. Her descendants, one of them the famous baseball player, Smokey LeBlanc, still lived in Chapelle. Joe and Nell were young and could wait for the Lord to act in a more natural manner, he suggested.

"No, they can't, Father. Nell's sister, she says now or never, and we gonna use every one of those little frozen babies, ain't we, Joe Dean?" his mama asked, having dragged Joe, Nell and all her daughters with her to plead her cause.

"Every last one, even if we end up with a dozen kids. I swore a holy oath to St. Jude and the Blessed Virgin." Joe crossed himself. Nell nodded weakly.

Allie came on forcefully. "Now isn't this just another kind of miracle, Father?"

"Well, I suppose you could look at it that way, but…" Father Ardoin scratched his thinning hair. Caught up as he was in the history of his church and the romantic days of its past rather than in the thorny problems of modern dogma, he was known for allowing more slack than some priests.

"I'm sure Nell will let all the children be raised Catholic," Eenie persisted.

"I, ah, well, maybe," Nell managed to get out.

"I may be married to an unreliable drunk, but he gave me my children, Father. My kids are why I get up in the morning. What if Joe should get his neck broken playing football like that Connor Riley, but end up dead or paralyzed? This could be Nell's only chance," Lizzie asserted.

"We should trust in the Lord to…"

"And if you don't let us have the novena in the church, we'll do it at home. Maybe the *traiteur* will help us," Izzy threatened.

Father Ardoin's resistance crumbled as if he had been tackled by the entire Sinners' line. Never would he give way for some mumbo-jumbo herb healer. He booked the dates and times for the devotional services.

As the Billodeaux mob left his office, he overheard Nadine tell Izzy, "Good idea about that *traiteur*. I think Madame Leleux is pushin' a hundred and don't go out no more, but her granddaughter, she got the power. We can stop off on the way home and invite her. Maybe get Nell one of her special potions for havin' children. I hear they work almost as good as a novena."

Father Ardoin shook his head and sighed.

****

The entire caravan of trucks, vans, and sedans

belonging to the Billodeauxs left the church and made the short trip to a humble white frame house on a nearby side street. The vehicles took up half the block's parking. The slamming of many heavy doors disturbed the peace of the neighborhood. Female in-laws escorted Nell up the cracked front walk to a sagging porch barely strong enough to hold up a wheelchair ramp of more recent vintage.

Joe Dean, bringing up the rear, stopped in front of a statue of the Virgin Mary sheltered from the weather by a half a bathtub buried in the ground and painted sky blue on the inside. The marigolds of autumn had been uprooted and replaced by purple and yellow pansies planted in a neat semi-circle around the Virgin's feet. Whitewashed rocks set off the flowers from the rest of the yard. Joe leaned down and put a roll of bills under one of the rocks. He believed in paying up front for good fortune. Giving a dazzling smile to the middle-aged lady who welcomed the women, Joe sauntered in behind the group.

The essence of freshly baked oatmeal cookies filled the little house. Joe could see several dozen cooling on brown paper torn from grocery bags on the kitchen counters. His stomach rumbled. Mama had made them all go to early Mass on an empty stomach to get God on their side before tackling Father Ardoin.

Pleasantly plain and dumpy in her flowered dress, Madame Leleux's fifty-year-old granddaughter showed them to seats on the worn sofa. She pulled chairs from the kitchen to accommodate the overflow and with a wink to Joe, set down a platter of warm cookies on the coffee table with its varnish worn thin in spots.

"I put a big pot of coffee on a while ago. Granny

and me, we knew there would be lots of hungry company today."

"But we just decided to come a few minutes ago," Izzy said.

Giving an enigmatic smile worthy of the Mona Lisa, the granddaughter left the room to get the coffee tray and reappeared as neatly as a magician a moment later with the exactly nine cups and spoons, a pitcher of sweetened condensed milk and a matching sugar bowl hand-painted with lush pink roses.

"Oh so pretty," Nadine complimented, examining the sugar bowl.

"I paint ceramics and sell them in the shops around town. The tourists love my magnolia blossoms, you know." The *traiteur* settled in a comfortable chair with a bag of crochet work hanging from the padded arm and picked up a cookie to enjoy.

Nell raised her eyebrows at Joe who straddled one of the kitchen chairs. She appeared to be sending him a message saying, "If these ladies are so prescient, why don't they buy lottery tickets or play the horses instead of painting china and selling potions?"

"Oh, that wouldn't be allowed, you see. I'd lose the sight just like that if I used my power for gain." The *traiteur* snapped her fingers and oatmeal cookie crumbs went flying.

From the back of the house, a rusty voice called out. "Rosema-rie, come see."

"Granny. I don't know if she's up to seeing so many, but I'll ask. Please, help yourselves."

Rosemarie disappeared down a short dark hall. The click of a wheelchair being positioned reached the guests. "Raise up all you can, Granny."

Joe Dean popped his second cookie into his mouth and went to help. A few minutes later, he pushed the wheelchair out into the living room. Madame Leleux, dressed in a nightgown and what sagging flesh remained on her aged bones, joined the party. One palsied hand sought Joe's on the handles of her chair. "You have *un bon coeur*, Joe Dean Billodeaux."

She adjusted an afghan of yellow, blue, and white daisies across her lap, and tugged down the long sleeves of her flannel gown. Two small feet covered with heavy athletic socks peeked out from under its hem. "I get so cold, you know. Come, just the happy couple in the room for a reading."

"Oh, don't trouble yourself, Madame. We come for a fertility potion like the one you give me twenty-seven years ago. Rosemarie can get it for us," Nadine Billodeaux shouted into *traiteur's* old ears.

"I said I was cold, Nadine, not deaf. I will see them, Joe Dean and his bride."

Joe stared at his mother.

"What, you think I was gonna take a chance on having more girls wit' your daddy pining for a boy? How many kids was I gonna have tryin'?" Nadine took a slurp of her coffee and motioned to the sewing room where Madame Leleux dispensed her charms and her prophecies. "Go on, Nell, go on. Don't keep Madame waitin'. Go, go."

Joe pushed Madame to her place at the small, scarred table with the worn spots where many a sweating palm had rested. Her little brown bottles of potions identified by colored ribbons, red, purple, blue, yellow, deep rose, green, lavender and white, sat on the shelves behind her. Holy cards, pinned up two and three thick, covered the remaining walls. Red glass votive candleholders overflowed with the waxy drippings of countless years. When Nell seemed reluctant, Joe Dean thrust out his hand. Madame Leleux slapped it away.

"I give your fortune before you went off to college. *Beaucoup femme, beaucoup pousse-pousse,* so much women and money no man deserves, but God give it to you. Use it right from now on."

Joe Dean smiled sheepishly. "Yes, ma'am." He turned to Nell. "My friends and me, we came over here the day after graduation. Boy, were they ever jealous. Lots of women, lots of cash, she told me."

"That certainly came true," Nell answered tersely.

"Come, *cher* heart, your hand." Madame Leleux beckoned. The elderly woman cocked her head. Two dark eyes set in her wrinkles like the raisins in the oatmeal cookies searched the lines of Nell's palm. For being always cold, her old hand, trembling gently against Nell's, gave off a surge of comforting heat. "All will go well for you."

"That's it? I thought we were supposed to find out about having a family."

"You will have a family, maybe this way, maybe that way, maybe all ways. You don't need my potion." Madame rested her eyes a moment. "St. Jude has you in his care." She tapped on a nearby holy card. "And the Blessed Mother."

"Maybe just for insurance." Joe Dean reached out for a bottle with blue ribbons. "I left some of my *pousse-pousse* out under the rock."

"Put it up, Joe Dean. Last person drank all of my elixir had seven with two sets of twins, one after another." The oldest of the *traiteurs* gave a cracked laughed that would have been witchy if it weren't so warm. "Here, *cher*, just a drop or two if you want, but like I said, you taken care of already." She pressed a tiny bottle with soft rose ribbons into Nell's palm. "Take me back to my room, Joe Dean. I need rest."

"Ah, before I do that, would you have anything to bring back a lost girl?"

Madame Leleux considered. Nodded to herself. "Burn some of her hair or a belonging wit' a brown candle. She come back to you if you believe. Better not use that to get yourself more women, Joe Dean, or I'll fix you good." The *traiteur* waggled a crooked finger at him.

"No, ma'am. I got the only woman I need and more *pousse-pousse* than I know what to do with."

****

Nell waited in the hall along with the baggage when she smelled something burning in the kitchen. She looked down at Deanie already strapped in his car seat. "I must have left the coffee on. Wait here, lovey, Mama will be right back."

Joe Dean leaned over the sink, his broad back hiding his actions. The stench definitely came from his direction. "What on earth!" Nell exclaimed.

"Hush! Blessed Mother Mary and all the saints, help us find the girl, Cassie Thomas, and bring her home." Joe crossed himself and blew out the candle he held. He turned on the tap and washed away a small pile of ash.

"Do you know how hard it is to find a brown candle in springtime? I been to shops I never want to set foot in again, places selling potpourri and aromatherapy products. I had so many offers to have

277

my chakra adjusted, it turned scary. I told them, no thanks, my wife takes care of all that. Finally, I got the lady at the Hallmark store to dig one out of the stored Thanksgiving merchandise."

"Idiot!" Nell punched his arm. "I thought the house was on fire. Whatever were you burning?"

"Some of Copperhead's hair. I found a few strands from his tail caught in the stall door. I figure if we find that horse, we find Cassie."

"Fine time for voodoo. Your mother will be here any minute to take us to the airport. What will she think?"

"Considering I was the result of one of Madame Leleux potions for a male child, she should think this is a good idea. Man, I still can't get over that."

"Coincidence or good luck, at least for me. Now I have to scrape wax out of the sink when we get back."

The bell rang and the front door opened. They could hear Deanie welcoming his MawMaw with a gibberish of sounds.

"Come on, y'all. We don't want to get caught in work traffic," Nadine shouted. "Poo-yie, this house needs airing out."

Joe loaded a month's worth of luggage into his mother's Honda while the women got the baby settled. They did miss the work traffic and said good-bye at the Lafayette Airport before Nell was quite ready to leave. With the tug on her heart as real as the plane ticket in her hand, she gave Deanie a hug and handed him over to her mother-in-law.

Joe kissed his son's head. "When we come back, we'll be bringing you some brothers or sisters to play with—guaranteed. Be good for MawMaw."

Deanie's parents stood at the top of the staircase and waved. The baby flapped both hands at them, then held out his arms. He whimpered. Nell's eyes began to tear.

"Come on, Deanie, we gonna have a good time at MawMaw's, no?" Nadine offered him his favorite comfort toy, a well-chewed terry lamb, and hustled them both out to the car.

After the flight from Lafayette to Phoenix, Joe and Nell rented a car and drove to the Sheraton luxury suite already occupied by Emily, who had gone ahead to begin the fertility treatments necessary for becoming an egg donor. Shot full of Pergonal and Lupron, she wasn't the most welcoming of hostesses.

She greeted them with, "I'm so horny I can't wait to dump these eggs and go have some fun." A magnificent silver Navajo squash blossom necklace studded with turquoise and coral and worn over a plain black t-shirt clinked as she paced.

"Lovely necklace," Nell said.

"Yeah. I charged it to the room. They have some awesome gift shops downstairs. Want to go shopping? There's a great mall with some good restaurants a couple of blocks away."

"Maybe later."

"Well, I'm out of here." Emily grabbed a purse and rammed into the bellhop with the luggage cart on her way out. "Watch it!" she growled.

Joe paid off the help and took a dismayed Nell into his arms. "Oh, Joe, this was not a good idea."

"Sure it is. And you know what? Our bedroom is way over there, and we have no restrictions on sex for the next couple of weeks. Let's check out the king-sized bed." He led his wife in that direction.

****

A week later, the suite phone rang. "Hey, the Sex Maniac around anywhere?" a gruff voice of indeterminate gender asked.

"That would be Joe?" Nell asked cautiously.

"Hell, yes. Tell him Bull Dyke is on the line."

"He's in the shower. May I take a message?"

"You must be the little lady and I mean that literally. I always figured Joe would end up with a tall blonde the way he put the moves on Stevie before she went with Connor."

"Really?" Nell stared at the bathroom door as if she could see through walls.

"Oops, didn't know about that, did ya? Water under the bridge, Nelly. May I call you Nelly since the tabloids do? You can call me Jackie. Joe's the only one can get away with Bull Dyke."

"Oh, Jackie Haile, the pro golfer, Joe's friend. I prefer to be called Nell."

"I heard Joe calls you Tink, short for Tinker Bell. Cute."

With some relief, Nell heard the shower cut off. Joe released a cloud of steam from the bath into the room as he exited, naked and toweling his dark hair. Her heart beat faster just looking at him, a sex god in the mist. They had to abstain from sex for the next few days. Emily's blood test indicated she was ready to ovulate. Nothing in her life seemed to come at the right time.

"You still there, Tinker Bell?" Jackie Haile bellowed into the phone.

"Yes. Here's Joe." She handed him the receiver.

280

"It's Jackie Haile."

"Hey, Bull Dyke! How did you find me in the wilds of Phoenix?"

"I passed through New Orleans on my way here and gave Stevie a call. She said you ran up a really big phone bill crying on Connor's shoulder the other night, and she thought you could use some neutral company."

Nell licked water droplets from the hollow of his back. Her hands moved over his hips and started around the front. His arousal was so instantaneous she might have pulled a rip cord.

He batted her hands away for the first time in their lives. "No sex," he whispered.

"You got that right. How about letting me beat your ass in a few rounds of golf?" Jackie answer.

"Come on, Jackie. You know I'm the only man you ever wanted. I'm naked and wet from the shower." Nell moaned and rubbed her face between his shoulder blades.

"You pulled that one before. Didn't work then, won't work now. Shove your dick into some jeans and get yourself down to the lobby. We tee off in an hour."

He put a hand over the receiver. "Ah, Tink, stop that!" Nell kissed the tip of his penis.

"Ummm, fresh from the shower." She smacked her lips.

"Jackie wants to play some golf. I think I could use the distraction. I really need to get out of here." Nell didn't raise her head to answer.

"I can be down in five minutes if I don't shave, Jackie."

"Doesn't matter to me. I'm driving, got my clubs. We can rent some for you."

"Brought mine along. Haven't used them. Give me ten. I got a situation here."

"Right. See you in ten."

"Nell, you know I have to save up. They're aspirating Emily's eggs as we speak. I need to have a fresh supply ready to go for the fertilization."

"You aren't any fun, Joe Dean Billodeaux!" Nell burst into tears.

"Sugar, I know you're all hopped up on estrogen and progesterone, but we can't."

"I feel fat. My jeans are too tight to wear. I hate you, Joe Dean!"

"Well, Tink, I love you and it shows. Let me put my clothes on and see if I can get my zipper closed. There now. This is safer." He patted the back she had turned to him. "Let me make you feel better."

"That's what you say to all your women. I'll bet you said that to Stevie!" Nell threw herself on to the bed and sobbed into a pillow.

"Nope. Stevie always belonged to Connor. She wouldn't have none of me."

"You say!"

"I say I'm going to make you feel better." He rolled his wife over and tugged at the knot on her loose drawstring pants. They came down more easily than jeans. Obviously, she had plotted to trap him with those black lace panties. He tossed them aside, parted her legs and dove into those moist dark curls face first. His nimble tongue went right to the spot and got to work. He called in one of his long fingers for assistance. His team set a new record for achieving orgasm in a minimum number of minutes. When Nell stopped writhing, he pulled the covers over her and lay down on top of the spread to cuddle her.

Emily's return put an end to that. She pounded on their bedroom door.

"I'm back. Are you having sex in there? You know that's forbidden. If I have to suffer, so do you. I've laid my eggs. I'm done with shots and blood tests. Joe Dean, I want my check."

"Sorry." Joe kissed Nell gently on the lips. "You rest up or work out or whatever. I'll take care of Emily. Then, I'm going golfing with Jackie. Afterward, I want to take both of you to the best steak house in Phoenix. Good red meat, yummy, yummy."

Despite her puffy eyes, Nell laughed. "Go. I'll be fine now."

Emily pounded the door again. "Are you laughing at me? I want my half million."

Joe had written the check when Emily left for the clinic. It only took a moment to get his sister-in-law out of his life and left him with a very good feeling. With Emily gone, Nell satisfied and the procedure on schedule, nothing sounded better than a nice round of golf with an old friend. He snatched up the bag of clubs that gathered dust in the closet and sauntered off to meet Jackie.

A dozen sets of female eyes followed Joe striding across the lobby and looking in each sitting area for the pro golfer. Dark hair, chocolate brown eyes, manly stubble, tight black T-shirt, snug black jeans, black running shoes worn without socks, who was this gorgeous guy meeting, they seemed to say.

Jackie with her fireplug build, cropped hair, Izod golf shirt and khakis, stood up and offered Joe a high five. They slapped palms. Jackie searched his face, then pinched his chin with two of her stubby fingers. Jackie held up the small, dark curly hair she'd removed from his face and murmured to Joe, "Maybe you *could* make a lesbian happy, Sex Maniac." She flicked the evidence away.

Joe roared with laughter and thanked the good Lord he didn't blush like the fair-skinned Connor Riley. "Let's go, Bull Dyke. I've been penned up with emotional women for a week. I've taken them shopping, to museums, to a play, and to a frickin' opera. I need fresh air."

They moved toward Jackie's rental car still parked by the entrance but were swept aside by a college-aged bellboy pushing a large brass luggage cart. Emily followed the worldly goods she had accumulated during her stay and charged to Joe's accounts. She gave the young man a lavish tip and a pinch on the behind when he bent over to load her luggage in the cab. Sliding into the back seat of the taxi, she waved good-bye to Joe with a flourish.

"I hope you and Nell saddle yourself with a houseful of kids. I'm off to Europe to have the time of my life. So long, sucker!" The cab pulled out leaving behind a waft of gas fumes.

"Yeah, this has been a fun week, Jackie. We get word yesterday that Emily is ready for the Transvaginal Oocyte Retrieval, and I need to abstain for a couple of days so I can do my part, you know. What does my bitch sister-in-law do but come on to me while Nell is taking a bath. Hey, she says, don't you want to do it the natural way with a real woman like you did the last time, Joey? I wanted to kill her."

"Because she called you Joey or because of the

transvaginal oo-whatever?"

"The TOR, the egg retrieval. I been to college, Jackie. You know I have to do my part tomorrow—in a cup."

"Big words coming from you, sports jock. Probably won't be your first time jerking off either. Bet you're good at it."

"I usually have women do it for me. You volunteering?"

"No way!"

Joe put his seat back and stretched out his legs. Jackie was like one of the guys. You could relax with her, not have to watch your language. He was set to enjoy playing SunRidge Canyon with a friend.

****

Jackie's presence made the next few days go easier. Of course, she beat his ass at SunRidge and enjoyed telling Nell about it at Don & Charlie's Restaurant out in Scottsdale that night. Joe was glad for the distraction because his wife hunted for bear in her little black slip dress. The hormones made her breasts bigger. They pushed against the nylon and flaunted their nipples. They jiggled as Nell clipped around in high gold heels to look at the sports memorabilia crowding the walls. He was positive she bent over to read all the labels on the cases containing baseball mitts and bats just to show off how the skirt clung to her rear.

When the manager asked for a picture of Joe Dean and Jackie to add to the collection, the group posed with Joe in the middle, his arms around the waists of the women. Jackie wore a blue silk shirt with dark slacks. Nell, apparently, hadn't put on underwear. He hoped his sports coat hid any unsightly bulges from the camera.

The women ordered the traditional shrimp cocktail, but Joe Dean selected the frog legs in garlic butter telling the waiter the appetizer would make him feel right at home. He hoped the garlic would ward off the vamp his wife was becoming, too. The twenty-ounce New York strip steak might make him logy enough to sleep tonight, but he had to watch the alcohol or Nell would take advantage of him for sure. Her bare foot beautifully pedicured that morning and smelling of some sort of rosy cream made its way up his thigh as he sucked on the delicate bones of the frog.

Jackie created a distraction by relating her adventures with Joe while bringing Connor and Stevie together. "And there he was chasing a paparazzo, his shoes all covered with smashed avocado. Didn't that damned photographer go and make it look like Joe and I were fighting over a woman."

She poked Nell hard enough in the side to make her drop her foot and settled in to enjoy a full slab of baby back ribs with fried onion rings on the side. Nell picked at her petite filet while Joe helped himself to some of the onion rings on Jackie's plate.

When Jackie complained about not being invited to their wedding, Joe told that story and promised her another chance if they ever married in the church to satisfy his mama. The meal extended into desserts no one wanted, but ordered anyhow and coffee Joe felt should have been stronger.

"So maybe I can be godfather to one of these kids you're going to have," Jackie joked. Joe watched Nell's expression go from hot-eyed to desperate in an instant.

"Tomorrow, why don't the three of us check out

how the Diamondbacks are shaping up?" Joe cut in while Nell loaded half of her meal into a go-box. "How about you drive us back to the hotel, Jackie? I had a little too much of that red wine."

In the parking lot, he held the back door open for his wife, shut her in, and took shotgun next to his pal. Nell stayed awfully quiet on the way back to the suite. For her own good, he would have to be quick and courageous tonight.

Joe made sure Nell entered the hotel suite first. Kissing her neck, he murmured, "Sleep tight, Tink," and slipped into Emily's former room locking himself in. She scratched on his door like a cat who wanted to come inside.

"Joe, please. If you let me in maybe we could make a baby tonight without going through all this mess."

Behind the door, Joe prayed for strength and crossed himself. "Tomorrow I'm going to start making love to you, and I won't quit until we go for the implant. Get some sleep, sugar."

She sobbed, making it hard not to go to her. At last, Nell moved away toward their room on the other side of the suite.

It took until two a. m. for the heavy meal to kick in and do its work. The scent of Emily lingered in the room even though the sheets had been changed. The smell of her helped him repress his urges until the sun came up. Joe opened the door quietly. Nell slept on the sofa closest to his room. She wore her old ratty Tinker Bell nightie and had covered herself with a huge blanket pulled from their bed.

He decided not to shower, dressed quickly and went to the café across the street for a plate of *huevos rancheros* and wheat toast, a whole lot of coffee and orange juice for energy. Joe took the rental car from the garage and waited first in line at the medical center to do his part in giving Nell a baby. With the memory of Nell's small white foot sliding up his thigh, her pink-tipped toes massaging his crotch, he had no trouble filling the cup in record time.

He rousted Jackie for another round of golf on a different course and returned to the hotel around noon sure he would now have something to offer his wife if she was still in the mood. He found Nell sitting in her pathetic nightshirt with a room service breakfast in front of her. The French toast had gone cold and the coffee lukewarm. She looked up at him with sad eyes.

"Joe, what if this doesn't work? What if I can't carry a child?"

"Then, we'll adopt. No big deal. Honest. Come on, we got a baseball game waiting—but first, let me keep that promise I made to you last night."

Joe held out open arms. She came to him, and he cherished her until the time came to leave for the game.

****

Good as his word, Joe made love to Nell so frequently for the next two days Jackie felt she interrupted something every time she rang their room. She was on the verge of packing her bags and leaving a good luck and farewell message at the desk when Joe asked her to stay until the next morning when the procedure would be done.

"Need somebody to hold your hand, Joe?"

"For sure, Bull Dyke. I'll be holding Nell's, but I may need someone to talk to—and don't tell me to call Dr. Fuck over at the Sinners' office."

"You want me, I'm yours."

"You know Nell and me, we can't have sex for the next three or four weeks after this. You might look pretty good by then."

"Yeah, but you'll still look the same, Sex Maniac. See you at the clinic."

****

Joe did hold Nell's hands throughout the painless but delicate implantation of the three microscopic pre-fetuses that might become their future family. The doctor was unwilling to go with more considering Nell's small stature and the possibility of multiple births. He remained cautiously optimistic, given Nell's youth and her good physical condition, at least one child would result—or two or three. If none, three more embryos had been stored cryogenically for another try.

During the mandatory hour's rest with feet up, Nell's hand went limp as she dozed off, sleepy from the previous night's activities. Joe went quietly from the room and sought out Jackie who was drinking weak coffee and trying to catch vending machine peanuts with her mouth out in the waiting room.

"Thanks for staying. Nell just about broke my fingers she was so tense. I'll have to call in a reserve when she goes into labor."

"Call me and I'll be there."

"I know I can count on you. Ever want children of your own, Jackie?"

"Naw. Peanut?" she offered him the sack and he shook a few into his aching hand. "I hope Stevie will let me help raise hers when she and Connor get around to having some. I'll make the same offer to you. Free golf lessons to any of your kids that want to learn and great gifts every Christmas and birthday and Saint's Day. When should I plan to take some time off the circuit?"

"Early December if everything goes well. I know I rushed too soon, but we had this narrow window of opportunity and I had to act. I guess everyone thinks this is a big ego trip for me, but honest, I couldn't stand the thought of Emily and maybe some other women making Nell feel less than complete for the rest of her life. I would do anything to make Nell happy."

"So how's it feel to be a grownup with a wife, and probably more than one kid, Sex Maniac?"

"Good. It feels good." He regarded Jackie Haile's plain face for a moment. She tugged at a small gold knot-shaped earring in her lobe.

"Stevie gave you those, didn't she?"

"Might have."

"You wear them a lot."

"Shows off my pretty ears. They're my best feature." Jackie gave him a rueful smile.

"It's always been Stevie for you, hasn't it? You'd do anything for her including getting her back with Connor."

"Now you sound like a girlfriend. Cut it out, Joe." Jackie launched another peanut into her mouth and choked on it. Joe slammed her on the back until the nut went down the right pipe.

"Look, my work here is done. I have to get on the road and win a few more championships so I can keep up with you, Mr. Super Bowl. Call me about the wedding or the baby. Whichever comes first. I'm outta here." She gave Joe a manly hug and went on her way alone.

Chapter Twenty-Nine

No sex for three weeks, the doctor said. Joe scrambled for ways to make the time pass faster. He rented a houseboat, and they sailed Lake Havasu for a week catching fish and watching sunsets like the retired couples who were able to enjoy such luxuries now that their kids were grown.

At the beginning of their second week of abstinence, Nell suggested they visit the red rock country of Sedona. For her, rough riding Jeep trips were forbidden and balloon rides were chancy, so they strolled among the galleries and admired the scenery. Joe treated Nell as if she were a precious work of art or natural wonder that could not be jolted or violated in any way. In the back of both their minds unspoken lingered the question as to whether or not Nell was pregnant.

When Joe stepped out to get a paper or bring his wife some treat he thought she would like, Nell stared at her naked self in the mirror front and sideways, searching for early signs, and found none. She had a good appetite now that the worst of the stress had passed. Nothing made her nauseous, not the sushi at the Japanese restaurant or the Mexican special scarfed up at a roadside diner. She had plenty of energy thanks to her enforced rest periods. Frankly, she wanted to go home.

Joe saw the poster for the rodeo. "Ever been to

one? Want to go?" he asked his antsy wife in his quest to find sedentary, non-sexual activities that wouldn't jounce, shake or bump any babies from her womb.

Horseback riding, jogging, even swimming in the hotel pool were on the no-no list. Surely she could sit in the bleachers and watch other people being tossed to the ground by bulls and broncos. Distracted by medical procedures, they'd had no time to think about Cassie.

Nell put a hand on her husband's arm. "Joe, we can look for Cassie. We can ask people if they've seen her. See if you can get a rodeo schedule."

He argued his investigator was covering rodeos in Texas and would pass this way eventually, but Nell insisted, eager to do anything useful. Immediately, they discovered a dismaying number of rodeos going on throughout the country, big ones, small ones, regionals and nationals. They even held them in places like Minnesota and Ohio, though not at this time of year. In two weeks, they could probably attend six at the most, but this is what Nell wanted to do, and so they did.

The couple drove from one dusty venue to another and searched with Joe keeping a firm grip on Nell's elbow as he guided her around the cow plops, horse nuggets and gobs of smokeless tobacco spotting the dirt and straw. No one they questioned, whether Navajo boy or Texan and proud of it, admitted to seeing the red-haired girl or her horse or the shifty guy in the mug shot. They figured Cassie must be dyeing her brilliant mop, brown most likely, the color it had been when Bijou sold the ponies.

In the end, they sat gratefully in an air-conditioned indoor arena with restrooms instead of portable toilets and a selection of chicken wraps and salads at the snack bars along with the usual hot dogs and greasy fries. Lately, Nell's stomach had been acting up, but she wrote it off to the hot tamales consumed at their last stop. The one problem with arenas was that rodeo riders had locker rooms and press conferences just like football players and were much less accessible for questioning. In the end, Joe's celebrity paid off.

He was caught on big screen and publicly welcomed to the event over the loudspeaker. Joe, ever the showman, waved a hand wearing a Super Bowl ring and gave the camera his dazzling smile. He applauded and cheered the good performances while Nell winced and gasped over every fallen rider or nearly gored cowboy. When the barrel racers performed, she searched her program for a familiar name and strained to hear the announcer when he mentioned the horses.

As the third female rider and mount shot out on to the cloverleaf course, Nell gripped Joe's arm hard enough to leave marks. "Joe, that's Copperhead," she shouted as the names were called—Norma Jean Scruggs on Copper Heart.

"I don't know, Nell. That horse is kind of dappled and the rider sure isn't Cassie." Norma Jean Scruggs had a long, black braid of hair flying in her wake and several inches in height over the lost girl. Although it was hard to tell under the brim of her hat, the face seemed older and wiser, too.

"Look at the way he moves and those strange blue eyes. We have to get backstage and talk to Norma Jean," Nell insisted. "If you won't come, I'll go alone."

She waited long enough for Norma Jean to post the second best time, then sprinted down the steep arena steps with Joe grabbing out for her arm to prevent a spill.

Joe asked a guard the way to the women's dressing room and got a sly wink in return.

"Still one for the ladies, eh, Mr. Billodeaux?" The guard took a step back when the little bitty thing hanging on Joe Dean's arm gave him a look she usually reserved for doctors who treated her clients callously. "Uh, let me walk you over there."

"Gals, you got a special visitor here in the hallway wants to talk to y'all. It's Joe Deeeen!" the guard called as if he were announcing the next even.

The quarterback was chest deep in cowgirls in five seconds flat. Some of the ladies barely had their shirts buttoned or jeans zipped. Some went bootless. Norma Jean Scruggs still had the flecks of straw and dirt on her face from her furious ride around the barrels. Nell homed in on her while Joe signed autographs on programs, number placards, the brim of a Lady Stetson, and a bra.

"Have you ever seen this girl or this man or this horse?" Nell questioned thrusting out her photos.

Norma Jean gave a quick glance, then rotated her eyes back to Joe and edged nearer to getting her own autograph. "Might have."

"For pity's sake!" Nell stood on tiptoe and waved her hand over the taller bodies surrounding her, all of them dressed or partially dressed like models for western wear. "Joe, I need you over here!"

"Sorry girls, the old lady is calling me."

He moved like Moses through the waters with women parting before him and arrived next to Nell. It was no accident she back-stepped on to his toes as she mumbled, "Old lady, old lady!" under her breath.

Despite the pain in his foot, he managed a charming Billodeaux smile for Norma Jean Scruggs. "Can you help us find this girl, Miss? It means a great deal to me." His voice lowered to bedroom intimacy level.

Norma Jean pried her blue eyes from his and studied the photos Nell handed her. "Well, the girl I'm thinking of is older, has mousey brown hair and is kind of chubby for a barrel racer. Most of us are sort of, you know, sleek."

Norma Jean ran her hands down the length of her trim, athletic body from the flowered yoke of her western shirt to the pants pockets of her jeans. She pulled the fabric of her blouse a little tighter over high, shapely breasts.

Joe Dean gave her an appreciative smile of encouragement. "Go on, sugar, about the man and the horse."

"Well the kid must have had some talent, though, because she scored enough points in wins at the smaller rodeos to edge into a better competition. The horse, now, has the same head and confirmation as Copper Heart. Could be his brother in fact. The guy though, he had reddish hair and a dark brown beard. Figured one or the other was dyed."

"How long ago did you see them?" Nell bobbed up and down in her impatience.

"Just last week. Bought Copper Heart from them since they were in kind of a financial bind and my best horse came up lame. Girl finished out of the money. Her old man was giving her hell sayin' how he couldn't feed her and the horse on what he made leading two mangy ponies around a ring for the little dudes. I gave 'em twenty thousand for the animal. Should keep 'em in grits and hotel rooms for a while. They slept in that big, fancy rig he drove. Me, I would have sold the truck and got something smaller before I gave up my horse, but I gathered they had more going on than money trouble."

"You might say that. Miss Scruggs, would you mind if we took a look at Copper Heart? I'm truly afraid you might have been taken advantage of," Joe Dean asked, exerting all his charm.

"I'd love to show you my horse, Joe Dean," the barrel racer assured him and took his arm, leaving Nell to follow behind fuming while the riders who had not gotten an autograph complained about Norma Jean having all the luck today.

A teen-aged girl was giving Copper Heart a light rubdown at the back of a trailer that put Joe Dean's vehicle to shame. Air-conditioned, it was painted a brilliant red and had Norma Jean's name on it framed by painted flowering saguaro cactuses. A fine bay quarter horse mare with one leg wrapped in bandages looked on while the dapple got all the attention.

Joe ran his hands over Norma Jean's mount, took a close look at the spots, then curled back the lips. He compared the tattoo with a number he carried in his wallet. As if to end any doubt, the horse head-butted him and gave a familiar nicker.

"I'm sorry Miss Norma Jean. This horse was stolen from me about three months ago in Louisiana. His name is Copperhead and he was taken by my cousin along with the girl and two ponies. Bijou knew how to doctor horses. I think he bleached most of his spots, but you can see they're starting to come out again.

Knowing this one, he didn't like having his head worked on so Bijou left rings around the eyes." Joe gave a friendly nose rub to Copperhead.

"Well, gawl darned! Taken for a fool and shut out of the runnin'. How am I supposed to ride now? I might have taken over first place next round." Norma Jean slapped her hands on her slim thighs. "Out twenty thousand and some mighty big prize money. Knew this animal was too big a bargain. But he had the papers and all, matched his license."

"Joel Beam Billodeaux?" Joe asked.

"Nope. Joe Bream Billod. The girl went by Callie."

"Look, sugar, mostly we want to find the girl. How about if I rent you the horse until you find another one just as good?"

"That's right generous." Norma Jean paused as if remembering she'd been conned by this man's cousin. "How much?" she asked suspiciously, flinging back the black braid she had been fingering.

"A dollar a month and you bring him back to my ranch when you pass that way."

"Deal." Norma Jean shook his hand as firmly as any cowboy, then ducked into the mobile home painted to match the horse trailer, came out with her tooled leather purse and paid her dollar. She handed over the altered papers for the horse as well.

"Here's where you can reach me to get directions to the ranch." Joe Dean scrawled a phone number on a slip of paper and out of habit wrote his name behind underlining his signature with the devil's tail heart.

"Stick around and watch me take the next round, you great big beautiful man." Norma Jean stuffed the phone number into the pocket over one firm breast and gave it a pat with her long tanned fingers. She kissed Joe full on the lips as if his little wife were invisible.

"Ahem," Nell interrupted. "Where did you last see Cassie and Bijou?"

"Oh, place outside of Phoenix. Got the idea they were heading to Mexico where they could live cheap and maybe find another horse. Poor kid. Should never have gotten involved with a cowboy."

"Some say the same about football players," Nell told her, but the woman's attention had turned again to Joe Dean.

"It's been a pleasure, sugar," he told the barrel racer practically kissing her fingertips instead of shaking hands in good-bye.

"All mine," she sighed.

"Phoenix!" ranted Nell moving away quickly. "They were right next door while we were trying to make babies."

"Don't get excited, sugar." Joe Dean caught up with her. "Watch where you walk."

"Don't call me sugar ever again!"

"Tink, don't get excited. You catch more flies with honey. That's all I was doing back there."

"You say! I'll be big and pregnant with little Deanie on my hip and slinky, gorgeous Norma Jean is going to show up at our place bringing her own bed." The tears started to flow.

"You know what, Tink? I think you are pregnant, and it's time to go back to Phoenix and find out for sure."

Chapter Thirty

Joe stopped at a small restaurant on the other side of the hills surrounding Phoenix when Nell said her stomach was acting up because she was starving. Nell ordered a grilled chicken sandwich, no fries, and a wedge of lemon meringue pie with hot tea while Joe took a chance on the chili, the apple pie a la mode and coffee. They savored all the food, but Nell complained of heartburn before they reached the city limits.

"Must be pregnant," Joe remarked, trying to keep it casual.

"It was those bad tamales. I'm still sick from them."

"I had the same tamales and I'm fine. And you're so touchy. The guys said their wives get touchy when…"

"I'm touchy because of your touchy-feely ways with Miss Norma Jean Championship Barrel Racer. Don't think I didn't see you slip her that phone number signed the same way as the note you gave me one year ago." Nell pressed her head against car window and pretended to watch the cactus-studded landscape pass by.

"I gave her the number for the phone at the ranch which you answer ninety percent of the time because she'll need directions, and I did not try to hide it from you. The signature is just force of habit."

"Admit you miss your old life! You must wish you'd never met me and Deanie had never been born. You only needed a mother for your bastard."

The words sat on the tip of his tongue to say he did miss the old days of wild women and drunken brawls simply to hurt her back, but the truth was, he didn't. He played the game with steadiness now, Nell was his match in every way, and he would never regret his son. He held in his anger and felt it melt away when he saw Nell's shoulders shake as she cried silently against the glass.

"Come over here, Tink. How can I tell you how much I love you and Deanie if you won't believe me?"

She came, slid down and sobbed into his lap. Nell slept in that awkward position until they pulled up in front of the Sheraton, their home away from home, again. Joe gently lowered her head to the car seat and slipped out. He opened the passenger door and bundled his wife to his chest. With a whisper to the doorman that he would be coming back shortly, Joe carried Nell to the suite without waking her, laid her down on the king-sized bed, and pulled off the sneakers with the straw and manure ground into the treads. He tucked the extra blanket around her and gave his wife a kiss on the cheek.

Scribbling a note on hotel stationary, Joe let Nell know he was going to put in a personal appearance at the Phoenix Police Department to ask for their help in notifying the Border Patrol to be on the lookout for the stolen truck even though Bijou had certainly changed the plates. He needed to add a new description of the missing girl whose appearance had altered since the first alert. He called his investigator on the way and told him to get his ass to Arizona. Now that Nell was out of hearing, he placed another call to the fertility clinic to let them know he would be bringing his wife in for her pregnancy test in the morning.

****

Nell woke up in a hotel bed with a resounding version of *When the Saints go Marchin' In* filling the room. She groped for her purse which Joe had slung on to a table nearby and located the blasting cell phone in its bottom. This was the number her old clients and friends tended to call while she used Joe's accounts more often than not.

"Hello?" she mumbled still groggy from her nap and disoriented about her location.

"Miss Nell? It's Callie, I mean Cassie," a timid voice claimed.

Nell came abruptly awake. "Cassie, my God, are you all right? Where are you, honey?"

"At the bus station in Phoenix. I only have enough money to get a ticket to Houston. Can you come pick me up there Saturday afternoon? Please don't tell me to call my parents. I can't face them right now." The burst of words came punctuated with a small sob.

"Listen, Cassie. I'm in Phoenix, too, with Joe. We found Copperhead and were looking for you. Stay put, we'll be right there. Promise not to leave," Nell urged.

"I won't. Oh Miss Nell, I'm so sorry."

"I'm coming. I'm coming immediately. Don't be afraid of what anyone will say. We'll get things straightened out."

"I don't think even St. Jude could do that, I'm so messed up, Miss Nell."

"Don't underestimate St. Jude, Joe would tell

301

you—or me. I'm on my way."

She disconnected, shoved the phone back into her purse, and groped for her shoes in the dim room. Flicking on a lamp, she saw the time was past seven p. m. and Joe had gone to see the police and offer the latest information. She had the doorman put her in a cab and once out in the stream of traffic, she called Joe with the news.

When he let out a whoop, she cautioned him, "Don't say anything to the police about finding her yet. Cassie sounds shaky, and I don't want to upset her anymore tonight. We'll report to them in the morning."

"I'll meet you in a few minutes then."

Joe closed his phone and looked at the officer who was dealing with the new information. "Whoopie! My wife found a place that serves boiled crawfish. We're eatin' there tonight in half an hour. Call me at the Sheraton if you need me. Got to go."

As Joe charged for the front door, Officer Rivera shook his head. "Cajuns and their crawfish," he remarked to no one in general, but he stuffed the notepad full of Joe Dean Billodeaux autographs for all of his relatives in a shirt pocket and picked up a phone to call the Border Patrol.

****

The cabbie knew the city and got Nell to the bus terminal in short order. She tipped him generously, but said he didn't have to wait as her husband would be coming soon. She stood looking up and down the bus docks for the slim, red-headed girl she knew, then shook her head and substituted mousey brown hair and chubby. The only teenager she saw leaned against a pillar and stared into the on-coming night.

Nell's heart went out to the kid. She wore a man's v-necked undershirt that spanned across her pregnant belly. Her low-slung jeans were half unzipped to accommodate the size of her stomach. The girl pulled an over-large denim jacket with the cuffs rolled up tighter against the chill desert evening.

The teen's hair looked as if it had chopped off above the ears in a bowl cut and the rest shaved leaving her neck naked and vulnerable. The top knot was dyed that dead black color so popular with Goths, and her makeup had the whiteness of a corpse with a thin red slash for a mouth. The girl seemed ready to weep under her tough exterior. A middle-aged man, unshaven and bald, unclean and unsightly, approached and whispered in her ear.

Nell turned her eyes elsewhere and scanned for Cassie, but a commotion snapped her head back to the pathetic Goth girl. "Let me alone! Go away!" The teenager pushed her hands against the chest of the guy who waggled a twenty-dollar bill in her face and crowded against her swollen belly. Nell recognized the voice.

"Cassie!" she cried out and came running. Nell grabbed at the molester's arm and shoved him away. His bourbon breath said the fellow had been drinking. It out-stank his body odor.

"Get lost, bitch! You too young to be her mama." The drunk eyed Nell's petite frame and large eyes. "Unless this is your corner and y'all want to give me a twofer. I got more money in my front pocket if you want to dive in and get it. It's a great big bill."

He laughed at his wit. Cassie turned her head aside and tried to move away, but he grabbed at her wrist and held on. His other arm shot out and smashed Nell against his crotch. Nell reached down with her small hand between his legs. The drunk gave her a "knew it all along" grin that lasted only until his alcohol numbed body registered the pain as she twisted his testicles. He shrieked and flung Nell away. Cassie escaped and ran awkwardly for the street while glancing over her shoulder. Nell collided hard with the pillar and crumpled to the cement floor.

Clutching her stomach and gasping for breath, Cassie got as far as the corner where she waved her arms and shouted for assistance. "Someone, please help us! Help, please help!"

A luxury car in the turn lane came to a sudden stop. A tall man all dressed in black jumped out and bucked the signal light, the curses of the other drivers, and a melee of cars attempting to go around the obstruction. He dodged, twisted, made the curb next to Cassie and ran right by her toward Nell.

"Mr. Joe," Cassie said. "Thank God."

Nell pulled herself up, shaking her head and gulping air, as Joe bore down on her. The drunk limped off into the darkness bent over like a stock hunchback in a B-grade horror movie. Cassie watched, forlorn and helpless, as Joe knelt beside his wife, ran his hands over her from head to toe, his face stark with fear.

"It's just a bump on the head, Joe. Please, get Cassie and let's go."

"Cassie?" He looked blank.

"There, on the corner."

"Jesus," he swore, taking in the changes. "May Bijou rot in hell, and I'll help send him there if he ever tries to come back to Chapelle. You sure you're all right, Tink?"

"Fine. I hear sirens. Let's go!"

Joe ran the gauntlet of automobiles and verbal abuse again to move the rental car to the curb. One driver gave him the finger with an up-held cell phone and shouted, "I gave your license number to the cops, jerk!" Nell and Cassie piled in, and they made tracks for the Sheraton. Joe pushed a large tip into the doorman's hand and asked him to see the vehicle was returned to the rental agency at the airport tonight.

In the safety of the suite, husband, wife and runaway breathed easier. While Joe seemed unable to take his hands off of Nell, she turned to Cassie. "Are you hungry, honey? Would you like a warm bath before we talk?"

Cassie nodded. Joe called in an order to room service while Nell put the girl into the second bedroom and showed her the voluminous terry robe hanging on the back of the bathroom door.

An hour later, Cassie put away an evening breakfast of ham and cheese omelet, toast, juice, and milk. The robe came down to her ankles but barely closed over her belly. With the ghastly makeup washed away, her freckles re-appeared. Her eyes emerged from the black shadows, blue and ashamed. Nell helped herself to a pot of hot tea laced with lemon and let the girl finish eating.

"It's not that Bijou didn't feed me. I'm just hungry all the time."

"Yes, I understand why." Nell continued to sip her tea calmly, but Cassie's naked face turned a fiery red under the dreadful cap of wet black hair.

"I wasn't sure for a long time about the baby. I

mean you told me I might be sterile like you. That's what I told Bijou, and he said it was fine by him because he hated using condoms."

If possible, Cassie's face turned even redder. She smashed a maraschino cherry inside of the fresh pineapple ring garnish with her fork and continued to talk into her plate.

"I know you said not to rush into things with boys, but Bijou was a man. He kept telling me I was pretty and spunky and a great rider. We didn't do anything at first, you know, just talked. He said if I was older we could go out on the rodeo circuit together. He'd be my manager, and we'd win championships with Copperhead. We did win at the smaller competitions. I had ribbons and buckles and some cash prizes, but it cost a lot of money to be on the road all the time and pay the entrance fees." She hung her head even lower.

"The sex started a few weeks after he began coming for me in New Orleans. I told my parents you were staying in Chapelle, and you would be there all the time to watch out for me, Nell. We kept doing it even after you caught me staying at the old house with Bijou. A hundred times I must have lied to everyone who cared about me."

"Don't worry about that now. Go on."

"By Christmas, I knew I was going to have a baby and told Bijou. He said Joe would beat the daylights out of him or have him up for statutory rape, and he was getting the hell out of Chapelle. I begged him to take me along. He said sure, why not stick it to old Joe Dean all the way? You'd probably lose your temper and blow the playoffs and the Super Bowl. Joe, I'm so sorry."

"You're not the villain, Cassie. Goddamn Bijou."

"I was pretty skinny so I didn't show for a long time, then it was like my belly just popped out. I stuffed my shirts with rags to make my top look as big as my bottom so I could keep riding, but I got heavier and couldn't keep my balance as well. It threw Copperhead off. Wasn't his fault we lost that big event. Bijou got really angry because the entrance fee had eaten up most of our money, and I didn't bring in a cent."

"You shouldn't have been riding at all. You could have injured yourself or lost the baby," Nell said outraged.

"I know. I don't think Bijou cared. When we were traveling with the carnival, he asked around about doctors who could fix things. I told him an abortion would be wrong, especially since he loved me and all. He took me to one of those places anyhow, but I cried and cried and told them I didn't want an abortion. I think he was afraid someone would recognize me even with my hair dyed brown because he hauled me out of there really fast. We stayed with his folks for a while. They gave him some money for a wedding gift when he said we were going to elope to Texas, but we never stopped at a Justice of the Peace. I was so stupid."

"There isn't a woman in the world who hasn't been stupid over a man once in her life, honey. Some of us are just luckier than others." Nell patted Cassie's hand, but looked over at Joe. They smiled across the remains of the omelet.

"When we finished out of the money here in Phoenix, Bijou said there was no sense keeping Copperhead because I had lost my touch and might never get it back after I had the baby. It was best to change our appearance again and head for the border because we could live cheap in Mexico on the money from the sale. I cried and begged, but he didn't seem to care about how I felt anymore. Once he cashed the check, he went out and got some things at the drug store, straightened my hair, dyed it black, cut it off, and used the mane clippers on my neck. I was already wearing lots of makeup to make myself look older and hide my freckles, but he wanted me to look the way you saw. He dyed his hair back to black, too." She paused to gulp orange juice and went on.

"We were staying at this cheap motel south of here with the truck and the trailer parked out back. He met some men there who wanted to play poker. He wanted me to sit by him for luck. One by one, he lost all his rings, then the old carnival ponies and the trailer, trying to win this big diamond pinkie ring one of the men kept flashing. They wanted him to put up cash or the truck. He said hell no, he needed those things to get to Mexico, but the winner could have his sister for the night if he lost again. I started to say all his sisters lived in Louisiana, but then I understood. I was so scared."

"Did he win?" Joe asked.

"No." Cassie turned pale under her freckles at the memory. "He lost and just walked out of the room, unhitched the horse trailer with the ponies in it and told the men he'd be back for me in the morning."

"Dear God!" Nell whispered.

"It's okay, Miss Nell. Isn't there a saying about God looking out for fools? These men, they wanted the cash and the truck, not me. They thought Bijou would keep going on as he had, not walk out. One of them called me knocked-up jail bait and said he didn't want any part of me. He went out to find a real woman. The second guy had been drinking and fell asleep with his face on the table. The third said he had a sister around my age and couldn't do it. Bijou drove off. I didn't know if he would come back at all. I told the last man my story. He dropped me off at the bus station and gave me some money. Told me to go back to wherever I came from. When I tried to buy a ticket to Lafayette, the ticket seller told me I only had enough to reach Houston. That's when I called you."

"Everything is going to be fine now. Let's get some rest. We'll make plans in the morning." Nell took Cassie to the bed, tucked her in, and gave her a kiss as if she were her own wayward daughter come home.

"Miss Nell, will you see about the old ponies? It's not their fault Bijou deserted them, too."

"We will. Sleep tight."

Back in her own room with Joe, she sighed deeply and feeling bone tired, went to shower. Joe was stripping down when the bathroom door reopened. Nell swayed on her feet.

"Joe, I'm bleeding. Call the clinic."

Chapter Thirty-One

In the commotion to get Nell to the hospital, Cassie woke and wrapped herself in the terry robe. She caught Joe by the arm as he charged out the door after the hotel wheelchair carrying his wife. "Please, what's wrong?"

Joe shook free of her grasp. "Nell is losing our babies. Stay put. I don't know when we'll be back." He slammed the suite door closed.

Shaken, Cassie sank down on the sofa nearest the door. She replayed the scene at the bus terminal in her mind: the drunken man soliciting her for oral sex, Nell coming to her rescue and being slammed into the pillar.

"What have I done now?" she whispered. "How can I ever make it up to Nell and Joe?"

Crying again, she hugged her belly with both arms and rocked herself back and forth in anguish. She always seemed to be crying, pitying herself for the results of her own stupidity. Her baby rolled and kicked under her hands. Everyone said life wasn't fair. They were right.

****

The clinic doctor gave one of those enigmatic hmmmm's after completing a very gentle, non-invasion examination of Nell's belly and nether parts.

"And what does that mean?" Joe demanded as he loomed over the examination table. Nell lay perfectly still with her eyes closed as if she were afraid to open them and face the facts. She had his hand in a white-knuckled grip again.

"The bleeding has stopped and was not excessive. Three weeks into a pregnancy, a woman may lose the fetus and assume her period simply came late and a bit abnormally, especially if she wasn't planning for a baby. In your case, Nell, we knew the risks. You say you bumped your head and had a fall?"

"Yes, earlier this evening. You can feel the lump on the back of my head, but it didn't bleed."

"You had no cramping before you experienced the bleeding?"

"No. I've had some stomach problems. An encounter with bad tamales, I thought."

"Nell, that was two days ago!" Joe blurted out.

The doctor gave him "a shut up or go outside look", then turned benignly back to Nell. "There is no doubt you lost at least one of your implants. The fall might have caused it, but there is always the possibility this one just didn't attach firmly to the uterine wall. What we don't know is how the other fetuses are doing. I'm reluctant to try anything invasive at this point. We took blood for a pregnancy test, but with the loss so recent it may not give a true reading regardless of the status of other eggs. I'd like you to get a few days of bed rest, then continue on normally for another week or two after which we will test again. How does that sound, Nell?"

"I'd like to go home," Nell said.

"After we are sure you are stable, you could do that. No rough activities though. I can recommend a few obstetricians in the New Orleans area to oversee your pregnancy once it's confirmed. A nurse will be in to get you settled for the night."

Feeling the physician was putting a positive spin on the matter for her sake, Nell nodded and refrained from telling him that she did not feel expectant. She allowed her hand to slip free of Joe's snug grip.

"I guess I've failed you, Joe—you and your mother, the entire Billodeaux clan and their ancestors, the Virgin Mary and St. Jude and all the saints in Heaven." She blinked her eyes to keep the tears away.

Joe raised her limp hand and kissed it. "You win some, you lose some. We got three more in reserve, remember?" he said lightly. "We can try again one day. Rest and don't worry about this." He stayed until she was asleep in a clean and sterile hospital bed before he drove back to the hotel.

Cassie slept on one of the suite's sofas. Her robe had fallen open slightly and a wedge of her ripe belly showed. Life had always been more than fair to Joe Dean Billodeaux. He couldn't complain over this one disappointment, but he wanted to for Nell's sake more than his own. He pulled the robe over the bulge of Cassie's baby and thought about his wife having to come back to the teenager who had conceived so easily and thoughtlessly. At this moment, he wished the girl had never been found, and that was so wrong. Ponies, he had two mangy old ponies to rescue, probably frying in the trailer behind some run-down motel. He'd better go find them.

****

As soon as Nell returned, she insisted Cassie call her parents and at the very least, tell them she was in good health and safe in Phoenix. Then, she dragged the girl to the clinic for a physical. Willing to indulge Nell after her disappointment, her doctor performed the exam.

He had a blood sample taken, palpated the girl's stomach and let her listen to the normal rapid chugging of the fetal heartbeat. Cassie's eyes lit with the wonder. He scheduled an ultrasound for later in the day. As the doctor scribbled prescriptions for iron pills and pre-natal vitamins, he asked a few pertinent questions.

"Well, Cassie, I'd say you and your baby are doing fine and dandy. You are a little anemic, but the iron pills will take care of that. Judging by what you've told me, I'd say you are going to be a mother around the end of June, say the twenty-seventh, give or take. Have you given any thought to putting the baby up for adoption? This is a fertility clinic and I can tell you many, many couples would be willing to pay your expenses and consider an open adoption where you could stay in touch with your child."

Cassie seemed startled by the suggestion. "Up until a little while ago I thought I was going to marry the daddy. Nell, I can't afford this. My parents barely get by now. They don't need another baby and a high school dropout to support." Panic invaded her voice.

"Cassie, dear, Joe will pay for this examination and the ultrasound. When you get home, you'll talk to your parents and come to a decision together. As for your being a high school dropout, I'd say they're more likely to make you repeat the eleventh grade than look for a job. Don't be afraid."

Once out under the turquoise blue Arizona sky, Nell suggested they go shopping for maternity clothes in order to return Joe's pinstriped dress shirt that Cassie wore, tails out, cuffs rolled, over her unzipped jeans.

"The money…" said Cassie.

"My treat." They shopped for cute coveralls, wild tops and maternity jeans. Nell insisted on getting the girl a bathing suit and two party dresses versatile enough to be worn for any special occasion that might come up in the next three months. Nell piled on stretchy underwear and low-heeled shoes so soft they would be kind to swollen feet.

"Enough!" Cassie declared. "I'm hungry."

They sat outdoors at an ice cream parlor and ordered banana splits. Cassie polished off her concoction and the half Nell didn't eat.

The teenager leaned back and let a small burp escape from her lips. "Excuse me. That was so good, Miss Nell. Thanks, thanks for everything."

"I wanted to do it. Now you can go home in style."

"Miss Nell, Joe said you lost your babies the other night. When I asked the next day, he said you'd be fine and not to say anything about it to you, but I need to know."

Nell studied the dry landscaping across from their table. A tiny hummingbird drawing nectar flitted among the sharp-needled plants and avoided all hazards.

"Joe and I were here because of the fertility clinic. My sister donated eggs to be fertilized with Joe's sperm so I could try to have a baby."

"A test-tube baby?"

"More like a petri dish baby, but yes. We were waiting to see if the implants took when we found you. I guess my body rejected them." Nell blinked her eyes a few times and concentrated on the hummingbird, so delicate but so tough.

"It was my fault you lost them, wasn't it? When

that guy who hassled me pushed you, that's when it happened."

Nell could tell Cassie wanted her to say it wasn't so. She could grant that wish at least.

"We don't know. It might be I'm unable to carry a child. I wasn't ready to have a baby anyhow. You sat for Deanie, so you know I have a wonderful adopted son at home—if he remembers me after all these weeks. Joe and I, we can try again later if we want. It's not that big a tragedy."

Cassie nodded as if she didn't believe a word of Nell's story.

"What do you think about finding the best beauty salon in Phoenix and seeing what they can do about your hair?" Nell said brightly.

"If you want to, I guess."

****

The novena brigade had gathered to greet them on arrival. Nell made out Nadine pressed against the window of the upper deck in the Lafayette Airport as she went down the steep and narrow mobile stairs pushed up against the small commuter jet from Houston. She could barely see over Joe's head. He insisted on going down first in front of the two women he treated like delicate Royal Doulton figurines in case either should take a fall. Deanie patted his small hands against the window with excitement. For the first time since finding Cassie and losing her babies, Nell felt warm and happy inside.

Joe lifted her down the last few steps making her feel weightless and airy. She seized her carryon bag from the porter and started eagerly for the terminal before Joe swung Cassie safely from the steps. He caught up with his wife in no time and snatched away her bag as if she were too weak to carry it inside.

Nell kept going. By the time she was inside the building, all of Joe's sisters, a couple of brothers-in-law, PawPaw Billodeaux and Nadine carrying Deanie clustered by the entry. Deanie's young, male cousins stopped playing on the escalators and joined the group. The bored teenaged family members pulled themselves from dawdling in the snack bar and made their way to the reunion.

Deanie bucked in his grandmother's arms when he sighted Nell and held out his arms. She went directly to her son and buried her face into his sweet, baby-powdered neck. Deanie made everything fine again. After a few minutes of nuzzling and telling Deanie how much Mama had missed him, Nell became aware some expected people were missing from the crowd of greeters.

She turned to locate Cassie who hung back. Deanie spotted his father and strained and held out his arms in that direction. Joe scooped him up and held him high in the air, not caring about the ribbon of drool making its way from his son's smiling open mouth to the front of his shirt.

"Nadine, where are Cassie's parents? For that matter, where are mine?" she asked her mother-in-law.

"Oh, yours are back at the house setting up a dinner. I think Episcopalians ain't too good at showing feelings in public. *Ca c'est dommage*, no? Didn't know Cassie's parents were coming. Where is that girl, anyway?"

Nell could understand Nadine not recognizing the teen. The best the stylist could do with Cassie's hair had been to shingle it in close to the head. A red-gold fuzz was beginning to grow over the shaved areas, but the permanent black dye permeating the rest of her strands presented problems. In the end, the stylist stripped a few long center locks and re-colored them in red hoping to blend the two colors as the hair grew out.

Knowing how much it would mean to the girl, Nell sprang for a makeup makeover, too. Cassie's freckles had been lightly subdued, her eyes lined in a subtle gray-blue shade and her lips glossed a light tangerine. Cassie wore small gold hoops in newly pierced ears. She'd covered her pregnant belly with a black maternity T-shirt crisscrossed by glittering silver and gold streaks and worn over black leggings. Probably, her own mother wouldn't have recognized her either.

"The pregnant one, Nadine. I think she's too embarrassed to come forward."

"Yeah, I remember you telling me. Damn Bijou!" Nadine pushed through her extended family and gave the girl a loving hug. "Welcome back, *cher*."

So many volunteered to carry baggage Joe didn't have to lug his own golf clubs. He did insist on keeping Deanie, not giving him up to Nell either. The procession of trucks, vans, and sedans exited the parking lot and moved on to Chapelle where the tearful Abbotts waited to serve a hot cooked meal.

The many Billodeauxs filled the trestle table in Joe's kitchen and spilled into the game and living rooms with overflowing plates in hand. Cassie followed the other teens to the game room with enough food for two in her possession. Deanie sat happily in a highchair and oozed mashed bananas from the corners of his mouth. Nell suppressed her heartburn and declared this to be Thanksgiving all over again.

She was more than glad when the bulk of the relatives left. In the kitchen with only Nadine and her own mother, Nell felt free to let her guard down and say what no one else had mentioned all evening.

"I'm so sorry about the babies. I should have been more careful."

"We are, too, dear, but Joe said you can try again someday when you are both ready." Mrs. Abbott dabbed her watering eyes.

"We done prayed our knees black and blue at the novena, *cher* heart. You might still catch a baby. Joe says you could still be pregnant but wanted to come home so bad he couldn't stop you. You supposed to check in wit' a doctor here, now mind." Nadine seemed absolutely positive her prayer efforts had not been wasted.

Cassie entered carrying dirty plates and collapsed soft drink cans from the game room. She ducked her head as soon as she saw Nell about to question her.

"Honey, did you tell your parents when our plane was arriving like I told you to?"

"No," the girl answered in a small voice. "I didn't tell them about the baby either."

"Cassie, you were on the phone for an hour yesterday. What on earth *did* you tell them?"

"About how kind you were to me. About Joe rescuing the ponies and having them transported to the ranch. How you got me new clothes and a makeover. I told them you let me pierce my ears. Mom wasn't too happy about that, but then said she didn't care so long as I was well and safe and coming home soon."

"When did you say that would be?"

"When Joe finished his business in Phoenix. I didn't say why you were there."

"Cassie, you can't handle things by pretending they didn't happen. I want you to call them right now and tell them you are in Chapelle."

"But they'll come here!"

"The next thing you are going to tell them is that you're pregnant, no matter how hard that will be. Cassie, you've never been a coward. You overcame cancer. You stood up to Bijou about this baby. Your parents aren't going to throw you out after they just got you back. Call." Nell held out the phone and Cassie took it.

"Mom?" she said hesitantly when someone answered on the other end. "Nora, go get Mom. This is Cassie." She took as deep a breath as her baby belly allowed. "Mom, I'm in Chapelle with Joe and Nell. Mr. Joe and Miss Nell. Yes, I know. And Mom, I'm pregnant."

Joe stood in the doorway of the kitchen with Deanie wrapped around his neck. He patted the baby's bottom and watched his wife as she stood beside Cassie.

"I want to stay in Chapelle, Mom. I don't want to embarrass you and Dad and my brothers and sisters. I can't face the nuns and the girls at school. Please let me stay here until my baby is born, please! Nell, she wants to talk to you."

"It's no imposition. We'd be glad to have her. I'll see she gets tutoring and goes to church, yes. No, no, the company will be great. This house is such a big empty place with so many bedrooms. Come visit us when you can. Have one of your older girls take care of the others. We'll work things out."

Nell sounded incredibly cheerful. Joe didn't say a word to disagree. He went to her side and placed Deanie in his wife's arms.

Chapter Thirty-Two

Nell shook hands with the couple who sat across from Mintay's desk. She knew she had done some good in explaining what the coming months would bring in the way of treatments and emotional ups and downs for their leukemia-stricken daughter. The impoverished family had two younger children being entertained in clinic's waiting room by Cassie. How wonderful to help someone else instead of dwelling on her own problems.

"Dr. Green is going to contact this great children's hospital and do all she can to have Starla admitted. Your daughter will get the best of care at no cost to you. I'm living proof your daughter can recover. You saw the young pregnant woman in the lobby? Another cancer survivor. Here's my card. Use the cell phone number to call me at any time." Nell rose and walked her new clients to the door.

Mintay waited in the office when Nell returned for her purse and car keys. "Tell me, who does a psychologist talk to when she has troubles of her own?" Dr. Green asked.

"What troubles?"

"Sit. Talk to me, Nell."

"Cassie is waiting."

"She's picking up the toys in the waiting room. We got time." Mintay leaned back in the office chair to show just how much time she had.

"Fine, then. Joe is still treating me like I'm going to break if he touches me. He can't accept I lost the babies. He's so full of hope I'm still pregnant when I cuddle up next to him and whisper dirty nothings in his ear, he says—not now Tink, I'm not in the mood." Nell deepened her voice and assumed a stance, a dead-on imitation of her husband.

Mintay crowed, "Joe Dean Billodeaux, that walking case of ragin' Cajun hormones, said that? I've lived to see the day! Hallelujah!"

"Maybe I shouldn't tell you this, but I've always liked it when Joe played a little rough with me. Then, I wasn't poor little Tink, the fragile cancer victim, but a woman he wanted very badly. Now, he doesn't want me at all—since I lost his children."

"Bullshit, pardon my French! The man is so worried he actually talked to Rev about his feelings. Of course, Rev talked to me and asked me to talk to you. Now, how about that?"

"You are good friends, and I appreciate your concern but…"

"No buts. Joe says you still show symptoms of pregnancy, and you've been home three weeks. He's says you are grouchy, and your stomach is upset all the time. He says your nipples are getting darker. Let me test you and put both of you at ease."

"I cannot believe he discussed my nipples with Rev!

"No big deal. The test, Nell."

"I'd rather not know right now. It would be failing all over again. As for the rest, having Cassie around is sort of nerve-wracking. That would account for the indigestion and the grumpiness. She isn't any trouble exactly. Since she can't ride she spends most of her time in the barn grooming the horses and those poor old ponies. I overheard her apologizing to Boo and Buttercup about leaving them with the carnival. Jet and Jazzy, the new ones, are thriving under her care. They aren't nearly as decrepit as we thought. As long as Cassie brings them carrots and sugar cubes, they all seem inclined to forgive and forget." Nell and Mintay smiled at each other.

"Cassie likes her tutor and does her homework. She helps where she can around the house. She offers to babysit Deanie if I have to go out. Really, she is a model guest."

"Except she's struttin' around with a big ole belly full of baby right in your face all day. Joe said he thought it was a bad idea to let her stay, not that he begrudges the money you spend on her. He's a generous man, but he says he sees this look on your face sometimes. He thinks you are in pain. Is he right, Nell?"

"Maybe. I'd hate to think I am so small and envious of a pregnant teenage girl."

"That would be natural. Heavens, I envy her when I watch her eat the entire office's supply of Easter candy I put out for the little ones…and not get sick. I'll bet all that baby weight slides off of her like jelly from a knife once she gives birth, too. Speaking of which, has she decided to keep the baby?"

"She hasn't said otherwise though I know she has talked about it with her parents. I'll ask Mrs. Thomas this weekend. She's supposed to collect Cassie for Easter."

"Fine, then. Nell, I'll give you three more weeks,

but then I expect you to get a pregnancy test. Just in case, let me give you some vitamins and…"

"Speaking of pregnancies, I was supposed to mention a little something to you when I could work it into the conversation."

"Don't tell me Rev has gotten Joe on his side."

"He's returning a favor, I believe. Though as far as I can tell, Joe thinks families should be started as soon as the ink is dry on the wedding certificate. He gave me three whole months before deciding radical action was necessary. You and Rev have been married a year now and the age of thirty looms ahead for both of you. Why do you want to wait?"

"Nell, being both Dr. Arminta Green and Mrs. Revelation Bullock is not as easy as I thought. Before Rev took me down like I was heading for the goal line with his team's football, I wanted to devote my life to medicine in a poor rural parish."

"Aren't you?"

"I am, but when it's the off-season, Rev wants to play around, go places, do things, and I can't simply take up and leave. Then, there's his family. Don't get me wrong, I love each and every one, but they are so churchy. I've always put my faith in modern science. After his career is over, I know Rev wants to assist his - father and later, take over the congregation at the AME. One of the things I admire about Rev is his faith and his vision of life beyond football, but I can't quite see myself as the minister's wife." Mintay sighed. "Adding children to the mix would be too much right now."

"I understand, but sometimes both God and modern science sends things our way more quickly than we anticipate. In vitro for me and a hellava guy with a big religious family for you. I think starting a family would take care of one of your problems. Rev is more likely to stay home and socialize less if you have children to keep him occupied. On the other hand, don't be pushed if you aren't ready. I know how that feels."

"But you did it for Joe?"

"Yes, and he would say he did it for me. That's love, I guess. Call if you want to talk some more."

"And vice versa."

****

Mrs. Thomas arrived in the battered family van to retrieve her seven months pregnant daughter for the Easter holiday. None of Cassie's many siblings had been allowed to ride along, and Mr. Thomas had not wanted Joe to drive his daughter to New Orleans. "You've done enough," he told Joe.

Joe wasn't sure if Mr. Thomas meant that in a good or bad way, but he did not argue. In the chaos of loading luggage and Easter gifts into the van, Nell was unable to speak to Cassie's mother alone.

Once they were gone, the huge house grew awfully quiet. Joe had taken L.B. out for some exercise. Later, he would ride Fatima around in the ring. Though expecting, the rotund little mare didn't appear much bigger than usual, and she certainly wasn't as grumpy as Nell. When Nell suggested she exercise Fatty, Joe said quickly he would do it as soon as he finished with L.B. All this protection was driving his wife mad. Joe still had hopes for adding to his family and would not let go.

When Joe, smelling of the barn and letting in a heady whiff of spring air, came for lunch, Nell lay in wait. As soon as the Thomas van turned on to the county road, she'd gone upstairs and found her under-used burgundy nightie. She didn't even bother with the bikini panties, just placed herself between Joe and the ham and pepper jack cheese sandwich waiting on the counter.

Joe took a step back and held up his hands. "Nell, I'm dirty and I reek of stallion. Stay back!"

She launched herself at his torso like a petite gymnast charging a vault. He had no choice but to catch her and hesitated to attempt to pull her legs from around his waist and her arms from around his neck.

"Make love to me, Joe. I know you want to." Nell let herself slip below his belt buckle to rest on the bulge in his pants, forcing him to cup her bare buttocks with his hands.

"Tink, I should wash up. Then, we can talk about this."

"I don't want to talk. I want sex."

Joe carried her to the counter and edged her rear on to the surface. He tried to back away, but Nell drew him tightly into the V of her legs. He had given her the advantage of placing her at lip level. She grasped the back of his head and brought him in for a kiss of depth and excessive juiciness.

When she ran out of air, Nell gasped, "I need love, and I need it now."

He groaned. "Fine, have it your way, but I don't want you to move a muscle. You let me do all the work." He escaped from his jeans, but didn't bother to take off his boots. He leaned Nell back on his two broad, long-fingered hands and probed gently between her legs so carefully and so shallow the motion became a tease.

Nell dug her nails into his shoulders. "Deeper," she pleaded.

He went deeper, but not as deep as she wanted. He kept her on the edge until she begged again. "Deeper!" With two or three thrusts as deep as she desired, she came, and he saw no reason to hold back. Joe Dean Billodeaux had been celibate six whole weeks for the sake of his wife, and Nell had taken advantage of that knowledge. They rested their heads on each others' shoulder, letting the counter bear the weight as they caught their breath and let their pulse rate return to normal. Joe raised his head first.

"Now, can I have lunch?"

Nell punched his arm and slid from the counter, but she could feel his hands enjoying an assist all the way down. By the time she stood on the top of his boots, her nightie had hung up on his belt buckle and covered very little of her. Joe ran his hands under the silky surface and massaged her breasts.

"Stop that! I'm tender and you need to wash your hands, cowboy."

"Tender? Just the way I like them." He nipped her through the fabric.

Nell groped the counter behind her and found the ham sandwich. She raised her hand and shoved a corner of the bread into his mouth. "Here, eat this. I'm probably ready to have my period. That's why I'm sore and horny."

"Now that just takes my appetite away, sugar. Tink, I mean, Tink."

"I'll tell you what, you can call me anything you want if we can do this again today."

"Never let it be said Joe Dean Billodeaux passed

up an offer like that." He crammed the rest of the sandwich into his mouth with a grubby hand and washed it down with the waiting glass of now warmish milk. Nell reached over and snagged the dill pickle strip on the side of the plate. She sucked it into her mouth and drew it back and forth.

Joe polished off the second half of his sandwich, never taking his eyes off the pickle and Nell's lips. "That doesn't look too strenuous to me. Maybe we could try something similar after we both take a shower."

Nell smiled with satisfaction. About time they got over their disappointment and got back to normal.

****

Since Joe Dean had the biggest house and the largest kitchen in the family, his mama and sisters commandeered the place and insisted on bringing all the food for the Easter feast. "Nell shouldn't be straining herself to entertain us," Allie told her brother in a whisper. He nodded in agreement and watched his wife ply Father Ardoin with another slice of the enormous ham his mother had glazed with brown sugar and ornamented with pineapple rings and cherries.

Nadine came up on his other side. "Nell seems better, more relaxed. She had that baby test, huh? Some women, they don't want to say before three months is up because something might go wrong. *Mais,* you know, Joe Dean, y'all should get married in the church before the baby comes."

"Let it be, Mama. Nell is still saying there is no baby, and I don't want to argue with her."

"Oops," said Nadine as she saw Father Ardoin pat the seat next to him and ask Nell to sit down.

"I was delighted to see you at Mass with Joe's family, Nell."

"How could you see me among all those people? You had standing room only for Easter."

"Yes, the holiday does bring out the casual, the lapsed and the visitors, but the Billodeauxs take up two rows. You are the shortest one in the bunch, easy to pick out in that pretty spring dress."

If only the priest knew what she had done the last time she'd worn that frock with the cornflower print. Nell turned a bit pink and fanned herself with a hand. "It's hot in here with all the people. Joe needs to turn on the air-conditioning."

"Certainly, in your condition he should do whatever he can to make you comfortable. You know, Nell, you would make your mother-in-law so happy if you took instruction and were married in the church before the baby comes. I'm not pressing you to convert, merely trying to keep peace in the family."

Nell shot a look across the room to where her husband and mother-in-law appeared to be plotting. "I guess you didn't hear I was unable to carry the babies, Father."

"No. I am sorry for your loss, Nell." Father Ardoin balanced his plate on a knee in order to take Nell's hand. A few grains of rice dressing slipped off the rim but two of Lizzie's nippy deviled eggs stayed put. "If you want to talk about it, I'd be happy to listen."

She didn't have the heart to say an unmarried, elderly priest would be the last person she would want to consult about losing her babies. "Thank you, Father. Can I get you some of the Watergate salad in a separate bowl?"

"That would be wonderful. I would appreciate it, Nell."

Glaring at her husband, Nell wove her way through the maze of children making themselves at home on the floor and filled a bowl at the dessert table. Joe came up behind and kissed her neck.

"It wasn't me, I swear. Mama is pushing the church wedding and a baby on the way would give her an edge is all. Let's not fight when we just got things back to normal. When everyone goes home, I'll show you what we can do with leftover cold banana pudding," Joe promised. Nell shivered beneath his hands.

Cassie returned around three. Her mother and father and half her siblings had come along and were shown the spread and invited to eat. The Billodeaux family, having digested the ham, turkey, stuffed Cajun roast, and all the sides washed down with coffee or iced tea, was considering second desserts. Bridget, Nora, and Kathy headed right for the table of treats. Ben and Brian hunkered down next to the enormous bowl of chocolate eggs and jellybeans on the coffee table. With her children set, Mrs. Thomas asked to speak to Joe and Nell somewhere alone. She looked around helplessly at the crowd of Billodeauxs covering every available space.

"Upstairs in our bedroom. We have a sitting area."

Joe led the way and closed the door behind the nervous parents and Cassie. The three Thomases squeezed on to the dark green rattan loveseat near the window overlooking the oaks while Joe and Nell sat in the comfortably cushioned chairs opposite. Nell expected them to announce Cassie was going home to have her baby and raise it among her brothers and sisters.

"Cassie should tell you," Mrs. Thomas said, ringing her thin freckled hands.

"I want you and Joe to have my baby. It was my fault you lost yours trying to help me. My folks really can't afford another child, and I want to finish school and do something with my life this baby can be proud of someday. I'd want to see him though. I want one of those open adoptions the doctor talked about. My mom and dad would want him to know they are his grandparents, too." Cassie collapsed around her bulging stomach as if all the air had gone out of her. She hugged her belly and waited for a reaction from the stunned couple.

Nell recovered first, reached out, and took Cassie's hand. "Honey, you shouldn't do this out of guilt. You may regret your decision later. That wouldn't be good for any of us."

"It's not just that I feel bad about the trouble I've caused y'all. My baby could grow up in this great house and go to any college he wanted. It's a boy, Joe. I saw when they did the ultrasound—for sure a boy, not a guess. He and Deanie would be so close in age. They could ride horses and chase the barn cats and go fishing in the bayou together like real brothers. I want my son to have that kind of upbringing, not grow up in a crowded place in the city with a teenage mother and no chance in life."

"Cassie, this is a great gift you are offering us, but I don't know if Nell is ready to…" Joe said, looking into the girl's baffled blue eyes.

"You don't want him? Is it because he might have problems because of my chemo? The doctor in Phoenix said everything looked normal. Did he tell you different, Nell? Is there something wrong with him? How can I raise a handicapped child with no money and no job? I'll have to quit school to help my parents raise him."

"No, no, dear. The doctor said the baby was developing normally, and he certainly had all his parts. As for other side effects, we'd have to wait and see. You heard him. If we adopted your baby, we'd accept that risk just as we did with Deanie being premature and a bit behind in his development," Nell soothed.

"Deanie is behind?" Joe said, upset.

"Not by very much. You know Izzy has been bragging about how long Randi has been crawling while Dean is just starting to get up on his hands and knees. Children develop at different rates, and a premature baby has some catching up to do. He'll be fine, Joe, and so will Cassie's baby." Feeling as if she were caught up in some kind of strange parental Twister game, Nell rubbed Joe's back with the hand not being squeezed by Cassie.

"Is it because Bijou is my baby's daddy?" Cassie asked with anguish in her voice.

"No, hell no. That would make him a Billodeaux, and we take care of our own. I was planning on setting up a college fund for the child anyway. We thought you'd be keeping the baby is all, and we could help out."

Nell watched a shadow cross Joe's face as he realized Cassie might give a Billodeaux baby to strangers. She spoke up quickly. "Cassie, Joe and I would be honored to adopt your baby and give Deanie a brother if this is truly what you want. Joe's lawyers can draw up an open adoption agreement, and you can stay with us until the baby is born. We'll plan his nursery together and shop for his clothes and pick out a name we all like. Mr. and Mrs. Thomas, we will make sure you're granted grandparents' rights. This is the greatest gift anyone could give us."

Joe unfroze from his shock and went into action. "It sure is. Why, Nell and I are well on our way to building our own football team. Now we have a quarterback and a receiver. This is great news. Can I tell my mama and the rest of the family?"

Cassie smiled for the first time since she'd entered the house. "Let's do it right now, make a big announcement on Easter Sunday to the whole bunch downstairs." She bounced to her feet and shot out a hand to catch her balance on the arm of the loveseat.

"Whoa, dizzy. I keep forgetting I can't get up that fast right now. Nell, I'm saving you a lot of trouble because it's a bitch being pregnant."

"Cassie!" her mother reprimanded.

Nell gave a slight smile. "I'm sure you *are* doing the hard part for me, Cassie. Thank you. Let's go tell the world the Joe Dean Billodeauxs are having another baby."

Chapter Thirty-Three

Nell and Cassie sat on the large bed in the guest room next to Deanie's nursery. The walls had been done in a masculine tan and the furnishings upholstered in leather, even the headboard and the tops of the night tables. Miss Ashleigh of Chapelle had envisioned massive football players sleeping here which explained the pigskin decor. They were about to play havoc with her design.

Cassie had the wallpaper book open to a border of cowboys on horseback chasing down a herd of cattle. "What do you think of this one, Nell? It would match the walls so we wouldn't have to repaint. With the little guy only three weeks from coming, I don't think we should mess with any fumes."

"I think I like the one with all the pretty horses better. You know like the old song—dapples and grays, pintos and bays. It would blend in, too."

Cassie ran a finger along the frieze of galloping steeds. "This one looks sort of like Copperhead before Bijou bleached him and made him so ugly."

Cassie's face clouded over. "Do you really think Norma Jean will return him to the ranch?"

"Yes, I'm sure she will if for no other reason than to get another look at Joe. I hope he's on the road somewhere when she shows up. Look, here's one like Buttercup."

"Hardly. They're both palominos, but Buttercup is a Shetland." Cassie rolled her eyes at Nell's ignorance. "Do you get jealous of Joe's other women very often?"

"There wouldn't be enough time in the day to do anything else if I did. No, he hasn't given me any cause to doubt him since we married—except that time with my sister, which I now understand completely. He was trying to get information out of Norma Jean, and I knew that. The hormones made me nuts. Have you given any thought to baby names yet?" Nell said to change the topic.

"I'd like him to give him my name, sort of. Maybe Cassidy or Cass. The baby name book says Cassidy means 'ingenious' in Irish, but Cass means 'vain'. I wouldn't want him to be vain. Ingenious would be great. Are they too girlie? Joe won't want a girlie name."

"That's true. Why don't we use your last name? Our son would be called Thomas Cassidy Billodeaux. Sound good to you?"

"Oh, yes! Thank you, Nell. He'll have both my names. Let's use the horse border. We can keep this big armchair and hassock by the window because it would be a great reading chair. Two normal sized people can sit in it and snuggle up. Maybe we can find a crib to match the wood on the dresser. We'd better do it soon. The doctor said I dropped, so it won't be too long now. Aren't you excited?"

"Very," Nell said, thinking she was also exhausted from trying to keep up with the teen who had twice as much energy as she did even in the ninth month of pregnancy.

"I'm hungry. What do we have for lunch?" Cassie

stood up in preparation for waddling to the kitchen. Her stomach had gone horizontal when the baby dropped, making her look twice as big as she had been last week.

"Nadine brought over homemade chicken soup this morning while you were still in bed. I told her light on the pepper sauce. Her gumbo was burning out the lining of my stomach."

"I like Nadine's gumbo. Isn't Thomas Cassidy going to be lucky to have four sets of grandparents? Could I have a peanut butter and banana sandwich with my soup? I'll make it and start heating up the soup."

Cassie went ahead leaving Nell with the wallpaper book and a moment of quiet. She wished she could stretch out on the over-sized bed and nap. Nadine insisted on feeding those she called her *T-mamas*, meaning little in Cajun. The excessive feeding was starting to show. Besides feeling sluggish, she had gone up a size in jeans since their return from Phoenix, and her bras fit too tightly. She'd made a secret trip to the mall to get bigger clothes claiming she had to meet a client at Dr. Green's office. Some competition she would be for Norma Jean if she got fat. Maybe, she would close her eyes just for a minute.

Joe shook his wife gently. "Cassie has lunch ready downstairs. Would you like me to bring you a tray?"

"No, sorry. I fell asleep while we were looking at wallpaper borders. Do you like this one with the horses?"

"Yeah, it's great. Not as good as the football players I picked out for Deanie's room next door, but still great."

"And we have a name. See if you like it—Thomas Cassidy Billodeaux. Our girl tells me Cassidy means ingenious."

"It's a good name. What does Thomas mean?"

"I don't know. It's Cassie's last name and a saint's name. That will make your mom happy." Nell yawned and scooted to the edge of the bed.

"I'd better see if Deanie is up from his nap before we go downstairs." She started toward the sky blue room with its border of football players. Red and black, she had told Joe, was not a good color combination for a nursery.

"Cassie has him. She heard Deanie whimper and brought him downstairs. He's spitting out his strained vegetables as we speak. The table is set and the soup is on. I think we even have peanut butter sandwiches on the side. You still seem groggy. Want me to carry you down?"

"Of course not. I really need the exercise. I should go riding or swimming this afternoon."

"You should go see Dr. Green. Cassie told me she's worried you don't have enough energy to take care of two babies. Nell, listen to me. If you aren't pregnant—well, I don't even want to say it because saying might make it so."

Joe looked too serious for her to make a joke out of his concerns the way she usually did. "You are worried my cancer might be coming back?"

He nodded, still not wanting to say the word.

"I'm fine. If it will make you feel better, I'll see Mintay as soon as she can work me in, okay?" Nell went down to lunch knowing she was almost as jealous of Cassie's health and energy as she was of Norma Jean's long legs and slim hips.

****

"Pregnant. Here it is in black and white. Read it and smile, Nellwyn Abbott Billodeaux. Everyone knew it but you." Dr. Green waved the file in her face.

"Then I didn't lose all the babies."

"You certainly kept one. From my brief exam, I'd say you are three months and already porking up, so watch the eating. I know in Phoenix they gave you some names of good obstetricians. Here's a few more. See one of them ASAP."

Nell fiddled with the notepaper containing the doctors' names. "Mintay, could we keep this quiet for now?"

"As a doctor, I can't say a thing. As a friend, can't I tell Rev?"

"I'm afraid this might upset Cassie. She might think we don't want her baby and we do. Joe, especially. He wanted to do something for his cousin's child since Bijou certainly won't, wherever he is. Keeping Thomas Cassidy in the family is very important to him. Our next son is due to arrive in two weeks, so could we not say anything to anybody until then? I swear I'll make an appointment in Lafayette and sneak up there for a checkup."

"I suppose the news will keep as long as you take it easy. No riding, understand?"

"Understood. Mintay, have you and Rev worked out your problems?"

"Well, sort of. He offered me a bribe last week. If we start a family in the next six months, he'll build a real infirmary for Chapelle with enough beds for poor women who can't afford the big hospitals to give birth with a midwife if they want and for others to recover from minor procedures. We could even have a hospice area. A facility like that would make it so much easier on those who have no transportation. He said he'd throw in a psychologist's office for you and we wouldn't have to share anymore. Rev certainly knows how to tempt a girl."

"An infirmary would be so great. I guess you are too moral to bribe."

"Oh, you know Rev will build the place regardless. The gesture reminds me what a good man he is. Is one little baby too much to ask? You said yourself I wasn't getting any younger."

"I sense weakening here."

"Let's take care of you first. At least, try to sneak these vitamins once a day."

****

Cassie went into labor on June 22nd, a full week earlier than expected. "How lucky is that?" she boasted when the pains were twenty minutes apart and irregular. When the spasms rolled across her belly in one-minute intervals after ten hours of labor, she wasn't so cocky about her luck or her choice of natural childbirth because it "would be better for the baby."

"Nell make them knock me out!" she pleaded as she gripped Joe's hand on one side and Nell's on the other.

"Try to relax. Pant, remember panting?" Nell prompted.

"Joe, force the doctor to come in here and get this baby out of me!"

"Cassie, it won't be much longer." With relief, he saw the doctor coming to check on the progress of the birth. This ordeal was worse than tearing a hamstring in the fourth quarter of the Super Bowl. To think he had wanted to put Nell through the agony of childbirth as a gift—a gift for Christ's sake!

"Here we go to the delivery room, Cassie," the doctor said.

"Then move your ass, Doc!" Cassie answered with a growl, followed by a groan and a series of pants. Her mother sat out in the waiting room too far away to reprove the language.

The procession of medical personnel and paper-clad parents-to-be moved down the hall and into the glaring lights of the delivery room. Joe stood in the puddles of fluids and blood that came with the birth process and watched his second son come into the world headfirst and capped with matted red fuzz. He smiled across at Nell. They lowered Cassie after helping her with the last big push.

"He's a winner, Cass. Great job."

They laid the baby on her thigh close enough to see all of his fingers and toes and his wide open crying mouth. "He's beautiful. Red hair like mine." Tears ran down her cheeks. "Oh, I'm having more pains. Is something wrong?"

"Just delivering the afterbirth and helping the uterus to contract," the doctor assured her.

Joe watched the afterbirth plop into the pan. The doctor examined the grisly slab thoroughly. "They use these to make shampoo," he told Joe Dean conversationally.

"Gross," murmured Joe under his breath and out of the hearing of the two women who seemed so elated after all this blood and gore.

Cassie released her grip on Joe and Nell and clutched her newborn when he was placed clean and swaddled into her arms. She hugged small Thomas to her chest. A few more tears slipped out. Then, she beckoned to Nell. "Here, you take him to the nursery.

Mr. and Mrs. Thomas, Mintay and Rev, Joe Dean and Nell, and MawMaw and PawPaw Billodeaux clustered around the nursery window.

"Fifteen grandkids for us, Frank. Course we got to share this one with Hal and Flo. They're good people even if their son is a stinker. How many for you folks?" Nadine asked the Thomases.

"Not so many yet. We have three others from our oldest children, all married. I guess with so many kids, we'll pass you one of these days," Mr. Thomas answered.

Ann and Gary Abbott arrived with a teddy bear and a bouquet they thrust at Nell. "For Cassie and the baby," they said pressing toward the glass. "We have three grandsons now, but no girls yet."

"Oh, I think some girls might come along. What do you say, Nell?" Nadine regarded her daughter-in-law who had worn baggy jeans and a cotton big shirt, tails out, for the ordeal.

"Oh, God willing, I guess."

Mintay dove right in and changed the subject. "What did you name him?"

"Thomas Cassidy Billodeaux."

"Good name," the Rev approved. "Looks like your old Saint Jude felt he had to pay up after you done won the Super Bowl for him, Joe Dean."

"Hmmmm," said Joe Dean, not quite over the gore he had witnessed at the birth of his redheaded son.

"Thomas after the apostle. Name means the Twin. And now you got two boys, and one of them's a twin."

Joe's big jaw dropped. "Mama, what did you pray for at the novena, just a live, healthy baby right?"

Nadine looked shame-faced. "Well, son, I know it wasn't right, but we prayed for twins in case Nell couldn't have no more, you see. Twin girls since you had a boy, but I'm not complaining, no. I'm lightin' a few candles on my way home for bot' the Blessed Virgin and St. Jude to say *merci'*."

"We have a lot to be thankful for," Ann Abbott added in her prim Episcopalian way.

"More than you know," Nadine replied.

****

Three days later, Nell glanced into the back seat as the sedan bumped over the back roads on the way to the ranch. Thomas slept curled over in his baby seat as if he were still inside Cassie's womb. The strong summer sun turned his red hair to fire. The rough ride getting home bothered him not one bit.

Joe had seen to it that Cassie was not rushed out of the hospital either, though when she hinted she wanted to remain the rest of the summer at Lorena Ranch with Nell and the baby, he sided with the Thomases. The time had come for Cassie to go home and restart her young life. He was positive about that. She could call and e-mail all she wanted. They would take weekly pictures of the baby's progress and send them to her, but Joe remained firm about Nell needing a respite and time to bond alone with the new child in their life. After all, his wife and child must come first.

Joe smiled as he watched Nell check again on Tommy. Then, he opened his mouth and said what he was thinking. "I never expected to get our twin boys by adoption, but I sure am glad it worked out like this.

That St. Jude, he knows what he's doing. I can't believe I wanted to put you through childbirth, Tink. What a dumb idea!"

"What? You never saw any of your sisters give birth?" Nell didn't seem as happy as she should be.

"Hell, no. Who would want to see their sisters down there squeezing out a baby? Man, that was brutal."

"You've seen plenty of other women—down there!" She spoke sharply.

He didn't have a clue what had gone wrong now. "Believe me, it's not the same. When you make love to a woman, they unfold like a flower, all dewy and moist. When they groan, it's with pleasure. That big hole opening up, all that blood and gunk and screaming, it's nothing the same, believe you me. If we want more kids, we'll adopt."

"Oh, will we? What if I want to experience giving birth—what then?" Nell sniveled against the glass of the window.

The drive through Arizona in search of Cassie repeated all over again. Joe shook his head as if to clear his brain after a bad hit. Outside the car, the sun sizzled in a cloudless June sky. They'd obtained a precious new baby without any physical suffering. Their other son who had started crawling waited to greet his new brother at his mama's house. In hindsight, Joe Dean Billodeaux knew he should have kept his mouth shut. It wasn't too late to start. He didn't answer his wife, but carefully steered around the potholes as well as he could to give them all a smooth, safe ride. Silence ensued.

Nell broke the peace. "Joe, I'm pregnant."

Joe screeched to a stop on the narrow dirt siding, nearly putting the car into the deep ditch filled with yesterday's rainfall and an overgrowth of weeds.

"For months, you've been telling me you aren't pregnant. Now you are. Did we make a baby by accident somewhere between Arizona and here?"

"Mintay thinks I didn't lose all of the babies. I've seen an obstetrician in Lafayette. Both of them say I should be due before Christmas."

Joe thumped his fingers against the steering wheel. "So, you are going into your fourth month and never said a word to me."

"I wasn't sure until a couple of weeks ago. I didn't say anything then because I didn't want to upset Cassie."

"But it's fine to upset your husband."

"I thought you wanted a big family."

"I do, just not all in the same year."

"Then you and your family should be careful what you pray for!"

"Aw Tink, it makes no nevermind to me, but you do know what this means?" He reached over and folded her against his chest.

"Now, we're gonna have to get married in the church, or we'll never hear the end of it from Mama."

Chapter Thirty-Four

What with taking the required instruction in the church and planning Tommy's baptism and Deanie's re-baptism because, Nadine said, you never could tell if they had done it right in Mexico, Nell approached her sixth month of pregnancy by the time she walked down the aisle at Ste. Jeanne d'Arc in Chapelle.

Nell stood in the church lobby waiting for the *Wedding March* to cue up and having second thoughts about her choice of gowns. She'd refused to wear white because she was not some quivering virgin worrying about her wedding night—her exact words to her mother-in-law who had backed off and told the rest of the family Nell was having pregnancy mood swings. The fabric in a soft yellow color did go well with her skin tones, big brown eyes and short brunette hair, but with her belly having gotten so big so quickly, Nell felt she resembled the harvest moon. The circlet of silk autumn leaves suggested by Stevie Riley to replace a veil wasn't doing much to draw the attention away from the cloth bunching under her high bodice beautifully embroidered with fall wildflowers. The final fitting had been only two weeks ago and for sure, she'd pooched out another inch since then.

Fingering the collar necklace of all shades of amber—honey and ruby, green and a tigerish brown—connected with fine gold links Joe had selected for her with the help of all four sisters, Nell realized she was as nervous as the first time around a year ago. Her father waited to take her arm. Mintay, clad in brown with glittering golden highlights woven into the threads, looked much more voluptuous than her slim form did in a lab coat or scrubs. The woman Nell regarded as her best friend reached the center of the church where the two main aisles formed a cross. Stevie already stood with the groomsmen in her gown of deep autumn red flecked with gold. Dear Father Ardoin, still distressed she had not been converted by his gentle teachings and so could have no full-scale nuptial Mass, opened the book containing the words for the service.

The agreement with Joe and Nadine had been that the ceremony would be private and small, a gathering of immediate family and the closest of friends. "And you hold out for that," Stevie told her. Even so, that came to fifty attending, all turned her way and waiting. Nell took her father's arm and began the processional march.

Where was Joe? She dreamt last night her super-sexy husband had run off with Norma Jean Scruggs in a motor home painted with cactus blossoms, and left behind his "old lady" with four sobbing children hanging on her legs. Joe woke her up when she cried out, "Don't go!" He soothed her back to sleep with an off-key version of *You're having my Baby* so badly sung he kept repeating the chorus because he didn't know the rest of the words.

Joe took his vows seriously, but perhaps vows taken in Las Vegas meant nothing and church vows meant everything. She couldn't see him waiting with the tall and wide forms of Connor Riley and Rev

Bullock blocking her view. Maybe, Norma Jean had chosen today to deliver Copperhead to the ranch. Then, she passed the Sinners' contingent and saw Joe, elegant in his black tux, backed up by Jackie Haile, looking very butch in hers.

Father Ardoin had expressed grave misgivings about allowing Miss Haile to be best man. Joe pointed out no written rules said the best man had to be male and a witness was a witness. Besides, this way he didn't have to choose between Connor and the Rev for the honor. Nell had no objections, not after the way Jackie stood by Joe in Phoenix. Stevie had given the groom a big kiss on the cheek for holding out for one of their best friends. After all, she said when out of Father Ardoin's hearing, it wasn't as if Jackie would try to seduce the altar boys. Typical Stevie.

Nell's doubts vanished at the sight of Joe's wide grin. She swore he hummed *You're having my Baby* under his breath during the entire ceremony and she whispered, "You got that right" when he arched his tall body over her pregnant belly in the awkward kiss sealing their vows.

Rather than the formal recessional, family and friends congratulated the couple in the center of the church. Rev Bullock in a moment of ecumenical fellowship put his massive arm around Father Ardoin's frail shoulders and said, "Unusual wedding, huh?"

"Oh, Nell isn't the first pregnant bride married in Ste. Jeanne d'Arc, and she won't be the last. I do believe this is my first lesbian best man, though."

"If every priest were as good a sport as you, Father, I'd convert."

"Heaven forbid, son. I'd never be able to face your

347

father across the table at the Chamber of Commerce prayer breakfast again if you were to do that."

"Only kiddin' you, padre, only kiddin'."

****

By the time the wedding party arrived, the blowout reception at the ranch was in full swing. Lizzie's children, well paid to do so, led the four ponies in an endless circle to entertain the youngest guests. A Jolly Jumper shaped like a castle, a Radar Frog where aspiring pitchers could test their fast balls and a rock wall kept the other children amused. Because at a Cajun wedding there were bound to be children, lots of children, Joe told Nell.

The All-American Cajun Zydeco Band rapped out a tune in the barbecue pavilion. Joe selected them on the basis they could play anything and they proved that was true. The musicians stopped in mid-chank to play their rub board version of *Here Comes the Bride* when Joe extracted his pregnant wife from the limo using both of his hands. The guests laughed. They formed a corridor when Joe scooped Nell up and carried her to a comfortable chair with a footstool deep in the shade of the live oaks. He held up his hands for silence.

"Yes, we are having twins, and we're fairly sure it's twin girls to go along with our two boys, so Nell won't be on her feet much today. Line up over there if you want to say hey."

Applause followed the announcement. Miss Maxine and Miss Lolly giggled and patted their ancient hands together. They shoved to the front of the line.

"Do you think they will name the twins after us since we helped with the novena, Lolly?"

"Doubtful. Nadine did all the arranging and the

most powerful praying."

Nell kept herself from rolling her eyes as she accepted their congratulations but she shuddered a little at the thoughts of having twins named Maxine and Lolita, Miss Lolly's real name.

Nadine overheard her name as she whisked by, her wedding finery covered with a dark green canvas apron, a Magnalite pot full of barbecued brisket in her hands. "I got two granddaughters wit' Nadine as a middle name, and you know my boy and his boy is named for me, too. They should call those babies something else so long as they each get a saint's name. Come eat."

Joe had done his best to convince his mama he could afford a caterer. But as soon as they set the wedding date for the first Saturday in September, Nadine pressured her daughters to empty their freezers of last season's venison and to fry up the accumulated fish so they could stuff in good homemade wedding delicacies. At least, Nadine allowed hired help to serve and do the cleanup and permitted the wedding cakes to be farmed out to Pommier's Bakery.

Beau's Blooms of Chapelle provided the vast white tent, the wooden folding chairs, tables and coordinated linens to match the decor of autumnal abundance. Shocks of sugar cane bound with gold wire ribbon sat amid banks of mums providing swaths of fall color even though summer would not release its relentless grip on Louisiana for another month or more.

The Sinners had come out in force, a little battered by training camp and pre-season games, but ready to party with wives and girlfriends. Precious and Sharlette, who had made up long ago, came to sit on either side of Nell for a visit. She hadn't seen either one since the

Super Bowl party. Precious, her usual self, was dressed resplendently in gold. Sharlette arrived very changed, but still chic in the last month of her pregnancy.

Sharlette shook a finger bearing a large topaz ring at Joe Dean and smoothed her other hand over an African print silk maternity dress knotted on one shoulder. "This is your fault, boy. You let Ace carry the ball and he came home still celebrating. He knows I don't bother with birth control during the season 'cause his mind is on the game, not on me. He's chasin' me around the house, and I'm yellin' 'Get a condom on, Ace.' Well, when a tight end takes you down in the hallway, there is no room for argument. You know what he said later—'Sorry, babe, I got carried away with being a receiver.' Good thing our girls were at a sleep-over."

"You look great, Sharlette." Nell regarded her own stomach and wondered how Sharlette could balance on those high heels without falling face first into the oak duff. She couldn't see her own feet clad in some kind of hard-soled ballet slipper her Prince Charming had slipped over her toes because she could no longer do it herself.

"I look like a pumpkin," Nell complained.

"Oh no, you don't," Precious swore. "Right now, you're only up to watermelon size, girl. By the end of November, you'll be a prize-winning pumpkin, one of those great big ones that weigh a ton. You show more 'cause you're short. Sharlette here, she never gains an extra ounce with her babies. Me, I'm wearing all four around my hips."

Stevie Riley, a little rattled by all the pregnancy talk, snapped a picture of the group. "Don't worry, I can airbrush out the bellies if you want," she assured the women.

"No use, those baby girls will just keep asking where they was when you got married. You might as well show 'em," Precious predicted. "Ooh! We got a big present coming."

Despite specifying "no gifts—your presence is all we ask to celebrate our happiness" on the invitations, a small tower of boxes accumulated by Nell's feet. One present, a pair of hand-carved wood ducks—the flamboyant male and his more sensible mate—rested in a basket filled with Spanish moss. Nell, feeling like a fat nesting hen, was relieved the carvings weren't of swans.

Now, Calvin Armitage and Asa Dobbs, carrying a wooden chest between them, set the offering at their quarterback's feet. As they bent over to drop the burden, dowdy Rosemarie Leleux appeared from behind their bulk.

"This gift is from Granny. She says she won't be around to see you use them all, so it's best to give you these now."

Joe raised the lid of the plain box, its thick reddish-brown finish patinated with scratches and nicks and perhaps, recently wiped of cobwebs. A stack of crocheted baby blankets, twelve in all, four blue, two pink, some yellow, some green, some multicolored lay inside.

"Dear God!" Nell gasped as if the chest contained a cobra. The prediction that she and Joe would have twelve children came surging back in her mind. She recovered quickly. "The blankets are so lovely. They must have taken years to make."

"No, only since last year this time when you and Joe Dean got hitched in Las Vegas. I never saw Granny crochet with such energy as after she heard the news."

"Please thank her for us. We're so sorry she wasn't well enough to attend. And do have something to eat before you go. Nadine is a wizard in the kitchen, just like your Granny is with afghans."

"Thank you. I know Nadine's cooking, and I know I make people uneasy, but I'll stop for a while."

The homely woman with the chicken-pox scarred face gave Nell a beautiful smile. She turned her stubby body toward Calvin Armitage who took a step back, something he never did, but she grasped his hand despite this move. "Hall of Fame," she said.

Asa Dobbs thrust his palm toward the *traiteur*. "It's a boy, positively," she told him, then turned and walked off to the feast.

"Yes, Yes!" Ace pumped the air and did his celebratory duck walk back and forth in front of Sharlette and Nell. "A son at last and you were going to make me wait to find out, devil woman!"

Calvin shuddered. "That's what the Rev said she is." He pointed a shaking finger at the retreating broad-hipped Rosemarie. "Some kind of voodoo priestess."

"*Mais* no, she's just a *traiteur,* my man," Joe Dean explained. "She does no harm."

"I don't give a damn!" Asa Dobbs exclaimed. "It's a boy!"

"Twelve, Joe. There are twelve blankets." Nell shivered even though it was eighty degrees under the oaks.

"We only got three embryos left in the freezer, Tink. Beats me." He grinned wickedly.

Looking shaken, Nell struggled out of her chair. "Excuse me. I need to use the bathroom—again."

Avoiding the trailer-sized portable bathrooms complete with sinks to wash up that were towed in for the guests, Nell waddled to the house and entered the dim hallway leading to the downstairs powder room. She nearly collided with Cassie who walked a tiptoeing Deanie up and down while Tommy watched from his baby seat. Deanie let go of Cassie's hand and toddled in a headlong rush to Nell's leg.

"Ma," he said happily. Pointing to his brother, he announced, "*bebe*," and flopped down beside Tommy. "Boo!" He puffed the word into the baby's face. Tommy blinked his eyes and smiled.

Both Nell and Cassie beamed. They hadn't seen each other since the baptism, and Deanie made this sudden reunion easier. "I came in to pee," Nell confided.

"See, I told you adoption went easier, but you had to have your own."

Nell was uncertain if Cassie joked or not. "You were right about that."

"You know when I gave you Tommy, I felt stupid for getting myself in trouble, guilty about what happened at the bus station, and very scared about the future." Cassie gazed at Nell's baby-filled belly.

Nell's stomach clenched. "Cassie, honey, it's only been two months, but we love him so. Look how Tommy's eyes have turned Billodeaux brown, just like melted dark chocolate. Deanie loves him, too, don't you, Deanie?"

"Bubba," Deanie said and blew another boo into the baby's face.

Nell went on a bit desperately, "Truly, I wasn't sure I was pregnant when you came to us, and I could tell Joe wanted to make a home for Tommy. He'd have a dozen if we could, but you know that won't be possible."

"For most people, Dean and the twin girls would be plenty." Cassie picked up her son and tucked him under her chin. Their red-gold hair matched perfectly where Cassie's natural color had grown out. Still, she seemed more likely to be the baby's sister than his mother in her short black skirt and snug emerald top, only a slight slackness of belly betraying what the teen had endured.

"You should be outside dancing and having a good time, Cassie. Let me find someone else to mind the babies."

"I'd rather stay here. People say things to me like how brave and generous I am to give up my baby. I was only dumb and scared." She held Tommy so tightly he began to cry.

"You'll always be a part of his life, Cassie. We promised."

Talk about scared. If Cassie chose to leave with the baby, she'd hardly be able to stop the taller girl whose figure had matured with her pregnancy. With the clang of pans in the kitchen and the blare of music from the band outside, Nell doubted if anyone would hear her call for help if it came to that.

"I got a letter from Mexico. Bijou said he's sorry, that gambling is a sickness with him. He told me how to find him and said I could bring the kid along if I wanted. It's cheap to live down there. He has a job training horses."

"Cassie, please…"

"You know what Nell? I'm not *that* dumb, and I never want to be that guilty or that scared again. I did the right thing giving you my baby."

Joe stepped out of the shadow of the stairwell. Deanie saw him first and got to his feet from a three-point stance on the floor. The boy tottered forward. "Dada!" Joe swung his son up on his shoulders where Deanie proceeded to muss a very expensive haircut.

"I wondered how long it took for someone as tiny as you to pee, Tink. Heck, you only went an hour an ago. LeJeune Pommier says we should come cut the cakes because he isn't sure how long the football-shaped one will stay up on the sugar tee in this heat. Some joker is vandalizing his other masterpiece by sticking plastic Mardi Gras babies in all the air-brushed grapes. You should see, two of them have little pink bows glued to their heads and someone put a daub of orange nail polish on the top of another so he looks like Tommy here. Can you believe, there are twelve in all. I tell you, the Sinners are the quickest team in the league to exploit a weakness."

"Go to your daddy, Tommy." Cassie held out her baby, and Joe tucked him under his arm in a football carry.

"Yes, let's all go see—after I pee," and Nell breathed out as easily as possible with two unborn babies pressing against her diaphragm.

****

The sun set. The party wound down as families with small children went home. Lizzie's kids gave the exhausted ponies good rubdowns and extra feed in the barn. The rental people arrived with their truck, and its crew deflated the castle-shaped jumper and the puffed-up radar frog. They broke the rock wall into pieces and placed it on a trailer. In the barbecue pavilion, Calvin and Ace danced with their wives to a slow nostalgic tune. Under the white tent, Nadine could be heard bossing the staff and dictating the disposition of the leftovers.

Nell watched from the balcony off her bedroom. She'd gone upstairs to rest and exchange her wedding gown for an airy white cotton dress that didn't make her look any smaller but did feel good against the skin.

Joe, Rev and Mintay, Connor and Stevie sat at a table and chairs purloined from the wedding tent and repositioned near the bank of the bayou where they watched a yellow autumn moon rise over the tall cane on the opposite bank. The grounds of the ranch had been thoroughly sprayed for mosquitoes, but it wouldn't be long before migrant insects across the river got their scent and forced the couples to retreat to the screened pavilion or the house. Until that time came, they enjoyed the night and the peeping of the tree frogs.

Nell went to join them. She took the chair waiting for her and swung her legs into Joe Dean's lap. He removed her slippers and began massaging her feet. She gave an orgasmic sigh.

"If I had a cold ginger ale in my hand right now, my life would be complete."

"Here, take what's left of mine." Mintay handed Nell a half-full aluminum can and sipped on her own drink from a plastic cup.

Connor nudged Stevie with an elbow as a signal he was ready to needle his friend. He poured himself more wine from a bottle they shared, put his arm around his tall blonde wife and said, "Football's greatest lover, Joe Dean Billodeaux, reduced to rubbing a lady's feet."

"Let me give you some advice, *mon ami*, rub a woman's feet, and they will do anything for you."

"I think I already have," Nell said.

"And just last summer on a night like this, you told me wishing wouldn't make things so. Since then, I've married you twice and given you a family of four children. These slackers are barely getting started."

"I wouldn't say that, my man." The Rev smoothed his wife's gown over the small, rounded belly its folds hid. "Lookit, only two months along and already showing. I think we havin' twins, too."

"You weren't supposed to say until next month after the ultrasound, Rev," Mintay protested.

"I can't stand when a Cajun boy goes smug on me. No harm done, my love. I'm callin' Connor and Riley for my twin names. Joe Dean, you think of something else for yours. One of mine is bound to be a boy and Riley will do for either, I figure."

"No worries. Since Nell, here, won't let me name the girls Revelationana, or T-Mintay, we're going with Jude Emily and Ann Marie. The Ann is for Nell's mama, Marie for her saint. Then, Jude for a saint and Emily for Nell's unsaintly sister. You and Stevie planning on a family, Con?"

"We'll get busy when I'm through playing. I want to be home with my family, and frankly, the thought of four kids in one year is kind of scary."

"You got that right," Stevie agreed.

"Hey, it took a lot of work to make these wishes come true." Joe Dean rubbed a hand over Nell's belly and felt one of his daughters respond to his touch with a small punch.

"Mintay would say modern science made these two. My mama would claim it was her novena. I'd say St. Jude gave me the wife I needed and my two boys. Whatever, wishes don't come true without some serious work and perseverance. That reminds me, I hope you guys are ready for another Super Bowl because I been praying."

Connor and the Rev groaned.

Nell, her face looking pale and fey in the moonlight, asked softly, "Do you really think there will be twelve children, Joe?"

"*Mais* yeah, Tink. Madame Leleux has already knit their blankets. They'll come, this way, that way, all ways, because you and me are forever—sugar."

Chapter Thirty-Five

Nell sat on the upper gallery waiting for Joe. She'd persuaded Corazon to move the wicker loveseat from the bedroom onto the porch. The stout young woman had done so without any help from her employer. Corazon Romero was a gem as the girl's aunt, Anita Pommier, had promised. Corazon deftly switched a tray with a toasted cheese sandwich and a cup of bland, canned chicken soup for two sleepy baby boys tucked under Nell's arms.

Fat and plain, the possessor of thick eyebrows and a light mustache, Corazon was good-natured, industrious, and devout. Nell heard her singing to Deanie as she put him down for a nap. Her sweet, sad voice seemed to say that having failed to find a husband in Mexico by the time she turned thirty, she did not expect to have children of her own. Nell had no idea what the Spanish words really meant. Yes, Corazon was a find—one that Joe Dean would have no interest in as a woman.

Silly me, Nell thought as she tucked the copy of the trice read *Goodnight Moon* under a pillow and took a bite of her sandwich. Her pregnant condition caused these jealous feelings. As Precious Armitage predicted, her belly had reached Great Pumpkin size while her actual stomach compressed to half its normal capacity because of all the room the twins took up. She no longer had an appetite and even insipid foods gave her heartburn.

Her obstetrician banned normal sex *way* back in October by saying it was best for the babies to stay inside as long as she could hold them. She'd done all she could to keep Joe happy, and he had done the same for her. But by this first week in December, the only urge left was to get the birth over with soon. Three more weeks to go. Nell sighed and sipped her soup. And no sex for six weeks after that. Poor Joe. Poor Joe like hell, he could find willing women wherever he went. Her hormones raged again, double damn it!

In November, she'd been assigned to bed rest after a scary encounter with early contractions. Allowed to come downstairs for Thanksgiving, she nibbled on what small portions her stomach could hold while Nadine and her own mother fussed over her and Joe coaxed her to eat a little more. What she wanted most right now was to see Joe drive through that gate, bound upstairs—and rub her feet. Maybe, just maybe, she would fall asleep on this balmy December day with Joe holding her exactly so, taking the weight of the babies off her insides. She hadn't slept really well since Joe left for the game last Friday afternoon.

She should have told him not to drive to Lorena Ranch today. The Sinners won their game on Sunday, but she knew enough about football to understand three turnovers and victory by a field goal were not acceptable to Coach Marty Buck. This morning, the team would be watching endless film on their errors. Tomorrow, Joe would throw the ball over and over to their rookie wide receiver, Dawson Hunt, who had been responsible for two fumbles, until the pigskin stuck to the new guy's hands like French Quarter Roman taffy. Then, the Rev and his gang would try to strip the ball from the kid until Dawson got it right. Maybe, the Sinners should have kept Jared Forte despite his problems with Joe. Regardless, Nell acknowledged being needy enough to ask her husband to add a six-hour round trip drive to his schedule. He intended to come home anyhow, he claimed.

****

Three days from home *was* too long to be away right now, Joe Dean figured as he sped along the highway watching for the exit to Chapelle. He had talked Nell into this pregnancy. He'd prayed and gotten twins just as he wanted. St. Jude must be a joker, though, to throw in three months without sex to make this little miracle happen, a small test of Billodeaux marital constancy. He could do this. Hell, last season, he had gone without for six months. Still, he'd never considered there might be no sex *inside* of marriage. He'd hang in there no matter how cute the temptresses on the road might be—and offer up his pain. If he had to drive three hours to make Nell happy after being chewed out by an irate coach, he could do that, too.

****

Nell heard the noise of an engine and pushed herself up awkwardly to listen. No, that wasn't the smooth sound of Joe's Porsche. A well-kept older model of a Ford truck with a gun rack holding two hunting rifles mounted in its cab came down the lane. Knox Polk, the retired army sergeant who had taken over the management of the ranch since Bijou's flight, sat behind the wheel. Sergeant Knox oversaw any of Joe's nieces and nephews who wanted to earn some cash by working for him. Joe had learned the folly of giving free rein to relatives, Nell thought, almost sorry his childlike trust in kin had been destroyed.

Knox waved to Nell as he passed. He continued on to the barn. A few minutes later, she could see Knox leading Fatima toward the paddock where she could crop the grass without being too far from her stall. Fatty's belly sagged earthward making the small mare look like a lumpy stuffed toy. She was full of L.B.'s foal and nearing her due date, too. All in all the horse seemed to be handling the discomfort better than her owner.

Another vehicle approached the gate, its engine as loud as a Mack truck. Nell couldn't see who was driving through the trees. Either Knox or Corazon had buzzed the noisy vehicle through to the ranch road. As soon as she saw the bright red paint with the frieze of cactus blossoms, her heart flamed into jealousy. Norma Jean Scruggs had arrived.

The driver laid on the horn belting out a bar of *Deep in the Heart of Texas* and brought the big rig with its matching horse trailer to a smooth stop alongside of the house. Nell tried to push up again from her nest in the cushioned wicker but couldn't find the best grip for the maneuver. She called out for Corazon. The maid came from a side door and marched gesturing and chattering in Spanish at Norma Jean, who emerged with a clatter of high-heeled boots from her impressive motor home.

"*Pardone me mucho,*" Norma Jean apologized, evidently speaking the lingo.

Corazon, mollified, fluffed the white uniform she thought proper to wear and flapped her red bib apron bordered in yellow rickrack she always placed over it. Then, she graciously invited that brazen woman into Nell's home. Knox, standing straight and tall in the barn door, shoved back his grubby white Stetson on his grizzled hair and watched with amazement and perhaps, appreciation as Norma Jean's long legs, clad in tight denim, carried her toward the kitchen door.

Nell succeeded in getting to her feet by the time the company made it to the balcony. She glanced at the road and hoped Joe Dean had been stopped for speeding along the way. By the time he talked himself out of the ticket and signed a few autographs, she would have Norma Jean out of St. Jeanne d'Arc Parish. Why couldn't this hootchie mama have shown up in June when Nell's breasts were getting bigger and her clothes tighter or in September when although large, she'd felt so very loved?

"Nice to see you again, Miss Scruggs. Come to return Copperhead? Corazon, would you bring some iced tea—or would you prefer coffee?" Nell offered, hoping her guest would refuse both.

Corazon set down a matching wicker chair carried from the bedroom for the guest and waited for the woman to express her preference in beverages.

"Well, I'll tell you, Mrs. Joe Dean. Sorry, didn't catch your first name last spring. What I could really go for is a nice, cold Dr. Pepper with plenty of ice, but if you don't have that, sweet tea will be fine." Norma Jean sprawled into the chair, her long, slim legs outstretched.

"I'm cramped up from drivin' all the way from the Texas border. Then, I got lost a few times on these back roads. Those danged cane carts are everywhere. Can't pass for miles. I called that number Joe gave me for directions, but the signal was busy."

"Oh, Corazon turns off the phone when the children are napping."

Norma Jean eyed Nell's big belly. "Children? How many you got? Looks like that big stud of yours knocked you up but good around the time we met and you say you got others? Did you have 'em before you got married? I seem to recall something in the tabloids about a love child, but not more than one."

"We have two adopted boys," Nell replied tersely when she really wanted to say it was none of the barrel racer's business. Then, an idea zipped into her had. "Joe Dean wants a dozen kids before he turns forty. He loves children and doesn't believe in birth control. He's very, very Catholic."

Norma Jean wrinkled her nose. "Honey, you can train 'em to wear a condom. No condom, no nookie. If they won't listen, I keep a pistol under my pillow. I don't threaten to kill 'em. I threaten to blow their balls off. Works every time. Haven't had to castrate one yet."

She stroked her long, black braid and crinkled her deep blue eyes when she smiled at Nell. "Where is that gorgeous bastard you got for a husband, anyway?"

Corazon set down a cut crystal tumbler chock full of crushed ice from the bar and a Dr. Pepper next to Nell's half glass of lukewarm milk. "More milk, *mamacita*? You have not finished your lunch," the maid asked with concern.

"Heartburn, but thank you. I'm fine." Nell faced her guest. "Joe is on the road right now. He'll be sorry he missed you. I'll have Knox unload Copperhead so you can be on your way as soon as possible."

"No rush now I've come this far. I'll tell you, I

kept stoppin' to ask directions. Everyone knew where Joe Dean Billodeaux lived, but no one could tell me how to get here. When I finally found the place, I overshot the drive and had to go clear into that little burg, Chapelle, before I found a parking lot big enough to turn my rig around. I never seen roads so narrow or ditches so deep. Nice place you got here." Norma Jean settled back in her chair, raised her arms above her head and stretched, raising her shapely breasts and showing off her flat stomach.

Nell looked at her own set of boobs. They had gotten bigger but had long since been surpassed by the size of her belly. Now, they just lay there like two goose eggs sitting atop a prize watermelon.

"Knox could show you around, then give you directions back to the highway. You don't want to be caught here after dark with the roads so bad."

"It's only one p. m. I was hopin' to make another offer on the paint. My quarter horse mare has mended fine, but she's getting older. Might be time to breed her before it's too late. Too bad Copperhead is a gelding. He's lookin' good since his coat grew out. Very flashy. Speaking of which…" Norma Jean tilted her head at the lane where Joe's Porsche revved toward the house.

So intent on getting rid of the rodeo queen, Nell hadn't even heard the engine. Too late. She sank back into her cushions and listened to the sound of Joe's feet taking the steps two at a time. He was with the ladies in moments.

Joe raised his wife's small, unhappy face and kissed her lips lightly. "Got here as fast as I could, Tink."

He turned to the barrel racer. "A woman as good as

her word. A pleasure to see you again, *cher*." He air kissed the back of Norma Jean's tanned hand.

"I know it's all bullshit, but that still gives me butterflies deep down, Joe Dean."

Nell's daughters kicked up a storm in sympathy with their mother's agitation. Joe patted the quivering belly. "Settle down girls. You'll make your mama nauseous. She hasn't finished her lunch."

Joe broke off a corner of the congealed cheese sandwich and fed it to Nell. "Eat, my sweet petite."

"Petite! That's more bull," Nell pouted.

"She's cranky," Joe told Norma Jean as if his wife wasn't sitting right there. "Not sleeping, I can tell by those dark circles under her eyes. Tink, why don't you go and lie down like the doctor wants you to? I'll unload Copperhead and show our guest around." He offered Norma Jean his arm.

"Knox can do that. I want you to rub my feet," Nell said petulantly.

Joe shuffled his own feet in embarrassment. "I won't be gone long, sugar."

"Don't call me sugar!"

"I forgot. You just rest until I get back."

The tall, fine-looking couple made their escape from the shrewish wife. At least, that was how Nell viewed it. She teared up. Hormones, simply hormones. She felt unattractive and highly emotional at this stage of the pregnancy game—in other words, completely normal. Still, she had no excuse for being bitchy to Joe after his three-hour drive. She heard the beautiful people emerge from the front door and stand a minute beneath the balcony.

"I'm sorry, sugar. The babies are making my wife

crazy. She's due in three weeks. Sorry, I shouldn't be calling you sugar either, Miss Norma Jean. I'm trying to give up the habit."

"I think it's kind of sweet."

They laughed out loud at that lame joke and sauntered off toward the horse trailer. Joe fooled around with the ramp and finally led Copperhead out into the mild winter sunshine. The horse gleamed from his mahogany head to his burnished black, copper and white spotted sides. The animal took a good look around the ranch, then head-butted Norma Jean.

"Yeah, I know. I'll miss you, too, my pretty boy."

Norma Jean unbuttoned a flap on her western shirt and reached deep down inside for a sugar cube. From Nell's vantage on the balcony, the woman could have been massaging her own breast or at least, showing one of them off.

"Here you go, lover, a little sugar."

Was Norma Jean staring at Joe while she said that? Nell couldn't quite tell. Joe let loose with one of his deep laughs. Norma Jean put a hand on Joe's upper arm much the way her sister had in the barn last year, and looked straight into his chocolate brown eyes. He was supposed to have eyes only for his wife.

"Would you consider sellin' this ole boy to me again? I'd go up to thirty-thousand."

Had she actually fluttered her eyelashes? Nell raised herself from the loveseat and put her back up against the verandah pillar closest to the trailer. She couldn't very well spy standing sideways in her condition, now could she?

"Sorry, can't. There's a lady would be very upset with me if I did," Joe answered, his voice a little huskier than usual.

Damned right, thought Nell. That lady was her, and she wasn't giving Norma Jean anything.

"Cassie has been fretting about this animal ever since my no-good cousin sold you a stolen horse."

"How is the kid? I take it you found her?"

"Yeah, pregnant and scared. Nell and me, we adopted her baby."

"You have a good heart, Joe Dean Billodeaux."

Nell peeked around the column. Those eyelashes went a-fluttering again. Nell was surprised they didn't stir up a breeze. She half expected Joe to duck his head and say, "T'weren't nothing" like some old time cowboy. Instead, he glanced at the horse trailer.

"I see you have your other mount with you. She mend all right?"

"Good as new, but I been thinkin' about breeding her. I don't want to miss the chance to get some good barrel horses out of her. As I was telling your little wife, it's just too bad this here gentleman is gelded." Norma Jean stroked her braid, up and down, up and down.

"I think I can take care of your problem. Come see what I've got in the barn, Miss Norma Jean." Joe led the way with Copperhead in hand.

Nell ground her teeth. That did it! She knew what Joe liked to show women in the barn. She'd been there rolling in the hay enough times with him. No, she was being paranoid. Knox was working in the stables. Still, Joe Dean had sent Bijou home when he wanted to be alone with his girlfriend. Bed rest or no bed rest, she'd make sure her husband remained faithful.

Nell made her way quietly to the carpeted staircase

and unlatched the baby gate at its top. Very aware of being off-balance, she clung to the banister and took each step carefully. The doctor said she was dilating faster and sooner than he liked. Corazon would give her hell if she caught *mamacita* out of bed.

Once down the stairs, she made for the barn to break up any clinches. She got as far as Norma Jean's motor home. Still on the far side of the vehicle, she heard footsteps approaching. So, that gorgeous couple came looking for a more comfortable place than the stable.

"He's fast and proven. He even got ahold of my wife's Arabian. She's due soon to produce a little half-Arab. Maybe we should call the foal a Quarter-Arab."

They laughed together over some horsey joke Nell didn't get.

"When your mare comes into season, you can bring her by, or I can arrange for a shipment of L.B.'s best if you want to inseminate. I'll give you my special stud fee."

Nell sucked in her breath as best she could. She imagined her husband's leer when he said that. Joe Dean Billodeaux hadn't changed at all. He was still a womanizing son of a bitch.

"It's a deal. I'll call when she's ready. Could you give me another number? This one is always busy," Norma Jean asked.

Joe was probably giving Norma Jean his private number and underlining it with a devil's tail heart this very minute. Why didn't they just back up against the trailer and start banging each other right now?

"Well, you showed me your barn, Joe. Would you like to see my rig? It's better than a motel when I'm on the circuit. I call her the Cactus Blossom 'cause she's tough but sweet," Norma Jean said breathily.

"Ah, sure. Why not? Maybe I should get one of these for family vacations."

They probably thought no one would catch on to the sexual innuendo in their conversation. Ha! Clearly, they'd settled on the privacy of Norma Jean's home on wheels as a trysting place. The door to the motor home stood open. Nell pulled herself up the steps and inside. She sucked in her gut as far as possible, got past the front seats, and scuttled as low as she could past the tinted windows toward the rear bathroom. When the lovers unfolded the bed, she would jump out at them. In her condition, the bathroom was a tight fit, but she could always stand in the shower stall until the right moment if necessary. Nell pulled the door shut and settled on the commode as the couple entered.

"Now I know you like Sinners' red. Even this fuzzy stuff on the walls is red. Used to be my favorite color, too," Nell heard Joe remark.

"I adore red. I have a nightie to match," Norman Jean replied, her voice sultry. "The couch folds out into a queen-sized bed. Very handy idea, don't you think?"

"This is an impressive place, but I need to check on Nell. She doesn't always do as she's told."

"Right, you're supposed to rub her feet. Big as she is, I'll bet you haven't had any sexual relief in quite some time, honey."

From her cramped space in the bathroom, Nell envisioned Norma Jean twining her long lean body around Joe like the snake in the Garden of Eden. Right at this moment, the barrel racer probably had one hand in Joe's curls and the other down the front of his pants.

"Playing football takes the edge off. I'm kind of tired. We got in late last night and had a long meeting and practice this morning. Then I drove three hours to get here—to be with my wife—who is expecting my twins."

"Yeah, yeah, all the good ones are taken. Shit. Ain't nothin' wrong with a little fun."

"Used to be my philosophy, too. In another place, another time, I'd be all over you, sugar, but I got to leave."

In the bathroom, Nell put her head in her hands. How could she be so untrusting, so suspicious?

"Would you at least guide me to the highway, Joe Dean? Got lost a few times tryin' to find this place. Maybe I'll stop at one of those mini-casinos I saw on the way here because I sure had no luck with you, gorgeous."

"No trouble. Follow my Porsche. I'll get you on the right road in no time."

Nell's head shot up in her bathroom hiding place. Right road, my ass! They were probably going to signal each other to pull over at one of the mini-casino parking lots and have at it right there.

The motor home engine fired up and the big vehicle swung in a wide arc. Unprepared, Nell slid from the commode and bumped to the floor. The engine went to idle.

Norma Jean shouted out a window to Joe, "Hey, wait up! I heard something bump in the back. Let me check my trailer hitch."

Afraid to move, Nell stayed on the floor. She'd been feeling off all morning and now felt just plain sick, whether from her lunch or from anxiety, she didn't know. The huge bus moved forward again. It bumped out on to the rutted blacktop parish road and swayed along presumably behind Joe's Porsche. Nell could tell where they were when the motor home took a long curve—still a few miles from the highway in that stretch with cane fields on one side and the wooded bank of the bayou on the other. Wouldn't be long before she caught Joe Dean Billodeaux up to his old tricks again.

****

Trying to get Norma Jean out of his life, Joe drove along quickly in his Porsche. She surely was a temptation and used to getting what she wanted. His resistance ran low after the hard game this weekend, the chewing out this morning and Nell's less than cordial welcome home. Still, he recognized the black-haired woman as just another test sent by St. Jude. At the highway, he'd wave her on to the road and not get out of his sports car. He put his foot on the accelerator and picked up speed in the long turn instead of slowing down.

Up ahead still on the curve, a massive silver pickup truck with an extended cab and bed passed a tractor hauling a load of cane at twenty miles an hour. The truck crossed the solid yellow center line and swerved for the Porsche. Joe Dean held the sports car steady as close to the edge of the road as he could, but the damned truck came right at him with the driver laying on the horn.

Joe mashed his foot against the gas pedal as he came out of the curve and gave the truck a narrow miss. He fought the wheel, but the right front tire caught in the edge of the road and steered the Porsche on to the soft narrow shoulder. Ground gave way. The sports car went airborne and descended into a steep-banked ditch. Joe braked as the car skidded along in six inches of water and came to a standstill a foot from a concrete culvert draining the cane field into the bayou.

He took a few seconds to throw his head back on the neck rest, still his shaking hands and think about Nell and the babies, born and unborn. In that brief moment, Joe witnessed the second crash in his rearview mirror. The great red motor home careened nose first down the bank and in slow motion fell on to its side. The horse trailer jackknifed, rammed the rear of the coach protruding from the ditch and miraculously rebounded still erect across the road.

Joe punched his safety belt, scrambled from his own wreck and sloughed through the muddy ditch. He rapped on the driver's side of the Cactus Blossom.

"Norma Jean, you okay? Speak to me, sugar."

The driver's window slid open. "I'm fine, just real shook up. Help pull me out. No way I can use the door."

Joe braced himself against the bank and grabbed Norma Jean's shoulders as she slithered head first through the window. Her feet came free and she bounced hard against his body.

"Thanks for the help, handsome."

The cowgirl's wet, red mouth came down on his with a hard, appreciative kiss. In the back of his adrenaline-clouded mind, he thought he heard Nell calling, "Joe, Joe, Joe!" He shook his head and freed his lips.

"No need to be that thankful, Norma Jean."

"Y'all hurt?" An old black man, his yellowed

eyeballs wide, peered into the ditch. "Wasn't my fault. Can't make dat tractor go no faster. Peoples here know to watch for cane carts dis time o' year. Dat silver truck—was his doing."

"We know," Joe said. "Give me a hand up."

The driver of the tractor held out a callused palm to Joe who clambered up on to the road. Joe offered Norma Jean an assist and she scrambled after him. Down the road, the tractor and cane cart sat parked half on the road, half on the siding, its engine still chugging away. Norma Jean clung to Joe's arm.

Again, Joe swore he heard Nell calling his name. Connor had told him once when he was about to lose his temper on the field, he imagined hearing Stevie's voice calming him down. Joe thought his own illusion came more likely from guilt over that unsolicited kiss.

"Better go check on your mare, Norma Jean. Either of you have a cell phone? I left mine on the hall table." Taking command did help, he found. For the moment, the voice inside his head stopped calling.

"No, sir, ain't got no phone," the farm hand answered.

"My cell is somewhere down in that mess," Norma Jean replied as she shifted off Joe's arm and trudged toward the horse trailer.

"Well, we're smack in the middle of Three Brothers Plantation. The closest house is my Uncle Wylie's about two miles that direction. Anyone have danger signs or traffic flares we can set up? Then, we can all ride the tractor over to my uncle's place and call the cops and a couple of tow trucks."

"I gots some." The old man hobbled on arthritic legs to the idling tractor and began unpacking reflective danger triangles to set along the road.

"Sweet Sue is fine, just shaken up. I'm glad I kept the bumpers on her legs. Help me get the trailer detached and out of the road, Joe." Norma Jean knelt near the rear of her motor home examining the twisted hitch. A low groan came from the same area.

"That your mare? Maybe she has internal injuries. Let's get her out before we try to move the trailer. We can walk her to that little bridge over the culvert and tie her up in the shade out of harm's way. We'll check her out."

"Good idea, but that noise wasn't Sweet Sue. Would you look at the hole that trailer punched into my plumbing? I guess I'll have to go to a motel tonight. Can you recommend a good one?"

"Jo-o-o-e!"

One mention of a motel and the voice of his conscience came back loud and clear. "Did you hear someone calling, Norma Jean?"

She peered into the gap in her motor home. "Joe, I think we have a stowaway aboard the Cactus Blossom. Looks like your wife down there lying in my shower. Did you have to go that bad, honey? Are you hurt?"

Nell groaned. Joe looked down at his wife's frightened face deep in her dark hiding place. "I think I'm in labor, but I wish I were dead."

"Say that again, Nellwyn Abbott Billodeaux and I'll really be pissed. What the hell…"

"Spying. I was spying on you and the rodeo queen."

"Have I given you any reason to…"

"Look, handsome, the girl says she's in labor. I think you should put off the marital spat and go find a doctor," Norma Jean advised. "I'll just take it as a compliment she was that jealous of little ole me."

"Joe, I'm hurting really badly. I feel pressure down there. I can't get up. A big piece of metal is pinning my chest. I think a baby is coming out."

"Y'all riding wit' me?" The old man had returned from setting up the triangles down the road from the trailer and the wreck. "You gots a pregnant woman down in dat hole? Christ Jesus."

"Can you unhitch the cane wagon and go to my uncle's for help? We need an ambulance first, then the cops and two tow trucks. Hell, we might need the fire department and the Jaws of Life. Get help as fast as you can Mr.—ah—"

"Windy. Everyone called me Windy. Not my real name, but I answers to it."

"Joe, I have a veterinary kit in the trailer I can leave you just in case. I guess babies come out on their own like foals, only head first instead of hoof first. You're a farm boy, you can handle it. I'll hop a ride with Windy, here."

"Water, I need clean water." Joe looked at his dirty hands and muddy clothes.

Nell, clutching the bar in the shower stall, panted, gave up and screamed.

Joe looked desperately at Norma Jean and Windy. "I need something clean to put on, rags, anything!"

"Gots a water jug and a roll of paper towels." Windy hobbled off again.

Norma Jean rushed for the horse trailer and returned with the vet kit, a saddle blanket and a garment still in a dry cleaner's bag.

"The vet kit has a good pair of scissors for cutting

tape, some Betadine, some sutures and those big curved needles they use to sew up horses. The saddle blanket is new. And this is my pageant jacket for when I ride out carryin' the American flag at the rodeo. Just had it cleaned. It was hanging in my tack room back of the trailer. Won't fit over your shoulders, Joe, but we could put it on backwards and cover your arms and chest. Could you try not to get blood and gunk all over it?"

Norma Jean stripped the plastic bag from the coat. The garment glittered in the pale winter sunshine. Encrusted with red, white and blue sequins, the back of the jacket had an American flag picked out in rhinestones. The arms and bottom hung with fringe, lots of fringe.

"Let me help you get it on," Norma Jean offered.

"I heard that!" Nell shouted, then went back to panting.

Joe held out his arms and Norma Jean slipped the jacket on backwards. "Try to be careful with it, okay?"

Windy returned with his contributions. He held the water jug and paper towels while Joe washed his hands. Norma Jean poured on some Betadine trying to keep the brown antiseptic away from the sequins. Just before Joe jumped into the hole to be with his wife and babies, Windy withdrew a pint bottle of whiskey still covered with a paper bag from the bib of his overalls and tucked it into the pocket of the coat.

"You be needin' dis more den me, boy. But I ain't been drinkin' on the job, no sir."

"Thanks, Windy." Joe lowered himself into the breach. "Hand down the kit and the blanket, Norma Jean, then you and the old man haul ass for help."

Joe squatted in the dim hole and let his eyes adjust.

He could hear his wife moan and smell her fear in the sweat gathering on her forehead. The tractor ground into gear and moved off. In the quiet, Nell's panting seemed sharper and more desperate.

"Tink, let's see what the situation is. I'm sliding this blanket under your hips. Now let's get your pants off."

Joe gagged and suppressed the sound. Nell's slacks were soaked and sticky and came off bearing the enormous stretchy underpants with them.

"Lookin' good down here. Have the top of a head showing. Just let me rub some antiseptic around. Feel good?" he said, trying with all his might to be cheerful and positive.

"No. Ooooh, I need to push."

"No, you don't. Just pant."

"Need to."

"Okay, just a tee-tiny push."

The head popped out. Nothing left to do but follow the game plan.

"Okay, we check to be sure the cord isn't wrapped around the neck, turn the head, and clean the nostrils."

"You listened," Nell panted.

"Thought I was sleeping during the orientation film at the hospital, no? I did close my eyes a time or two, but not because I was tired. Couldn't shut out the sound though. This isn't working. Give me another little push."

The tiny body slipped into his hands so quickly, he almost fumbled. His daughter came into the world slimy, very wrinkled and purple-hued. Worse than that, she didn't seem to be breathing on her own.

"Sorry, *cher* heart, but Daddy is gonna spank you."

One quick slap on the behind, and the baby quivered, opened her mouth and hollered. Joe laid her on Nell's naked thigh.

"Let me see, Joe."

"Got to cut the cord first, Tink. Do you hear a siren?"

"No, only the baby."

"Wishful thinking. Okay, scissors and string to tie off the cord. No string. Some sutures then."

"Tie off two places. Cut between."

"Thanks for the reminder. Here goes. Done."

The baby screamed louder as he sterilized the cut with the contents of Windy's bottle.

"Must be Jude Emily. She screams like my sister," Nell said attempting a joke.

"*Mais*, yeah! Keep the baby warm," Joe told himself. He unrolled a yard of paper toweling and wrapped the infant until she looked like a mummy child, a howling mummy child. "There. All finished."

"Joe, the second baby is coming. I can feel it."

"Was that a siren?"

"No, Joe. That was me. I need to push again."

"Can't you just cross your legs? The ambulance will be here soon."

"Joe."

"What?"

"I'm sorry I doubted you. You're my hero."

"Aw, shucks, Miss Nell. Give me another tee-tiny push."

****

The ambulance got to the accident scene first, followed directly by the fire department vehicles bearing the Jaws of Life and two squad cards. The police blocked the road in both directions. A small crowd gathered at the barricades as tractors hauling cane chugged to a halt and passenger cars taking the back way to the interstate parked along the blacktop.

The audience applauded as Joe Dean handed up one Bounty-wrapped baby, then the other. A female paramedic prepared to go down into the gap to check on Nell as soon as Joe got out of the way. She laughed when she saw him crawl from the hole.

"That you, Cousin Joe Dean? When did you buy a motor home? All that money and you let your wife give birth in a ditch," Uncle Wiley's second to last daughter teased him.

"Not funny, Marlene. You better take good care of Nell, or I'll lock you in the old outhouse like I did when you were a little brat."

"Who was the brat, Joe Dean?" she challenged as she slid into the hull of the motor home. "Oh, good. You saved the afterbirth all wrapped up in paper towels. If you ever quit football, we need more paramedics."

"I'd rather break every bone I have on the playing field before I do this again."

The firemen moved him aside and applied the Jaws of Life to widen the gap in the Cactus Blossom. Someone made a ruckus at one of the barricades.

"No, no, they're making it worse!" Norma Jean, her black braid whipping, waved and called out. "And I forgot my horse. How could I forget my horse? Joe, could you check on her?"

His knees shook like mayhaw jelly, either from kneeling for so long or from the ordeal, but he checked on Sweet Sue still in her trailer. The mare was calmer than he, what with being used to rodeo crowds and noises and all that stuff. Joe walked over and leaned on the barricade in front of Norma Jean.

"She's fine, a real sensible creature for a female. Want your jacket back?"

Norma Jean looked at the fringe wet with some kind of gook and the splatter marks on the sequins. "Why don't you keep it and give it to your babies as a souvenir from their Aunt Norma Jean."

"Joe," Nell called weakly as the paramedics lifted her from the hole.

She looked pale and—deflated. They placed her on a stretcher and carried her to the ambulance. Joe started to go to her when a brown, wrinkled face pushed up behind Norma Jean.

"Would you still be needing dat bottle I give you?"

"I used a little to sterilize the cords, but most of it's there. Just a second." Joe withdrew the flask from the pocket of the pageant jacket. He uncapped it, took a good swig and handed it over to Windy who looked around, then slipped it back into his bib.

The old man squinted. "You dat football player? What won two Super Bowls? I ain't never gonna drink dis. Got a grandson could sell it on e-Bay and send hisself to college."

"Good luck with that. If this doesn't bring enough, tell him to call me about a scholarship. Thanks for your help." Shedding his sequin and rhinestone persona as he went, Joe walked to the ambulance.

"Not even a good-bye kiss for me." Norma Jean turned her charms on the policemen guarding the barricade. "Oh, officers, I need to see to my horse and motor home real bad." She batted her eyelashes like she was swatting flies.

Nell looked from the barrel racer to her husband kneeling at her side. "Joe, I'm so sorry I risked the babies because that woman irritated me. Aren't they beautiful?" Nell tuned her head toward the paramedic unwrapping the first twin.

Honest to God, the first words that dropped into Joe Dean's mind when he saw his daughter in the light was a mental picture of naked mole rats—skinny, hairless, pink things with closed bulging eyes. As a sign of his increasing maturity, he bit his lips and said, "They are gorgeous just like their mother."

Nell looked pretty bad. Her short dark hair was plastered to her skull and the dark circles under her eyes had gotten worse. Something that looked and smelled like vomited cheese sandwich spilled down the front of her huge, sunny yellow T-shirt with the arrow pointing downward and the slogan, "Yes, it *is* twins." Still, she gave him the loveliest smile, as if every molecule of her body suffused with joy. He thought his answering grin might display that same happiness.

"Thanks for saying that. Thanks for my babies." She took his hand and kissed it, gunk and all.

Thanks for months of discomfort and an hour or more of pain. He would never understand women entirely. Instead of talking, he squeezed Nell's hand and kissed her forehead.

The ambulance dipped as another person climbed in through the open doors. Joe Dean's cousin, attending to the babies, scolded the new arrival.

"No visitors, we need to get to the hospital. Oh, it's you Sheriff LeDoux."

"Need to get a statement from Joe Dean, so I'll just ride along. One of my squad cars is going to clear the way for you and take me back to town. About this hit and run Miss Scruggs reported, I don't suppose you got a license number either?"

"Actually, it wasn't a hit and run. I mean the driver of the truck didn't hit either of us, just sort of drove us off the road. The back side of the truck was covered with mud. Even if I hadn't been driving for all I was worth, I couldn't see the plate."

"Yeah, that's what ole Windy said, but I had to write him up last harvest for overturning a cart when he'd had a few. He said the vehicle was a big fancy rig, extra long cab and bed, probably a Chevy. White man driving. The lady with the motor home supports that."

"Me, too. The driver had no cause to swing out like that. He was already past the tractor."

"Joe," Nell interrupted.

"Hush, Tink. I can barely hear the sheriff over the sirens and the babies."

Nell jerked the hand she held hard.

"Hey, that's my throwing hand, and playoffs are coming up!"

"Joe, Sheriff, do you think Bijou is back? That description sounds like our stolen truck."

The men stared at each other.

"He'd be a fool to show up around here. We have a dozen raps we can charge him with including stealing your truck. He got away lucky once. Why would he come back?" Sheriff LeDoux asked.

"To take our son. Joe, I think Tommy is in danger."

Chapter Thirty-Six

Corazon swung her wide hips in time to the beat coming from the Spanish language mix on the lime green iPod she had bought with her first paycheck. Her brothers would be so envious. She ran a finger around her waistband. Yes, she had lost a few pounds running after small Dino, as she like to call the very active boy, and trudging up and down those stairs when Rojito, her pet name for Tommy, cried for attention. Being hundreds of miles from her mother's freshly-made tortillas and refried beans helped, too. One day, she would go home to Mexico as the rich and slim American aunt, Tia Corazon, and spoil the children of her brothers and sisters with her largess.

For now, she remained content with a free hour or two while the babies slept and Miss Nell rested. Corazon removed a pan of her special enchiladas from the oven. Extra cheese bubbled on top of the tortillas. She added a liberal sprinkling of sliced jalapenos for color and heat. *Mamacita* could not eat them, but Mr. Joe Dean would indulge as would Knox Polk, a fine figure of a man.

Knox had a stern mahogany face and a straight military bearing. She suspected him to be more than the ranch manager, maybe a guard, too. She certainly felt safe when he was around. He liked the food she prepared and always complimented her after a meal.

Corazon Romero knew she was not pretty, but she could cook—and pray for a husband.

When the tall man came from behind and put an arm around Corazon's waist pulling her tight against his hard body, she murmured a prayer of thanks that she had not dropped the enchiladas and made a brief plea to the Virgin that he would be gentle their first time. When the knife point dug into her throat, she screamed. Knox was a retired soldier, but he would never do this. The hand near her waist moved upward and clamped over her mouth. She could tell her attacker said something because she could feel his jaw moving close to her ear, but the vibrant salsa music obscured his words.

The hand covering her mouth ripped off the ear buds. Corazon, using all her weight, butted him backwards and screamed again. She wished her legs were longer so she could flee, but knew they would not grow longer just because she wanted them to. Instead, the nursemaid pivoted and flung her hot enchiladas at a man who was neither her boss of the questionable reputation or the quiet Knox. This man she did not know, but he stood as tall as the others. The bubbling cheese hit the middle of his chambray-covered chest, not his face. Even though the hot food must have burned his skin, this stranger kept on coming. Corazon let loose with two more screams before her assaulter pinned her against the kitchen counter. *Madre de Dios! Madre de Dios!*

Tearing off her oven mitt and shoving it into Corazon's mouth, the man with the gold tooth got right in her face. "Be glad I'm not a killer, bitch. I come home hoping for some good Cajun food and a lot of *pousse-pousse* for my signature on a piece of paper, but what do I get, me? Another fat Mexican broad and enchiladas down my shirt. One more scream and I might be pushed into slitting your throat, *comprende?*"

Bijou removed the oven mitt. "Now, you tell me where my kid is and I'll be going."

The *senora* is upstairs calling the *policia*. The babies are crying. Mr. Joe will come to see."

"Mr. Joe might be dead in a ditch by now. Could be I got carried away and killed the golden goose. As for his little wifey, I hear she is so knocked up she needs help going to the bathroom. I'll be gone before the parish *policia* put down their donuts. If the woman who works with sick kids wants my healthy one, she'll have to pay for him. Won't be kidnapping since he's mine, and I'm just laying claim like Joe Dean did with his bastard. I never agreed to no adoption, you hear?"

Corazon nodded. This must be Rojito's true father, an evil man they called Bijou. She hoped the *senora* had called the police. She prayed the *senor* was not dead as this man said. She hoped Knox Polk had heard her screams way out in the barn and would come to her rescue.

Bijou gave her a nudge toward the stairs. Heavy-footed, they went up to the second floor together. The intruder looked into both rooms with screaming babies. Deanie tried to climb over the rails of his crib, a trick he had mastered earlier in the week. Tommy lay on his back, kicking and very red in the face. Pushing Corazon into the room with the younger child, Bijou ordered the nursemaid to pack a diaper bag for the trip.

"Please, do not hurt Rojito. He is a good baby, but with a temper if Dino teases too much."

"Rojito, cute. I wouldn't hurt one red curl on his head. He's my own flesh and blood even if he does look like his mama. Not much Billodeaux showing in him. Besides, you know what kind of cash a healthy white baby like this will bring?" Bijou wrinkled his nose. "And give him a diaper change before we go. He might not get another one until I'm across the Rio Grande."

Bijou's eyes scanned the room. "Good, no phones. What's this thing?"

"For to hear the baby when I'm downstairs."

"You just stay here, then. I'm going to pay a visit to the little mother, let her know my terms for getting this kid back."

"Please, *senor*, she is sick. Leave her alone."

"I feel so sorry for that baby-stealin' bitch, me, I probably won't bother to rape her. Don't care for pregnant women, you see. And you, you're plain too ugly. Got a better *senorita* down south. Don't you leave this room, you hear."

Bijou expected the master suite to be locked. It wasn't. He flung the door back hard just in case little Miss Nell hid there with an upraised poker or a handgun. She was small but feisty, he recalled. She certainly led Joe Dean around by the nose.

Her bed was empty. He could see no one in the bath through the open door. The gallery appeared to be unoccupied. For the first time, Bijou noticed the blue truck. In too much of a hurry to be observant, he'd driven up the old cane field road, across an open lot and then walked along the bayou to get to the house. Joe Dean wouldn't drive an old heap like that. Who? Returning to the hall, he caught Corazon moving away from Deanie's now locked bedroom.

"What did I tell you? Stay in the baby's room! *Comprende?*"

"*No comprende.* Sorry, *senor.* I do not want the other child to get out and fall down the stairs."

"Ain't you the good little nursemaid? Maybe I need to take you along. You're probably an illegal anyways. Want to go back to old Mexico, huh? Give me the bag. You take the baby and step out here on the balcony. Go, go, go, *andale!*" He gave Corazon another prick with the tip of the hunting knife. Her neck ran red with small rivulets settling in the creases.

Comforted by his nurse's cushiony chest and a clean diaper, Tommy peeped over her shoulder at his father. The man did not smile, and his voice was rough and deep. Tommy buried his big brown eyes in Corazon's shoulder as if that would make the scary man go away. He peeped again. Still there. He began to wail.

"Is Joe Dean losing his taste for fancy rigs, or does that truck belong to someone else?" Bijou crouched closed behind Corazon using her and the baby as a shield.

I may be fat and ugly, but I got good eyes, Corazon thought. *Bueno.* Knox had heard her plea for help over the monitor and gotten into position. A rifle is missing from his gun rack and an odd, bumpy shadow is being cast by the afternoon sun behind the truck. I need to get out of the way.

Bijou prodded her again with the knife. "Whose truck? Answer me!"

"It belongs to the handyman. He is very old and has a bad leg. He can't hurt you." God forgives lies told to save the innocent, surely. Then, cradling Tommy, she dropped to the floor boards. A bullet took a chunk from the slick white railing of the gallery, surged on, and lodged in the brick of the house.

Bijou crouched beside the maid. "Old and lame, fuck! Give me the kid."

Corazon held Tommy tightly to her chest as Bijou pulled at the crossed corduroy straps of the baby's overalls. He held his knife up to slash at the maid's arm and raised his head slightly above the railing with the motion. A second bullet carved a groove across his forehead and threw a curtain of blood over his eyes.

"Shit!" He released Tommy and wiped his face with the sleeve of his free arm.

Corazon turtled backward until she reached the side of the balcony. She raised her bulk up to the railing, pushed her hips on to the edge and murmuring, "*Madre de Dios,* hear my prayer," let her weight carry her and the baby backward over the edge. They landed in a clump of thick, glossy gardenias professionally planted in a bed with three feet of mulch. Tommy, still enfolded on Corazon's bosom, seemed to enjoy the ride. He ceased crying and raised his head to look around. His small hand reached out for the clump of leaves crowning his nursemaid's head, then drew back as a squad car came screaming down the drive. He burrowed into the pillowy chest again.

Now they come, thought Corazon, the wind and heaven knew what else knocked out of her. Forgive me, Holy Mother, for not being grateful for my fat behind. She closed her eyes.

On the balcony, Bijou stayed low and ran to the opposite side of the porch. If a fat old maid could do it, so could he. Bijou jumped feet first into a matching clump of gardenias and mulch. He bent his knees as he hit and rolled to one side, his knife carving a deep hole in the loose dirt. Hell, this was like the good times when he did bull riding and Joe Dean was a pissant high school wannabe pro quarterback. He gained his feet and took off toward the bayou path.

Behind the fugitive, the sheriff, two patrolmen and Joe Dean Billodeaux unloaded from the squad car. They gave chase with first the sheriff wheezing to a halt, then the first and second patrolmen as they came up to L.B.'s pasture. The stud horse was gone. Joe spotted a flash of red going into the trees.

He pursued, his feet slipping in the duff. What he would give for a good pair of cleats instead of these fancy Italian loafers covered with gunk right now. Millions. He whistled shrilly hoping to get the animal to pull up short. L.B. did jerk to a stop long enough for Joe to catch at his cousin's leg. Bijou struck downward with his knife catching Joe in the right shoulder. L.B. reared and bolted leaving the knife buried in the wound. Joe kept running. He ran until he collapsed in the glade where he once made love to Nell. Nell. The moss soaked up his blood.

Chapter Thirty-Seven

"I have to say, Al, wearing Joe Dean Billodeaux's number on their helmets didn't bring the New Orleans Sinners the luck they needed. The team seems leaderless without him. Green Bay's defense fully contained Sinners' reserve quarterback, Jim Jennings, who had only one win in the last three games of the season. The Sinners made the playoffs on Joe Dean's legacy. Of course, this dome team didn't care for the Wisconsin weather either, driving snow and temperatures in the low thirties. Made that football as hard as a rock and slippery, too."

"The weather was a factor, but if Joe Dean had been here in more than spirit, the Sinners might have had a chance for redemption, Hank."

The sports commentators chuckled. "What a guy, that Joe Dean. The women always thought so, but you have to give credit to a man who delivers his own twin daughters, then chases his adopted son's would-be kidnapper, and goes down with a knife in his shoulder. Sounds like one of my wife's romance novels—not that I ever read one."

"Heaven forbid, Al. I think Joe Dean's story is more action/adventure. They should put him in the Hall of Fame now for best off-field performance. Here's Rita Fortunado with wide receiver, Connor Riley, who carried the ball for the Sinner's only touchdown in today's game."

"Connor," said Rita, standing a little too closely. "Did the loss of Joe Dean Billodeaux cost your team another Super Bowl?"

"Those of us who are married, especially the ones with children, understand what Joe Dean had to do— protect his family." Connor reached out an arm and pulled Stevie next to him from her position slightly off camera.

"Family, then football. The team did their best without him. But Rita, you know, there's always next year."

****

"*Mais*, yeah!" Joe Dean shouted from his seat on the sofa beside Nell. He pumped his left arm. "Next year, baby, once I get this shoulder loosened up again. Still, I think I could have helped if Coach had let me go along to Green Bay and sit on the bench."

"Sure and crack that wound open again in the cold with you flailing your arm around every time you got excited? I had to sit on your hand to keep you still in this nice warm game room. Hush, now. You'll wake the girls." Nell gave him the warmest, most loving smile he'd ever seen on any woman in or out of bed.

Joe Dean looked at his daughters sound asleep in their baby carriers, their small faces now pink and plump after a long hospital stay. Making fish faces against the glass, Deanie played under the coffee table. Tommy dozed just below Corazon's neck brace as the maid sat in the best recliner with her feet up.

Nadine Billodeaux scraped the last of the chili-cheese dip into the bowl sitting between her husband and Knox Polk. Knox loaded a chip with dip and fed

Corazon. Then he offered her the bent straw stuck into a chilled can of diet ginger ale.

"Here you go, Brave Heart."

Corazon raised her newly plucked eyebrows and gave him a smile that showed off her waxed upper lip and fine, white teeth. Nell, bored during her recovery and getting plenty of childcare help from the Billodeaux women, had given her a gratefully received makeover. With her brave heart, she had survived the leg waxing, too.

"You know, this brace is helping me lose weight, I think," the maid remarked with a sidelong glance at Knox.

"Women should have a little padding. You might have broken your neck, not just sprained it if you were thinner," Knox said.

"Knox," she said. "You are my hero. In America, any wish can come true."

"That means trouble, Knox. When a woman tells you that, she expects you to do big things," Joe Dean answered. "Speaking of which, I think I have a winning team here. I want to give you and Corazon these rings for all you did to protect my family."

He twisted off his two Super Bowl rings leaving only his wide wedding band behind on his fingers. He tossed the one with the S picked out in rubies to Knox and handed the second one glittery with diamonds to Corazon.

"No, no, we cannot take them, Mr. Joe," Corazon protested, though her sprained back wasn't allowing her to get up and hand the ring back.

"No, sir. I can't accept a gift like this," Knox Polk agreed.

"Keep them. I plan on getting another one next year." Joe stretched out, caught Deanie between his legs and drew him from under the coffee table. "Go get the Nerf football, son. Daddy needs to practice his left arm throws. You can receive. Get the ball. There you go."

Nell put hats on the girls and pulled their pink, crocheted blankets up around their necks in preparation for giving them some fresh air. She raised Tommy off of Corazon's chest.

"You must be numb by now," she teased the woman.

"It is a good hurt, *señora*," Corazon answered.

When all the children were bundled and Corazon helped to a rocker on the porch, the Billodeaux family gathered to watch another sort of game. In a corner of the training ring closest to the house, Fatima craned her neck over the fence to assess the cause of all the commotion. A red colt with a long white blaze on his dished Arabian face stayed tucked to her side. L.B. stood nearby showing his stuff.

Frank Billodeaux directed Tommy's eyes toward the foal. "See Drummer Boy, Tommy? He come on Christmas Eve wit' lots less fuss den your baby sisters. He be your horse one day."

"Yep, L.B. produces a fine product. Good thing he found his way home safe after Bijou ditched him for a truck. Too bad I didn't kill that bastard of a kidnapper when I had the chance. He's probably hiding in Mexico again," Knox remarked as he leaned against a pillar.

"He won't bother us again, I'm sure," Nell said. "Not with all the great people we have on the ranch protecting us."

Out on the grassy part of the lawn, Joe threw a

wobbly left-handed pass high in the air with the spongy ball. "Go long, Deanie, go long!"

Arms up, the dark-haired little boy scrambled across the grass. The ball hit him in the chest and bounced to the ground. Deanie jumped on the ball, then held it up, and gave it a spike. The gallery of fans applauded. Joe patted his son's rear and gave him a high five.

"Next one is a short shovel pass, Deanie. Stand right there and get ready."

The child held out his hands. Joe Dean Billodeaux, star quarterback of the Sinners, paused to look at his family before making the play. Less than two years ago, he thought he had everything a man could want, but now he had even more than he had wished.

A word about the author...

Once a librarian, now a writer of romance, Lynn Shurr grew up in Pennsylvania Dutch country. She attended a state college and got a degree in English literature. Her first job really was working in a burger joint. Holding one humble job after another, she traveled to Europe and across the U.S., finally buckling down and getting an M.A. in librarianship.

She found her first reference position in the Heart of Cajun Country. For her the old saying, "Once you've tasted bayou water, you will always stay here" came true. She raised three children not far from the Bayou Teche and lives there still with her astronomer husband.

When not writing, Lynn likes to paint, cheer for the New Orleans Saints and LSU Tigers, and take long road trips nearly anywhere. Her love of the bayou country, its history and customs, often shows in the background for her books.

She is the author of the popular Sinners sports romance series, the new Roses series, and the stand alone contemporary romance, A Trashy Affair. You may contact Lynn at www.lynnshurr.com or visit her blog at lynnshurr.blogspot.com.

~*~

Other Lynn Shurr titles
available from The Wild Rose Press, Inc.:

Goals for a Sinner *The Convent Rose*
Kicks for a Sinner *A Trashy Affair*
Paradise for a Sinner *A Wild Red Rose*
Love Letter for a Sinner

Thank you for purchasing
this publication of The Wild Rose Press, Inc.
For other wonderful stories of romance,
please visit our on-line bookstore at
www.thewildrosepress.com.

For questions or more information
contact us at
info@thewildrosepress.com.

The Wild Rose Press, Inc.
www.thewildrosepress.com

To visit with authors of
The Wild Rose Press, Inc.
join our yahoo loop at
http://groups.yahoo.com/group/thewildrosepress/